The Promises A Man Makes

David looked up at Kate, his eyes taking on that familiar devilish gleam. "Somehow, some way, Irish, I'll make it to the biggest, fanciest house in San Francisco. I'll buy you silk dresses from France and your own landau with a matched team of white horses. I'll smother you in emeralds as green as your Irish eyes."

In all his promises, Kate longed to hear only one—one she knew she never would hear: *Marry me, never leave me! All the silks and emeralds on earth aren't worth as much as that.*

If David noticed her pensive air, he didn't show it as he scooped her up and carried her to the bedroom. Pulling off her simple calico dress, he laid her back on the big bed. They tumbled together in a tangle of arms and legs, laughing and gasping in sheer animal pleasure...

It was always like this. Kate didn't want to think about when he was rich and powerful enough to confront his father, his whole family— then what? Where did that leave an Irish saloon girl? But now she couldn't think, she could only feel and want.

*   *   *

"An unusually powerful and moving romance...a worthy heroine, vulnerable and appealing...an excellent first novel. FOUR STARS! (highest rating)."
—*Romantic Times* on *Golden Lady*

Also by Shirl Henke

Golden Lady

Published by
WARNER BOOKS

Love Unwilling

Shirl Henke

WARNER BOOKS

A Warner Communications Company

WARNER BOOKS EDITION

Cover art by Max Ginsburg

Warner Books, Inc.
666 Fifth Avenue
New York, N.Y. 10103

 A Warner Communications Company

Printed in the United States of America

First Printing: April, 1987

10 9 8 7 6 5 4 3 2 1

For James T. Henke,
who is all my heroes.

Remember, O Lord, what is come upon us: Consider and behold our reproach.

Our inheritance is turned to strangers, our houses to aliens.

We are orphans and fatherless, our mothers are as widows.

We have drunken our water for money; our wood is sold unto us.

Our necks are under persecution: we labor and have no rest.

Lamentations 5, 1-5

AUTHOR'S NOTE

The characters of this story are fictitious, but the problem of Californio landholders retaining title to their estates was real. In 1848, Mexico lost a brutal, bloody war to the United States and signed a peace treaty giving nearly half of its territory to the victor. Yankee laws and lawyers arrived in California, neither of which augured well for the property rights of the Spanish-speaking population.

The lament of the Old Testament prophet Jeremiah reflects similar circumstances. In the April 11, 1855 issue of the *Southern Californian,* Don Juan Bandini quoted those words verbatim to express his desolation.* Most Hispanic Americans throughout the Southwest faced similar losses, but in no other state or territory of the Mexican Cession was it of such magnitude; the fabulously rich land grants of California were as large as fifty thousand acres.

A handful of Californios in the southern cattle country did manage to keep title to their lands by a variety of means, marriage alliances being one. The Kane-Alvarez family of this story is a composite representing what such mixed marriages might have been like.

*As quoted by Robert Glass Cleland in *The Cattle on a Thousand Hills,* (San Marino, California, 1951), p. 41.

PROLOGUE

Spring 1848, Cien Robles

David Kane took off his stained, wide-brimmed hat and wiped the sweat from his brow with his forearm. The sun glinted on a thatch of long, shaggy hair that he shook carelessly from his face. He replaced the hat, for there was no other shade on the hot, dusty ride. He was home at last. Home: Cien Robles, Hundred Oaks—the vast rancho of his family, held by his mother's people since 1784 when the Spanish governor of California, Pedro Fages, had awarded it to Diego Alvarez, David's great-grandfather.

He surveyed the majestic scene. Buttercups covered the hills in a blaze of yellow. The mountains on the far horizon glowed pale lavender in the haze, and two streams meandered across the valley floor, still nourishing the same ancient stands of oaks. Just over the next hill a big adobe with a red tile roof and wide, cooling veranda beckoned him. *Nothing's changed in five years. This is still my birthright, mine and Miguel's.*

1

As he thought of his brother, David impulsively guided his bay off the main trail leading to the big house. He headed toward a branch of the stream on the valley floor. It twisted tortuously and formed a pool at the base of a small hillock, surrounded by the huge oaks that grew in profusion in the shallow valley. Had anyone ever counted them? Were there truly a hundred? Miguel probably knew, David mused. Miguel knew every rock, tree, creek and piece of livestock, every blade of grass or wild mustard on these dozen leagues. *I used to know it, too,* he thought, *although never as intimately as my brother.* David dismounted by the pool, letting the bay drink. As he knelt down and reached his hand toward the invitation of the water, a voice startled him, familiar but deeper than he remembered.

"David, is it you?" A young man emerged from behind the thick underbrush that lined the side of the pool.

David was instantly on his feet, amazed to look eye to eye with his brother. Miguel had been only thirteen years old when he left; now he had grown to a man's full stature. "*Hermano!* I wondered if late afternoon would catch you dreaming here by the water like it used to."

The two tall, slim men embraced. Then, the older one released his grip, holding his younger brother by the shoulders, at arm's length for inspection.

"Your habits may be the same, but you've certainly changed! God! Look at you! Tall as one of those oaks and shaving, too, by the looks of it. I left a boy and I return after five years to find a man."

Miguel had a swarthy countenance, coal black curly hair and thick black brows that arched over his dark blue eyes. A high forehead, straight prominent nose and sculpted lips completed the picture of a haughty Californio, grave and courteous even when smiling, yet possessed of something more, something elusive beyond the obvious Hispanic inheritance of the Alvarez mother. His brother's looks provided a key to the rest.

David's dark gold hair was straight and thick; his brows were golden slashes over deep-set eyes. Although darkly tanned, his complexion was fair where the sun did not touch him. His midnight blue eyes danced devilishly and his generous lips curved often in casual laughter. David was as full of charm as a Yankee trader, a legacy from the New England father.

Their long-legged, lean frames and hard, jutting jawlines were reminiscent of the harsh Massachusetts coastline, yet both young men were tempered by the warmth and courtesy of more hospitable California climes. Miguel was the more serious and quiet of the two, while David was the reckless and flamboyant brother.

As David grinned crookedly, he roughly scraped his brother's cheek with his knuckles, teasing, "I never realized I'd come back to find you grown up so fast or I'd have brought you a razor. Or a woman!" He gave a wicked laugh.

Miguel looked into David's eyes, older eyes, still full of humor yet unsettled, as if their blue depths had seen too much. David had left five years ago, an eighteen-year-old college boy bound for the eastern coast of the United States to receive the formal education their sea captain father wished for him. He returned a veteran of the Mexican War. Miguel perceived the difference of more than the passage of time in his older brother's face.

"You're changed also, *hermano,* not so much physically, but you're different . . ." Miguel stopped, hesitating to broach a subject both knew they must speak of.

David's eyes were almost opaque as he turned with casual grace to slide down the trunk of a comfortable old oak and lean back. Silence. He lit a cigar taken from his shirt pocket and offered one to Miguel, who sat down beside him. The youth refused the smoke as David knew he would. The kid never did have any vices. He would have to work on that.

Clamping the cigar between even, white teeth, David said, "War makes you different. Only damn fool boys like I was think it's fun. College boys, out for a lark, wanting to escape their books, just like the farm boys want to escape their plows. Amounts to the same thing. Only we end up with commissions and they end up as privates. Funny, we bleed the same, though.''

"Mexicans bleed the same, too." The minute he said it, Miguel wished he could call back the words, but David only laughed, a hollow, sad sound.

"You sound like Mama. I fought a war against my own kind, I know. It wasn't so bad at Palo Alto. At least it was from a distance." He paused and ran his fingers through the thick shock of hair, then went on. "But at Resaca de la Palma, there I came face to face with them in that fucking mire of brush and mud. Boys! Jesus, they looked like you, Miguel! By the time we reached Monterrey I'd had enough. Enough poisoned water, enough stupid orders, enough of the stink of death, enough of that fat old Whig, Taylor, running for President." Unconsciously, he ran his right hand across his thigh, rubbing the fresh scar where a musketball had slashed him. It still ached.

Miguel looked at David's face, changed in some indefinable way. "Then, why? Why did you run away from school and join the Americans to fight Mexico? You're Californio, born and raised. It wasn't our fight, especially not *ours*, half Yankee, half Mexican."

"Hell, Miguel, you weren't there! You were a sixteen-year-old boy on a ranch in California, isolated, surrounded by Mama and your priests, your books, your horses. I was sent to Maryland, surrounded by Americans, attending an American college, trying to become the gentleman Papa wanted me to be. I was good at gambling and women, but bored to death with school. It seemed to be a logical way to redeem myself. 'An officer and a gentleman.'" He snorted in self-derision. "A way out of the country."

"And a way to strike back at Mama—at the Mexican side of your heritage? You were always on *his* side, against her." Miguel had a fierce Latin temper.

David took a long drag on his cigar and exhaled, flicking a length of ash carelessly into the clear greenish depths of the pool. "I take it nothing's changed. I'm not forgiven for joining the army of General Taylor, despite the stupid excesses of youth. Papa's letters reached me.

Shit! Did they reach me!'' David laughed, throwing his head back. His white teeth flashed in his darkly tanned face while he again clenched the cigar in his mouth. Then he paused as his mood darkened. Removing the cigar, he said softly, ''Mama never wrote. I guess that means she's even given up lighting candles for me. She'll never forgive me. God knows, I'll never forgive myself. The stupid thing is, once you're there, you're ... there. You have these men—hell, boys—depending on you and you can't just fucking resign. You stay and do what you have to.'' He sighed. ''It's over now and I'm home. What's it like at home? Same as ever?''

As a boy, Miguel had never imagined the hurt he now saw etched in his brother's face. But he suddenly realized that it had always been there. *I knew Papa loved him more. He knew Mama loved me more*, he thought to himself. *They hurt us both with their private war.* Miguel was moved to a combination of sorrow and laughter which drew him closer to David and further away from the parents whose mutual antagonism had begun the torment.

''Mama was very unhappy when she heard you'd joined the American army. She didn't stop the prayers and candles, though, David. She never will. She'll never understand you, but she does love you in her own way. Papa was livid, as you learned through his letters. He wanted you educated, not shot.'' Miguel's dark blue eyes, so startlingly like David's despite such different coloring, suddenly lit with humor. ''I think he was proud of you despite your disobeying him and leaving school. Oh, he'd never admit it, but the adventure appealed to him even if he's not happy about California becoming American. You always were the doer while I was the bookworm.''

David looked at his eighteen-year-old brother, physically a man, but still a boy in experience. ''And what of Miguel, *hermano*, do you forgive me?''

Miguel's serious expression did not change, but his eyes were warm as he gazed levelly at David. ''There's nothing to forgive. I was here, as you said, a world away from the conflict. You were there. I don't pretend to understand all the complications of life in the United States, even if this is American territory now. Let's learn together, David.''

They clasped hands under one of the hundred oaks of their inheritance.

CHAPTER
1

December 1851, Bent Fork

Kate Muldoon stepped into the kitchen, her arms laden with firewood. She dropped the heavy load beside the hearth, then threw one log on the sizzling fire and sat down in front of its orange blaze, rubbing her hands to warm them. It was a raw, foggy night in Bent Fork, the usual for this time of year in Southern California.

"If only I was in the warm room up front," she muttered aloud in resentment. But as she thought about the crowded bar and its sodden patrons, she knew she wanted no part of them or of her Uncle Will, the owner of the sleazy cantina who watched her with crafty eyes, leering and rubbing his stubby chin whiskers. It was a sin that Aunt Tess, her father's kind and loving sister, had been forced to marry the likes of Will Bolton in order to provide for her orphaned niece.

Tess and Kate had slaved for years to keep Bolton's cantina going while he did nothing but drink up the profits.

At least while her aunt lived, Will had kept the whores out. But Tess was not cold in her grave before he moved several unsavory women into the upstairs quarters. Although Kate was a virgin she was not naive. She knew what they did with the men in those rooms, coupling like dogs or horses. It was cheap, fast and dirty—as dirty as Lil or Bernice themselves.

In the past two months since her aunt died, Will ordered Kate to relinquish her room to Lil and move into a servant's attic, then to work harder in the kitchen and to serve drinks in the bar, something she had never done while Tess was alive. Will grew nastier and more demanding with each passing day.

What if he turns me out? Where will I go? The good folks of Bent Fork'll be wantin' no part of an Irish girl raised in a saloon. Kate had no education, not even the rudiments of reading and writing. Her only skills were cooking and scrubbing. She considered her alternatives.

There was Abe Durkin, who had asked her to marry him. But Abe was an impoverished farmer barely able to support himself, much less a wife. If she married him it would be a last resort, for he was homely and uncouth. She was repelled whenever he tried to put his arm around her or kiss her.

Too bad I'm not a Catholic like the Mexican women. I could enter a convent. She laughed in spite of her grim predicament. Although most Irish immigrants were Catholic, Kate was a Methodist from Belfast. She had never really been religious and the thought of being locked away in a house full of nuns appealed to her adventurous blood even less than marriage to Abe.

What wonderful choices I have! Sure there must be something better than what's here. She looked around the bleak kitchen in disgust. It was a large dark room with two doors and a couple of small windows. A graniteware dishpan full of cooling water with stacks of dirty plates beside it sat on the rough oak table.

"What you doin' sittin' here like Good Queen Bess

holdin' court! Dishes ain't even done." Will's tirade interrupted her thoughts.

Bolton was a short squat man with hairy arms and an uneven bristle of whiskers across his face. His thinning hair was the pinkish gray color common to older redheads. Piglike bloodshot eyes and an enormous paunch attested to how he spent his time. He stood in the kitchen doorway glaring at her.

Kate had learned from her aunt to stand up and look him in the eye. At five feet five inches she was tall for a girl.

"I've washed dishes for half the afternoon and I just came in from choppin' firewood for more heat. Until the water is hot over the fireplace I can't be doin' any more dishes. You know well I'll be gettin' the kitchen clean before I go up to bed."

At the mention of her bed, Will's eyes shifted and he grinned. "How'd ya like ta fergit 'bout them dishes, an' choppin' wood an' t' other chores? I could hire me a Chinee ta do thet."

Kate felt the hair on the back of her neck prickle in warning, but she kept her green eyes fixed on his face. She forced a calmness she did not feel into her voice. "Why would you be relievin' me of all my chores, Uncle Will? You were always complainin' to Aunt Tess that I never earned my keep."

"Oh, ya'd earn yer keep, right 'nough. They's ways an' they's ways. Some's better'n others. Pay's more too."

"What might you be meanin'?" she asked with all the haughtiness a nineteen-year-old could muster.

"Ya know Hank Clune?"

Indeed she did. Oafish Hank was over six feet tall. All his front teeth had been knocked out in a brawl and his mouth was scarred. "I know Hank Clune, always leerin' at me. He has no manners."

"Has no manners," Will mimicked her voice sarcastically. "Well, let me tell ya, girlie, he's taken a shine ta ya. Be grateful. He's got gold ta spend an' it might's well be here as anywheres. Ya git yer prissy ass up ta yer room an' wait fer 'em. When th' game's over in th' front, he's comin' up fer ya.''

"Like hell! He'll have to break down the door and I'll be waitin' with a poker to bash in his brains! How dare you, you trash! You—you bastard!''

Kate had been raised around profanity, although her aunt strongly discouraged her use of it. Now her fierce anger, combined with real fear, erased her inhibitions. So this was what the crafty consideration was about! He'd make her into a whore and retire on what she brought in by serving those filthy men in the cantina. *Like hell he will!*

Bolton snarled an oath and moved toward her but Kate took up the poker from the hearthside, determined to face him down. Something in her manner made him reconsider. Always a coward, he backed out of the room and vanished down the hall.

Kate shook fiercely as the bravado left her. Sinking down on the stool by the fireside, she lay the poker across her lap. With her head in her hands, she sobbed. *God, what can I do? He'll only keep after me.* She must gather her meager belongings and flee. Time tomorrow to think about where to go and how to survive. Kate rose and walked to the back door. Just as her hand touched the latch, the door flew open, knocking her backward.

Will's bartender Mike Wallaby burst in and reached for her. She swung the poker at his head, but he raised his massive forearm and deflected the blow. With a feral grunt, he wrenched the rod from her hand and threw it across the floor with a clatter.

Will stood behind Wallaby and rubbed his hands across his greasy denim pants, his eyes glinting with avarice. "Now, we'll see, Miss High 'n Mighty. Ya fuckin' Irish trash. Ya'll git yer comuppance, yessiree . . .'' A rope dangled menacingly from his hands.

Five men sat around a poker table in a small private room of the cantina. Noise from drunken revelers filtered through the thin walls as a sloppy blonde in a stained satin dress served a round of drinks. Three of the men watched her sway her ample hips seductively.

Hank Clune was thinking of the pretty little piece of Bolton's waiting for him upstairs. No more frizzy-haired, blowzy old hags for him. But first he must win back the money he had lost to the rich bastard sitting across the table. He thought again of Kate Muldoon and raised another twenty dollars, wanting to end the game. He had a good hand.

The stranger reclined in his chair, shoving his hat back on his head. He waited while the other players disgustedly threw down their cards. "Price of poker just went up another forty dollars—American," he said casually, picking a piece of lint from the sleeve of his immaculate black broadcloth coat. He grinned, then lit a fat black cigar and clenched it between his teeth. His dark blue eyes gave away nothing.

Clune cursed as he pushed his money across the table and called.

The old rancher and his foreman whistled when the stranger spread out his hand.

"Flush, pretty diamonds, ace high." He cocked his head, waiting for Clune to show his hand, knowing from the draw he'd taken that he should have nothing better than a straight.

In agitation, Clune threw down a "wheel," an ace through five straight. "Your luck beats all hell, Kane," he ground out.

Before Clune could say more, the sounds of a scuffle turned everyone's attention to the door. Will Bolton shuffled in with Wallaby behind him. The big man had a girl carelessly slung over his shoulder, tied hand and foot. She was squirming fiercely and breathing hard.

David Kane kept his indolent pose, leaning back in his chair as he watched the scene unfold. He noticed that the man on his right, Rice Brighton, had an anticipatory gleam in his eyes.

Pushing his sandy hair from his forehead, Brighton spoke up. "Thought you promised Hank here she'd be all ready and willing in her room upstairs. What happened, Will? Can't deliver the goods?'' He barked a harsh laugh, his handsome face taking on a cruel caste that distorted his features.

Will fidgeted nervously. His right hand had bloody teeth marks and he limped. Even the huge Wallaby sported a long nail scratch that seeped red across his face and down his neck.

Bolton's first impulse after they had subdued Kate was to beat her unmercifully, but she was worth more money to him unmarked. A plan had quickly formed in his mind. He'd be rid of her, once and for all. He would earn more from her if he kept her as a whore, but it wouldn't be worth the trouble.

Hank Clune looked Kate up and down. ''I was fixin' ta have her tonight, Bolton. Said I'd pay ya good. Ya welshin' on yer word?''

Will spread his fat hands in a placating gesture, wincing at the pain from Kate's bite as he did so. ''Now, Clune, ya know I ain't fool enough ta do thet. I jest got me a better idee, thet's all. She's only good fer one thing, won't do chores or serve drinks. Now thet her sainted aunt's gone ta her reward, I cain't handle 'er. But yew'd know how ta break 'er good. Give me five hunnert in dust 'n she's yers.''

''You bastard, you cur whoremonger vomit! You can't be sellin' me! I'm no African slave!'' Hate radiated from her fierce green eyes.

Brighton chuckled while the older rancher looked distinctly uncomfortable and shifted in his chair. The foreman just gaped silently.

''Five hunnert in gold's a lot o' money fer a female I never even tried before. I dunno, Will . . .'' He looked at her, standing where Wallaby had dumped her while still holding her bound wrists. Her torn dress was hanging loosely about her legs, baring the slim calves and ankles. Her arms were uncovered, and one shoulder and the top of a breast were exposed through a large rip in the cheap green calico.

David watched her also. God, she was wild and lovely despite her disarray! She was tall and slim with fair skin touched by a golden tan. Great masses of dark auburn hair glinted like fire in the light of the tallow lamp. When his careless inspection reached her face, blazing green eyes met his and held him fascinated. Then, unexpectedly, she blushed and looked away. He smiled and set his cigar in a dirty ashtray on the table. *Yes, she is a piece!*

As he watched her strain against the ropes and saw the painful red weals rise around her wrists and ankles, David realized this was no act to get Clune to pay more. Her uncle really meant to sell her against her will!

As she spat some remarkable oaths at Bolton, Wallaby and Clune, David Kane sat in deceptive calm, taking in the scene. What would happen next?

Brighton asked incredulously, "You really mean to pay that much for her?"

"Git th' dust. Ya know where it is," was Clune's reply.

Brighton reached behind them and picked up a leather sack filled with gold dust that he handed to Bolton.

Clune said, "I figer thet's at least yer five hunnert American. I got no more cash. Ya want it weighed, ya take care o' it tamorra."

Unfolding his ill-proportioned frame, Clune started to get up, but the stranger in black interrupted him. "You lost at least that much to me tonight. Want a quick chance to win it back? It'd pay for the girl." He sat, legs outstretched beneath the table, hat now pushed forward over his face, obscuring his eyes as he spoke.

"What's yer offer, Kane?" Clune slowly sat down again on the edge of his chair.

"One hand of showdown, all five cards up. If you win, I shove all these United States banknotes back to you. If you lose, I take the girl." The silky soft tones were almost taunting in their casualness, as if the stakes were nothing to him, and only the game mattered.

The struggle between greed and lust was written plainly on Clune's face as he looked between the struggling girl and Kane's winnings. How long could one hand of show-down take?

"Shit! Deal the cards."

The rancher and his foreman stood up and backed off, fascinated but nervous. The tension in the air was so thick it could be sliced and fried.

David looked calm and indifferent. Hadn't he always been a lucky gambler, winning more than he wanted to keep from college friends and fellow soldiers? His hands were slow and steady as he motioned for Will Bolton to deal the cards, but his palms were sweating. He had better win or else—what? *Why the hell should I risk my life for a saloon girl who got herself in over her head?*

Kate quieted in Wallaby's brutal grasp to watch the stranger. His speech was educated and his clothes expensively tailored. Even her untutored eye could discern that much. He had the face and manners of an aristocrat and was the most strikingly handsome man she'd ever seen. She stared at his shock of dark blond hair, sculpted, hawkish face, and those eyes, dark blue like summer midnight. God, she'd turned earlier from their searing gaze. *Well, he'll not be ownin' me!* Unbidden, the thought flickered through her mind: *Would you rather belong to Hank Clune?*

Everyone watched Will Bolton's fat, stubby fingers shuffle the cards and lay the first one in front of Hank Clune. The ace of hearts. Then, a king of spades to David Kane. Clune grinned wolfishly as the next three rounds were dealt. Three aces and a queen lay in front of him. David had a king, jack, ten, nine.

"Odds on makin' that straight inside are piss poor, Kane. Ya sorry now?" Clune edged up on his chair, eager to collect the bet. His last card was a deuce.

Everyone in the room was breathless. The rancher and his foreman stood frozen in one corner, Kate and her captor Wallaby in the other. Clune waited expectantly. David was still leaning back in his chair, legs stretched beneath the table, hands resting on the chair arms. A sapphire ring on his right hand winked in the dim light as he carelessly flicked the ash from his cigar onto the floor.

Shakily, Bolton turned up David's last card. The queen of hearts!

"King high straight," breathed the old rancher in awe. "Beats three aces."

"I think my lady here just won me your lady there, Clune." David gestured from the queen on the table to Kate across the room.

"Ya bastard! Yew 'n Bolton here cooked this up!" Clune's voice rose sharply in rage and cracked like an adolescent's as he stood up and grabbed the revolver from his belt.

Bolton choked out a terrified denial, overturning a chair in his haste to get out of the line of fire.

David didn't move until Clune was standing with his gun almost cocked. Then, in a blurring move, he produced a .36-caliber Manton pistol from inside his coat and fired once. Hank Clune sank to the floor with a surprised expression on his face, crumpled in a heap of protruding bones between the table and chair. His .44 clattered down beside him.

Rice Brighton knelt quickly and stretched his companion out, checking him for signs of life. Finding none, he whirled with a snarl to look down the barrel of Kane's gun, scant inches from his nose.

"Don't be a fool, Brighton, unless you want to join him. Jesus, nothing I hate worse than a poor loser!" As Brighton reconsidered and backed away, David looked from him to Wallaby.

"Let her go." His words were no longer casual but bitten off.

Kate furiously shoved herself away from Wallaby. The old rancher shamefacedly walked over and used his knife to cut the bloody ropes from her hands and feet.

"Everyone here see this fight?" Kane looked from the rancher to his foreman, then to Bolton, Wallaby and Brighton. "It wasn't me who started it. I think we all agree? Also, the girl is mine. Bolton, you realize you have no more claim to her?''

David's cold blue eyes and clipped tone made Will nod a quick assent.

"Then I think this party's over, gentlemen. Brighton, why don't you collect your friend and make arrangements for him?''

Rice Brighton hefted Clune over his shoulder with a grunt, then hissed at the man holding the gun, "You damn Kanes think you own the earth. You can take anything you want. Someday, Kane, you and your old man'll face a reckoning.''

"You know my family? This far from home I'm flattered to be remembered, Brighton.'' A fleeting look of quizzical interest flashed in David's eyes as Brighton stomped out with his burden.

The ranchers followed him silently, eyes downcast, ashamed of their passive part in the ugly incident. Bolton shuffled past Kate and out the door, leaving her alone with her owner in the smoke-filled room.

She stood mute in shock, her rage now burned out, leaving her spent. Absently, she began to rub at her tingling wrists as she watched David casually slide the gun back into his coat and scoop up the banknotes from the table.

He lit another cigar, then smiled at her as he stepped across the small space separating them. "Ah, Kate, my lovely queen, what am I to do with you?''

Defiance once again flashed in those bright green eyes. "You don't own me!''

"Would you rather I give you back to your *uncle* so he can sell you all over again?'' The way he said the word *uncle* spoke volumes.

She was instantly furious, but swallowed her harsh retort, realizing even in her desperation that this man controlled her fate. He was right. If she went back to her old position, Will would try his treachery again and God only knew who might be her next captor. She shivered at the thought of Hank Clune's sadistic laugh and coarse body.

David watched Kate in perplexity. She looked so vulnerable, not at all like a saloon doxy. He'd heard the Irish brogue in her speech and her clothes told of poverty. But she was young and fresh. Her skin was clear, her darkest red hair was lush and her tall coltish body was sculpted just to his tastes. He'd enjoy his winnings for the night, then leave her enough cash in the morning so that she could get a stage out of Bent Fork and a new start away from Bolton.

Gently, he took one slim wrist in his hands and turned it over to examine the abrasions. "There's some ointment in my saddlebags upstairs. I rented a room this afternoon. I expected the game to go on well into the evening and thought I'd spend the night. Will you come with me?"

Kate hesitated. Then looking at his handsome face and dazzling smile, she was beguiled. He was asking her, and after all, where else could she go? "It's sure and I can't stay here alone." She took a step, then winced. Her ankles were tender after being tied so roughly.

When she swayed, he caught her and whisked her into his arms, easily carrying her out a side door and around to the back of the building. Kate found herself holding on to his neck and snuggling her head against his chest. The broadcloth jacket was soft against her face and he smelled of whiskey, tobacco and another faint, unidentifiable essence, clean and compelling. It felt good to be held.

Quickly, he climbed the rickety outside stairs and kicked open the door to a long, narrow hall on the second floor. She heard the low laugh of a man and the coy giggle of Bernice. Ignoring the sounds, she closed her eyes and held tightly to David as he walked down the hall. He carried her through a door in the middle of the corridor, then deposited her gently on the bed. As she huddled there, forlorn, gathering the shreds of her dress around her body, he rummaged through a hand-tooled black leather saddlebag carelessly tossed on a splintering chair.

She suddenly realized he didn't fit in this place. It was

musty and cheap, often washed but never clean, smelling of mildew and lye soap. He was elegant, from the top of his blond head to the expensively crafted leather boots on his feet.

He turned, approaching her with a small vial of salve, and gingerly rubbed it into her wrists. *Strange*, he thought, *her hands are delicate, but work roughened, more like a scullery maid's than those of a whore.* Next he removed her slippers and repeated the ministration to her ankles, noticing that she wore no stockings despite the winter chill.

"That feels good, umm." Not since childhood had Kate been waited on. It was a luxurious feeling.

He slid her back on the bed and slowly removed the remnants of her dress. It was in tatters and no loss, a cheap, flimsy thing to his mind.

To Kate, who owned only three dresses, it was a serious loss. She felt very self-conscious at his deft movements, realizing that he had a great deal of practice at this while she had none at all.

Once the dress was in a heap on the floor, he reached first for her right wrist, then her left, lightly kissing around the abrasions. When he turned her hands up and kissed the sensitive palms, she began to relax, reveling in the strange new feelings he was creating.

"Kate, the fairest Kate in Christendom," he breathed the words softly, dimly remembering them from an old play he'd read in college. She was slim and long-legged, made for pleasure. Still, that aura of vulnerability haunted him. Her chemise and pantalets were much mended and of poor quality. Absently, without thinking of what it implied, he imagined the beautiful, lacy undergarments he'd buy her.

With one hand he stroked her arms and her breasts while supporting his weight with the other hand. Then slowly, still looking into her eyes, he lowered his face to kiss her. She closed her eyes under the intensity of that mesmerizing blue gaze and gave herself over to her feelings. Her arms crept around his neck to hold him to her. She wanted to melt into him. Just as he softened the first warm pressure of his lips, she opened her lips for a breath and felt his tongue touch hers.

By this time, Kate was beyond coherent thought. She had been briefly pecked but never really kissed. Her proper mind told her to feel shocked indignation, but her physical instinct told her this was good, wonderfully, excitingly good. She returned the caress, gingerly following his lead, increasing the pressure of her lips. Her hands wound through his thick golden hair. The room was getting unaccountably warm for December and her breathing became fast and erratic.

David slowly ended the embrace, sprinkling quick, light licks and bites down her throat and breasts, then stood up, shed his coat and pulled off his boots. She watched in fascination as he began to unfasten his shirt studs and let the snowy silk garment fall carelessly. His chest was thickly furred with the same dark, tawny hair as his head, and his muscles were lean and hard. Catching her staring as she had downstairs, he flashed her a dazzling white grin. She blushed and looked away.

David sat on the edge of the bed and turned her face gently in his hand, forcing her to meet his gaze. Almost of their own volition, her hands came up to rub against the hairy expanse of his chest, to feel the sinewy texture of his muscles, to reach up and cup his shoulders, then lightly glide down his biceps. This time he swooped down and took her lips fiercely. She held him tightly and met his fire with her own. Kate was dimly aware that he had eased her chemise off, but when his lips connected hotly with one dark, rosy nipple, she gasped and arched her eager young body up to meet his.

"Ah, Katie, I must have you," he said with a low sigh, as breathless as she was. He stood up to slide off his trousers and hose, but this time she didn't dare look. He stretched full length alongside her on the narrow bed. His body was warm and hard as it rubbed from thigh to chest against her own. He kissed her and wrapped their legs together, rolling them over in a frenzy of passion. Then he removed her pantalets. When his hand reached between her legs and began to stroke, she was at first amazed, then eager. It felt so good, yet she ached—for what?

She writhed and bucked, making little, incoherent sounds deep in her throat. All at once he was between her legs, probing at that incredibly sensitive, wet place, but now it wasn't his hand. Kate knew enough about how animals joined to realize what he was doing, but the sudden sharp stab as he penetrated her was a shock. It had felt so good a minute ago!

If Kate was shocked, David was stunned. He could feel the pressure when he entered her, despite her wet eagerness. *God! She's a virgin!* One look at her stricken face was enough to confirm the fact and to still his passion to gentleness. He held himself immobile, supporting his weight on his elbows, while he caressed her neck, earlobes, eyes, then nuzzled her lips with soft kisses. She continued to hold him tightly, her arms wrapped around his shoulders as the initial pain quickly subsided.

For several moments he was still inside her. Very slowly then, he moved in her, watching and feeling for her response. The aching pleasure of earlier began to build once again as she kept pace with his thrusts, at first slow, then increasingly frenzied. Kate whirled in a vortex of wild, beautiful sensations, gasping out her pleasure until a final, glorious explosion hit her in succeeding waves.

David sensed her climax, then gave way to his own after the agony of holding off for so long. The wait only seemed to intensify his orgasm. He collapsed on her, then rolled them onto their sides without breaking their joining. As they regained their breaths, he ran his hand up and down the slim curve of her spine, murmuring love words in her ear and kissing her softly.

When he regained his senses, David realized he was a fool not to have recognized her inexperience. The blushes and the shy, tentative way she had responded were a dead giveaway. He'd seen her vulnerability, but never dreamed an Irish saloon girl would be an innocent! *And that bastard*

Bolton was going to sell her to Clune! He stiffened in rage at the thought.

She sensed the nuance of change in his body tension and looked directly into his eyes with a question of her own. "Was—was I—I mean, was everything all right?" She swallowed hard, looking down again in mortification. Kate didn't know if her awkward reactions and responses were adequate. He had doubtless known far more skilled, sophisticated and beautiful women than Kate Muldoon!

David's voice was warm with a hint of supressed laughter vibrating in his chest. "Oh, Katie, my lovely Irish lass, you were quite perfect. You're a passionate, sensuous woman. Just follow your instincts and you can drive a man wild." He paused, unsure of how to proceed, or indeed, if he should. He took her chin in his hand and gently kissed the tip of her nose. "Did you enjoy it?" He had to ask, even though he was sure she had, at least at the end. But damn, he wished he had known she was a virgin!

"Yes." It was barely a whisper and her downcast green eyes were shielded by her thick, dark red lashes.

"Kate, if I'd known you had never been with a man before, I wouldn't have hurt you so much. I just never thought when you agreed to come with me that you didn't know . . ."

"I *knew* well enough, but what other choice did I have? After all, you 'won' me, even killed a man for me!" She was sitting up now, holding the sheet across her breasts, rigid in anger, looking self-righteous and wronged.

Damn! He'd saved her life and planned to do right by her when he left in the morning. "Would you rather I let Clune have you? Then he'd be alive, and you'd still be minus your maidenhead, but I bet you wouldn't have enjoyed it at all!"

She gave an outraged howl and raised her hand instinctively to slap his arrogant, handsome face. With a blurringly rapid movement, he grabbed her wrist and held it.

"I wouldn't. You really must learn to control that Irish temper, Kate, or they'll be calling you 'Kate the Cursed' instead of 'the fairest Kate in Christendom.' "

She whimpered involuntarily at the pain in her lacerated wrist. He released her at once. She jerked it back and began to massage it with her other hand as she bit off her words furiously.

" 'My Irish temper,' you say? Yes, and sure I'm Irish and bein' Irish and bein' in a saloon, that makes me a whore, just like that." She snapped her fingers furiously. "My uncle, as you so sneeringly called him, is truly that, God save me. He married my Aunt Tess. After she died he had his plans for me. You saw what he had to do to get me there! And you might be takin' notice, Mr. Fancy Rich Britches, Will Bolton is *not* Irish!"

Her fierce pride touched him. He watched her green eyes shooting sparks, her magnificent darkly burnished hair falling in tangled curls to her waist. Her hands were tight fists, clutching at the sheets. She was lovely and vulnerable.

"Ah, Kate, you're not the only one with family troubles, Irish or not. I didn't mean to insult your ancestry. God knows, I grew up hearing enough about my own 'unworthy blood.' " His jaw tightened and something tense and hurt in him seemed to surface, then vanish as if he willed it away.

Despite her volatile temper, Kate was drawn to forgive David. His pain seemed to reflect her own. "Who are you?" She blushed as the obvious implication suddenly struck her; she had been to bed with a man whose given name she didn't even know. "I mean, I never saw you in Bent Fork before, but Clune's friend Brighton seemed to know you."

"I dimly recollect him now, from the St. Clair place. I think he ramrods there and knows my family, at least my father, Alexander Kane of the estimable *estancia*, Cien Robles."

"Oh!" She let out a small gasp of amazement. She knew he was rich, but she had not realized how wealthy. The name Cien Robles was known even this far north of Los Angeles. It was the biggest ranch in Southern California.

"I've heard of the ranch, but I still don't know your

given name, Mr. Kane." Again the flush brightened each
cheek.

"David Alexander Kane, at your service." He grinned
wickedly.

"You live on that huge ranch?" Try as she might, Kate
could not keep the awe from her voice.

His expression changed to a grimace. He reached for a
cigar and lit it, then leaned back against the rickety
headboard of the bed and drew her to him, putting an arm
about her shoulders. She snuggled against him, and offered
no resistance.

"Yes, I'm heir in fact, the first born, but I have a
younger brother wasting his life trying to become a priest.
My fondest hope is that he comes to his senses before it's
too late! One way or the other, though, I'm the one
destined to run the ranch, marry and provide a family line
to carry on the inheritance—my mother's inheritance,
really." He hesitated a moment, but after making love to
Kate, he felt close to her, close enough to confide in her.
"That's the real problem. My lady mother is Maria Teresa
Esperanza Alvarez de Kane, one of the oldest names in the
Spanish conquest of Mexico. Her bloodline can be traced
back five hundred years. Pity she was forced to marry a
Yankee and contaminate it with me."

She looked at him quizzically. Despite his blond hair
there was something exotic and foreign-looking in his
features and bearing: his Spanish blood. "And you have a
brother?"

"Miguel is five years younger. Luckily for him, he
resembles the Alvarez line, not nearly so diluted with the
crass Yankee strain. He pleases Mama while I please
neither her nor our father." He stopped and laughed in a
sharp, deprecating bark, then flashed the dazzling, boyish
smile that brought out her protectiveness.

"Why ever shouldn't you please your father?" Kate
could not imagine why any man as educated, attractive and
charming as David Kane would not delight a parent,
especially if he resembled his sire.

"Katie, look at me. Here I am in a saloon, wasting my

time gambling and drinking. I just shot a man and frankly, I don't even care."

"And you're with an Irish saloon girl, and sure that's no recommendation." Despite the bite of the remark her lips curved in an unwilling smile. "Scoundrel, seducer of virgins," she teased boldly. She turned her head to his chest and felt the rumble of his laughter as he kissed the top of her head affectionately. He ground out his cigar while she waited expectantly.

His mood shifted and he held her tightly, stroking her hair, then kissing little trails down her temples and throat, around her neck, moving to her breasts, pulling the concealing sheet down. Her insecurity faded with his gentle persuasion.

"Kate, beautiful Kate," he murmured softly as he slid them down to a reclining position on the bed. Once more the heat invaded her senses and she responded. She knew now what to expect. When he took her hand and placed it around his pulsing shaft, she complied with his unspoken directions and stroked it eagerly, enjoying the feel of heated velvet, then guided it inside her. This time there was no barrier, no more pain, just a joyous surge of pleasure.

CHAPTER
2

December 1851, Bent Fork

Rice Brighton arrived at the Clune place well past midnight with Hank's body tied across his horse. It had been a long, slow ride and his hate had simmered all the way.

"Damn that son of a bitch Kane! Winning the girl. Shit, if Hank had kept her, he'd have shared her when he was done. Bad enough he'll get Ellie, but he even has that pretty tart!" He cursed out loud.

Ellie. Fury at his deprivation ate into his guts as he thought of her. Ellie, a beautiful, spoiled child-woman with hair pale as moonlight. God, how he'd looked forward to initiating her into the joys of the flesh! He almost succeeded once, but she backed off, saying he had to talk to her father and they had to be married first. Hellfire, he was willing! Inheriting her father's big spread wouldn't hurt. He could settle down in the St. Clair place and live like a king with Ellie for a wife. As old Adrian's only child, she'd inherit everything. Rice Brighton would be a rich man, not grubbing for nickels and dimes as a ramrod.

But all his plans had collapsed last month when the old bastard had arranged a suitable marriage for her with Alexander Kane's son and heir, David. The two largest ranches in the Los Angeles area adjoined one another. The marriage would consolidate them into one vast holding. Where did that leave Rice?

He swore again, then laughed aloud to himself. "We'll just see, Adrian, you old sidewinder, we'll just see . . ."

The banging on the door finally roused Tom Clune from a drunken sleep. He looked outside, saw the moon up and swore. It was the middle of the night and the sour taste of corn whiskey backed up in his throat. Stumbling across the hard-packed clay floor of the adobe, he looked cautiously out a front window. It was Rice.

The door swung in and Brighton was greeted with a string of oaths. "Ya could've spent th' night in town like Hank planned. No call ta wake a body up at this piss ass hour!" Looking over Rice's shoulder, he said, "Where's Hank?"

"Hank's dead, Tom. Shot by that rich bastard, Kane's son. Over a woman in Bolton's place. I'd 'a done for him, but he got the drop on everyone and sent me out with Hank's body."

At once Tom was sober and awake. He knocked Brighton

aside to charge out the door to the horse where Hank's long corpse was hung. He pulled up its head to look at the face, dropped it, then stamped and swore. "Ya say Kane's whelp did this?"

"I ought to know who he is. I've worked on the St. Clair spread right next to his for ten years," Brighton replied arrogantly. "He needs killin', Tom. But he's fast and got a hidden gun. I figure we take Lon with us and ride back to Bolton's quick. He's all cosied up with that red-haired piece of Will's. It'd be easy to catch him with his britches off if we move now."

Daybreak. Pink and mauve streaks of light jaggedly inched their way across the eastern sky where the foothills rose in waves. Dim early light fell across the bed illuminating the small, tawdry room on the second floor of Bolton's cantina. Kate awoke suddenly, feeling that something was not right. She felt the heat of another body against hers, an unfamiliar sensation. She had never dreamed she would wake with a man in her bed until she married.

In the soft light David looked like a sleeping god, all tawny, from the thick straight hair on his head down to the curly fur on his chest. He slept flat on his back with one arm under her head, the other slipped carelessly off the side of the narrow bed; the covers were below his waist. His broad, muscular torso was exposed. The full length of his body pressed intimately alongside hers as she lay on her side facing him. His head was rolled to the left and she ran a finger gently along his profile, the high forehead, strong hawk's face, and forceful jawline glinting with bristly whiskers. His hand cupped her shoulder. She could feel his bicep flex under her head as his arm moved. He stirred but did not awaken.

The past night's events, her wild response to his skilled seduction and his offhand remarks of surprise at her virginity rushed back to her. She shuddered, remembering Hank Clune as the marks on her wrists and ankles burned faintly. She might have wakened in bed with him. There was no doubt, as David had arrogantly told her last night, that she preferred to be with him, but how long would he keep an Irish saloon girl? *Kanes don't marry Muldoons*, a small voice niggled. She dismissed the idea angrily. *As if I'd be marryin' the likes of him anyway. Snob, arrogant womanizer*, she thought to herself.

Once again he stirred in his sleep, his head rolling to the right, so near she could meet his slightly parted lips with her own. Like a magnet, the beautifully sculptured mouth drew her. She had to get away, have time to think. She sat up gingerly; the covers fell below her waist revealing her smooth, naked flesh. How pale she looked next to his tawny skin. As she slid carefully from the bed, she pushed a mass of dark red hair from her eyes with one hand. Now that she had moved from the heat of David's body, Kate shivered in the cold room.

She tiptoed silently across the floor gathering up her clothing. In consternation she realized the dress was too ripped to cover her. Disgusted, she threw it down and paused, listening for sounds in the early morning stillness. Will was doubtless passed out drunk. He'd be no threat for now. She heard no night customers stirring in the other rooms with the whores. She would simply have to sneak up to the third floor in her underwear to get another dress. After that, she was unsure of what she'd do. *One thing at a time, Katie, me girl*, she thought as she stole from the room without looking back.

Clad in a worn blue cotton dress, Kate slipped down the outside stairs and entered the kitchen. There was a small pot of clean water on the stove from last night's work. She used it to wash her face and brush her teeth.

After finishing her simple toilet, she braided her hair into one long plait over her right shoulder, peering into the dull cracked surface of an old hand mirror. *Strange, I don't look any different from the way I did yesterday. Or, do I?*

She inspected her eyes and face critically. Just then she heard voices outside, nearing the stairs that went up to the second floor from the alley, the stairs David had carried her up last night.

She peered cautiously out the kitchen window and saw

three men dismounting quietly, talking in low voices among themselves. One was Rice Brighton and the other tall lanky fellow was Tom Clune. The third was a squat, ugly brute she did not know by name, but she recognized him as the Clunes' foreman. Kate could hear Brighton, who seemed to be the ringleader.

"These stairs are squeaky, so mind you don't step in the center of the planks. Quietlike, so that murdering bastard doesn't wake up. And don't touch the girl 'til we're sure he's dead. I get first chance at her, just remember that."
They began to climb slowly and quietly.

God in heaven! They mean to kill David and take me!
She dropped the dingy sun-faded curtain and whirled from the window. Mike Wallaby kept a shotgun under the bar. She dashed down the hall into the main saloon where Will Bolton snored in a chair, head and arms sprawled across a table.

Kate swept past him and knelt behind the big scarred oak bar to pull the heavy shotgun free. She'd seen Mike load it, but she had never handled it or any other firearm herself. At least she knew it took little aim with a ten-gauge. The shotgun was heavy, but Kate hardly noticed that as she dashed across the floor and up the front stairs from the taproom to the second story.

As she turned the landing on the stairs, she heard a slight sound from the middle of the hall. They were opening the door to David's room. She used both thumbs to pull back the resistant hammer, cocking one barrel of the gun. As she fell up the last few steps she screamed. "David—look out. Brighton's going to kill you!"

As Kate yelled, she hit the top step and fired from her prone position. The recoil of the gun felt as if it had broken every bone in her body and her ears rang from the shot's loud report. The heavyset foreman took most of the force of the load and fell against Rice Brighton. He was dead before he hit the floor.

Tom Clune was inside the door, silhouetted against its frame when David aimed his Dragoon Colt and fired. David had wakened shortly after Kate slipped out and had heard quiet footsteps in the corridor. He had instinctively grabbed his gun from his open saddlebags. The sound of Kate's scream and the shotgun blast coincided with Clune's sudden lunge into his room. David killed him with one shot. As he turned his aim to Rice Brighton, the man was knocked out of his line of fire by the third man who crumpled next to Tom Clune. By the time David got to the door, Brighton had fled down the back stairs, peppered with buckshot but not badly wounded.

Kate was lying on the stairs, her long red pigtail askew over one shoulder, the shotgun on the hall floor. For one heartstopping instant, David was terrified that she had been hit. As he ran to her, she stirred slowly, groaning as she moved her arms gingerly to lever herself up from the sharp edges of the filthy steps.

He dropped to his knees and shoved the barrels of the shotgun to one side. "Katie, are you hurt?" Her only reply was one long agonized hiss of pain as he carefully helped her up.

"That's a mighty big gun for a little lady, but I'm sure glad you used it, Irish!" As he spoke, he examined her for injuries. "Good thing you were down when you fired it or it would have knocked you all the way to the bottom of the stairs."

"Not much good it did me, even though I was down," she gasped as he held her. She looked over his shoulder at the two bodies.

"It did *me* a lot of good, Katie. You saved my life." He turned her face with one hand so she looked at him, not the carnage behind them. "Thank you." He kissed her softly on the forehead.

She wrapped her arms around him, realizing suddenly that he was partially dressed, with his pants on, but no shirt or boots.

"You were awake? You had a gun?"

"I shot the tall one, you didn't get two with one blow. Don't hog all the credit, Irish. Or the blame. Is he any relation to the fellow I shot last night? They look alike—plug ugly."

"His brother, Tom. That was Rice Brighton with them."

"For a fellow I scarcely know, Brighton seems to have taken a real personal dislike to me. Wonder why?"

As they stood at the top of the front stairs, embracing and talking, one of the doors at the far end of the hall opened and a pasty face peered out. Bernice's garish yellow hair stood on end. The rouge on one cheek was rubbed off while the other side was still intact. Her eye makeup had run in black circles beneath the hollows of her eyes. In her bright purple robe she looked like a frightened circus clown.

"What hap—oh!" She gasped at the two bodies on the floor outside David's room, then turned as Lil emerged from her room at the other side of the hall. Lil silently looked from the dead men to David and Kate, eyeing the discarded ten-gauge and the Colt in David's belt. Without a word, she took the shaky Bernice by the shoulders and ushered her past David and Kate downstairs to the bar.

Will Bolton had heard the commotion upstairs, and was still shaking his head to clear it when Lil and Bernice descended the stairs. "What happened? I heard screamin' 'n shootin'."

"Thet pretty stranger 'n yer niece shot Tom Clune 'n Lon Zeltman," Lil supplied laconically, then gulped a shot of whiskey neat. Bernice sat on a stool, holding her drink in both hands, trying to steady them so she could take a sip.

Bolton stood up none too steadily and swore virulently as he staggered behind the bar.

Lil stopped him by saying, "She's took th' shotgun. Used it upstairs by th' looks of th' hall 'n Zeltman."

The Clunes and their foreman were some of his best customers. That damn high and mighty chit of Tess's had defied him, caused him to lose money and now even shot up his place! Damn her and that rich son of a bitch Kane. Wallaby did not come in until evening, but Will decided he could handle matters for himself. By now he was too livid to think straight.

David had finished dressing and was tending to Kate's

wrists with the salve when Bolton broke in on them like an enraged bull. "Yew slut, too good ta do what yer uncle needs ya fer, but ya'd kill fer the likes o' fancy pants here. I'll see ya hang, Kane, 'n then I'll take a belt ta yew, missy. Ya'll whore fer him, ya'll whore fer me!"

David stepped across the room and grabbed Bolton's shirt collar in one hand, almost hoisting him off the floor. The stench of Will's breath almost made the younger man gag as he glared at Bolton's suddenly frightened face.

"Yew leave me be, Kane. I ain't armed. Yew 'n her shot them men. Sheriff'll be askin' questions. I sent Lil ta fetch 'em."

"I shot these men when they broke into my room to kill me," David said evenly. "A third one got away—Hank Clune's pal Brighton. I figure when a man is attacked by three other armed men in his own room, he has a right to shoot."

Will backed off, inching toward the door, his fury still held at bay by his cowardice. He would come back when the sheriff arrived, but as he cleared the door, he couldn't resist one parting yell. "Yer word agin' mine! The Clunes was well thought o' men in these parts. So's Lon. Yew say Rice's here. No one else seen him."

As he shambled rapidly down the stairs, Kate came up to David and put her hand on his arm. "He's right—he'll bring the law down on you. Bent Fork's a little town not likin' strangers to be shootin' their own folks. They'll believe Will, not you or me."

Her disheveled hair had come loose from the plait and was curling around her shoulders, her face seemed pale in contrast and her eyes were fearful. What could he do?

David grinned as he turned and walked calmly to the bed. He quickly tossed a few toilet articles into his saddlebags. He slipped the .44 Dragoon Colt into a holster, then wrapped the gunbelt carelessly around his slim hips.

"Kate, I always had a hankering to see the goldfields up north. Maybe this is the excuse I've been needing to break free of my family, once and for all. My father arranged a wedding for me with another rancher's daughter, a property merger of sorts.'' He tossed the saddlebags over his shoulder and continued, ''Guess that's why I've been on such a tear lately, drifting through little back country cowtowns, gambling and drinking—avoiding the hacienda and my parents. I don't want to settle down. Come with me, Irish? We'll have a high time, maybe even find a pot of gold, who knows?''

As he waited for her to reply, she sensed a welter of conflicting emotions in his dark blue eyes. He was making the gesture only because she'd saved his life and he felt he owed her for it, that and perhaps her lost virginity— although she doubted the latter. He obviously was not asking her to marry him, only to be his temporary amour. But what choice did she have? To stay and face Will's wrath was unthinkable. A small voice in the back of her mind taunted, *You want to go with him, don't be denyin' it, girl. You want him.*

Aloud she replied, ''What else might I be doin', David Kane? Stay here and let the likes of that dull-witted sheriff hang me?''

Her fierce, hands-on-hips stance, such a sudden switch from her earlier fearfulness, took him off guard. Damn the little bitch, she had a changeable temper! He was crazy to take her with him, but she was lovely with her green eyes glittering and her proudly tilted chin set stubbornly.

He laughed. ''Katie, you've far too beautiful a neck to be stretched by a hangman's noose.'' He swept her in step with one arm tightly around her small waist. Strange, how perfectly she seemed to fit against him.

They descended the back stairs and crossed the street toward the stables. David saddled his horse, carelessly tossed a few coins onto the livery owner's bench for the night's care of his mount and swung into the saddle. Reaching down, he lifted Kate up in front of him. She clutched her small bundle of possessions in one hand as they trotted out of the stableyard into the bright morning light.

It was a clear day, dry for winter and pleasantly warm. David was exhilarated despite the sordid killings. He was off—beyond the reach of any Southern California sheriff, on his own and damn his family! Let Miguel marry St. Clair's daughter. At least it would be better than the boy staying a virgin at age twenty-one! He laughed, thinking of how furious their mother and Father Sebastian would be! Of course, Alexander Kane would be furious, too. Alex didn't like his plans thwarted, but David knew how his father thought. If forced to abandon number one son for stud, he'd go to number two. Miguel was always one for doing his duty. David was not.

As they left Bent Fork behind, a thought suddenly occurred to him. Katie hadn't known his given name last night; he still didn't know her surname. "What is your full, beautiful Irish name, Katie, my love? We've not been properly introduced."

She whispered, "Kathleen Anne Muldoon," blushing furiously and burrowing her head against his chest. Once again, she could feel the rumble of his teasing laughter as he chuckled at her naiveté.

Yes, indeed, things were going to be fine, just fine. The luck of the Irish was riding with him.

CHAPTER
3

December 1851, Cien Robles

Alexander Kane took a gulp from the glass of rum in his hand and grimaced as it burned a fiery trail down his throat. The grimace was more from the letter he held in the other hand than from the rum. Good Jamaican rum could not leave the raw burning ache in his gut that the letter before him did—the letter and the news that preceded it by two weeks.

First there was an official visit from the sheriff. It seemed David was wanted for murder in Bent Fork, nearly a hundred miles to the northeast! He had shot two brothers over a card game and a saloon whore. The sheriff was deferential, and Alex remained calm. He had waited patiently, assuming David would return to Cien Robles. The boy had always been wild and impulsive. As an unruly twelve-year-old, he ran off to sea on one of Alex's whaling ships, finally turning up in the Sandwich Islands. The captain brought him back a year later, tanned and more defiant than ever.

Alex laughed bitterly and silently to himself. David had always been independent from both the mother who disowned him and the father who tried to mold him in his own image. But through it all—the running away, the fights, even when he left college to fight in that damn fool war—David had shown such spunk, such ingenuity and intelligence that the old man had always admired him however much he wanted to disapprove.

Alexander Michael Kane had lived the nomadic life of a sea captain for many years after leaving New England as a boy. He scarcely felt close ties to the United States, especially after he became a ranchero in Mexican California. However, he felt no loyalty to Mexico either. Alex was purely and simply a Californio, like hundreds of other American expatriates who married into the native Hispanic population. There were no patriotic loyalties to the winner or the loser. He shared the political isolation and neutrality of most Californios—Mexican and Yankee. But damn him, he did feel proud that the boy acquitted himself well with General Taylor's army. Certainly Maria's horror at the treachery of her son shooting at her countrymen did not diminish his pride.

David returned from the war more distant than ever. He wasted his time drinking, wenching and gambling. He was lucky with cards and women, but nothing could make such a wastrel an acceptable eldest son. David must settle down and learn to run the ranch he would one day own. He should have been finished with sowing his wild oats; he should have been ready to marry and produce grandchildren.

But now Alex's plans were in shambles. David was not coming home. He would not honor the marriage contract with the St. Clairs. Despite the fight Alex had with his son two months ago over the scheme, the old man had been sure that David would come to his senses at last. After all, he was twenty-six years old—hardly a boy. He'd had enough time to realize that he must do his duty and claim his inheritance. Alex took another swig of rum and reread the letter for the hundredth time.

Dear Papa:

By now you have probably been told by the authorities I'm wanted for murder in Bent Fork. I did kill Hank and Tom Clune but not without cause.

After I won a card game, Hank Clune pulled a gun on me and I shot him. I spent the night at the cantina and in the morning Clune's brother and two friends came to kill me as I slept. Miss Kate Muldoon, the saloon owner's niece, gave me warning, shot one of the men and saved my life. I owe her. I would never get a fair trial in their town, if I got a trial at all.

You know how restless I've been since coming home from the war. I was never meant to be a stockman. I tried to tell you how I felt about marrying Miss St. Clair. Now things are out of both our hands. I'm off for the gold camps up north. *Quien sabe?* I might strike it rich. At least, you can consider me disinherited. I won't live off your largess and I won't be the dutiful son.

You neglected Miguel. He understands duty

and he loves the land in a way I never could. Get him the hell away from Mama and his priests. He's worth the trouble, Papa. I am not. Forgive me if you can.

Good-bye,

David

Cursing roundly at the well-remembered handwriting, Alex balled the missive and threw it furiously onto the desk. He considered David's words. It was done now, that was for certain. Even if David could be found amid the thousands of argonauts flooding the goldfields, Alex could not bring his son home as a wanted man.

The tall old man slumped in his chair. At age fifty-seven, his gold hair was liberally sprinkled with gray. His lean, hawk visage was lined by the salt spray of a hundred voyages across the Pacific and burned by the hot sun of a thousand rides across the vastness of Cien Robles. Cien Robles: a land as limitless and full of promise as the sea itself. Alex had found a home here, a heritage for his sons. Now he must have grandsons.

David was right about one thing: Miguel. Damn, he did have two sons, even if the younger looked like an Alvarez and was devoted to Maria. He was a Kane, blood of his blood. This inheritance was Miguel's also, priesthood be damned! Yes, David was right; Miguel did understand duty and tradition. The ties to the land were his Alvarez heritage. Alex had a bad heart and did not know how much time he had left. There was no other way. Bowing to the inevitable, Alex slowly stood up and walked to the big desk. Sitting down behind it, he picked up a pen and began to write.

"You are mad!" Tiny Maria Teresa Esperanza Alvarez de Kane stood in front of her tall husband, dwarfed by him, but never intimidated. Her black hair was severely swept back into a huge coil on the top of her head. A widow's peak and the wings of silver on each side were a dramatic accent. Her obsidian eyes flashed fire as she held an ivory rosary clenched in her small fists. She was thin and fine boned, once beautiful in an ethereal way, but years of bitterness had hardened her to flinty edges.

Alex looked down with the cynical smirk he wore as a barrier to her wrath. God, she looked like an angel, one from hell, not heaven. He almost laughed at the thought.

Before he could say anything, she furiously whirled from him and moved across the *sala* to stand by the window. "You cannot mean to do such a thing! Miguel is in his last year of study. He will be a priest of Holy Mother Church within the year. Father Sebastian will be beside himself."

"As are you, my dear." He spoke to her in Spanish, a language he used fluently when it suited him. Usually he spoke English and had insisted both boys learn it first with Spanish as a second tongue. Maria spoke to him in Spanish and he replied in English; they understood one another, but today, in this confrontation, he wanted no excuses for misunderstanding.

Telling her of his plans to remove Miguel from the seminary and have him marry Eleanor St. Clair gave Alex great satisfaction. *The boy will become a man. She wants her son to be as asexual as she is. Well, damn her, she won't have her way!* Maria had been cold and unyielding in his bed all those years past, her lips moving as she said a silent rosary while he tried desperately to evoke a response from her. Ellie St. Clair would heat up Miguel's blood! Alex would bet his life on it. He relished Maria's impotent rage.

"I never interfered with your directing Miguel's life before, my dear, but surely you see now why I must step in?" His voice was filled with silky solicitude. "All well and good for the second son to be a priest and please you and Father Sebastian while the elder took over the ranch. But David is gone and will not be back." His voice cracked here.

Maria knew how much that fact hurt and pounced.

"Yes, your precious David! The image of the great Alexander Kane has deserted you, turned his back on his heritage. Now you take *my* son, the Alvarez you scorned and never understood—take him and drag him from holy vocation to do what David should be doing!"

"Would you rather we allow the land commissioners to rule our title to Cien Robles invalid? Where would your grandfather's proud inheritance go then? To strangers?" He bit off each word.

"Find David and make him marry the St. Clair girl, or have your high and mighty Yankee friends go to San Francisco and use their influence on those Yankee politicians. Our title is unblemished, a direct grant from the Spanish Viceroy." She held her head defiantly high in pride.

"Spain no longer rules here, or hadn't you noticed, beloved? Nor does Mexico." His voice was taunting now. "This is a state of the American Union and land titles, by act of the United States Congress, are being examined. Even titles as venerable as those of the Alvarez family."

Maria winced under his withering sarcasm, yet refused to accept the unthinkable—that a Yankee court could take their vast estate from them. *My husband is one of them. He can make them understand without marrying my son to a gringa!*

"You arranged this marriage for David and you failed. Try something else! You were always good at getting what you wanted. You cannot take Miguel from me, not after all your years of neglect. He is an Alvarez! You cannot have him!"

"Shall we see about that, my beloved wife?" His voice held an edge of challenge that chilled her to the bone.

Father Sebastian was a graying, emaciated man, gaunt in his severe black robes. An even blacker scowl knitted his thin, straight eyebrows into one black slash across his forehead. He stood in the *sala*, surrounded by the opulence of the Cien Robles hacienda, as out of place as a crow in an aviary full of peacocks. Turning to Maria Kane, he said soothingly, "Surely Don Alesandro will not go through with this! The boy will refuse him. He owes a higher allegiance to his God than to his father."

Maria let out a harsh, quick sigh of frustration. "Ha! Alexander Kane thinks he *is* God, at least on Cien Robles!"

The old priest crossed himself at this bit of sacrilege. "You do not think, my daughter, that Miguel will listen— will bow to his father's wishes? No." He shook his head in stubborn resolution. "I have taught him since his youth. He and his father were never close. Miguel will not fail in his devotion."

Maria twisted her hands in agitation and said softly, almost to herself, "I—I do not know. He is an Alvarez and the ties to the land are strong. If Alex can convince him . . . I am not sure." She put a scented handkerchief to her face and suppressed a shuddering sob, then looked through the open arch of the *sala* at the huge oak door to Alex's study, now ominously closed this last hour. The old priest followed her gaze.

Inside the study Miguel sat in a high-backed chair in the corner, surrounded by bookcases. It was the very chair he had used as a boy when selecting books from the library, books he had taken to his room or down to the pond. This time it was not a book he read, but David's letter. The bitter taste of bile rose in his throat as he held the missive, thinking back over his abrupt summons home from the seminary. No hint was given of why he must interrupt his studies, just a crisp, decisive note to Father Dominic from Don Alesandro Kane, informing the head of the school that Miguel must come home because of an emergency .

This was the emergency! David had fled to the gold-fields in disgrace—wanted by the law for murder! As Miguel reread the last part, reminding Alex that he had a second son who must be rescued from their mother and her priests, he had to smile sadly in spite of his anger. Misdirected as it was, Miguel could still feel the protective concern that David had always showed him. He remembered all the times David had tried to get his younger brother to join him in carousing. *David always felt I was*

*missing something because I didn't share his enthusiasm
for women—and liquor and cards.*

The words that said their father neglected his second son
had a bitter ring of truth for Miguel. *Yes, I understand my
duty to our heritage,* hermano, *in a way you never wanted
to! Now I must pay the price for your irresponsibility.*
Miguel sighed. He could never really stay angry with
David. It was toward their father that he directed his
fearsome Alvarez temper. In seminary he had tried to
subdue it, but now it rose in him.

He stood to confront Alex. "I assume that you mean to
take my brother's advice." It was not a question.

Miguel knew the answer, but he would wring from the
old man an admission that at long last he needed his
younger son because the elder had failed him. If Miguel's
life was in shambles, all his plans thwarted, he would have
that much satisfaction.

"You plan to substitute me for David in the marriage
contract with the St. Clair family. Don't you think the
bride might object? After all, I'm not the golden, glamorous David. I'm the dark, brooding Alvarez."

Alex sat calmly behind his big oak desk. "You're a
Kane," he interrupted. "You are my blood and this land
belongs to you, too. As to the St. Clairs, I've already
spoken to Adrian and he sees no problem in you taking
your brother's place."

"And what about Eleanor?" Miguel raised one eyebrow
quizzically, his body looming over the older man seated in
the chair.

"Ellie will do as her father tells her," Alex replied in
dismissal. He took a scrutinizing appraisal of the tall, dark
youth standing before him. Alex was startled at how much
like a Kane Miguel looked—simply a dark version. "Besides, you'll do well enough. If you'd ever leave your
books and praying to look in a mirror, you might be
surprised. Women will find you considerably more than
passable."

"So David used to tell me, but my vocation is the
priesthood. It's better if I never follow the venial side of

our ancestry that you and my brother are so taken with."
His expression was self-righteous and haughty.

Alex stood up angrily, pounding on the desk. "Pah,
you're a boy! A twenty-one-year-old virgin, so sequestered
and hounded by blackrobes you've never known your own
mind—or body. Unless you get out in the world and see
what's there, how the hell can you know the truth of your
vocation?"

Alex's withering scorn bit deeply, but Miguel stood
face-to-face with his father, refusing to back down. "As
David pointed out, Papa, you paid little enough attention
to me in the past. When Father Sebastian guided me
toward the church, you never cared. You need me because
your firstborn failed you! Suddenly you notice I'm alive!
You looked right through me for twenty-one years, just
like you did Mama. We never mattered to you. Well,
maybe it's too late now."

Calmly, almost wearily, Alex sat down again, then said,
"Let's leave your mother and me out of this argument.
Our failures are our own. You're right, though. I neglected
you and favored David. I got him, she got you." He
paused and smiled sadly. "It was a compromise of sorts.
But now everything's changed. David doesn't love the land
the way you and I do. And," he went on relentlessly, "he
never understood duty the way you and I do. You know the
situation, Miguel, just as well as I. Either you marry Ellie
St. Clair and tie Cien Robles to Adrian St. Clair's lands,
or we stand a damn good chance of losing everything to
the government. The land commission meets within the
year to rule on the titles of all Spanish and Mexican land
grants. Our grant's boundary descriptions are a trifle imprecise, to say the least—'from the big oak by the meadow
to the rock pile by the ravine.' Ha! On a dozen square
leagues named One Hundred Oaks, that's a hell of a way
to record a survey!"

"It was always the custom. Until the Yankees came, it
served Californios well enough, whether Spain or Mexico
ruled us. No one contested the extent of Alvarez land."
Miguel's voice had calmed. He was bowing to the inevitable.

"Well, they're contesting it now. Old Adrian has only one child and he wants a good marriage for her. He drives a hard bargain. He wants a merger of our lands in return for using his influence with those men in San Francisco to secure our title."

"Damn!" Miguel swore as he turned away, hating himself for his lapse into profanity. Then he faced Alex once more with an accusing look in his cold blue eyes. "You might get Adrian to help you without this marriage. Have you even tried—or do you want to double the size of the estate just as much as he does? This marriage suits you as well as him. Maybe even more because you can hurt Mama in the bargain. You know how proud she was of my becoming a priest."

"How much she didn't want your blue Alvarez blood contaminated with more Yankee strains, you mean," Alex interrupted dryly. "As long as it was David marrying to secure the title, she was all for it. But her Miguel marry a gringa?" He chuckled. "At least the St. Clair family is Catholic and Ellie is a beautiful child. Look at the bright side. You might actually find her pleasing, even if your mother does not."

Miguel looked squarely at Alex. "It doesn't really matter whether I do or not, does it, Papa? You hold the threat of losing Cien Robles over my head if I don't marry the girl."

Two pairs of midnight blue eyes locked in a final, deadly showdown. Alex played his last ace. "Would you care to defy me and see your mama turned out onto the streets of Los Angeles, destitute, losing her proud Alvarez heritage? She'd be completely dependent on me, on my shipping income, my crass Yankee dollars. What do you think that would do to her haughty Castilian pride? You choose." Alex waited, and held his breath.

Bitter resignation was written all over Miguel's face. His voice was calm as he bit off each word. "You win, just as you knew all along you would. I'll marry the chit. I'll do my duty, not shirk it like my brother. But remember this. You play with other people's lives and someday you'll pay. I agree to this marriage because of Mama. It would kill her to live in Los Angeles. Tell me, Papa, would you move your Chilean mistress out, or would you make Mama live in the same house with her?''

Alex flinched in amazement at that unexpected sally. "How the hell did you find out about Dolores?"

"Just because I don't share your vices, don't think I'm so stupid as to be unaware of them," Miguel sneered in disgust.

Alex replied coldly, "I don't expect you to understand about Dolores and me so I won't dignify your self-righteous accusation with a reply. You're a green boy who's never lain with a woman, never loved one. You know nothing."

"You never loved your wife! And you want to preach to me about my inadequacies? I will never forgive you for this!" With that, Miguel turned and stormed from the room, slamming the door.

The silence was heavy around Alexander Kane, who suddenly felt years older. He was a good card player. He had won. Why did he feel so infinitely sad at the victory? The familiar pain in his chest caught him suddenly. It had been quiescent for the past week, even after his fierce fight with Maria. Strange that it now stirred again. Slowly he stood and walked over to the bar behind the desk and poured himself a shot of rum.

Alex was dumbstruck at Miguel's knowledge of Dolores Santiago—Dolores, the shy, sweet young woman from Chile who had taken his eye in a cantina five years ago. He'd given up his random whoring after that. All the restless, desperate unhappiness of the years with Maria seemed to recede when he gazed into Lorry's calm doe eyes. *She is my haven, my safe port. David knows about her and he never condemned me*. He grinned weakly. *The pot can hardly call the kettle black!* Alex now discreetly confined himself to one loving woman, but Miguel would never understand that need for solace. *Then again, perhaps he will. Wrenched from Maria, the boy may become a man, with a man's needs.*

Ellie St. Clair was lovely. They'd make a striking pair and have beautiful children. Of course, he remembered sadly, he and Maria had made a handsome couple and had two beautiful sons. Well, even if his son's marriage were as empty as his own it would still save the boy from becoming a humorless aesthete like Father Sebastian. *Running Cien Robles is in his blood. Miguel knows every inch of the place. He'll be a fine ranchero.*

Alex drank deeply of the rum, lost in thought.

CHAPTER
4

December 1851, Twin Rivers

"You only care about the land, not my happiness! You'll have the two largest estates in Southern California tied together for your grandchildren, you and that hateful Alexander Kane!" Ellie St. Clair shrieked the accusation at her father.

Stoically, the portly, dignified Adrian St. Clair bore this temper tantrum as he had so many others through the years since Althea's death. "It's been hard raising a girl alone without a mother. I've always let you have your head, Ellie. I guess I spoiled you in the process, but I did it out of love. I want your happiness, but a fortune-hunting cad like Brighton won't make you happy. He'll run through your money, let Twin Rivers go to ruin and disgrace the St. Clair name in front of the whole community."

"I suppose that wild David Kane is a much better

choice? Oh, I've heard talk in town about his carrying on, don't think I haven't! Convenient, he's heir to a huge ranch bordering ours. You can overlook a lot of faults for that," she shot back, interrupting him.

"The Kane and Alvarez names are established and respected ones in this part of the country. David is a fine young man, educated, good looking, acquitted himself well in the war. He'll settle down and be a good husband for you. Blood will tell. I've known his father for twenty-five years. The Kanes have business sense as well as honor. He'll know how to run both ranches. Brighton is only after your money. David Kane obviously doesn't need it."

She seethed, stamping her foot in fury, "Oooh, that's flattering! A man could only be attracted to me for this ranch or for my money. God! I must be as ugly as Medusa. If you don't make this merger, heaven only knows who I'll be forced to wed out of desperation!"

At this, a hint of a smile tugged at the corners of the old man's mouth beneath his thick, brushy mustache. "Eleanor," he replied gravely, "you know you are beautiful, just as your mother was. But you're young and impulsive and you don't understand what a man like Rice is capable of."

"Then why did you make him ramrod?" she shot back instantly.

Adrian hesitated, then answered. "I never planned to discuss such things with you, Ellie, but I want you to understand why I would forbid a marriage to Brighton under any circumstances. Rice Brighton is a gunman. He has a reputation from here to the Mexican border. We've had frequent problems with rustling in the years you were away at school. Bands of cutthroats roving across the eastern desert have stolen whole herds of prime stock, driving them to those blasted Mormons in Utah. Brighton has trained some of the hands to use firearms and hired a number of his unsavory friends to keep the thieves at bay. So far, his reputation and a few minor skirmishes have done the trick. Our losses have been minimal."

"It sounds to me like Rice is quite capable of running

this ranch. I don't care about his past. I love him and he loves me!''

Finally, Adrian lost his temper. "Here I explain to you my very real fears for your safety and Brighton's disreputable past, but you still prattle of love. You are a willful child and know nothing of life! You've been sheltered and cosseted and now you fancy yourself in love with a man you know nothing about! One who will only use you!''

"Of course I've known David Kane all my life!'' she answered sarcastically. "We're strangers. I can't marry a stranger. I love Rice and I'll marry him.'' She finished on a mulish wail.

"You will do no such thing! You need a strong hand to bring you to maturity. God knows, I've failed. Miss Jefferson's school has, too. You will marry David Kane and he will deal with you. That is my final word!''

"I'll tear up your precious contract in front of his horrified eyes! You'll have to haul me in tied to a board!''

"How would you like to spend the rest of your life sleeping on a board—living on bread and water and precious little else? I'll send you to the Carmelite Convent in San Luis Obispo. You choose. Be a wife or be a nun!''

Ellie's eyes widened in shock as she stood mute, staring at her father, the daddy she'd always been able to wind around her finger, cajole for anything she desired. He was like a stranger now. He truly meant it! He would pack her off to that dreadful place! She shivered in shock at this change in him, then turned on her heel, tears blurring her eyes, and ran to the stables to saddle Moonlight.

She whipped the small white filly into a furious gallop, racing across the wet ground, heedless of slippery mud and treacherous rocks. Once again she and her father had fought over the marriage agreement with the Kanes. *Damnation*, she swore to herself, leaning down across the horse's elegant neck to run her hard, working her own frustrations out through the animal's pounding hooves. After a few minutes, she slowed Moonlight and began to think.

Ever since she returned home from school last fall, her

father had been watchful and fussy about her. Now she was a grown woman. When she left for Miss Jefferson's Academy in St. Louis, she was fifteen, a child sent East to be polished into a lady. Her father could not provide the necessary refinements on a ranch in Southern California. Ellie's mother had been killed in a carriage accident when she was three. She had only dim memories of a pale blonde woman of delicate beauty and placid manners. Placid Eleanor Leona St. Clair was not! She had her father's stubborn pride and fierce temper, even if she was tiny of stature, fine-boned and fair like her mother.

Ellie had adored Rice Brighton since he first came to work for her father as a cowhand, when she was a spindly child. She worshiped him from afar and her father laughed at her schoolgirl crush. But when she came home a young woman of eighteen to Rice's twenty-nine years, the infatuation no longer seemed so amusing to Adrian St. Clair. During her absence Rice had become ramrod of Twin Rivers, the huge St. Clair estate. In the past months he had noticed the boss's daughter and had begun to court her.

But an odious alliance with the Kanes of Cien Robles was all her father would consider. Ellie had a faint recollection of David Kane and his father, the formidable Alexander. She remembered the elder son as a yellow-haired, teasing youth she'd met briefly at a fiesta long before she'd gone to St. Louis. She vaguely remembered that he was pleasant to look at—but to marry a man she did not love! It was unthinkable.

Anyway, the Kanes were overbearing and snobbish. Elegant old Alexander was a cold Yankee and the Alvarez side of the family was even worse. Doña Maria considered herself too good even to speak with the upstart St. Clairs, whose French ancestors did not possess exalted bloodlines like her Castilian ones. What Ellie knew of the Kanes was more than enough. She would never marry into such a family.

But her father would never let her marry Rice. He categorically forbade her to see the ramrod, saying Rice was impoverished and unsuitable. Then, he caught them defying him, kissing in the stables one day last week. Ellie had not planned to meet Rice; it was an accidental encounter, but Adrian was livid, threatening to fire Rice and keep Ellie under lock and key.

Reddening in mortification, she recalled an earlier incident in one of the line shacks. *If Dad thought a simple kiss was so horrible, what would he have done if he'd caught us then?* She shuddered. Rice had all but undressed her and it took every ounce of her willpower to call a halt to his feverish kisses. She pleaded that they wait and get her father's blessing. Now she almost wished her principles had not won out. Perhaps if she had let Rice continue, her father would have allowed them to get married. She had heard all sorts of stories about shotgun weddings at school in St. Louis. Growing up on a ranch, Ellie knew the facts of life, at least as far as breeding cattle and horses went. The same general methods doubtless pertained to men and women. Besides, she enjoyed it when Rice kissed her.

Ellie sighed. It was no use. She had a sense of honor, and blackmailing her father with the threat of an illegitimate grandchild went against her instincts. No, she would have to wait until she could marry Rice Brighton.

"I won't sign any cold-blooded contract! I'll steal away to Rice and tell him what Dad plans to do. We'll just have to get married without his blessing and leave Twin Rivers. Devil take the place!" As she formulated her plans, she slowly cantered back to the ranch house.

Rice had been gone for nearly a week. The men had told Ellie they didn't know why he wasn't back. He often left for a Saturday night outing, usually in Bent Fork, which was only a few hours' ride northeast of Twin Rivers' land. However, this past Sunday evening he hadn't returned.

Well, it was Wednesday now. Surely he would be back in a day or so, Ellie reasoned. As she walked back to the house she fretted over his absence, silently praying the rustlers her father mentioned had not waylaid him and shot him. The sunset was a purple and gold blaze of splendor in the west and the high mustard swayed in the evening breeze. Rice could lay wounded in some field, hidden where no one could find him. She forced the thought aside as foolishly morbid.

It was Friday when Rice returned to Twin Rivers. Adrian was looking for him, furious over his unexplained absence. Brighton told him a cock-and-bull story about a run-in with some Utah cattle thieves and a shooting fracas, explaining that he'd had to stay with a doctor in Santa Benita until his buckshot wounds were partly healed. The old man, ever gullible about his tales of thieves, accepted the lie.

Little did that stupid old bastard know, the cattle thieves whom Rice was hired to drive off were his friends! He had worked a deal with the Clune brothers over a year ago when he needed cash. He simply let a few head of prime beef wander into the high mustard for their gang to corral and sell. It had been so profitable that he, Tom and Hank had a regular partnership going. It was easy cash on the side since Rice as ramrod knew the location of each herd. As long as he didn't get too greedy, it was easy to steal from Adrian St. Clair.

Of course, if he could maneuver that pretty little chit Ellie into his bedroll and marry her, he could forget the risks of rustling or hiring out his gun or any of the other things he had done to survive over the years. But David Kane might still spoil his plans. That rich bastard took a lot of killing. Both Clunes and Lon were dead and his own wounds still made him feverish and achey. He owed that Muldoon bitch, too, if he ever caught up with her again, but he'd think about that later. For now, there was the old man to placate and Ellie to woo.

But how to get to Ellie without the old man finding out? Every time he caught her alone Adrian was on them instantly. He was sure protecting the merchandise for Kane.

Then, one morning a few days after his return, Rice saw Ellie ride slowly toward the east fork of the river, a favorite spot of hers. Just as she went over the hill, Jeb Greenly, who usually saddled her horse, came up to Rice with a note. Rice tossed him a plug of tobacco, Greenly's usual bribe for a favor, and quickly read the note.

Rice:

Meet me at the line shack on the edge of the east fork in half an hour. There is something urgent I have to talk to you about.

Love,

Ellie

He chuckled. Talk, huh? He'd do a lot more than talk this time. No more waiting. He would get her into bed and she would damn well wheedle her old man into making him a son-in-law. Whistling casually, Rice saddled up and headed west, then cut through the mustard toward the east fork.

When he got to the deserted shack, Ellie was there, nervously pacing the crude floor, which creaked and groaned under her slight weight. It was made of splintery, dry boards nailed to logs and simply provided a platform a few inches off the dirt which would turn to mud in the rains. As Rice stepped through the open door Ellie ran into his arms.

Ellie had gone to great pains this morning, feigning a headache when Adrian rode to town. Then she gave her maid the slip, saying she wanted a sleeping draught and to rest undisturbed all morning.

"Oh, I thought I would never get free, Rice! Dad is determined to go through with this mad scheme of his."

He held her securely and stroked her hair, kissing her temples. When he spoke, his voice was low and urgent. "You could always bring him around before. You can now. Let's just do what we held off on last time, darling. Then he'll have to let us marry!"

He turned her face up and covered her lips in a kiss before she could utter a sound.

Breaking off after a minute of the fierce, hypnotizing assault, Ellie shook her head. "No, no, Rice, you don't understand. We have no reason to expect Dad's blessing. He's never going to give it. We might as well go to Los Angeles and get married right now."

Taking her roughly by the shoulders, he held her at arm's length. "What do you mean, 'no reason to expect his blessing'?"

She cast her eyes down at the harsh question, then began in a low, hesitant voice, "He—he's become like a stranger, threatening me. He said you were a gunman and he'd never let you inherit Twin Rivers. He offered me a choice. Either I marry David Kane or he'll force me into a convent!" She threw herself back into his embrace, flinging her arms around his waist. "Oh, don't you see, if I don't make this marriage, I'm disinherited! Well, I don't care! He can give this accursed ranch to the convent. We'll be together, Rice. That's all that matters!"

Rice stood very still. Then after a minute's pause, he questioned, "You're absolutely sure about this? He's really going to disinherit you if you don't go through with the marriage to Kane?"

Something in the tone of his voice made her look up into those gray eyes. He was the same handsome Rice, with curly, light tan hair, straight, clean-cut features and broad, muscular shoulders. Yet he looked different. Or was she seeing him as he really was for the first time? The handsome mouth and chin a bit weak, the eyes cold, the manner glib and wary?

"Rice, I told you. We had a horrible fight while you were gone. If I don't escape soon, I'm afraid he'll lock me up and I don't even want to think what he might do to you! We have to get away, now!"

Brighton did some quick calculating. If he ran off and married her, that old bastard might just be ornery enough to disinherit her. Then he'd be saddled with a penniless wife. On the other hand, if she married Kane and then her husband met with an "accident," she would be free and richer than ever. He began very carefully.

"Ellie, we can't just cut and run. I'd have no job, no way to support us. And besides, you can't just desert your

father. He's your only kin. He loves you and is trying to
do what he thinks is best for you." He gathered her more
closely in his arms and began to rock them gently together.
"It doesn't mean we can't be together. We can seal our
love right now. then you'll have the memory of that to
sustain you, little girl. I'll still be nearby, and who knows,
something might happen to Kane . . ."

Before he could go any further, the full implication of
what he was saying hit her. She broke away, stunned. "You
mean I should lie with you now and then marry David
Kane and continue as an adulteress, just so we'll both be
secure? So you'll keep your job and I'll be heiress to two
ranches? You can't mean it!" Furious, she ran the back of
one small hand across her mouth as if wiping away the
contamination of his kiss. No! It was too much to bear.
"Dad was right! Oh, Rice, Dad was right!"

Before he could stop her, she whirled and fled. He
would have caught her and taken what he had waited for
so long, now that his plans were in ashes. However, as he
lunged across the rickety wood floor after her, his greater
weight caused one of the rotten planks to give way. His
foot was caught between the boards. By the time he freed
his boot, Ellie was galloping Moonlight across the meadow, driving the filly in a frenzy of anger and hurt.

He swore and limped toward his horse. Well, he would
have to bide his time and make the best of it. She would
come around. After all, he had been her idol since she was
a skinny kid. This forced marriage could not change that.
She would see, after Kane was dead, how much more
sensible it was to have waited. In the meanwhile, he had to
work on his sideline of rustling. He had met the gang from
Utah that the Clunes dealt with. If he went into Bent Fork
in a couple of weeks, he could leave word with Bolton that
he was still interested in continuing their partnership,
despite Hank's and Tom's deaths. The rustlers just might
be helpful in dealing with David Kane when the time
came. Yessiree, real helpful.

Ellie cried so hard on the way home, it was a wonder
she didn't break her neck and the terrified little filly's as

well. She rode the horse into a mad gallop, unable to see anything in her path. She had to get away from Rice. *Oh, Rice! Dad was right about you all along. You only wanted me for Twin Rivers, not for myself. And now, it's either a convent or a loveless marriage.*

By the time she arrived at the big house, Ellie was calm. She made no attempt to hide her actions from the household help. Let them tell Adrian. What difference did it make now? She had nowhere to go, no one to run to.

On the way back she began to recall the few childhood memories she had of David Kane. He had seemed pleasant enough, more laughing and carefree than his aloof father and mother. He looked like old Alex, she remembered. Well, she must make her peace and go through with it. The other alternative was too hideous to contemplate—a nun, indeed!

With the resilience of youth, she bathed and changed to face her father upon his return that evening. She chose a green dimity dress that emphasized her youth and innocence. He'd be furious when her maid tattled about her outing that morning. She must agree to the marriage and be conciliatory, but she would salvage her pride, never admitting to her father that he was right about Rice Brighton. She would do her duty and make the best of it, head held high. Damn him, Rice, Alex and David Kane. Damn all men!

"Eleanor, I know about your disgraceful escapade this morning. God only knows how you got past Mattie and out of the house, but I promise you, it will *not* happen again." Adrian stood at the dinner table. His manner was deceptively calm, but Ellie could sense the anger.

Equally calm, she faced him and replied, "There will be no need for it to happen again. I met Rice briefly to tell him of your ultimatum. He understands that we can never marry."

"Am I to understand all you did was talk?" His clipped, controlled accusation broke her resolve to be calm.

"Would you like to have a physician examine me to verify my virginity! As you will, sir. I'm at your disposal in all things, it seems!"

Adrian whitened at her vicious thrust. She looked so much like her sweet mother, but she had inherited her wicked temper from him, he feared. All his life he had struggled to control that temper and felt, in large measure, that he had succeeded. He shook his head. Ellie was worse than he had ever been, even as a foolish youth.

Adrian considered Alex Kane's younger son, whom he had not seen in three years while the boy was at seminary. Miguel was quiet, well-spoken and had his mother's Hispanic coloring and Alex's blue eyes. That was all he remembered. Adrian prayed the boy had the patience of Job.

Throughout the strained meal, neither father nor daughter said anything nor ate much. Adrian was lost in thought, unsure of how to broach the subject of the switch in bridegrooms to his already furious hellcat of a daughter. He had reluctantly agreed to the substitution of Miguel for David that morning in town when he met Alex.

His old friend told him about David's flight and the unlikely possibility of recalling him. Alex assured Adrian that Miguel was studious and obedient, devoted to the land and far more aware of his family duty than David. As to the matter of Miguel's vocation, Alex said that his son's love for Cien Robles was far more significant. They both agreed to postpone the signing of the betrothal agreement for a month to allow Miguel to settle in at Cien Robles. Then the two young people would meet.

This marriage seemed the only solution to Adrian. He had to get Ellie safely married and out of the clutches of that ruffian Brighton. She was rich and inexperienced, a likely target not only for Rice, but for other unscrupulous men.

To be honest with himself, Adrian also had to admit that he wanted the land merger. He squirmed a trifle uneasily in his seat as he absently stirred cream into his coffee. Cien Robles was the most magnificent estate in Southern California, but the boundary lines of the old Spanish land grant were imprecise. The new land commission in San Francisco might well rule it invalid. But if the two ranches were tied by a dynastic marriage, there would be far less chance of an unfavorable ruling on the Alvarez title. Adrian had friends in high places. He could easily deal with the land commissioners.

So could Alex, who was not without his own political influence. Adrian sighed. Both he and his old friend were greedy Yankees at heart. The thought of the land merger that their grandchildren would inherit drew them to manipulate their children's lives.

Adrian looked again at Ellie. He was doing what was best for her. The Kane and Alvarez lines were both blue-blooded and honored. Their child and his were fitting mates. It would work out, could be a good marriage, once Ellie curbed her cutting tongue and vicious temper. Perhaps Miguel Kane would even make a genteel lady of her. Heaven knew her father and teachers had failed, but then as Alex had said, Miguel was the quiet, dutiful son, a perfect husband for her, patient and understanding.

CHAPTER
5

March 1852, Cien Robles

Miguel burst from the stable, kicking the door shut with a resounding slam that sprayed gravel across the courtyard as he strode over to his big black stallion. Swearing in Spanish, he swung into the saddle in a fluid motion, smooth yet indicative of cold fury. Just as he turned to ride off, Alex stormed out of the same door, yelling at him to come back.

Cursing roundly, Miguel reined in and glared down at his father. "We've said it all, Papa! You want to save your hard-earned Yankee dollars and keep breeding inferior cattle, so we do it your way."

"Dammit, Miguel, I don't trust those bastard Mormons. Who says their stud bulls are better? I don't like doing business with them."

"Then don't. You make all the decisions about the stock business, just like you run the shipping business. All I'm here for is to be a stud myself, so you can turn the real running of Cien Robles over to a grandson!"

With that, he wheeled the black stallion furiously, nearly knocking the older man to the ground. As Alex watched his son ride away he had to grin in spite of his anger. *The boy has spunk. And a temper! Whew!* There was more Kane in him than Miguel would ever own up to. There was also a quiet, resolute strength and an almost uncanny judgment about animals.

Alex had to grudgingly admit that Miguel was probably right about the bulls. If they bought half a dozen from that Mormon stockman, they could increase the size of their beef cattle by as much as thirty percent over a few years. He hated dealing with Mormons, sharing a mistrust common to his countrymen for a generation. Well, they'd talk about it at dinner tonight. Alex admitted to himself he wasn't allowing his son enough say in running the ranch. His well-concealed but rapidly failing health attested to that. Miguel was proving to be a first-class ramrod. It was time to give him more responsibility.

Alex smiled as he remembered the afternoon in January when he had called the vaqueros together to announce that his younger son was the new *mayordomo*. Miguel would have the responsibility for running the ranch—organizing the rodeos, overseeing the vaqueros and buying and selling livestock and equipment. Since everyone had expected the war-toughened David to assume this role, not the bookish younger brother, Miguel was greeted with quite a few skeptical looks. The smirking vaqueros remembered him as a boy gone off to be a priest. Now he was going to ramrod Cien Robles? He would have to prove himself.

Alex recalled Miguel's well-chosen first move. His son had gone to the stable every day since he returned from seminary to feed, groom and talk to the black stallion that he had left behind three years ago. Miguel had gentled the horse as a colt, breaking him to bridle and saddle, only to have a brutal vaquero abuse the animal in his absence. By the time the man had been fired, no one could ride the black devil horse. Alex had always known that his son had a special way with animals, but what Miguel did that warm January morning put even his skills to a difficult test.

Miguel had gambled that the stallion was intelligent enough to remember him. Alex had watched in apprehension as Miguel saddled the black and brought him to the breaking corral in full view of all the hands. *By tomorrow, he'll either be a laughing stock or in charge of Cien Robles*, Alex thought. The horse's gleaming ebony coat had inspired Miguel to name him after the Dominican brothers, who were known as blackrobes. Alex had often wondered how Father Sebastian felt about Miguel's name for the beast.

Alex had watched as Miguel stood very quietly in the center of the corral, allowing the nervous stallion to smell him. As Dominican calmed, Miguel began to croon soft words and rub his muzzle ever so gently. After that, watched by the vaqueros gathered around the corral, he led the horse in ever-widening circles, coming nearer to the fence as he did so. If he had sold seats for a bear baiting, he could not have collected a larger audience. Although many of the hands pretended to be passing on the way to other chores, they all stayed to watch the show. Undoubtedly, some were betting that the kid would be dumped on his ass. Old Rafael, who had cared for the ranch's horses for years, watched Dominican, searching for any change in his mood.

After walking a few rounds in the corral, Miguel stopped and again talked to the big horse. "All right, Dominican.

From now on, boy, you belong to me and we'd better learn to work together.''

No quirt, no spurs, no sharp bit in the horse's mouth. Miguel never used pain to force an animal. He was counting on the keenly intelligent stallion remembering his handfeeding and affection. Slowly, he put his foot in the stirrup and easily swung into the saddle. Miguel had been raised on horseback like all Californios, but the ground had never looked as far away.

The sweat rolled down Miguel's brow. Continuing his low, musical conversation and stroking Dominican's neck, he used his knee to guide the big black around the corral. Several times Dominican shied, but the patient rider kept a firm, steady hand on the reins. When Dominican was collected, Miguel urged him into a trot, then a canter. Finally, satisfied with his control over the horse, Miguel had signaled Rafael to open the gate. He rode past the crowd of onlookers, galloping hard across the open ground. The big stallion's long stride had eaten up the distance as they raced toward the horizon to the cheers and shouted congratulations of the vaqueros. No one had been able to ride that horse since Martinez left, and he had used a razor sharp bit to do so.

Alex overheard Joe Hooker swear in surprise, "Maybe the *muchacho*'ll do better 'n we'd a figgered.''

The gnarled Rafael spit a big splash of tobacco from between several widely spaced teeth and replied in his heavily accented English, "Why would you doubt it? He is Don Alesandro's son, no?''

Alex turned his thoughts to the present, berating himself for his favoritism toward David all those years. David, his firstborn, his image, and the son who felt no love for the land. Miguel loved Cien Robles with the same passion Alex did, as one loved a woman.

At that Alex had to smile. They were going to Twin Rivers in two days. That might account for some of his son's temper. The bridegroom was nervous at the prospect of meeting Ellie St. Clair and signing the betrothal contract. The wedding was only months away and Alex was sure Miguel was still a virgin. He recalled David's unsuccessful attempts to get the boy to accompany him to the bordellos in town. At one point the old man had considered forcing the issue and dragging the boy in to be initiated, but he decided against it. Such an embarrassing encounter could end with a youth humiliated and impotent. He'd seen it happen in the rough camaraderie of sailors. Alex had let it drop and abandoned Miguel to Maria and Father Sebastian.

Now Alex laughed. He had never found out exactly what Miguel told his mother and Father Sebastian, but it settled once and for all the issue of his leaving the seminary and marrying Ellie St. Clair. Tight-lipped, sorrowing, the old priest went about his duties at the hacienda with far less zeal than before, looking like a soul already consigned to eternal perdition.

Miguel, for his part, spent little time in the company of his spiritual mentor. Once committed to becoming the new *patrón*, he lived the part. He was up every day riding Dominican before the first pink streaks of light glowed on the eastern horizon. He knew every hand's name in the main bunkhouse and was learning to know all the outriders in the lineshacks. He had adopted several of their habits which horrified Maria and Father Sebastian. He swore, smoked hand-rolled cigarettes and even joined Alex in drinking before supper.

Not that Miguel was any more cordial toward his father than he'd vowed to be the day he agreed to the marriage, Alex sadly admitted to himself. Still, the boy was enjoying the work. He loved the land and was a natural leader. Perhaps a reconciliation between them would come in time. Tonight, Alex vowed he'd make a conciliatory move and admit the deal with the Utah breeder was a good idea. Miguel could arrange the purchase.

"Damn, if I'm not mellowing with age, just as Miguel's hardening with it." The chest pain gripped him again, but Alex laughed despite it. Life was good.

*   *   *

On the long ride to Twin Rivers, neither father nor son spoke. But when they entered the small valley at the fork of the two rivers and saw the two-story frame house that was old Adrian's pride and joy, Miguel snorted in derision at the out-of-place Yankee architecture. "It looks as hot as an oven. I bet you could fry eggs on the second-story floors in summer. Thank God we don't have to live here!"

Alex laughed. "No, you'll take Ellie to our cool, practical adobe with its two-foot-thick walls and open, tree-shaded courtyard. Be thankful, but please don't deride Adrian's taste. He had the place built to exact scale, just like his father Morton's house back in Massachusetts."

"That's where he should have built it, in Massachusetts." *And had his daughter live in it,* Miguel added silently to himself.

Alex let the comment pass.

Ellie looked carefully in her mirror. She forced her clenched jaw to relax. Despite her foul humor she wanted to look her best. For February it was a balmy day and she wore a turquoise silk dress, one of her most elegant spring gowns.

Hearing horses, she went to her bedroom window and looked through the lace curtain. As befitted Kanes, the two men were mounted magnificently. Ellie almost forgot her anger as she admired the younger rider's black horse. They rode alongside Doña Maria's elegant carriage, which Alex had imported on one of his ships all the way from New England. Ellie would have been just as glad to postpone meeting her future mother-in-law indefinitely.

Of course, that went double for her bridegroom! A ringer! A second son run in to replace the elder who fled at the dismal prospect of marriage with Ellie St. Clair!

Adrian, fearing his daughter's deviousness, thought she might find a way to run off once he announced that Miguel would be substituted for David. At least she had met David years earlier. Therefore, he did not inform her until the day before the Kanes' arrival that the second son, whom she had never met, was to sign the betrothal.

Adrian had expected tears, screaming, recriminations,

but he received only icy, shocked silence from his daughter. Nevertheless, he ordered Mattie to spend the night in Ellie's room and not to let the girl out of her sight all morning.

When Ellie walked down the long staircase, beautifully dressed and coiffed, Adrian breathed a sigh of relief. It seemed she was cooperating. Still, he was wary as he took her cold little hand in his at the bottom of the stairs and led her into the large parlor where the papers and writing instruments were set out.

As she passed through the hall, decorated with vases of freshly cut spring flowers, Ellie seemed oblivious to them. She did not answer when Adrian complimented her, apparently unaware that he had spoken. In spite of his fears about her ill-checked temper, Adrian wished she would show more of her usual animation.

Once in the parlor, Ellie sat so she could see through the front windows, curious in spite of herself. From the upstairs window, the two figures on horseback had been indistinct. Now she could see the two men clearly as they dismounted. When one of the stable hands took the horses' reins, the big black horse Ellie had admired from the window began to toss his head. The young rider, Ellie assumed he was Miguel, patted the horse's neck and the stallion calmed magically. *Well, at least horses seem to like him. That's something.*

The man's face was obscured by his wide-brimmed hat and since she could see nothing of his features Ellie turned her attention to the others. Adrian went out to greet the Kanes and to usher them into the parlor.

Alex had changed little from Ellie's childhood memory. He had grown grayer, but still stood straight and tall, a graceful and elegant man. Doña Maria was aloof and haughty. Her black eyes were cold despite the forced smile on her lips.

However, it was on their son that Ellie fixed her attention. He was presented to her last and he was quite the opposite of what she had expected. Ellie never met him, but had assumed that he was blond like David. She was taken aback as she realized how he resembled his mother, Hispanic and alien in looks and manner.

He did indeed look like a *criollo,* a Californio aristocrat with curly black hair and hawkish, sculpted features. Only the midnight blue color of his eyes under those thick black brows resembled Alex Kane. That, and his tall, lean body. He was dressed to accentuate his Alvarez heritage in a tight-fitting black charro suit, with flared pants and a short jacket trimmed in silver. A white ruffled shirt open at the throat, a colorful red sash and elaborately tooled leather boots added to the aura of foreignness.

If Ellie was stunned at Miguel's obvious Hispanic darkness, he was equally surprised at her startling fairness. He'd attributed Alex's descriptions of her blonde beauty to the optimistic attitude of a matchmaker and was prepared for what David had offhandedly once described as ''Adrian's pinch-faced, pale little girl.''

The young woman in turquoise silk curtsying at their formal introduction was certainly no "little girl," nor was she "pinch-faced"! Her body was small. Indeed, she was barely taller than his mother. However, she was beautifully formed with a high bosom, slim waist and softly flared hips. When she met his gaze, he squeezed her tiny, cool fingers and was dazzled at her clear turquoise eyes. They were a light, changeable blue-green that now matched the rustling silk of her dress. Her hair was the color of sun and moon melded together, a silver-gilt blonde, gleaming as the light hit its long silky coils. She wore it caught with a ribbon at the back of her neck, falling in a glorious cascade to her waist.

If her beauty struck him, so did the hesitant, almost wooden manner in which she greeted him. The delicate silvery brows arched over veiled eyes whose thick lashes hid the turquoise depths. Her mouth, barely hinting at a smile, revealed even, small white teeth. For all its loveliness, the face was stiff and cold.

So, he thought bitterly to himself, *she's not happy at the substitution of a greaser for a gringo. Well, too bad; it doesn't please me either.*

Ellie was unaware that she radiated a reserved sort of shock that might be mistaken for hostility. She could only sense Miguel's own leashed anger and the alien courtliness of his Mexican formality, so like that of Doña Maria.

"I've had Mattie bring in some cool wine to refresh you after your journey." Adrian broke the uneasy silence as he escorted Doña Maria to one of the overstuffed chairs. Soon all were seated and served as banalities were exchanged about the unseasonably warm weather and the ride from Cien Robles to Twin Rivers. Adrian and Alex did most of the talking. When they discussed cattle prices, the spring calf crop and semiannual roundup of new calves, Miguel joined their conversation. He was quite interested in the cattle business.

Just think, by agreeing to marry me, he'll double his total livestock tally next year, Ellie thought waspishly to herself.

As the men discussed a joint rodeo set for April, to begin on Cien Robles, Doña Maria interrupted Ellie's reverie for the first time and addressed a question to her.

"I understand your Grandfather St. Clair came from Massachusetts. Was your mother's family also from New England? I never heard anything about them."

A third degree of pedigrees. Well, hers was as fine as the Alvarez one! Ellie smiled back archly at the small, cold woman she had already decided to dislike. "Oh, no, the Waggoners came from Virginia. Some of my mother's ancestors fought in the American Revolution and one even signed the Declaration of Independence. Dad's side were New England shipping merchants. That is, until Grandpa St. Clair decided to move to the beautiful land he had visited so often on his early voyages. He converted to the Catholic faith and qualified under the terms set by the Mexican Government for ownership of a large tract of land. He was very careful to secure exact boundary markers for Twin Rivers, unlike so many of the older grants."

She couldn't resist a jab at the tenuous status of the Alvarez claim in the American courts. Let it be clear right at the onset that the St. Clairs were doing a considerable favor for the Kanes.

Ellie's jibe did not sit overly well with Miguel. Seeing Maria stiffen and then force a smile at the brazen little chit angered him further. Before they had left the ranch that morning, his father and mother had a fearful argument over her conduct when meeting the St. Clairs. As if his mother would ever behave other than as a lady! She had been bullied and coerced by his father into taking whatever the St. Clairs dished out, but damn if he would! Turning away from Adrian and Alex, Miguel shifted his attention to the two women seated on the adjacent sofa.

"Our rather cavalier system of establishing boundaries worked in Spain from the time of the Reconquista in the fifteenth century and has served Mexican landholders for nearly three hundred years. It's only the Yankee fixation on legal technicalities that's created a problem now." His dark blue eyes were mockingly earnest.

Before Ellie could reply to his historical evaluation and rather argumentative point, Alex questioned him about the stud bulls the Mormons were selling and he was drawn back into the stockmen's conversation.

With eyes glittering, Maria saw a chance to reaffirm her ties to her son and drive a wedge between him and his prospective bride. She picked up where he left off. "You must realize, my dear Eleanora," she Hispanicized the name in dulcet tones, "that a family name as old and revered as Alvarez has always stood above reproach. No one ever questioned our birthright from the time of Philip II in Spain. My great-great-grandfather was a chief military advisor to His Majesty and came to Mexico in the sixteenth century. Ever since then, in the New World as in the Old, we have exercised our prerogatives as we earned them. It is only now because of the dreadful war that we must prove we own what everyone of any account always knew we owned."

"Everyone of any account" made crystal clear to Ellie just how all the Yankee intruders, including the St. Clairs, were classified. Ellie bit back the urge to mention that if an Alvarez was Philip II's chief military advisor, small wonder Elizabeth I of England trounced his Armada in 1588! However, sensing the divisions the recent war must have caused in a family half Mexican, half Yankee, she knew she had better not reopen that ugly wound, no matter how much she disliked the old harridan.

Trying for more conciliatory grounds, Ellie responded blandly, "I'm afraid our political and social customs must be quite different."

Before she could elaborate, Maria seized on a favorite topic. "Californio social customs are like those of all the Spanish world, quite strict, especially where young people are concerned. Sons owe their fathers complete obedience, no matter what is asked of them, and daughters are chaperoned every minute of their lives until marriage."

At this point it was Alex who interrupted, quelling Maria with a withering glance. God! If she started on the loose morals of American women who grew up without benefit of *dueñas*, who knew where it might end!

"I think we should do what we all came together for and sign the betrothal papers. Then, let the two young people get to know one another, perhaps spend a little time after dinner walking in the garden?"

As he spoke, his cold blue eyes conveyed volumes to Maria, who nodded in assent. This sharp interchange between his parents was not lost on Miguel. The little silver she-cat did not like his mother and Alex was stepping in to quell both women.

The signing took only a few moments. As he wrote his name Miguel felt the taste of bile rise in his throat. Beautiful or not, Ellie was a spoiled little child, a rude *Americana* who would never show his mother respect. *As if Mama doesn't have enough to deal with already, married to Alex.* He set the pen back in its stand and looked levelly at Alex. They both understood.

Ellie was still seething from Maria's slur and the implication of Miguel's great sacrifice in obeying his father and agreeing to marry her! *My life is signed over to them, mother and son allied against me.*

Dinner was a sumptuous but stilted feast with Alex and Adrian still carrying the conversation. Doña Maria was subdued. Across the table, Ellie and Miguel stole covert glances at each other, half hostile, half curious in spite of themselves. Ellie watched his impeccable table manners, the way his slim elegant hands held a wine glass. Not daring to raise her gaze higher and meet those startlingly blue eyes, she found herself wondering, *How would those hands feel if he touched my body?* She was tantalized but shocked by the images of his hot dark flesh pressed to her pale cool skin. Scarcely daring to breathe, she prayed he could not sense her shameful thoughts. Determinedly, she concentrated on her dislike of his cold, hateful mother, trying to put his disturbing presence from her mind.

She's proud and spoiled, but damn! She's beautiful! Her beauty took Miguel's breath away. He looked at her silvery head, bowed as she concentrated on her food. *And I expected her to be plain!* Never had he seen a woman with such dazzling coloring. *She looks like a statue made of moonbeams.* Angry at the irrational emotional reaction she evoked, he resolved not to look at her during the rest of the meal. He did not succeed any better than she did.

Although everyone praised the meal, no one could have said what he or she ate except Adrian, who missed much of the hostility between Alex and Maria. He was enjoying the sneaked glances between his daughter and her future husband. Alex was right. They were a stunning couple. What splendid grandchildren he would have!

Perfunctorily, Ellie did as Alex asked and offered to show Miguel the grounds after dinner. They followed a winding flagstone path into the large formal gardens. Neither he nor she paid any heed to flowers, but walked side by side, not touching yet nervously aware of one another. Each was lost in thought.

After several minutes of silent, desultory wandering, Miguel felt constrained to try and ease the tension between them. They were committed to a life together and this was a bad beginning. Perhaps if she were a plain, mousey little thing, he might find it easier to deal with her, but she was beautiful and far more outspoken than he was accustomed to.

Of course, Miguel's experience with women was very limited. Maria was always soft-spoken and deferential in his presence, even when she confronted Alex. Only when she was alone with her husband did she openly defy him; her son never saw that side of her personality. To Miguel she was a madonna, prayerful, devout and loving, taking his side against his harsh father.

Ellie was the opposite of Maria in all ways that Miguel could see. Her open defiance of his mother seemed to indicate that she was coerced into the marriage as was he. Perhaps, even if the groom had been David, Ellie would have resisted all the same. He had not considered it from that perspective before, thinking only of what he had to sacrifice.

He began tentatively, uncertain of how to phrase what he meant. "Eleanora—Ellie," he amended, recalling that she did not like the Spanish version of her name, "we have to make the best of this arrangement and we're off to a poor beginning. I did not choose—"

Before he could say more, she whirled furiously on him, her blue-green eyes flashing. "*You* did not choose! I guess not, considering you were a substitute brought in when your brother ran off! Well, *I* did not choose this marriage either, *Don* Miguel. I don't care how big the combined ranches will be or how many salable beef cattle you get next year!" She stamped her small foot, bruising her tender instep on a sharp rock in the path, but she was too angry to cry out in pain.

His face darkened in anger as he shot back, "You think all I care about is the land, cattle, making money? You think I'd marry you just to get rich! I was only months away from an irrevocable vow of poverty. I studied for and dreamed of entering the priesthood since I was a boy! I don't want your money, your land or you. I gave up my vocation, my life's work for my family duty. If I don't make this marriage, Miss St. Clair, my grandfather's ancient land grant will be disallowed. My mother will be turned out of the hacienda her family has lived in since 1787!''

His anger over David's desertion, his frustrations over his mother's unhappiness, his aggravation and sorrow at having to leave the seminary all spilled out. But most of all, his hurt after a lifetime of being second best in Alex's sight was now compounded by a beautiful girl who did not want him.

But Ellie knew none of this. She saw he was a young handsome man who implied that he would rather be celibate than consummate a marriage with her.

Coming so soon after the terrible moment when Rice showed his true colors, this was the last straw. Bad enough that David ran off to escape her, but now her father drafted a seminary boy! She lashed out, using the first weapon that came to mind.

"So you had your life planned and your dreams shattered. Well so did I and the man I love. I was going to marry Rice Brighton, Dad's foreman. We've been together since I was a child. When I came home from school last spring we took up where we left off when Dad sent me away. Then Dad caught us and gave me a choice—you or a convent. Isn't that ironic? Any man should be better for me than Rice, or so my father seems to believe, as long as he gets Cien Robles in the bargain!''

When she delivered the fast, furious monologue, Miguel whitened as the implication of her words hit him. She'd lain with another man, had a lover that her father forced her to abandon! His mother was right about gringa women and their morals. And he, who had never allowed himself the luxury of giving in to his baser physical instincts, was betrothed to such a one! Father Sebastian had always warned him about the sins of the flesh. Here stood living proof. *Bitch, beautiful whoring little bitch!*

Ellie finished her tirade and then grew silent, suddenly aware of the taut set of Miguel's mouth. His clenched fists were held impotently at his sides, while his pantherish, lean body towered over her as if ready to spring and smash her. She had gone too far. She had actually lied and told him—or at least clearly implied—that she was soiled, not a virgin. After all she had done holding Rice at bay to protect her honor, this was a cruel jest!

Just as she was about to relent and admit that it was a lie, he turned silently and walked away, his long legs carrying him swiftly up the path toward the house. She picked up her silk skirts to follow him, then pride stopped her. *No. I won't run after that arrogant, rude, bullying . . . priest! Damn him, it serves him right!*

When Miguel came in alone, face dark as a stormcloud, Alex decided that it was time to ride home. The boy was probably full of prenuptial jitters. Well the marriage date was set just after the June rodeos. By then, Alex vowed, his son would damn well not be a virgin!

CHAPTER
6

March 1852, Los Angeles

Alex need not have worried about his son's lack of experience, or concern himself with educating an unwilling youth. A grim, tight-lipped Miguel announced the very evening of their silent ride home that he was going to town. Alex had a pretty fair idea why Miguel wanted to go to Los Angeles and smiled to himself.

But Maria was upset. Her son was becoming like a stranger, indulging in many evil things that he had never done before, drinking and smoking, even using vile language when he did not realize she could overhear him.

Now this. Maria was narrow and provincial, but she was not stupid. She knew why Alex went to Los Angeles and why any young man would ride off for a late night in town. Alex had corrupted Miguel's immortal soul. David had always taken after his father and his venal ways, but Miguel had been good and decent. Now he not only abandoned his holy studies, but was fast becoming as immoral as his father and brother.

Miguel paced Dominican steadily on the long ride to Los Angeles, thinking the same thing. If truth were told, he wanted to exceed the reputations of his father and brother. It would hardly do to come to that St. Clair slut's bed an inexperienced, bumbling innocent!

He had fallen into the petty vices of the cowhands naturally enough when in their company and away from the influences of Father Sebastian and his mother. To use tobacco, profanity, even imbibe in a good stiff drink at an exhausting day's end—these were natural habits that he unconsciously adopted as he began to live as a ranchero. In surprise and disgust he realized that it had been alarmingly easy to put the seminary behind him.

However, he had never had a woman. A few pretty girls worked at the hacienda as maids and cook's helpers, but his own inhibitions had always kept him from approaching them. Miguel had always been shy around girls. Alex and David were outgoing. They charmed the females wherever they went, turning their fickle heads, seducing them, then leaving them. Miguel had watched his father and brother with disgust, and a small measure of envy and awe, always the outsider.

Since boyhood when he had tagged after David, worshiping him the way most younger brothers do, Miguel believed that everything came easier to his tall, yellow-haired brother than to him. The girls flocked around David while no one noticed his younger brother. Miguel gradually withdrew into a world of books and tending sick and injured animals. Shy and introverted to begin with, he was a natural pupil for Father Sebastian.

But since he had left the seminary and returned home

everything changed. He took readily to the life at the ranch and loved his job as *mayordomo,* despite long, hard hours. He enjoyed working with the men and winning their respect. He was good at running Cien Robles, successful where David had failed. *Finally, I'm doing something that pleases my father.* He cursed, breaking off that train of thought. Why the hell should he want to please Alex? Then, a voice nagged him, saying: *Perhaps he did you a favor. You belong out in the world, not sequestered in a church.*

Miguel mulled over his life as he rode, unable to keep his thoughts from the silver-haired slut who was soon to be his wife. He would deal with her when the time came, and it would not be as a fumbling fool. He rode up to David's favorite whorehouse with a sense of grim determination— as if he were about to wrestle a longhorn to the ground for branding.

Rosalie's was a plain gray stucco building, shaded by tall sycamores on a dusty side street. There was no name on the door or sign of welcome on the outside. The clientele knew of its existence strictly by word of mouth. Years ago it had been called something else. Just before David left for college he brought his virgin brother here. God, it seemed like yesterday. Miguel broke out in a sweat, despite the cool night air as he remembered. An insistent David, already wise beyond his eighteen years, practically dragged the terrified boy in the front door. When a tall, very voluptuous redhead sauntered across the room toward them, Miguel broke and ran. He could still hear the ring of the redhead's laughter as David called after him, ''You'll never know what you're missing 'til you try it!''

Miguel could still see the redheaded whore, enormous breasts almost hanging out of her low-cut, white cotton blouse. They bounced with each measured step she took. Her wide red smile and big square teeth seemed to magnify her laughter. He wondered how old she had been. *Pray God she's retired by now! Maybe she won't remember me.*

Reluctantly, he dismounted. Suddenly he was struck by

a question. What if the banknotes he had on him were not adequate payment? He considered what he knew of stud fees and felt reassured. Surely it could not cost more than *that*! Could it?

Rosalie Parker was bored as she sat in the front parlor of her house. How had she ever ended up in this godforsaken hole? She had a brilliant career as the mistress of a prominent San Francisco banker, until his heart gave out on him one night. Unfortunately, it happened while he was in her bed. His wife was vindictive and Rosalie retired in haste for parts south. After the glitter of the gold town, Rosalie found Los Angeles exceedingly dull. It was hot, dusty and foreign with more Spanish- than English-speaking people.

Stifling a yawn, she stood up, catching her profile in the large gilt-framed mirror across the hall. At thirty-seven she still looked good, a well-proportioned, full-busted brunette of medium height with pale, clear skin and hazel-green eyes. Patting her hair, styled in a sleek pompadour, Rosalie inspected her posture for sags and her face for wrinkles. It was a nightly ritual. A few more good years, maybe five if she was lucky. She sighed and turned down the hall toward her office. Might as well count receipts. Somewhere in the night a caballero was strumming a guitar, no doubt for his ladylove. A dog barked. The boredom was oppressive.

Then a knock sounded and the front door slowly opened. Expecting one of the girls to be around, Rosalie continued down the hall until a low, musical voice stopped her.

"Pardon me, ma'am. Is this Rosalie's place?"

He sounded young and nervous. Sighing and aggravated that Susie or Lita hadn't answered the door, she turned— and stopped dead in her tracks. She had expected the usual callow cowboy with slicked-down yellow hair and a cowlick, wearing a stiff new plaid workshirt, his Sunday best. She saw instead a tall, elegant man in his early twenties with curly black hair, wearing an expensive silver-trimmed charro suit. His face was beautifully sculpted and his lean body moved with unconscious grace despite his nervousness. He walked across the hall, fingering the flat-crowned, black hat in his hands.

"This evening might just be redeemable after all," she said softly and smiled invitingly. Then more loudly, "Yes, this is the place and I'm her. Welcome." There was something naggingly familiar about him, his movements, build, the eyes, the set of the jaw. He was dressed and looked like a wealthy Californio. She prided herself on remembering rich men but could not recall him. His English was clear and unaccented. A mystery.

Down to business. "You're a little late, honey, but for one as pretty as you, I'll gladly stay up after hours. My girls are all, ah, occupied, but I'm free for the rest of the night, if that's all right with you? It's five dollars—U.S. banknotes or hard coin."

Miguel smiled uncertainly and nodded his assent. If he was going to learn anything, it might as well be from the most practiced teacher, the woman who owned the place. Besides, she was striking-looking and her friendly manner appealed to him.

As she linked her arm in his and they began to stroll down the long hall, a door to the left opened and a pert blonde with ringlet curls stuck her head out.

"Ooh, Rosalie, I thought everyone was gone. I'll be glad—"

"Get your beauty sleep for the weekend when the cowboys get paid, Susie. I'll take care of this customer."

The look that flashed from her hazel eyes quelled any protest from Susie. With a pout and a wink at Miguel, she said, "Next time, darlin'," and shut her door.

When they entered Rosalie's room, Miguel looked around, surprised at its subdued, tasteful decor. He expected red velvet curtains or black satin bedcovers. The pretty yellow calico curtains and bedspread were homey, in Yankee fashion. She lit a small lamp on a bedside table, then walked silently across the braided rug on the floor to where he stood with his back against the closed door.

"Now, why don't we get comfortable?" As she spoke, she began to pull the pins from her hair, letting the

shimmering, brown coils fall artfully around her shoulders.
When he made no move to undress, she stopped in front of
him and took his hat from his hands, tossing it on the
washstand next to the pitcher and bowl. *So, he's in no
hurry, a classy young gent. Well, good.* Looping her arms
around his neck, she pressed herself into him and pulled
his head down for a light, experimental kiss. His movements were stiff and awkward for one who walked and
looked so naturally graceful.

The question was evident in her eyes when she loosened
her hold and gazed up into his face. He swallowed and it
felt as though his dry throat closed up like a mine shaft
cave-in. *Damn! She knows, just that quick!* He took a deep
breath and disengaged himself from her embrace, walking
over to the window to stare out in the darkness, standing
with his fists clenched rigidly at his sides.

"I—I've never been with a woman before. I guess it
shows. I thought this was the best place to learn."

"You were right, honey. It is. I usually guess right off,
but you threw me, what with the fancy duds and that face.
Hard to believe women could keep their hands off you for
so long. How old are you?"

There was no mockery or false solicitude in her voice,
just a heady warmth he found appealing. "I was twenty-
two last month. Does that seem rather old for the first
time?"

"Not always, but in your case . . ." She shrugged, taking
with gratitude what the gods dropped in her lap.

"I studied for the priesthood. I've been away at seminary for three years."

"Obviously you've had a change of heart," she supplied dryly, waiting for him to tell her as much as he
wanted.

"It wasn't my choice to come home, at least, not at
first, but I'm happy on the ranch. Maybe I was meant to
be a stockman, not a priest, *quién sabe?*" He shrugged.

Taking in the expressive gesture and the tall, slim build
from the back, that nagging sense of familiarity again

touched her. "Is your place near here? I've never seen you in town." She walked up behind him.

"Cien Robles isn't far. I was just never interested in town or . . ." He turned to face her, gesturing around the room, indicating the nature of the place.

"Cien Robles! You're Alex Kane's boy, the younger one. I knew you looked familiar! Your darkness threw me, but now I can see it, yes." As she spoke, she caressed his face with one hand, her eyes running over him from head to toe. "Those same dark blue eyes, that stubborn jaw, the long, rangy frame. You must have your mother's coloring, but you're Alex's get, no doubt about it. David's brother, as alike as two pups in a litter, one yellow, one black, both too damn handsome to do a woman any good." She chuckled fondly.

He stiffened as she mentioned Alex and David. He could not stand another competition with them. Would he never be free from their shadows? "I should have realized you know my brother, not even be surprised you know my father."

The tone of his voice was deadly. At once Rosalie realized her mistake. Nothing a man liked less than to be reminded he was last in line at the watering hole! Soothing him with a soft, brushing rub down one arm, she laughed huskily. "Darlin', I've only seen your pa from a distance. And someone had to teach David everything he knows. No man's born that good; it takes a woman to teach him and I'm a great teacher, if you let me show you. I promise, you'll like it . . ." She punctuated her words with sensuous rubbing movements, first up and down from his shoulders to his forearms. Then, with palms flat, she kneaded little circles across his chest. Slowly, as he made no move to stop her, she began to unfasten his shirt studs, sliding her hands inside the shirt, soft fingers brushing his hard, furry chest. "That's it, just relax." She helped him shrug off his jacket, then eased his shirt open further to rub her face against his chest, planting small, moist kisses while her lower body connected with his, matching the smooth, caressing motions.

He put his hands on her waist, uncertain of what to do, but liking the sensations that were rioting through his body. The faint essence of her perfume seemed to drug him. He found himself running his fingers through the long hair hanging down her back. She raised her face and again kissed him, this time with steady, even pressure, raising her hands to knit them together in back of his neck, pulling him down, deeper into the kiss. When she could feel him respond, she broke off to whisper, "Now, open your mouth, yes, like that."

As her hot, probing tongue entered his mouth and entwined with his, Miguel began to lose the self-conscious awareness that had held him in check. It seemed natural to move his mouth over hers and return the intimate caress, even as his hands moved up and down her back. He'd never felt a woman's body before, so wonderfully pliant and soft. It seemed curved to fit his eager hands. He placed one around each of her well-rounded buttocks and squeezed experimentally.

Rosalie seemed to melt into him, swaying with him. After the first exploratory exercise, she gently disengaged herself to allow him access to her breasts, fitting his hands over the appropriate places, then helping him with the silk frog fasteners so he could reach inside her brocade dressing gown and feel her nipples tense in anticipation.

Miguel felt the generous thrusting mounds in his hands, and was intrigued by the hardening at the tips of them. Eagerly he began to slide the gown to her hips, then slip the thin camisole straps over her shoulders roughly, tearing one in the process. He wanted to see the soft breasts that felt so good.

"Easy, darlin', easy. This is pure silk, all the way from China. We have all night. Here, let me." She gave one lithe swish of her hips and the brocade gown fell to the floor in a crumpled heap. Next, she undid the small silk-covered buttons of the camisole before his hypnotized gaze. Without thinking, he reached up to cup the freed breasts in his hands as she tossed the flimsy silk garment on a nearby chair.

It was becoming very hot in the small room, despite the cool February night. As if reading his mind, Rosalie took his shirt off and unfastened the wide sash at his narrow waist. He grabbed her tightly, rubbing their bodies together in a swaying, frantic rhythm. By this time her experienced senses told her that he had moved beyond his earlier stiff, frightened self-consciousness and was simply a young male animal, eager for satisfaction. She could have performed the perfunctory copulation quickly, taken his money and sent him on his way, thinking he knew all there was to know. But she would do better.

Despite all the customers through the rough years, Rosalie Parker still liked men. She was a rarity in whores. Most men sought in a paid embrace what they never found in their prim, cold wives. However, few men knew how to satisfy a woman's needs any more than their wives satisfied them. It had been a long dry spell in Los Angeles, full of fat, bald old men, hard-eyed gunmen and gawky, horse-faced boys, none of them in the least worthy of her extra attention. She had not lied to Miguel when she said she was a good teacher, and it was seldom that she had such superb raw material to work with. The things she could show him! He was hers to mold.

Slowly, murmuring soft words of endearment, she disengaged from their frantic embrace and gently shoved him down in a big overstuffed chair next to the bed. Then she stood in front of him and began to finish undressing, slipping off her shoes, garters, stockings and finally her lacy pantalets. As she stood naked before him in the dim flickering light, she could sense his primitive male desperation as he devoured her with his eyes. When he started to reach for her she shook her head, blocking his attempt by kneeling in front of him. Slowly, giving him an excellent view of her ample breasts, she began to pull off his boots and stockings; then she ran her hands up the tight black pants on the insides of his thighs. By the time her fingers arrived at their destination, she feared stripping the pants from him might prove difficult. She stood and extended her hands to him, pulling him from the chair. Then she unbuttoned his fly and worked the last articles of clothing off, kneeling in front of him to complete her task.

When he stood naked, she found his lean, dark body one of extraordinary male beauty. As Rosalie slowly rose once more, she licked her lips with the tip of her tongue. Her gaze traveled up the long, slim legs, pausing at the pulsing, engorged penis, then up that narrow column of black hair that ran from his hard lower belly to the thick black forest on his chest. His breathing was labored and his nostrils flared, his eyes darkened to midnight with passion, a lock of raven hair tumbled across the high forehead. Lordy, what a man!

He gave a low, moaning growl and swept her onto the bed. Again, she slowly calmed his rough movements and exerted her gentle guidance by taking his shaft in her practiced hands. He let out a gasp of pleasure so intense it stilled his whole trembling body. Carefully, she guided him into her and they began to move. She knew the first time it would be over quickly, but then, as she had told him, they had all night.

The sun was well over the horizon and blazing against the thick walls of the building. Rosalie wore a thin, peach silk wrapper as it was unusually warm for so early in the year. She paused, silent as a cat in the doorway, looking at the young man still asleep on her wide bed. His long body was dark and hairy against the smooth white sheets. A few curly black locks of hair tumbled across his forehead and one hand dangled carelessly off the side of the bed, its long elegant fingers limp in relaxed sleep. He had kicked most of the covers off after she rose and went to fetch coffee. Admiring the view and chuckling over their previous night's exertion, she decided that thirty-seven wasn't so old after all.

Not over the hill yet, not by a damnblasted sight! What a night it had been! The first time he had come quickly in a few hard desperate thrusts. Almost immediately he was ready for more. All the years of deprivation seemed to give him incredible stamina. Playfully, she had slowed him down the next time, explaining how much better it was when a man took his time and let all the slow, languorous sensations build up. The third time she took it one step further.

"It's better for you if your woman enjoys it, too," she whispered, nuzzling him and stopping his quick move to enter her again.

Miguel looked frankly puzzled. "Do women...do you?" He had not considered *that* possibility!

Her hazel eyes danced. "Not always, but with the right man, you bet I do!"

Ever so carefully she instructed him, guiding his hands and lips until she was ready. Then she showed him that what she said was true, an invaluable lesson.

"A satisfied woman wants a second helping, too. Someday you'll learn to appreciate that."

Realizing this had been his first venture out on his own and that his illustrious family was probably worried, Rosalie knew he had to go home. She put the tray on the table, then sat down on the side of the bed and ran one hand across his chest. When she moved her hand upward to his face and stroked the black stubbly beard, he reached up suddenly and grabbed her wrist, pressing the palm to his lips.

She smiled. "Mornin'. Thought you might sleep all day and even a town lady like me knows a ranchero rides at daybreak."

"Not when he rides all night before."

She let out a whoop of delighted laughter as he pulled her to his chest, silencing her with a kiss as he rolled her over him, full length on the bed.

"Umm, you are a randy young stud, sure enough. Not tired anymore?"

"I figure I have a lot of wasted time to make up. The ranch can wait."

"What about your family? Won't they be worried?" she asked teasingly.

He appeared to consider for a couple of seconds, but knew what he'd do as he kissed her again and ran his hands inside her wrapper, which was now askew.

Later, they sat drinking coffee at a small table in the far corner of the room, by an open window. The sun filtering through the sycamore outside made moving patterns on Miguel's face as he held the cup in those strong, slim hands. She thought how artlessly natural it was for him to hold the fine china cup, unconscious of his beautiful manners, graceful in every movement. Well, perhaps not *every* movement, at least not the first time. Nevertheless, he was as good a pupil as she was a teacher.

"What are you thinking?" He broke into her reverie.

Rosalie smiled. "Oh, just that you look the part of a don, *patrón* of Cien Robles, so careless and elegant sitting there."

"Even if I'm a little wet behind the ears, you mean," he supplied, as if reading the rest of her thoughts.

She chuckled a hearty, warm laugh and said, "You're learning right enough and I think you know it."

He looked down into the cup, then back up at her, his facial expression turning abruptly grave. "I'm surprised. You see, things never seemed as easy for me as for David. He was supposed to be the new *patrón,* not I. When he ran off, well, that's when Papa dragged me out of seminary. Sort of rediscovering that he had another son."

"You closer to your ma?" She had hit the situation. From her knowledge of the old man and David, she could guess a great deal.

"Yes. I'm the Alvarez. David's the Kane."

She shook her head. "No, there's where you're wrong. You may be dark, but there's a lot of old Alex in you in spite of that Spanish name, Miguel. Seems too formal. Your pa named David, your ma named you?"

He nodded. "Another of their compromises. They each got one son to raise."

"But you're running the ranch and it sounds like you love it, so you must've learned something besides praying."

"I sure did last night!" Rosalie brought out a devilish streak in him that Miguel never dreamed existed. He enjoyed it, as he enjoyed her open, easy company.

She laughed with him, then snapped her fingers suddenly. "I have it! You need a new name for that new Americano side of you that nobody ever knew about before. Miguel, Michael, no, Mike—I'm gonna call you Mike. Miguels and Michaels are saints, Mikes aren't."

Grinning at her over the edge of his cup, he agreed. At Rosalie's, he would be Mike.

In the months that followed, Miguel went to town two or three times a week despite the long ride. However, he seldom stayed overnight and never as far into the next day as he had the first time. That had provoked a scene when he arrived home in mid-afternoon.

Maria was frantic and Alex watched her discomfiture, relishing every minute of it, knowing it meant another apron string rent. When an unshaven, disheveled Miguel rode lazily up and dismounted at the stable, he handed Dominican's reins to a stableboy and turned toward the house. Maria swooped down on him like an angel of wrath with a grinning Alex slowly ambling behind her.

As she neared her son she could see that his shirt was unfastened and he had his good suit jacket slung carelessly over one shoulder. Disgraceful! Did he seem to walk with more assurance than ever before, with less tentativeness and caution, even be cavalier in his greeting to her as he ignored her black scowl and his father's knowing grin?

"Sorry I'm late, Mama, Papa. I stayed over in Los Angeles. I'll change and get out to the west corral." He began to walk past her, but Maria would have none of it.

She put one tiny, beringed hand on his arm with a deceptively strong grip for one so petite. "Where have you been? Look at you! Half-dressed, unshaven. For the *patrón* of Cien Robles to come home looking so!" She berated him rapidly in Spanish. Then seeing the look in his eyes, her finely honed intuition told her she had overstepped a strange new boundary between them. At once she returned to the role of frightened, long-suffering mother. "I'm sorry, Miguel, but you look exhausted and I was so afraid something terrible had happened to you."

"Something terrible did, my dear," Alex interjected,

almost purring. "At least, terrible from *your* point of view."

Giving her husband a look of mute, furious venom, she turned back to Miguel. "You must eat luncheon and take a rest. Then you will feel better."

Patiently, feeling the crackling tension between his parents and heartily sick of Alex's baiting, Miguel replied to her, "I've already eaten, Mama. I'm fine. I have a lot of work to do today and I'm late." He was polite and even conciliatory in tone, but the gentle finality of his voice brooked no further opposition.

As she watched her son stride up the hill toward the house, Maria's shoulders slumped.

Almost kindly, Alex said, "It had to happen someday, Maria. Even if he'd entered the church, you'd have lost him."

"But not this way, to some—harlot. The shame of it!" Her outburst began in anger but ended on a sob.

"Perhaps when he marries, there'll be no more need for his visiting whorehouses." She flashed him a look of wounded fury and he shrugged. "I see. I don't think you want him lying with Ellie any more than with the whores in Los Angeles. You can't make him like you, Maria. He's *my* son." The words were delivered in a level, weary tone.

At that her head snapped up. "*Your* son, indeed, in all these late-discovered vices, perhaps. He would still be a decent boy if you had not interfered."

"He's not a 'boy' any longer. He's a twenty-two-year-old man, distressing as that is to you."

"You may have corrupted him, taken him away from his vocation, but he does not thank you for it. I may lose him, Alexander, but you will not gain by it. He despises you!"

That hit the mark. Alex could still feel the bleakness in those blue eyes, see the accusing set of Miguel's face as he agreed to Alex's plans that day in his study. No. He had lost the right to Miguel's love long ago—a stupid, wasteful mistake on his part. Now the best he could hope for was to free the youth from Maria. Alex might not gain his son, but she would lose her control over him.

Miguel busied himself arranging the spring rodeo, or roundup. Every large landowner, by state law, was required to hold at least one rodeo a year at which all calves were branded with *fierro* and *señal*, hip and earmarks. Cien Robles held several a year on their farthest boundaries. All the neighboring ranches, whether near or far, were notified of the date of the rodeo nearest to them, so they could come to claim any of their stock. Because the cattle roamed on unfenced range and most of the land grants were in excess of fifty thousand acres, the confusion between herds was great. A *juez de campo*, or plains justice, was called in to decide disputes over the livestock. Cien Robles was nearly two hundred thousand acres with a herd of over fifty thousand head of cattle. The work was monumental.

Setting up a big rodeo served to keep Miguel's mind off his impending marriage. Up each day before sunrise, dropping off to sleep at midnight, it was not impossible to forget Ellie St. Clair.

Alex, understanding his son's need to feel in command, allowed him free rein with the vast enterprise and was continually amazed at how well Miguel handled things. Alex was also delighted to have Miguel come to him for advice about the assignment of hands, or the idiosyncrasies of a given *juez de campo*. Father and son were not close, but at least they were developing a sound working relationship and earning each other's respect.

When Miguel did not have enough time to ride into Los Angeles to Rosalie's, he began to take notice of several of the young women who worked at the ranch. One kitchen maid named Sarita had long noticed him and was delighted when he made advances to her one evening. She took him to her small servant's cabin, well-removed from the watchful eyes of Maria or Father Sebastian.

Sarita was a voluptuous, dark-skinned young woman with a thick mass of straight, gleaming black hair that fell below her waist. Her slanted black eyes and high cheekbones gave a faintly Oriental cast to her handsome face. She was striking and men were always drawn to her. It had piqued her vanity that the young *patrón* never noticed her before. His older brother had always appreciated Sarita. When Miguel finally succumbed, it was a triumph for her.

The week after their first encounter she emerged from her toilet at the stream just in time to see him embracing her young cousin Luz. He gave the girl an affectionate swat on the buttocks and proceeded toward the big house, whistling carelessly. So, that was why he had not come to her this past week! She accepted his visits to unknown women in Los Angeles, but a rival right here on Cien Robles! Unthinkable!

She launched herself at her smaller cousin, knocking Luz to the ground with a filthy Spanish curse. The two women rolled in the dust, kicking and squealing, their full cotton skirts swirling around their thighs. Luz yanked Sarita's long hair viciously while Sarita ripped the thin blouse from her cousin's breasts.

The melee was ended by Father Sebastian, whose morning offices in the chapel were rudely interrupted by the noise. Shocked and appalled, he pulled Luz up, only to have Sarita lunge at her cousin while he held her. Stepping between them, he finally brought both panting girls to their senses.

"What is the meaning of this, Luz? Sarita?" His liquid eyes were wide with amazement and concern. "What if you injured each other?"

Luz was tongue-tied in humiliation as she tried to cover her naked breasts with the remnants of her shredded blouse. She could not meet the look of disappointment she knew was on Father Sebastian's face.

Sarita had always been more devious and clever. She crumpled to her knees in supplication, crying piteously, "She attacked me and I defended myself, Father. I'm sorry we fought."

Luz's head jerked up and she blurted out, "You lying whore! You leaped on me and beat me when you saw the *patrón* leave my cabin!" The instant she spoke, Luz crimsoned, ashamed and angry, for she saw the gleam of triumph in Sarita's eyes. *Why have I always fallen into her traps, ever since we were children?* Resigned, she forced herself to meet the priest's eyes.

"I think, Luz, that you have some things to confess," Father Sebastian prodded gently. As she nodded in dejection, he turned his attention to her smirking cousin. Although Sarita resumed her sobbing, the canny old priest was not fooled. In his sternest voice he commanded, "Stand up, Sarita. I suspect you have as much to ask forgiveness for as does your cousin. If only your contrition was as heartfelt as hers." Before he turned to leave, he said softly in a tone that was not a request, "I shall see you both this afternoon at confession."

"What a penance we'll get," Luz said bleakly.

Never concerned with spiritual matters, Sarita brushed the twigs and dust from her torn skirt and shrugged. She stalked off a few paces, then whirled and hissed at her cousin, "Just stay away from Don Miguel! He's mine! If you don't, I'll fix it so you have a lot more to confess to Father Sebastian, pious one!"

As he returned to his chapel, Father Sebastian pondered what to do. He was under no illusions when it came to Sarita. She had been a child of Satan all her life. He prayed for her soul, but held little hope that she would ever change. Luz, on the other hand, was a good girl who attended Mass regularly. He hated to see her falling into the same wicked habits as her cousin and he felt especially saddened that she had committed a mortal sin with Miguel. He must have a stern talk with her about the Church's teaching on morality. That should turn her from the path to destruction.

But what shall I do about Miguel? It will break his mother's heart if he continues this way. The old priest felt the anguish tear at him, for he had devoted his life to the saintly *patrona* and her younger son. Now he watched helplessly as she grieved over Miguel. Not only had he forsaken his priestly vocation, but was falling into wickedness. *He is as lost as Don Alesandro or David.*

Ever since that mysterious confrontation between Miguel

and his father five months ago, things had gradually worsened. The old priest would have given a great deal to know what passed between father and son. Miguel had agreed to abandon his studies, marry the St. Clair heiress and take David's place. All that was sad, but understandable to preserve the Alvarez holdings. However, the evils of drink, profanity and fornication were incomprehensible to Father Sebastian. Now Miguel was a stranger who made obligatory confessions of serious mortal sins with little apparent remorse.

At first I pleaded and I reasoned. Then I thundered and I threatened. But his repentance is not sincere. Now I must treat Miguel as I do other men who come to me, who only go through the motions of penance. It saddened Father Sebastian beyond measure. He had such high hopes for his favorite.

As a boy, Miguel had taken to heart the priest's admonitions about curbing the evils of the flesh. When he fell from grace and confessed lying with a paid prostitute, Father Sebastian excused him, telling himself that it was done away from home, merely a way of sowing wild oats. The youthful excess could be kept from Doña Maria, and soon the boy would be married and settled down to his proper duty.

But now this, two young girls whose families have been employed on the ranch for generations, fighting over Miguel in sight of the hacienda! With a heavy heart he decided what to do. He would tell Doña Maria. Despite the pain it would cause her, it was better that she hear it from him than from the eternally gossiping servants, or worse yet, from her vindictive husband! If anyone could talk some sense into Miguel, it would be his mother. He turned with leaden feet toward her apartments.

"How can you turn your back on everything you always held sacred, valued above all else? You were meant to be a holy priest," Maria cried.

Miguel looked away. Through the window of the sitting room he could see the ranch land stretching across the horizon.

Finally he admitted the truth to her and to himself. He

looked into her jet eyes, glistening with tears, so woeful yet angry. "Mama, I don't think I ever wanted to be a priest."

"You don't know what you are saying!" Her voice rose hysterically.

He walked across to her and took her clenched hands in his. Gently, he eased her down into a chair and knelt beside it. "Yes, I do know, I was always so jealous of Papa's love for David, always in the shadow of both of them. It seemed natural to turn away from their life, their ways. You've always been so good and loving and Father Sebastian was patient and kind to a reclusive, uncertain boy. But I was drifting then, Mama, not making a real choice. A grown man must, you know.

"I admit I was furious about Papa's high-handed summons home to take David's place and I don't want the marriage, but that's not the issue now. I was forced from one kind of life into a totally different one. I've been exposed to both now. Mama, I like my life here better. Maybe I found out by default that I love running Cien Robles, but I belong here, not in the church."

"And what about the rest, the wild sinful life with these rough cowhands, the..." she took a shaky breath, "...the women? Do you 'love' them also?" Her own indelicacy shocked Maria, but how else to confront him and bring him to shame for it?

Surprising her greatly, he smiled sadly and nodded his head. "I'm afraid I have to claim all the vices I used to condemn, Mama. It's just something a man does. It has nothing to do with you or any good, decent woman. Please, just try to forgive me and not think about it. Or, if you will, pray for my soul."

"Pray for my soul." He said it as glibly as Alex or David would have. Her heart ached and she knew she had lost him. Miguel was a man now, no longer her gentle, loving boy.

If the interview upset Maria, it also upset Miguel. However, the state of his soul was his lesser concern. He thought about his words to her, "any good, decent woman." His episodes in town or with servant girls had nothing to do with a lady like his mother. But what about women like his soon-to-be wife? She was no better than Sarita or Susie, certainly far less honest than Rosalie. Ellie was a member of the illustrious St. Clair family, rich and respected, raised with every advantage, yet she behaved as if she were a cheap tart. He felt his bile rise and nearly choked on it.

CHAPTER
7

January 1852, Wilderness City

A monotonous drizzle fell from the foggy skies. For three weeks David and Kate had been in Wilderness City, a helter-skelter gold camp of tents and rickety frame buildings on the American River. Wilderness City: a perfect name for such a cold, wet, evil place. The mud was so deep mules foundered in it and the fog so dense in the morning hours a man could not see his hand in front of his face.

The focal point of the boomtown was a big tent in the center of the camp where miners came to drink and gamble and a motley assortment of whores also peddled their wares. One wit dubbed it the "Civic Center." Men panned and sluiced for gold with varying degrees of success. Those few lucky enough to hit rich strikes usually sold out to big mining companies and hightailed it back to civilization. The argonauts came from all over the world, although most were Yankees. A few Chinese had filtered into the camps, but they were not allowed to stake gold claims, and so did menial jobs. The Mexicans, Germans, Swedes and other "furriners" faired somewhat better—at least if they came in large groups and were armed. Claim jumping, even between Americans, was commonplace and frequently men were found with their heads bashed in or shot from behind, their pokes stolen. Some just vanished without a trace and others took over their digs.

It was a violent society, loosely held together by the golden cement of greed. Men worked hard at backbreaking labor for uncertain return. Food was always scarce and dear. Whiskey of uncertain age sold for a dollar a shot and eggs were a dollar apiece. Tools, clothing and the simplest amenities such as soap were as costly.

Life was dangerous and expensive and boring, especially during the rainy winter season when little mining could be done. Many who had been lucky enough to accumulate sizable pokes by the fall lost all their hard-earned dust or nuggets by mid-winter as they indulged in the vices of the camp.

David supported himself and Kate by playing poker in the Civic Center every afternoon and then returning again after supper for a late night round. The place never really shut down. Men who were holed up in rainy tents waiting for a break in the weather had no regular hours to keep.

David had discovered his skill and natural luck with cards as early as his college days. Now that he had to live off his winnings, he honed the instincts of a born gambler to a fine edge. So far he'd done passably well, making enough in the past weeks for them to have hopes of renting a frame cabin in a month or two. The wet, miserable tent they now occupied made Bolton's Cantina seem a luxury hotel.

Kate never complained to David, but he knew she felt alone and useless in the camp, unable to do any work besides camp cooking over a sputtering fire. She was used to running the big kitchen and doing the heavy cleaning at

Bolton's, and now she had nothing to do. The first time she had gone down to the river with a bundle of washing a crowd had gathered, whistling and making catcalls. David quickly hired a Chinese to do the laundry. She could not mix with the rough miners or whores, but if he could get them set up in a cabin she would at least be able to pass the time keeping house.

David had never before made plans for his future nor had he worried about money. When he was at Cien Robles or in college, his father's wealth was always available to him. Even in the army, he had been fed and sheltered. But now his whole life was changed because of Kate. For the first time David was responsible for another person and he wasn't sure he liked it. No matter that he chafed under the responsibility; he had to admit that Kate was quite a woman, sensual and lovely, even laughingly puritanical at times.

She never said a word about the physical hardships of the gold camp but eventually the boredom became intolerable and her fiery Irish temper flared. After weeks of sitting quietly in the tent, she insisted on accompanying him to the Civic Center to watch the game. "Why can't I come? Lord knows I'll be doin' nothin' sittin' in this tent. At least there I can be with you and watch the people. It's not like I was wantin' to walk out in the camp unescorted for any drunken miner to molest me."

David sighed. He knew how she hated inactivity. "It just isn't safe, Kate. I can't concentrate on my game and worry about you at the same time."

Hands on hips, her green eyes flashed a warning as she stood her ground. "As if to say I'll be battin' my eyes and wigglin' my bottom at every stray miner who walks in the place! What do you think I am?" She turned quickly away, to hide the blur of tears. She had always thought of herself as strong and resilient, but it seemed she could not cope with life in the goldfields. How could she be so weak? God, she hated the sound of her own angry, accusing voice!

David came up behind her, running his hands up her arms, cupping her shoulders, then kissing the back of her nnck as he lifted the mass of dark hair away. "I know what you are, a very beautiful, desirable woman. All you'd have to do, love, is be there and men would flock to you like crazy. You wouldn't have to invite them, but I'd have to fight them off. Then what time would I have to play cards?"

As he talked, he nipped tender little kisses at her temples, neck, shoulders, then turned her around into his embrace. "Soon," he crooned. "Soon we'll have enough money for a real cabin. In a month or so it'll begin to clear up and then the digs will really open up again. We might even strike it rich."

"Are you really serious about staking a claim? Somehow I can't see you as a toiler in the dirt. What would you be doin' when your britches got dirty or your hands callused?" The gleam in her eyes had turned warm now.

He laughed, throwing back his head in that careless way she loved. His thick blond hair fell across his forehead as he leaned down to plant a kiss on her mouth.

"You're probably right, but there was a time when I worked hard and got very dirty. You forget I was raised on horseback. All Californios are. My father put me on my first pony when I was barely three years old. By the time I was ten, I was working alongside the vaqueros, branding stock, driving them to market, even helping butcher the fifteen or twenty steers a month it took to feed all the people on the ranch. I worked and sweated plenty."

"Do I get the feelin' you never wanted to be a rancher any more than you want to be a miner?" Teasing, her eyes nevertheless questioned him.

"Nope, guess I didn't. That's why I ran away to sea on one of Papa's ships when I was twelve years old. Spent a wet, miserable year in the Pacific on a whaler. Didn't like that either. Ah, Katie, I'm just a worthless, footloose misfit. You should never have gotten mixed up with me." Beneath his banter lay pain and confusion.

"Considerin' my choices, sir, I think I have me a pretty fair bargain." She kissed him languorously, twining her fingers in his hair, which now fell nearly to his collar. There were no barbers in Wilderness City.

Her quick passion always delighted David, perhaps because he knew that she had been with no other man but him. Since neither had fully dressed yet, it was easy to discard clothing quickly. David peeled off the man's flannel robe Kate wore, a practical item he'd bought from a drummer. He was clad only in his boots and pants. She savored his hard, furry chest, rubbing her face against it as she reached down to unbutton his pants. He pulled off both boots and the pants in a few swift movements, then pressed her back on the rickety cot.

"One of these days we're going to break this thing," he said, nuzzling her breasts.

"Umm, better get us a place with a real bed, I guess." Kate didn't sound concerned.

He felt her urgency and quickly slid into her, finding her wet and ready. They moved in a rough, straining rhythm, causing the cot to squeak and crack in protest. Miraculously, it did not break. He levered himself above her, hands gripping each side of the cot, straining to thrust in her as she locked her long, pale legs tightly around his hips. His dark blue eyes were gazing hypnotically into her green ones as a shock of straight gold hair fell across his forehead. Running her hands up his rigid, muscular arms, she raised one hand to push the hair from his eyes, but it quickly fell again with his exertions. When she arched up and gasped as the sudden waves of orgasm hit her, he feasted his eyes on her pale, quivering flesh. The rose-brown tips of her breasts were rigid and upturned, her face was flushed and her thick reddish lashes fanned over her magnificent eyes. Kate's hair spilled in dark undulating waves across the pillow as her head thrashed from side to side in ecstasy. He gave several long, convulsive shudders and slowly bent his arms, lowering himself on top of her, gasping for breath. He carefully rolled them on their sides, taking his weight off her slender body, but holding her to him tightly and tenderly. Her hands dug into his shoulders, kneading his hard muscles.

He took one hand and raised it to his mouth, kissing each fingertip in turn. "So soft and pretty now," he murmured.

As Kate nestled alongside his body, she considered one long slim hand, the fingers now smooth and the nails grown out. "Now that I'm a lady of leisure, with no dishwashin' and laundry to do for a whole cantina, amazin' it is that I can have hands like this." Never in all her lifetime of hard physical labor had Kate been able to have soft hands and long fingernails.

"I'd hardly call this a life of luxury, Irish, but I guess it is less work than at Bolton's."

"Umm, much nicer cookin' for one man than a whole cantina full of people, for sure," she added.

He laughed. "As long as it's the right man, you mean," he said smugly.

"Conceited bastard!" She reddened the minute the epithet was out. A canvas city overrun with rough men and prostitutes left everyone's ears burning. Kate found she had started to swear as readily as she had taken to living as David's mistress. *Pretty soon I'll be smoking cigarillos and drinking whiskey.* She vowed with renewed determination to act like a lady. If only her life could conform as easily as her hands had!

David never showed any concern with her use of strong language. Kate was sure he attributed it to the fact she was a saloon girl of dismal pedigree. *He doesn't expect any better of me,* she thought bitterly. *Kanes don't marry Muldoons.* The unbidden thought taunted her once more. She pushed it out of her mind.

Feeling her stiffen and withdraw, he held her securely and chuckled. "Kate, you are always an amazement to me, more worried about slipping out a swearword than shooting a man."

"But that son of a bitch Brighton needs killin'!" she burst out. Then she sighed. "Oh, drat! I'm just hopeless, damned to perdition like Reverend Morgan used to warn Aunt Tess."

She fumed and he laughed. "Oh, Irish, don't ever change, not for me!"

When David was gone, Kate considered her life, not just the immediate boredom of sitting in a tent watching it rain, but her position in David Kane's life. He was quite taken with her now, finding her eager responses in making love delightful and her unsophisticated outlook on life refreshing. But he was an educated man from a socially prominent family. Someday he would become bored with her, embarrassed at her lack of breeding and refinement. Then what? Would he keep her only because of gratitude for saving his life? Out of pity? Kate cringed as her fiercely independent pride was stung.

Finally, she admitted what she'd tried so vehemently to deny for the past month. She loved David Alexander Kane with all her heart. And she knew he would never marry her. But at least she had this little time with her splendid, beautiful David, time to share a private world, a world of love. Yes, it was all worth it, even if it lasted all too briefly. She'd worry about the future later. But now, she would do her chores.

Kate picked up a wooden bucket and went toward the stream, about a hundred yards from their tent. It was the cleanest source of water, coming from a spring that surfaced in the river. Even so, she boiled it before cooking with it just as an added precaution. David explained the dangers of contaminated water. After his sojourn in Mexico with the invading American army, he knew the risks firsthand.

As she walked through the camp, Kate pointedly ignored the leers, catcalls and suggestive taunts, varying in their crudity. She had never been accosted on her brief walk for water but she hated it. Holding her head up proudly, she fixed her eyes straight ahead as she walked. Everyone knew that she belonged to the gambler who carried a fancy, ivory-handled Dragoon Colt and knew how to use it.

"Lookee here, purty firehair. Ya Irish, honey?"

"Damn, lookeet them titties bouncin'!"

The remarks were the usual, but there was one big hulk who watched her each day in silence. She feared him more than all the loud, crude men. He was whitehaired with pale eyes and chalky skin, an albino named Dutch Joe. He had never uttered a sound, but looking into those fathomless eyes made her shiver. He was well over six feet tall, big boned and fat. Striding rapidly, she passed him and continued on to get her water. When she retraced her steps up the path, he was gone. Strange.

The heavy rope handle of the bucket cut into her slim fingers. She switched the bucket to her right hand and opened the flap of the tent. Before Kate could turn around, she knew someone was inside the tent with her.

One big white paw came out and grabbed for her coat, tearing the sleeve free from the tunic in one resounding rip. It was Dutch Joe! As she began to scream, he yanked her hair in one hand, then reached for her face, to cover her mouth. As they grappled, she realized the oak bucket was still in her hand.

With hysterical strength, Kate swung, leaving a wide arc of water in her path as she lunged free of his grip. Her hair was almost torn out by its roots and her face was gouged where his nails dug in, but the heavy bucket flew backward, connecting with sickening impact against the side of his head. The force of the blow threw Joe out the door of the tent onto the soft, muddy ground where he landed with a sucking thud.

The right side of his face was bleeding, but his skull must have been two inches thick, for he slowly began to rise, wiping blood from his right eye. "I get you, woman!" he growled in a thick Germanic accent. Kate stood in the door of the tent, the handle of the defunct bucket still clutched tightly in her hand.

He lumbered toward her until a low, deadly voice stopped him. "Dutchman, ya be in a peck a trouble if'n ya move agin. I purely swear it." The speaker was a small, wiry man of indeterminate age, with a greasy gray beard, a seamed face and weatherbeaten clothes. He held a ten-gauge shotgun loosely crooked in one arm.

The albino turned to face him like a great, confused bear. At a distance of four feet, the ten-gauge would make refried beans of a man—even a man of his size.

He stopped. "What she to you? I want. Why not I take?" It seemed reasonable to him.

" 'Peers ta me she ain't yer woman. Her man'd kill ya, Joe. I seen 'em do it afore. Now, jest ya scoot whilst ya got yer hide half-ass yet. Ya cotton ta thet?" The gun never moved, but the threat was palpable and tension hung like fog in the early evening air as a crowd gathered to watch.

The albino's face was bleeding profusely. The blow to his head had caused a concussion and he was now beginning to wobble from foot to foot. Suddenly, there seemed to be two—no, three old drummers with guns. Ponderously, he considered. The woman, even with her wondrous red hair, was not worth a ten-gauge in the belly. He slowly staggered off.

As the onlookers dispersed, the old man lowered the gun barrels to the ground, and approached a pale, shaking Kate who stood in the tent opening. Realizing she still had a deathgrip on the rope handle of the bucket, she dropped it.

"Thank you, thank you very kindly. It's grateful I am, knowin' no one else here would turn a hand to help me, not to face down that beast." She shuddered again. "I'm Kathleen Muldoon and it's right happy to meet you I am, Mr.—?"

"Jebediah Hooter, Hoot ta my friends, ma'am. Glad ta help. Old Joe ain't all bad, jest a mite slow. When he gits him an idee, wall it purely takes some whompin' loose, yessiree it does. I 'spect ya remind 'em a someone back in th' old country, ma'am. Yer man hereabouts? Think ya might oughta go ta him 'n stick right close fer awhile, leastways till the Dutchman fergits ya."

Kate flushed, realizing that he knew she was the gambler's woman. Everyone knew. Yet this kindly old man struck a chord with her. He was not condemning or lustful, just kind and concerned. In gold camps like Wilderness City, such goodness was rare.

Kate nodded. "Yes, I'll go to the big tent now and stay there with David until suppertime. Would you be doin' us the honor to eat with us, Mr. Hooter—Hoot? We'd be pleased for your company."

He grinned, shaking his head. "I purely 'preciate sech a nice offer, ma'am, I do, but Baker and Bitsy are waitin' fer me—my mules, ma'am. I got ta make Pine Bluff afore dark an' I'm right late now." He tipped his battered hat, revealing thinning, stringy gray hair. "I was goin' yer direction, past th' big tent. Right proud ta walk ya there, ma'am, it'n ya want?"

Glad of his protection, Kate smiled and nodded.

After the incident with Dutch Joe, Kate accompanied David to his card game every afternoon and evening, unless he could find a reliable man to stay nearby and guard her. In Wilderness City there were only two men David would trust—an old preacher called Bible Sam and a young Irishman, Pete O'Mara. Pete was really a boy, awestruck by his beautiful countrywoman and would gladly have died for her. His puppydog adoration was almost as hard for Kate to stand as the hellfire and damnation of the preacher. Bible Sam only stayed with her so he could attempt to bring her to repentance. After all, she was a kept woman. Kate certainly did not want daily reminders of that fact! But it was better than going with David to the Civic Center.

As Kate packed the leftover food from supper—salted-down pork, sourdough bread and beans—she thought with dread about the night ahead. David had been right about the men and how she drew them. The only thing standing between her and any number of filthy, burly miners was the threat of David's guns. Kate shuddered, remembering Dutch Joe as well as a dozen other coarse leering men who would bore smoldering holes in her with their eyes when David wasn't looking their way. She knew what they were thinking—if she had been won in a card game, could she be lost in another? David would never use her as a stake, of that she was sure, but one day he would tire of her—and then what would she do? Resolutely, she pushed the thought out of her mind. She would cross that bridge when she came to it.

David slipped on his coat and lit a cigar as he watched Kate fuss with the dishes. *God, but is she lovely!* He wondered how he could have brought her to this place, but he was not ready to leave yet. He would never go home impoverished and beaten. But Kate deserved better than being mauled by the likes of Dutch Joe. He should take her to San Francisco and find her a job of some sort in a decent hotel or restaurant. Yes, as soon as spring came, he must take her to San Francisco, he promised himself. Then he wondered why the thought of her safely in the city made him feel so empty.

That evening two Germans from Feather River country came to the Civic Center to try their luck. Karlstadt, a large, jovial blond, suggested a game of draw poker in his broken English. David agreed; he preferred the game to the three card monte, which most miners chose. Karlstadt's partner, Streicker, a slight dark-haired fellow with hard gray eyes, said no more than necessary as they played. Two other miners, both Americans, also joined in the high stakes game.

They played steadily for over an hour with the crowd getting increasingly raucous, especially Karlstadt who drank seemingly endless quantities of beer. His smaller companion, however, stayed sober and watchful. David, who was always careful of his ability to win and to protect Kate, drank sparingly. Streicker focused his attention on Kate, and when she returned his rude stare, he gave her an insolent, leering grin. An evil foreboding came over her. He reminded her of Dutch Joe and Hank Clune. She shivered and moved closer to David as he raked in a good-sized pot, his third in a row.

"Ya win the pot and the deal, Kane," Abe Forker said good-naturedly. His creased face broke into a freckled grin when he spoke. "Yore pretty lady must bring ya luck."

Absently, David gave Kate's fingers an affectionate squeeze. Then he reached into his vest pocket for a cigar and bent over to light it. When he raised his head and exhaled, he caught the little German staring at Kate. A warning look was exchanged between cold gray eyes and dangerous dark blue ones.

Another hour passed and David won fairly steadily. Forker and the other American dropped out. Well into his cups by now, the big blond German stayed, although his compatriot suggested, sotto voce, that he quit. Finally, Karlstadt bowed out, but Streicker wanted to play more.

"Now, I think we get down to business, ja?" The dark German spoke so quietly that no one in the noisy room except for those close to the table could hear him.

"What did you have in mind?" David queried with deceptively calm amiability.

"Five card stud, minimum bet one thousand dollars. Herr Forker will deal, if he would be so kind?"

Abe nodded in agreement and looked at Kane.

"Pretty rich stakes for a man who's lost a lot already," was David's only reply.

"Perhaps now that it is between you and me, luck will smile on me, nein?" The sibilant voice almost purred the dare.

Clenching his cigar in his teeth, David had a premonition of sorts. "Deal." He grinned his whitest smile through the smoke.

By this time all the men drinking at the bar, the other monte gamesters and the prostitutes were clustering around the small corner table. David had never looked more boyish and appealing, Kate thought jealously as she watched all those hard-eyed, painted faces in the crowd, each woman drinking in his lean golden body. *He could be charmin' the underpants off Queen Victoria herself,* Kate thought furiously, but only smiled archly from behind his back, her hand resting on his shoulder.

As each card was dealt the bets rose accordingly. On the second card up, the little German had two kings showing while David had only a queen and a jack. Streicker bet two thousand and David matched it. On the third card up, David was dealt a ten and Streicker a deuce.

"Pair of kings high. Bet," Forker said to Streicker, looking in fascination between the small brooding German and the lean indolent Yankee.

"Another two thousand."

Again David matched the bet and a gasp went up around the table. Even in a gold camp full of rich, bored men, this was a high stakes game.

Streicker's last card was a jack. Kane received an ace and the tension mounted palpably in the smoke-filled canvas enclosure.

One grizzled old miner swore, "By damn! If'n ya got th' king down, ya got a ace high straight, Davie."

David's blue eyes, nearly black in the flickering lantern light, indicated nothing. He remained in the same casual pose, slouched back in his chair, his hand draped loosely over his hole card while the ace, queen, jack and ten sat in mute promise on the weatherbeaten table in front of him.

Streicker fingered and rubbed his hole card nervously, his gray eyes gleaming with a feral, silver glint. His two kings were still high on board. The bet was his.

"A strong hand for five card stud, mein herr." David's voice was as expressionless as his eyes.

The German laughed. "You think to bluff me with an unlikely twist of the odds? *Ja?*" His chuckling subsided and he shoved out a pile of nuggets, neatly weighed out by the assayer who doubled as the general store owner. "Three thousand dollars."

David matched the three thousand and then raised three thousand more. Streicker paled and began to count. He had in his poke only a little over three thousand. Hesitantly, he shoved it out as his face darkened. It was all he had left because of his wild betting earlier in the game. Damn! Let everyone here think that lucky Yankee had a king buried for that straight. The odds were against Kane because Streicker had a third king in the hole to give him three of a kind—and the winning hand, a damn big one, over twelve thousand dollars! The last thing he wanted now was for that bluffing gambler to raise again! House rules decreed three raises were allowed.

David raised, only another thousand, but more than the German had and Streicker knew Kane was aware of it. After all his careful plans! He fumed inwardly while forcing an outward calm. He was a far better card player than his previous performance indicated, but he'd deliberately lost earlier in the evening, along with that idiot Karlstadt to lull the winner into this kind of a game for high stakes. On several other occasions since he'd joined up with his unsuspecting countryman, it had worked perfectly. Tonight his plans were thwarted.

He *knew* he had the winning hand and the huge pile of dollars on the table made him nearly salivate in spite of himself.

"Aw, go on honey, rake it in. The Kraut ain't got a pot ta' piss in!" The guffaw came from an orange-haired harlot, leaning her heavy bosom over the table, smiling provocatively at David.

Kate looked scornfully at the tawdry, dyed red hair, comparing it to her own lustrous locks, almost black in the wavering light reflecting off the canvas walls.

Streicker, too, made the comparison, distracted by the interchange between the two women over the handsome Yankee. Well, when he won, that whore would be talking out of the other side of her painted mouth and even Kane's beauteous redhead might come around. All women responded to money, if one had enough of it. Streicker smirked and made a snap decision.

"I have not enough nuggets on me to call you, but I have a claim deed to the source from which they came. Might that serve, Herr Kane?"

He extracted a paper from a sack at his feet and shoved it toward David. Gold claims were seldom formal affairs in the rough, unsettled wilderness of 1851 California, but this one had been meticulously recorded in Sacramento for a specific area one hundred feet square, on the Feather River, in the heart of one of the richest gold veins yet unearthed in the state.

David studied it intently and shoved it back. "Sign it over and see my hand."

Streicker's hands trembled as he endorsed the paper in front of a room full of witnesses. As soon as it was done, he eagerly fingered his third, hidden king, beginning to toss it over, only to be taken up short when the indolent Yankee flipped up his hole card next to the four face up on the table. The case king. Kane had his ace high straight!

Streicker whitened visibly as the grinning gambler stretched his long arms forward and raked in the huge mound of banknotes, nuggets and the deed to the claim. It couldn't be! Incredible, against-all-odds luck! Frantically, the German clawed the remaining cards from Abe Forker's hands and flipped through them, looking for the real fourth king. Surely the Yankee had held a spare up his sleeve!

David's chilling dark blue eyes watched the small man intently through his fruitless search. Kane said nothing, waiting to see what the loser would do.

Throwing the cards down on the table with considerable force, Streicker stood up. He glared into the calm, expressionless face of the Yankee, who sat very still.

David waited, right hand never leaving his side. Streicker looked into the face of certain death and backed off. He turned sharply on his heel, scooped up the pack at his feet, hissed a few words sharply in German to his big companion and stalked out of the tent. The drunken blond giant staggered after him, hiccuping loudly.

After the Germans were gone, the crowd erupted in boisterous cheers for the young gambler's good fortune, relieved that the tension was over without any shooting in the close quarters of the tent.

Old Abe Forker, gathering up the scattered pasteboards, grinned a whiskered smile at David. "Ya be mighty lucky, young fella. Ya fixin' on bein' a miner now?"

"Don't rightly know yet. That part of the country is rich in open veins, so I've heard. If this," he paused to heft a handful of the nuggets, "is any indication, I just might check it out."

"Lady luck shore smiled on ya," a weatherbeaten

old-timer chimed in, along with like comments from a host of other onlookers.

David turned to Kate, taking the cigar from his mouth and depositing it carelessly in an ashtray on the table. "Here's my lucky lady right here." With that, he drew her to him for a quick, hearty kiss. The crowd roared its approval as Kate backed off, flustered.

"Watcha gonna call the mine?"

"Dutchman's Folly!" one wit volunteered.

"Kraut's Bluff," another chimed in.

Abe supplied, "Lucky Lady."

Grinning, David nodded, then said, "Nope, but close. I'll call it 'Luck of the Irish' and I'll make a present of it to the lucky lady responsible. I think she distracted him so much he made all those damn fool bets too early. What say, Kate?"

A rousing cheer went up around the room as miners, drummers and even the motley assortment of whores joined in to celebrate Kate's good luck.

"Anyone got a pen?" David reached for the pen Forker handed him. He endorsed the deed over to Kathleen Anne Muldoon and pushed it across the table for her signature.

"Just sign under my name, here. Come on, Irish. I want it to be yours." David waited, pen outstretched toward her. Kate stood riveted to the floor. Everyone was caught up in the spirit of the magnanimous act, yelling, toasting the gambler and his lady and generally being raucous.

Sensing something was wrong as she stood immobile, David reached out a hand toward hers and pulled her to the table by his side.

"What's wrong, Kate? We'll work the mine together. I want to give it to you as—oh, hell, as a sort of good luck token. Just sign it, for me. Please?" He looked almost wistful, years younger in his boyish entreaty, eyes alight in exuberant happiness, face flushed with success.

Kate blushed a deep crimson and murmured very low in David's ear, "I—I cannot sign my name, David."

"Sure you can, Irish. I have all this money, must be

over twelve, fifteen thousand on the table, beside the mine. It's yours, sweetheart."

Her head flew up and her eyes flashed both hurt and anger at his density. *Spoiled, thoughtless rich man's son!* "I can neither read nor write, David Kane. That's why I cannot sign your deed!" With that she broke free of his handhold and whirled, fleeing the room.

Gales of drunken laughter and well-meaning advice followed David as he gathered up his winnings and left the Civic Center in haste to catch up with Kate.

"Tell her ta jest make her mark like I do," one yelled.

"Honey, I'll sure work your claim with you, any day," one blonde in a pink satin dress volunteered.

"Aw, women, who kin figger 'em!"

The babble of sounds died down as David took purposeful, long-legged strides down the muddy street toward their tent.

"For Chrissake! How the hell was I supposed to know you couldn't read or write? You act like I did it just to belittle you. I was trying to give you a present—a damn handsome one, too!" David stood facing Kate across the table, his hands out in vexed supplication, anger and bewilderment warring within him.

Kate's hurt and humiliation were so intense since she fled the raucous catcalls of the Civic Center that she could scarcely see, much less think straight. Her eyes were glazed with unshed tears and shot sparks.

"Damn your arrogant hide, David Alexander Kane, you high 'n mighty rich man, with your educated airs! What do you know—what have you ever thought of the likes of me? There's no more time nor money in New York than there was in Belfast for schoolin' girls. The boys go to church schools, if they're lucky and their parents can pay. Girls learn to sew and clean and cook. Niver do they learn readin' or writin'!" Her brogue thickened as her anger rose and she planted her hands on her hips, her feet squarely apart, defying him.

"Then why the hell did I see you with those so many evenings when I came home?" He gestured toward the small cache of books he'd accumulated since they arrived in camp. "I thought you were reading them. You certainly gave me every impression you did!"

Kate dropped her eyes, beginning to run her hands across the back of the crude wooden chair in front of her, fidgeting in an agony of embarrassment. "I—I only pretended to read. I love to look at books and imagine what it would be like. The readin' of them, that is." Her voice dropped to a strained whisper.

David considered the beautiful young woman standing so near, yet so far away from him. Would he ever really know her? He said softly, "I'll teach you to read, Irish. It's not hard and Lord knows you're bright enough." He paused and that old teasing grin spread in dazzling whiteness. "Besides, what else is there better to do on rainy mornings or late at night?"

A look of wistfulness and awe infused her face with rapt wonder. He stopped short, his easy smile erased when he saw what his offer meant to her.

"You—you really mean it? I mean, could you—would you teach me? Oh, David!" With that she was around the table and chair, catapulting into his arms.

He caught her in a fierce embrace and swung her tall, slender body up and around. Then he lowered her back down and kissed her tenderly at first, then with increasing intensity.

"Yeah, I mean it, Irish."

As they waited for the winter rains to clear, David taught Kate the rudiments of reading and lettering. The first lesson was writing her name so that she could sign the deed. After a long afternoon of practice, she was able to write *Kathleen Anne Muldoon* in an even, childish script. Before his pleased eyes, she signed the paper, insisting stubbornly that her share be only half with him and no more. She didn't really feel as if she owned anything at all. The possibility of sudden wealth was unimaginable. Also, if they were partners, it kept them together.

David was amazed at her quick mind and boundless

curiosity about every conceivable subject. His own intellectual bent had always been superficial. He was bright enough and readily absorbed a wide variety of knowledge from his tutors, much as a sponge does water, but it was only because of the inescapability of the lessons. Miguel had been the bookworm who diligently plied his studies beyond the forced rigors of the classroom. At every opportunity David had played hookey. Indeed, he thought back grimly to his enlistment for the war, realizing that it had been another way of playing hookey.

But now, with Kate, he was rediscovering the delight of learning new things. He helped her master the alphabet. Then they turned to the more arduous task of learning words. In a week, she was reading simple sentences. By the time she could read a paragraph from Jonathan Swift's *Gulliver's Travels* without requiring his help, she was radiant with joy. He was triumphant sharing her pleasure.

As her abilities increased in the following months, David began to buy books of any sort, even old newspapers and magazines from back east. Their store of reading materials contained fine books, plays and poetry as well as tawdry tabloid materials. Kate also practiced her penmanship, although she lacked skill in the art. Indeed, her writing looked like chicken scratching once her train of thought outran her unskilled hand. Gritting her teeth, she would slow down and begin over again.

One morning in late April, while Kate was absorbed in just such a frustrating exercise, David came home. "Katie, love, I just talked to Ira Walton and he says the roads are clear enough for us to get to our claim. He's got three men who'll be willing to work for me and run the sluice. We can leave in a few days as soon as we provision up."

Still absorbed in her writing, Kate looked up. "What's a sluice?"

"It's a bigger, more efficient version of a long tom—oh, a long series of connected boxes that water and dust are sifted through, designed to trap the heavier gold in the bottom and wash the sand and mud free. You'll see it in action soon enough. Kate, I have a lucky feeling today.

Think I'll go up to the Civic Center for one last game. Who knows, I might win you a new pen and some fancy India ink! Want to come?''

Smiling, she declined. "No, I'd rather start to pack. Send Mr. O'Mara over if you can find him, please. He's a much more tolerable protector than Sam.''

In point of fact, Bible Sam had become quite a nuisance of late, exhorting her to read only the "Good Book," now that she was becoming lettered. Last week when he caught her reading one of Lord Byron's poems—a rather naughty one, she blushingly admitted—he had threatened her with hellfire such as she'd not heard since Reverend Morgan's heyday when she was a child in the church pew next to Aunt Tess.

"I'll see if I can find Pete, lovely. I know Sam's busy. He's got a funeral this morning. Seems a couple of miners got drunk at Willy's last night and had a fight. One was unlucky enough to fall against a cast-iron stove and break his neck.''

Kate shuddered at the violence of camp life as David bent and kissed her lightly, then swung around and sauntered out. Her eyes drank in his retreating figure. *How much longer, oh, how much longer will we stay together?*

Pete O'Mara, her adoring young Irish bodyguard, came to the tent agog with an incredible tale.

"'Top o' th' mornin' to you, beautiful colleen! Niver guess what I was witness to with me own eyes!'' He rolled his brown eyes dramatically. For all his boyish enthusiasm, Peter Sean O'Mara was a fine-looking young man, tall and muscular with a wealth of curly brown hair and a neatly trimmed beard. Kate always suspected he grew it to hide his youthfulness.

"Pray tell, Mr. O'Mara, what did just happen?'' Kate dimpled at his excitement.

"Oh, Miss Muldoon, a wild and wicked place this is, not safe for a lady. Even that rascal heathen preacher, Sam Buller, isn't safe to guard the likes of yourself.''

"What's poor Bible Sam done now, Pete?'' If she did not think about it, Kate used his first name. Usually, to ward off his earnest romantic pleas, she resorted to strict formality, but he was really like the charming, ingenuous younger brother that she wished for but never had. It was hard not to forget herself now and then.

He was so full of his tale he failed to notice her lapse. "Oh, and right shockin' it was and the poor man not cold in his grave when it happened."

"What happened? To who? And what did Bible Sam have to do with it?"

"Him it was, doin' the burial service, if you can call it that. A couple a clumsy prayers he says and two men start to throw dirt on the body with their shovels. Not even the decency of waitin' 'til someone could make him a proper pine box. Then, just as the poor soul was half laid to rest, out on the far side of the pine knoll we were, someone near the edge of the grave up and yells 'color!' The whole crowd went wild. That so-called preacher jumped down into the hole and yanked the body out almost single-handed, him grabbin' a shovel from one of the miners and beginnin' to dig! Afore any decent soul could even think or speak up, half the men there were clawin' and diggin' all round the grave for gold whilst the poor dead man's body was rolled up on the ground and forgotten!"

At this point, Kate, imagining the spectacle and inured to the harshness of gold camp life, had to stifle a chuckle at Pete's outrage. She pictured a rudely discarded corpse in the midst of flying picks and shovels. She forced a straight face and inquired, "Poor soul! What became of his body?"

Pete crossed himself and went on righteously. "Well, there was no gold, just a bit o' iron pyrite and once that was cleared up, they calmed down. Just as unruffled as you please, that so-called preacher drops his shovel and doffs his hat, kneelin' in prayer, him realizin' a little belated that he'd forgot his holy office. A couple of the others rolled the body back down the hill and filled in the hole. And a lot bigger it was, too, than they'd dug at first for the dead man!"

At this point Kate turned her back on Pete to hide her mirth. So, that righteous old hypocrite was guilty of at least one of the seven deadly sins himself—greed. No one, it seemed, was immune to gold fever! Next time he berated her for living in sin, she'd fix him, right enough!

As it turned out, Kate did not need to worry about any more of the preacher's bombast, for in a scant two days they were packed up and on their way to the "Luck of the Irish."

CHAPTER
8

April 1852, Boomer Gulch

David hired three men from Wilderness City to work the claim. The first was an old man, Joe Mullanphy, tough and wiry, who'd spent half his life in gold camps across North America and Mexico. The second, Zebulan Monroe, was an easygoing young argonaut, down on his luck ever since he hit California after traveling around the Horn from Boston. The third man worried David a bit, but finding a man willing to work someone else's claim was not easy. He had to take what he could get and Stoker Lawrey was it. A big, brutish man of middle years, he had a reddish beard and narrow eyes, almost yellow in color, sunken deeply in his head. His frame was beefy and he shambled around the camp.

Kate detested Lawrey the first moment she laid eyes on him. The two-day trip was a misery for her. She felt his leering stare on her back as he rode behind her, and he watched her out of the side of his vision when she cooked over the campfire. But he was careful to stay clear of David, so Kate did not complain about him.

The "Luck of the Irish" claim was not what Kate expected, although she would have been hard put to say just what she thought it would look like. It was in a narrow valley with a creek meandering through a stand of tall pines. At one side of the stream there was a wooden trough, about a foot or so wide and over thirty feet long, with crossbars of wood nailed in the bottom of it at regular intervals. At the lower end of the sluice a perforated metal plate caught any matter flowing down with the mud and water. With luck there would be gold among the debris.

As they stopped next to the crude mining equipment by the stream, Kate could see around the incline of the hillock where a small, sturdy log cabin sat nestled among the pines. With a squeal of delight she jumped from the back of Featherweight, the small dun mare that David had bought her. "Is the cabin part of our claim, David?"

David smiled. The gleam in her eye was worth waiting for. When he checked the details of their new property and found it included a two-room cabin, he decided not to mention it and let her be surprised. He hadn't expected it to be this well built. That mean little German was a damn fool at betting his cards, but he sure knew how to pick a pretty spot and make it a comfortable place to live. Now, if only there were gold in the ground, it would be splendid. "Yep, the cabin's ours too, Irish. Now you can put all those frustrated domestic talents to work. I'm still going to hire a Chinese from the camp to do the heavy chores for you, though. Go look at it and see what you'll need while the men and I unpack the gear and take a look around."

She ran up the hill and threw open the cabin door. The place had been closed up for months and was filthy. The stale, sour smell of fireplace ashes dampened by rain permeated the interior. Suddenly Kate sensed someone in the room with her. Whirling, she looked into the cat eyes of Stoker Lawrey. Before she could regain her composure, she let out a small gasp of dismay and backed away from his formidable height.

"Now, missy, take it easy. Boss man jest sent me ta see if'n ya want th' bedrolls 'n sech brung up now."

"No, no, Mr. Lawrey. I want to sweep and scrub the place and air it out first." She knew her voice still betrayed agitation and cursed herself for being intimidated by this brute. "Please bring up the pack with soap and brushes."

Lawrey grinned a knowing grin and shambled noiselessly out of the room.

Kate inspected the cabin—their first real home—hers and David's. As Kate remembered how puzzled she had been when David had packed cleaning supplies, she smiled. How silly of her not to guess his surprise. Then forcing her thoughts away from wistful romantic notions that could only come to naught, she began to plan the day's attack on a year's accumulation of dirt. In truth, she had to admit that for a man alone, Streicker had been a fairly good house-keeper. Most of the filth was the natural result of the place being deserted for so long.

How stupid that man was! Minin' a bankroll out of such a spot and then leavin' it to gamble his hard-earned gold in another camp! And what if we strike it rich? What if it was really rich? Kate closed her eyes and tried to imagine it. If she were a rich lady dressed in silks, might David marry her? *No. Kanes don't marry Muldoons, rich or not.* She shook herself and went in search of the broom.

The first week passed in a flurry of activity as Kate cleaned and scrubbed till the cabin fairly sparkled. The nearest camp town was only five miles up the valley, called by the odd name of Boomer Gulch. There Kate purchased all the domestic supplies she needed to set up housekeeping—yard goods, a big feather mattress for the bed and assorted pots and pans as well as pottery, dishes and cutlery.

David hired a Chinese servant, Chin Lee, to do laundry, chop wood and help Kate with all the heavier chores. The small, wiry man from Canton spoke little English, but he was incredibly strong and very bright. He soon devised a simple system of sign language combined with a few

English and Spanish words he'd picked up in California. He and Kate and David had no trouble understanding one another.

By the fifth day Kate had the place furnished. She made cheerful curtains of yellow gingham and had Chin replace the oiled paper on the windows with real glass panes. The simple oak table and two chairs were polished to a soft luster with beeswax and a bright red pot filled with wildflowers adorned the table. Iron skillets and pots hung neatly around the fireplace and there was a braided rug in the center of the plank floor. The back room was smaller and held only their bed, a simple chest and bedside table. It, too, was cosy and charming when Kate finished with it. As she stood in the door between the two rooms, looking into the bedroom at her newly made up bedspread, she was content.

That evening Kate could see that David was exhausted and disheartened. The claim might indeed be played out, but she knew how much money they still had from his winnings at cards, so she did not feel the failure as acutely as he did. She watched him stare moodily into his plate and cup, ignoring the fragrance of fresh-baked bread and beef stew with wild onions. Running her fingers through his thick gold hair, still damp from his pre-dinner bath in the creek, she tried to console him. "It's not as if we were starvin', David. There's plenty of money to last us until somethin' else turns up."

"Ah, but Kate, I don't want to keep living hand-to-mouth. I've been doing a lot of thinking here lately. I know my winnings seem like a lot of money to you, but the way I was raised, it won't last that long, believe me." His face became thoughtful. Then, the already dark blue eyes darkened even more in anger. Or, was it a hint of pain?

"I could always crawl back home, I guess. Papa'd take me in after a whopper of a penance, work my ass off and find me a 'suitable wife,' now that my brother's taken over the arrangement with the St. Clairs. I always favored the sea over ranching, even when I was a kid. I guess now that

Miguel has Cien Robles, Papa'd set me up in his shipping business.''

Kate's heart lodged in her throat. He'd leave here, leave her behind, go back to all the wealth he had given up. *A suitable wife*. She swallowed back her tears and stood by his side as he went on, almost unaware she was there, thinking out loud to himself.

''But I won't ever do that. That's what I've come to realize in the past months. I guess it really began the night I won this claim. I had a premonition of sorts, not about a gold mine exactly, but about making it on my own and never again being beholden to the high-and-mighty Kanes and Alvarezes.

''I guess that's why I'm down now. There may not be gold here, but even if this isn't it, I'll take the money I do have and go to San Francisco. There's more to be made in supplying the mining industry than in panning gold.''

He stopped and looked up at Kate, his eyes taking on that familiar devilish gleam. ''Somehow, some way, Irish, I'll make it to the biggest, fanciest house on Stockton Street. I'll buy you silk dresses from France and your own landau with a matched team of white horses to pull it. I'll smother you in emeralds as green as your Irish eyes.''

In all his extravagant promises, Kate longed to hear only one—one she knew she never would hear: *Marry me, never leave me! All the silks and emeralds on earth aren't worth as much as that*.

If David noticed her pensive air, he didn't show it as he scooped her up and carried her to the bedroom.

''David, your dinner, the stew . . .''

''It'll keep on a low fire, Irish. I have another high fire only your own sweet self can bank.''

Slowly, he set her on her feet alongside the soft feather-bed and began to nibble at her earlobes as his busy fingers worked the buttons down the back of her dress. He smelled of soap and shaving lather, still fresh and damp from bathing. The faint aroma of an unidentifiable male smell that always accompanied him to her bed was a heady sensation. She clutched him to her and eagerly twined her fingers in his long thick hair where it met his shoulders. As she deftly unbuttoned his shirt, he shrugged it off, allowing her access to his thickly furred tawny chest. She nuzzled it while he pulled her simple calico dress off and worked her petticoats loose, Lifting her out of the tangle of clothes, he laid her back on the big bed. As he finished undressing, she watched, still marveling at her own boldness and the pleasure she found in the beautiful symmetry of his body. The lean, hard muscles moved smoothly as he walked back to the bed, pausing in mid-stride to shake his hair off his forehead.

She raked him with a scorching look from head to toe and back up, provocatively licking her lips with the tip of a small pink tongue. Kate felt wanton and wonderfully wicked as he let out a low, growling laugh and grabbed her by her waist as she knelt up on the bed. They tumbled together in a tangle of arms and legs, laughing and gasping in sheer animal pleasure as they rolled across the big, soft feather mattress.

He dug his hands into her tousled dark hair, tangling it and drawing her mouth to his. With slow, intense pressure, he ground his mouth over hers, then traced a rough path of bruising kisses down her throat and across her breasts. She arched against his mouth's demands, moaning in fevered ecstasy.

It was always like this. Kate couldn't think, only feel and want. Yet this time she sensed a desperate urgency in David, as if he was using her body to assuage his pain, a pain she only dimly understood. He rolled her on top of him, then grabbed her buttocks in his hands and impaled her. With each thrust and retreat, thought receded further until she was as mindless in need as he.

Just when he could feel her stiffen and begin her orgasm, he pulled her down to him in another fierce kiss, spilling his seed deep within her in surfeit. Her hair covered them in a burnished blanket of dark russet, splashing onto the stark white pillows as she lay on top of him, panting in exhaustion and pleasure, all mixed together with an odd sort of hurt.

The following morning, the feeling of being used still haunted her. It was not that she minded his intense sexual release, for he gave her great pleasure in return. He was a splendid lover who aroused her to heights of passion Kate never imagined. Rather, she was disturbed by his desperate drive for independence from his family, a family he would never ask her to join. She was close to him only physically, never emotionally. She swallowed the lump in her throat. *I please him in bed. That is enough to please me. It has to be.*

Kate did not want to think about what would happen when he became successful, but neither did she doubt that a man like David Alexander Kane would make his mark in California. When he was rich and powerful enough to confront his father, his whole family—then what? Where did that leave an Irish saloon girl?

Weeks moved into months and the summer passed in a slow golden cavalcade. The sluice yielded just enough in dust and flakes to keep them breaking even and hoping. Kate was happy as the small vegetable garden she planted in late April yielded its harvest of peas, beans, cabbage and other fresh vegetables. She settled into a routine of rural domesticity. The cabin afforded such privacy that she could ignore being in the midst of a gold rush. Even Lawrey's brooding presence no longer disturbed her. She studied diligently by lantern light at night and David tutored her. His thoughtfulness in securing her books and newspapers never ceased to delight her. Kate put any thoughts of the future out of her mind. This time might be only a brief idyll, and she wanted nothing to spoil it.

One morning, just after she had hulled wild blackberries and began to roll out pie crust dough, Kate heard a commotion from down at the creek. When she got to the door, David was sprinting up the hill, bare-chested and soaked with sweat in the hot August sun. His grin was a mile wide.

"Lucky Irishwoman! We've done it! Oh, Katie, we've done it—pay dirt! Really rich! Solid ore in a deep crevice! We can use penknives to dig it out, it's so pure! All the flakes and dust were just what leached down to the creek!"

He swung her up in his arms and whirled her around and around.

That night they celebrated with a special dinner. David invited Joe, Zeb and Stoker. Other miners who lived nearby and had befriended them joined the party.

After all the men left and Kate began to clean up, David sat at the table, toying with a spoon. There was something he wanted to tell her, she could feel it. "Well, out with it. What's eatin' at you, David?" She knotted the dishtowel in her hands as she waited.

He lit a cigar and sat down. "Katie, what would you say to taking on another partner to run the mine? I talked to Kurt Watchner about it. He's made enough on his vein to have over a hundred thousand in a San Francisco bank. Now his mine is played out and he wants to invest for a percentage of 'Luck of the Irish.' "

"If he did, what would that mean?" Her manner was hesitant.

"It would mean capital for heavier equipment to pursue the vein deeper. But more than that, Kate, it would mean we'd have someone here I could trust to run the mining operation honestly. His reputation is solid and I've already checked into his finances. We could move to San Francisco sooner, within a month or two. We wouldn't have to spend another damnable wet winter in these hills."

"I like these hills. It's lovely here and we have our cabin." *I know it had to end, but must it be so soon?*

Half amused, half exasperated with her, David drew her into his arms. "Oh, Irish, remember when I told you about silk dresses and matched teams and mansions? You'll be the toast of San Francisco. Forget this miserable cabin. I'll buy you a palace!"

"But I love this—'miserable cabin,' as you so kindly put it! I've been happy here and I thought you were, too, but it seems I was mistaken!" Her temper, in check for so long, burst inside her in white-hot fury. Scorn her attempts at making a home for him, would he, the rich bastard!

Realizing she actually wanted to stay and play house in the wretched wilderness when he was offering her all the glitter of San Francisco, David was first incredulous, then angry. He'd finally struck it rich and all she wanted was a log cabin! Dammit, he ought to leave her. When she broke free of his embrace and whirled to fly out the door into the still darkness, he sat down and uncorked one of the half-full bottles left over from the earlier celebration.

He was unsure how to deal with Kate. He was certainly fond of her. Indeed, he'd never stayed with one woman for anywhere near this long before. What was it about her?

Most obviously there was the matter of bed. God! He loved teaching such a delightfully responsive pupil. He also admitted that taking her virginity still bothered him, but he pushed that aside. *In Will Bolton's place, a lot worse could have happened to her.* But her mind delighted him as well. In teaching her about literature, history and mathematics, he discovered an intellectual curiosity in himself that he had never been aware of. They learned together and he found their discussions about Shakespeare and Shelley almost as diverting as their lovemaking. Well, not really. . . .

Despite it all, she shackled him. He felt bound to her, but he wanted no wife. He had seen what his father's life was like with his mother. Duty, ties, children. It all boils down to guerilla warfare! No thanks. *Anyway, that's absurd. I can't marry an Irish orphan I won in a card game!* But a small nagging voice whispered to him: *Then why won't you give her up?*

There was a full moon and when Stoker, still drunk from his private after-dinner party, had gotten up to relieve himself, he had seen Kate run from the cabin. He'd watched Kate's redhead all night with veiled, hungry eyes as she served dinner, moving with unconscious grace and sweet female allure. She'd stoop over Kane's shoulder and put her hands on him so lovingly. The absentminded intimacy of their casual touching inflamed him. Damn rich boy, a gold mine and that woman to boot! Well, if he couldn't have the mine, he'd just encountered a piece of luck on the other item. Kane had not followed her. With a sudden sobriety born of lust, Lawrey stalked his prey.

Kate's tears blinded her as she ran toward her garden on the other side of the hill. Somehow it was a symbol of permanence, belonging. This was her first real home and now this security was being torn away from her. She didn't want to be paraded across San Francisco as David Kane's mistress, for everyone to see and whisper about. She knew many women would envy her, but she preferred her secluded life here.

Kate knelt in front of the garden plot, running her hand idly through the rich, warm soil at the edge, reassured by its feel. Suddenly, she heard a twig snap behind her and turned her upper body while still on her knees. Stoker Lawrey loomed over her. His features were malevolent in the wavering moonlight and the ugly grin of lust on his face was unmistakable. He moved so quickly she only had time to scream once before he crushed the breath from her. He covered her thrashing body with his own as they rolled in the garden, smashing her lovingly tended plants beneath them.

She bit his hand and flailed her arms and legs, all to little avail. His brutish weight pinned her, cutting off her breath until consciousness began to slip from her grasp. Just when she thought the enveloping blackness would win, she was dimly aware of a grunt of pained irritation from Lawrey and a shrill cry of warning in frantic Chinese from Chin Lee. Stoker lurched up to confront his assailant, leaving Kate bruised and gasping for breath.

Chin looked very small silhouetted in the moonlight next to the hulk of Lawrey, who literally made three of the Chinese. Nevertheless, he spat furious invectives in rapid-fire Cantonese as he lashed out at his mountainous opponent with a wickedly gleaming stiletto. Stoker tried to parry the thrusts bare-handed. Soon he was covered with cuts and bleeding profusely from the deep puncture in his shoulder where Chin's blade had first stabbed him.

Then, as Chin thrust once again, Stoker deflected the blow with his forearm and knocked the knife to the ground. He grabbed the smaller man and began to tighten his hold around Chin's thin neck. Suddenly a voice cut through his homicidal lust with such penetrating force that he froze.

"You squeeze and I squeeze, Lawrey." David's finger was pressed to the cocked Dragoon Colt's trigger, only a couple of feet from the man's shaggy red head. He'd come up on them while they were absorbed in the fight. A shot at that range would blow off the back of Stoker's head.

Lawrey released his hold on the Chinese, while Kate slowly sat up. Then, just as she stood up, Stoker lunged, shoving the Chinese at David. His shot went wild as Chin collided with him. He cocked the gun and took aim again, but Lawrey ran toward the woods, knocking Kate aside as he fled. She hit the ground with a sickening thud and lay still. When David fired, her groan distracted him and he only grazed Stoker, who kept on running. He let the man flee; his immediate concern was for Kate. He knelt by her side and looked at her torn dress and scratched body, suddenly terrified that she might be seriously injured.

Chin, dazed and with a decidedly sore throat, picked himself up and also hurried to Kate's side.

"Kate, Irish, where are you hurt?" David's hands reached down to where she held her side, her face drawn with pain.

"Ooh, I think that bastard broke me ribs. Damn his scurvy hide to hell, mmm." She hugged herself, breathing in searing little gulps.

As he gingerly helped her up, David sighed in relief. If she could swear that vehemently, she must be all right. Thank God!

Kate leaned against David and looked at Chin, who calmly reclaimed his fallen knife and then bowed politely before them. "Oh, Chin Lee, you saved my life! It's my everlasting gratitude you have."

"And mine," David added. "If you hadn't tackled that brute and gotten him off Kate before I arrived, he'd have crushed her for sure." David realized Lawrey nearly crushed Chin, too. It took great courage for the slight Cantonese to go up against a hulk like Stoker Lawrey, armed only with a small knife.

Chin bowed again. "This one pleased evil one gone."

He made a motion of disgust toward the woods where Stoker had vanished.

"Well, maybe the son of a bitch will bleed to death. At least we can hope so, Chin. Between us we did some damage to his filthy carcass," David replied.

When Kate tried to take a step, she let out an involuntary moan. David tried to pick her up, but she cried out again, convincing him it was better for her to walk than to have her cracked ribs bend as he carried her.

Later, after Dr. Jensen had been summoned from Boomer Gulch to tape her ribs and clean the abrasions, Kate lay pale and limp on the bed in their cabin. David sat on the side of the bed, holding her hand in his.

"Now you see why we can't stay in this place? God, Kate, he could have raped and killed you out there all alone! If Chin hadn't followed him when he stalked you and held him off, I'd never have reached you in time. You can't go wandering off like that so far from the cabin."

"We owe him a generous reward, David."

"I know. I offered, but his stubborn Oriental pride won't permit it. I did get him to agree to move with us to San Francisco and stay on as a servant at a good raise in salary. He's got quite a loyalty to you, it seems."

At the mention of moving to San Francisco, her eyes darkened, but she sighed in resignation. David was right. With Lawrey still about, it was hardly safe for her here. And David was determined to keep her with him. That was as much as she could ask.

Brightening, she said, "And when do we leave for the gold capital of the West Coast?"

CHAPTER
9

June 1852, Cien Robles

The land commission met in Los Angeles five days after the betrothal agreement between Miguel and Ellie was signed. The three-man commission made a special trip from San Francisco to Los Angeles to settle the huge land grant boundaries and corresponding claims of ownership in the southern cattle country. Although much litigation would remain pending in the courts for years to come, many of the oldest and largest grants were confirmed to their owners, among them Cien Robles to Alexander Kane and his heirs.

Adrian St. Clair had dinner with two of the commissioners the night before the Alvarez grant was assured to the Kane family. Everything went as planned. In the months that followed, a survey of the land was made under the careful surpervision of Adrian, a lay expert in California land law.

Alex and Maria both breathed easier after the final papers were filed in Sacramento, even though neither would admit so to the other. As for Miguel, when his father told him the good news, he simply gave Alex a level, penetrating stare, nodded in assent and went upstairs to change for dinner.

It was nearing the end of spring rodeo and the wedding was only two weeks away. Alex still assumed Miguel's moodiness, drinking sprees and peccadillos with servant girls were due to prenuptial jitters. When it came time for the backbreaking, dust-eating, sweaty labor of the roundups, Miguel worked tirelessly, like a man driven. Alex watched from the sidelines, grateful that his son took so well to the job. He knew his own rapidly deteriorating health would quickly have become evident if he had spent each day on horseback. He noticed with pride that the other ranchers and the vaqueros all respected the young *patrón*.

Alex was content, but his son was not. Miguel's estrangement from his mother and Father Sebastian continued. He was unfailingly polite to them both, something untrue of his exchanges with Alex, yet both mother and priest sensed a widening breach they could not mend. Father Sebastian blamed it on the harlots who had corrupted the boy and led him to his repeated, blatant sins of the flesh.

But Maria was sure that Rosalie and Sarita were symptoms of her son's fall from grace, not the cause. She knew that his impending marriage to that Americana, that Ellie St. Clair, with her loose, hoydenish ways was ruining her son. If only Miguel could somehow break the betrothal now that their lands were assured.

"I signed my name and pledged my honor, Mama. It's done," was Miguel's quiet reply to her entreaty.

"But surely, if you and she both do not want it, it will be no true marriage, even if the sacrament is enacted in the Holy Church."

With a trace of pity, Miguel looked at his mother and said bitterly, "If that's true, Mama, then I'm afraid it makes both David and me bastards, doesn't it?"

"Aah! How dare you say such a thing to your own mother!" Maria paled at the barb, realizing how true it was. God knew, she and Alex had never wanted to marry and thus received no sacramental blessing on their union.

Miguel was immediately contrite. His pain should not be taken out on her. She had not created his problem now any more than she had chosen to marry his father twenty-eight years ago. But he had given his word. If the St. Clairs had no honor, he did. "I'm sorry, Mama. I shouldn't have said that, but what you ask is impossible and you know it. Let's not think about it. We only torture ourselves over what cannot be changed.''

That night, Miguel rode to Rosalie's for the first time in two weeks. Now that the rodeo was over and he no longer had to work, he found that he missed the activity. He had finally proven himself, yet with that done, his mother's entreaties brought thoughts of his impending marriage back to him.

He sat in Rosalie's front parlor, long legs stretched out in front of him, slouched in one of her big, overstuffed chairs, a brandy in his hand, brooding. As she entered the room, Rosalie observed his preoccupied, casual pose and recalled the shy, nervous boy of five months ago. Quite a contrast to the self-assured man in front of her now. She was a bit smug about her part in his transformation, but realized that he still had some real blind spots and was too damn caught up in religious claptrap and guilt for his own good. That was probably what bothered him now. He had most likely come as much for talk as for sex.

"Howdy, Mike. You look like a Santana wind blew you in, darlin'. Rodeo goin' all right? You look beat.'' As she spoke, she poured herself a brandy from the sideboard and walked over to his chair.

Smiling at her, he reached one long arm up and pulled her down on his lap, absently stroking her neck with the fingers of one hand as he sipped his drink.

"I'm not fit company, I guess, Rose. I am tired, but that's not what's wrong. The rodeo is over, complete until fall. Went great. Alex let me run the whole show.''

"Then what's botherin' you?''

He didn't answer, but put down his glass, took hers and set it down also, then proceeded to kiss her fiercely. "Let's go to your room,'' he said, his voice hoarse with urgency.

Rosalie didn't argue. His strange, almost violent compulsion needed to be assuaged. They went to the room at the end of the hall and both quickly undressed. He fairly fell on her, kissing her with passion and quickly pulling her onto the bed where he entered her feverishly. Sensing his mood, she rode with him, only slowing him a bit toward the end so as to catch up with his frantic passion. Despite the haste, when she felt him swell and explode within her, she followed him over the brink.

Afterward, they lay in the dim, flickering light, she on her side with one arm propping up her head as the other hand traced patterns in the black mat of his chest hair. He lay on his back with his arms behind his head, staring at the ceiling, lost in thought.

It wasn't like Mike, this fast violent way. Oh, it had been the first few times, just as it was with most men, but she had convinced him the pleasure was greater if slowed down, prolonged. This swift, rough sex was out of a deeper need, having nothing to do with pleasure or even physical relief.

As she waited for him to talk about it, she remembered his first half dozen visits, when they'd discussed his upbringing and study for the priesthood.

"I still confess what we do as a sin, you know," he said one time.

Rosalie had looked at him expectantly.

Miguel laughed and said, "I don't mean I plan to stop doing it."

"Then why 'confess' it? Seems natural enough. Living like your Father Sebastian seems unnatural, if you ask me!"

"You wouldn't understand. Old habits die hard, I guess. I grew up in the shadow of the church and Father Sebastian. He was the epitome of everything educated, spiritual, saintly. I wanted to be like him, but now I find I'm not like him at all."

"Or like your ma?" she questioned shrewdly.

"You wouldn't understand my mother. Women like her don't understand a man's needs or failings. They don't feel what you feel, Rose."

She made a coarse sound of disgust. "Bullshit! You're *criollo*, a real blueblood. You think your vaqueros enjoy women more than you do because they're poor and you're rich?"

He scoffed. "That's not the same thing. A man needs a

woman, no matter what his station in life. Women are different.''

"You think you know all about women, just because I'm a whore and I like it and your ma's a saint and she doesn't? Seems to me that leaves a lot of females in between somewhere, rich and poor. Women need men, just like men need women. Course, there are some exceptions in both sexes, like your saintly Father Sebastian.''

The argument had become circular and useless, but at least his religious guilt had let up some, heavens be praised. One day she had jokingly asked him about "confession" and he had made one. "I guess I'm taking your advice to heart despite myself. I felt like a damn hypocrite for so long, I quit going.''

She laughed. "There's hope for you yet, Mike. What does Father Sebastian say to that?''

He snorted in disgust at a joke she didn't fully understand. "That he can't perform the marriage until I make a complete confession. So, I suppose sooner or later, I'll have to.''

A few times he had mentioned the arranged marriage between himself and the St. Clair girl, but he never wanted to talk about it. Rosalie had seen Ellie St. Clair in town on a number of occasions. The girl was a beauty, but because old Alex had forced the match, apparently Mike didn't favor it.

Her thoughts returned to the present and she gently stroked his chest once more. Something was deeply wrong and she had a gut feeling that it was related to Ellie St. Clair.

Finally, he turned to her on the bed and spoke. "A week from Saturday I'm getting married.''

"Don't make it sound like a one-way ticket to hell, baby. I've seen the girl. She's gorgeous. And don't worry. You'll be able to show your new bride quite a good time. I ought to know.''

He stiffened. "I doubt there's anything she hasn't already tried.'' The words were clipped.

Ouch! So that's the lay of the land! His blushing bride had something to blush about, did she? What a blow to his pride! How the hell had he found out? The girl certainly seemed proper enough. Not a whisper of scandal had ever been breathed about her in town and little gossip escaped Rosalie's place.

Rosalie felt his anguish and wanted to offer what comfort she could. If it was not to be conversation tonight, all right with her. Slowly, she began to run her caressing hand lower down his chest, over that flat, hard belly, lower still. He groaned in pleasure when she wrapped a deft hand around his shaft and began to stroke it back to renewed life. Then sensuously, she slid down and took the sleek, hard flesh in her mouth. For now, she would take his mind off Ellie St. Clair.

As the day of the wedding neared, Ellie was extremely unhappy. She tossed and turned each night in bed, fearfully conjuring up that dark, hawklike visage with lips whitened in fury. She could feel the barely leashed anger in his midnight eyes as he stood over her that day in the garden. She dreamed of their hurtful encounter and her nightmares always ended as he stalked up the path to the house, leaving her alone under the peach tree, shaking as if she had an ague. Yet for all her anguish, she could confide her fears to no one, least of all her father. *Why, oh, why did I make up those terrible, childish lies?*

The girls at her school back east had speculated, whispered and giggled about men. Because she had been raised on the ranch, Ellie felt superior. She knew about cattle and horse breeding, but in point of fact, she was woefully ignorant of what went on between men and women. When she returned to the ranch and fell under Rice's sway, his kisses seemed wonderful. She had felt no fear then, only a delicious shiver of anticipation for the unknown.

But now Rice had betrayed her and the man she was betrothed to believed she was a harlot. And to cap it all off, he was a damn priest! Well, *almost* a priest, a reclusive celibate. She probably knew as much as he did! What a laugh their wedding night would be! Even worse than the physical aspect of their marriage was the emotional one. He hated her, had never wanted to marry, and he blamed her for the complete disruption of his life.

All these thoughts churned around in her mind one morning as she rode into Los Angeles for her final fitting on the elaborate silk wedding dress Adrian insisted she have. Wanting to spare nothing in the marriage of his only child, he was throwing the biggest fiesta of the year in a land famous for its lavish entertainment. The wedding was to be in the largest church in Los Angeles with his winter villa in town being opened and readied for the gala to follow. After the feasting with friends and family, she and Miguel were to return to Cien Robles to begin their new life. New life. Her mouth puckered wryly, then quivered. She shook herself and dismounted from Moonlight in front of the seamstress's shop.

Señora Valdez was the best dressmaker in the area and she disapproved with typical Hispanic rigidity of Ellie's riding horseback to town for her fittings. She was appalled at Ellie's split riding skirts and practice of riding astride. No decent Californio's daughter would dream of such a thing.

Ellie swished the full tan broadcloth skirt freely as she walked up to the shop, smiling archly in spite of herself. *Just wait until my new mother-in-law sees one of these outfits!* If Adrian had a fit when she brought one home from St. Louis last year, imagine what Maria Kane would say! She couldn't help letting a wicked chuckle escape her lips despite her depressed mood.

Ellie was politely ushered into a fitting room by one of Señora Valdez's young helpers, who cast eyes big as saucers on her remarkable attire. She helped the young *patrona* out of her blouse and the shocking skirt. Then Ellie stripped off her sturdy linen undergarments and donned the lacy thin chemise, pantalets and layers of petticoats that went with her wedding dress. The seamstress's assistant helped Ellie change and marveled at the pale silvery beauty of the tiny Americana. So this was Don Miguel's bride-to-be. She was certainly lovely enough, with startling coloring, turquoise eyes and all that wealth of silver-gilt hair on her head, as well as its matching counterpart at the juncture of her legs. The dark servant girl stared in awe. Oh, to be in her place!

If Ellie was aware of the girl's perusal, she did not show it. The rigors of a girl's boarding school had long ago inured her to jealous evaluations of her unusual beauty.

When all the frilly undergarments were in place, Ellie instructed the girl to let the señora know she was ready to try on the dress. She thought of the breathtaking sheer silk, inlaid with hundreds of tiny seed pearls, inset with hand-made lace of the most gossamer delicacy and sighed. For such an occasion as this, she should have a mother or close female friend, someone to soothe her nerves. Instead, here she was, alone as usual.

Of course, Aunt Beatrice was arriving next week for the wedding. She was Dad's widowed sister from Oregon Territory, a prim, distant figure Ellie had met only a few times in her life. Ellie knew her father wanted a woman to tell her about "delicate matters," but she was glad Aunt Bea would not be arriving for four or five days. She remembered a thin, bloodless woman with none of her dad's gentleness or humor. Her aunt would certainly give no consolation.

Her reverie was interrupted when she heard giggling voices carrying down the long hall from the rear of the building. "Eh, Rosa, I just helped her undress for her fitting. She wore the most incredible skirt, split up the center, like men's pants! She rides astride!" Ellie recognized the voice of the girl who just waited upon her. The exchange was in Spanish, which Ellie could understand quite well.

The girl named Rosa tittered. "I wonder if Don Miguel will ride her or she him! What does she look like, Anna?"

"Oh, she is quite pretty for a gringa, if you like all that pale hair and skin. Her body is small and well enough formed, if a man likes a small nibble instead of a big feast."

Gales of giggling laughter followed. Ellie reddened.

"Oh, but what I would not give to be in her place! To be his wife!" The breathless voice of Anna was almost dreamy.

"Ha! Better wish to be Rosalie or one of the whores who work at her place. It is said he takes them all on some nights. My cousin is a cook at Hundred Oaks and she tells me he takes a different serving girl to bed each night when he's home. He'll probably be too tired to bother with his pale little lady after all that exercise!''

"Still, just to get the eye of that one, ah, such a body, and that face! He is the most beautiful man I ever saw, even better than his brother, who was too much the Yankee. If I were his wife, I'd know how to hold his attention!''

Ellie was riveted to the floor. The tittering exchange went on, but the two girls must have walked into the back courtyard because their voices gradually faded. She stood in the new silence. *So! Some priest! He's abandoned his chaste inclinations quickly enough. Every trashy servant girl and prostitute in the area knows the dazzling Don Miguel, damn him!* And, worse yet, everyone expected him to be bored with his American wife. He was a typical Hispanic philanderer who would never honor marriage vows. Tears of shame and self-pity mingled, running down her flushed cheeks, but when Señora Valdez entered the room, Ellie quickly turned and dashed them aside, silently cursing Miguel Kane.

CHAPTER
10

June 1852, Twin Rivers

The wedding day dawned bright and unseasonably cool. Adrian St. Clair stood on the front porch of the Twin Rivers ranch house and took a deep breath of the clear morning air. What a good omen, such a lovely day! Ellie had been so touchy lately, sharp-tongued, jumpy as a cat. After Bea arrived last Monday and had her "little talk" with the girl, Ellie had been even more nervous. Better to get a skittish young girl like Eleanor safely married and have done. After her fears were laid to rest, she would feel better.

Upstairs, Ellie was preparing for the two-hour ride to their villa in town, trying not to think of this afternoon and most especially of tonight. She almost laughed, remembering Aunt Bea's whispered conversation with her the other night. Ugh! All that stilted, euphemistic language to describe what a man did to his bride on their wedding night. It was disgusting and terrible, but a good, dutiful wife had to submit to it over and over for the rest of her married life. It was her sacrifice to assure that she would have children, if God blessed them so. Aunt Bea was childless. Ellie could not help but wonder if Aunt Bea had "sacrificed" very often.

Recalling her reactions when boys had kissed her at dances in St. Louis, and certainly how she had felt when Rice took her in his arms, she didn't agree with her aunt's terrible description. Was she a bad woman? Ellie didn't think so, but realizing that Miguel thought of her as such brought her up short. What would it *really* be like? *At least he's not a green boy,* she thought grimly, *a would-be priest! One of us will know what to do, anyway.*

The journey into town was a blur of images flashing through Ellie's mind as she rode in the carriage with Adrian on one side and Aunt Bea on the other. She saw Rice, at first loving and tender, then with his face contorted in rage as he lunged after her that terrible day at the line shack. She saw Aunt Bea, rolling her eyes as she described the terrible intimacies of marriage. She pictured the pretty, laughing faces of the two Mexican girls at the seamstress shop as they whispered about Miguel. Most of all she pictured Miguel, soon to be her husband, his handsome face furious at her lies. *Oh, God! My stupid lies!*

*   *   *

At Cien Robles, Doña Maria knelt in the chapel and prayed, yet felt her words hollow, not rising to heaven at all. How did one pray for a blessing on a marriage that should never be? It was as accursed as her own had been twenty-eight bitter years ago. Her father had forced her to wed the Yankee sea captain whose wealth could restore the rancho. All he ever wanted was to hold the land, even if it meant bringing in foreign blood, a heretic, an Americano from a class of merchants!

And now another American, further dilution of the proud Alvarez bloodline. It was for Miguel that she felt the most sorrow, Maria told herself. He should have been a priest now, happy in his holy orders, not sweating on horseback sixteen hours a day for this land, working himself to death for Alex's dream. Of course, she could never think of losing Cien Robles. But it should have been David, not Miguel, *her* Miguel, who had to make this sacrifice.

Outside, Miguel strode toward the stables, dressed in simple riding clothes. He would change into his resplendent wedding attire after the dusty ride into Los Angeles. Father Sebastian was already there, making final arrangements with the parish priest for the nuptial mass. The priest who had wanted to assist in Miguel's ordination would now assist in his marriage.

Miguel walked into the dark interior of the stable, blinking at the sudden shift from bright light. The smell of horses and hay was familiar and comforting. He heard Dominican neigh and moved over to stroke the horse's nose absently, lost in thought. Last night when he heard Alex and his mother arguing again, he fled the house and rode hard and fast until very late. *Perhaps in hopes of breaking my neck?* He laughed bitterly. Then, considering the magnificent big black he was stroking, he said aloud, "Hardly fair to you, old friend, eh? No, I'll just have to see this through and hope my father can leave my mother some small measure of peace." Of his own peace, he thought not at all.

* * *

The church was shaded from the hot mid-afternoon sun
by huge sycamores that sheltered its vaulted roof. Its
coolness and tranquility remained undisturbed by the arrival of the wedding party. The interior was large and
ornate, Spanish rococco, with elaborate beaten gold al-
tars. Crucifixes gleamed dully in the flickering light from
hundreds of candles.

The two men standing at the side of the high altar were
subdued. Alex looked at his son, now attired in his most
elegant black charro suit, heavily trimmed in silver. White
silk ruffles ran down the shirt front to the red satin sash at
his narrow waist. Heavy silver shirt studs winked in
splendor to match the trim on the high-cut jacket and
thigh-hugging flared pants. At first glance, the old man
thought anyone would take Miguel for a pure-blooded
Californio. However, the Kane resemblance in dark blue
eyes and stubborn jaw were clearly discernable. This was
his son and he was proud of him.

"Do you have the ring?" Alex's words were laden with
meaning.

Miguel produced a heavy gold band inset with rubies. It
was a small size, to fit a tiny finger. "Everything is taken
care of, Papa. Nothing will stop this wedding but an act of
the Deity." Was there a hint of caustic humor lurking
behind his pious words?

Nothing stopped the ceremony. Ellie came down the
aisle in her gossamer concoction of French silk and lace,
silvery white and breathtakingly lovely. All those present,
including Maria, were dazzled by the girl's beauty. Miguel
stood at the foot of the altar, stunned as he watched her
float toward him like an angelic vision, chaste, pure and
perfect. He took her small, cold hand from her father's
arm and they knelt before the two priests, a beaming
Father Francisco and a crestfallen Father Sebastian.

Ellie glanced up into Miguel's darkened eyes. Their
expressionless depths betrayed no emotion—but told her
everything. Quickly, she looked down at his hands as they
covered hers. She studied their contours, beautifully sculpted

and strong with fine black hair in patterns on the backs. Remembering those erotic images from their betrothal dinner, she blushed. They were in church! During the ceremony she concentrated on his hands as he placed the antique ring on her finger. *If only he weren't so forbidding, so angry.* She spoke her vows and went numbly through the intricacies of the ritual like a sleepwalker.

Miguel watched her throughout the ceremony. After that first fleeting glance when he took her hand, she kept her veiled head down, unable to meet his level gaze. He had carefully schooled his emotions, trying to show neither the sadness nor the anger he felt. They were in church and what must be done, must be done. *But why does she have to appear so withdrawn? Just like the day we signed the betrothal. She couldn't meet my eyes then either.* Deep inside him the hurt festered. She was marrying him, but she wanted another.

Then, before either realized it, they were sitting side by side in the St. Clair carriage, heading to Adrian's villa a few blocks away for the big fiesta. The noise of mariachis and cheering crowds of well-wishers receded as they became aware of each other. Surreptitiously, Ellie stole glances at him, saying nothing for the brief ride. Miguel looked out over the crowd, refusing to look at her, but acutely conscious of his beautiful new wife. They were careful not to touch, sitting woodenly on opposite ends of the seat.

They greeted guests for hours in the palm-lined courtyard of the St. Clair city house. Virtually all of the ranchers, politicians and bankers in California were there, from the oldest, most aristocratic Mexican *criollos* to the most crassly nouveau riche Yankees.

Adrian spread a magnificent feast which reflected the cultural merger of Hispanic and Yankee in the best Californio tradition. The revelers dined on roast steer, suckling pig, tortilla dishes with hot chilies, New England steamed breads and freshly churned ice cream, native-grown oranges and sparkling wines from Alex's vineyards.

As they sat at the banquet table and the endless toasts

went on, Adrian and Alex watched. "They make a splendid couple, Alex." Adrian beamed, seeming unaware of Ellie's pallor and nervousness.

"Yes, my friend, that they do." Alex remembered twenty-eight years ago and another wooden, frightened young bride. *Pray God I've been right to do this. It can't turn out like my marriage with Maria!*

Ellie continued to cast quick, appraising glances at her husband when he was not aware. He was wonderfully handsome, she would give him that much. In spite of herself she imagined those lips, now spread in a dazzling laugh, pressed to her own, that lean, dark body lying beside her. *What is it about this man that brings out such a wanton streak in me?* Even when she had believed she loved Rice, she had never imagined such things about him. When Miguel shifted his attention back to her, she nervously pushed the food on her plate back and forth, unable to taste or swallow, much less meet his gaze.

"Some wine for your bridal nerves, *mí esposa*?" He formally offered her a crystal goblet filled with dark red liquid, grown and bottled on Cien Robles. "The very best fruit of the vine from our own cellars."

His voice was deep and resonant yet there was a controlled note to it that she detected. "Yes, thank you." She took a tiny sip, more for the gesture than because she wanted wine. "It's very good."

"It was bottled the year my parents were married. Fitting, don't you agree?" The edge to his voice was unmistakable now.

Ellie's pride was stung so fiercely that she refused to back down at the deliberate insult. Everyone in the huge courtyard knew of the wretched marriage between Alex and Maria, of his mistresses and philandering. She looked her husband squarely in the face and said sarcastically, "Your hope for our success over their failure is touching, *mí esposo*."

His eyes darkened perceptibly and he rose, taking her hand in his, pulling her unwillingly from the chair. "I think it's time we went home to Cien Robles. After all, it *is* our wedding night."

It was dusk outside, but in the brightly lit central courtyard of the villa the music and laughter only grew more raucous and would go on until daybreak. Ellie knew it was customary for newlyweds to steal away from the merrymaking early, but she was less and less prepared to do so as he maneuvered them across the patio toward the *sala* door. Just as they neared the door, Adrian came upon them, heartily placing his arm over Miguel's shoulder.

"You two must have a bridal dance to start the festivities for everyone else. No one can dance until the bride and groom do. It's an old New England custom I'm fond of." As if on cue, one of the groups of strolling mariachi came up and began to play a slow Mexican folk piece, haunting and sensuous.

Miguel gave a resigned nod and bowed to his wife, then took her in his arms and they began to move in the traditional steps of the dance. At first both were grave and stiff, unaccustomed to the physical contact. However, with the increasing tempo of the music that Ellie had loved since childhood, she began to dance with more expression, moving in rhythm to the hypnotic beat. Some subliminal part of her mind wanted to prove to her husband that she was as desirable as the women at Rosalie's. She, too, was a woman worthy of his attention.

Miguel was naturally graceful at dancing, although it was not an accomplishment that he had practiced more than his tutors demanded. His limited experience had been with plump matrons and scrawny cousins when he was a boy. Now he watched Ellie, entranced by her sensuous, fluid movements. Her beautiful little body was warm and enticing as all the earlier coldness fled. She was Eve, Lilith, Delilah, every woman whose corrupt, wonderful flesh ever tempted man to perdition. *Damn her, but I want her!* And in the wanting, his anger was fired anew along with his desire. *How many other men has she seduced? Is she looking at me and imagining Rice Brighton in my place?*

As the music ended abruptly he swept her up, all her silver glitter and gossamer softness, and carried her from the courtyard. Ellie was stunned and breathless, held effortlessly in those lean, corded arms as he strode through the house. Outside, his black devil of a stallion was tethered, pawing the ground nervously.

"We aren't, you can't mean to—" Ellie paled.

She could say no more before he put her down. Holding her wrist in an iron grip, he swung fluidly onto the towering height of Dominican.

"My dress, you'll ruin it! I'll fall!" she shrieked as he swept her up in front of him.

Amid the shouts of the throng that followed them outside, he whispered in her ear, in what appeared to be a loving gesture, "The bridal dance was your Yankee custom. Riding home on the bridegroom's saddle is an old Californio custom. We begin with a compromise, no?" At a touch from Miguel's heels Dominican took off at a wild, swift gallop for Cien Robles.

Miguel stood in Alex's study in his shirtsleeves, leaning against the desk, pouring a brandy. He had allowed himself nothing stronger than a glass of wine all day, even at the long, arduous reception, exerting careful control over his emotions so as to get through the stinking ordeal. Now he needed a drink. On that mad, headlong ride home, holding Ellie so close, inhaling the lilac fragrance of that silvery hair, he was able to think about nothing but her enticing little body. He closed his eyes and once more saw her at the fiesta. God, *how* he needed a drink!

He sipped slowly, imagining her upstairs, ensconced in her new bedchamber adjacent to his. The maid was helping her undress and prepare for him. He had planned simply to perform his duty and consummate the marriage briefly and emotionlessly. He did not love her and she certainly did not love him, so he'd make it as painless as possible for both partners. That's what he had been trying to tell himself during the past weeks. But tonight he had felt an intense surge of desire sweep over him when she warmed to him in that dance!

He muttered a vile Spanish oath and took another gulp of brandy. What a joke! *She wasn't warming to me—just using me as a substitute for her damn foreman.* She did not want him, but he wanted her, damn if he did not, more than he could remember wanting a woman—and in the past five months Miguel had made up for a great deal of lost time where women were concerned.

Finishing the drink, he walked slowly out the study door and up the stairs toward his bedchamber at the far end of the east wing. The gleaming parquet floors echoed the click of his boots as he entered his room. He heard no sound from next door. Roughly, he pulled his shirt studs out and shrugged off the garment, tossing it carelessly on a chair. Boots and stockings followed. He wondered if he should don a dressing robe, but decided not to bother. The hell with any more polite conventions. He had spent the day posturing, smiling and making banal conversation. He was through with pretenses. Just get it over with.

Ellie smiled uncertainly at her new maid, Luz, as the pretty girl helped her undress. It took quite a while to undo all the tiny buttons and untie all the petticoats. The gorgeous dress was ruined: wrinkled, torn at the seams, and covered with dust from that insane ride back. *Well,* she mused to herself, *I'll certainly never wear it again anyway, so what's the difference?* She flexed her aching muscles, cramped from sitting across the big saddle for two hours. *Bastard! What was he trying to prove?*

By the time Luz assisted Ellie into the sheer white batiste nightrail and matching robe embroidered with silvery flowers, the serving girl was in awe of her beauty. Luz's jealousy was forgotten, for she thought the young *patrona* was kind and even a bit frightened. She smiled to herself, thinking of how lucky Doña Eleanora would soon be.

With a quiet *"muchas gracias,"* Ellie dismissed the girl and sat down nervously on the edge of her bed. *At least I have the privacy of a separate bedroom.* Was she happy

for that or not? When she heard footsteps pass her door
and continue down the hall, she jumped off the bed as if
burned and began to pace silently across the woven rug.
The room was lovely, with leaded glass windows that
opened to catch the breeze, intricately carved oak furniture
and ivory stucco walls. The bed had big bolsters on it and
was quite large. She wondered if all the beds at Cien
Robles were specially built to accommodate the long legs
of the Kane men. Somehow she suspected that Doña
Maria's was not.

The bed. She stared at it as if hypnotized, listening to
the faint rustling of clothing emanating from next door. It
would not be much longer, she knew. Her fear suddenly
blossomed to full-blown terror. He was upset at her dancing, she had realized too late. He probably thought her a
hoyden for making the foolish display. Then that terrifying
ride back. His monster of a horse could have broken both
their necks! What next?

As if in answer to her question, the narrow door between the two bedrooms opened and Miguel stepped into
her room. Ellie could not have said just what she expected,
but his half-naked body was a surprise. He was barefooted
and barechested, clad only in the tight black suit pants.
Her eyes riveted on his chest, densely furred with curly
black hair descending in an arrow to his waist. Embarrassed
to let her eyes travel lower, she looked up abruptly into his
face. A lock of raven hair hung over his forehead and
those thick black brows were creased in a frown, shadowing
his dark eyes. He stood still in the center of the room,
looking very handsome and very dangerous.

A small thrill of primitive excitement raced through her
veins. Rice had never stirred her senses as Miguel did.
When they had danced at the villa, she felt a strange new
sensation, like a magnetic pull between them, male and
female, soon to be joined in the most ancient dance of all.
Part of her welcomed the culmination, wanted to know the
mystery, said, *Come, take me*. Yet for all the attraction,
she was still afraid. He was embittered, believing her
soiled and deceitful; he was angry with her inept attempt to

attract him with her dancing. *If only I hadn't lied to him. If only he wanted me.*

Miguel watched her shiver when he fixed her with a penetrating blue stare. He said nothing, scorning her vaporish air. *It's a little late to play the frightened innocent,* he thought grimly. But she looked so ethereal and lovely that he was wrenched anew. He fought to control his desire, afraid she would see his weakness and scorn it. He must be calm and consummate this marriage emotionlessly. However, nothing at Rosalie's had prepared him for how to proceed. What should he do? What should he tell her to do?

Ellie was confused by his hesitation after his menacing entrance. What did he want her to do? With a jolt she realized that he believed her a whore who would know what to do. Choking on that awful thought, she blurted out with an air of false bravado, "I await your instruction, sir."

He flinched at her nerve, then said coldly, "Take off your clothes."

She did not move.

He paused a moment more but still she stood her ground, motionless. He took a step toward her and touched the fastener of the peignoir. Shoving his hand away, she stepped back. As if dancing once more, he moved after her. "You lead, I follow. It should be the other way around, I think." Miguel forced himself to speak evenly as he reached for her shoulder, planning to pull her closer so he could unfasten the robe.

Divining his intent, she jumped backward in instantaneous reflex. His fingers caught in the sheer white batiste, separating it like gauze, leaving her shivering. Clutching the shredded remnants of the bridal peignoir to her breasts, Ellie spat with a stubborn tilt of her chin, "Don't you dare touch me!"

He scowled. "Ah, *querida,* I must do a great deal more than touch you."

She let out a shocked gasp of indignation, her turquoise

eyes flashing angrily at him. She had not dreamed he would be this crude!

He grew increasingly impatient with the charade. "Surely, my love, the command to undress can't be a new one for you. How many times have you done it for Rice Brighton? And how many others, I wonder? While you danced tonight half the men in the courtyard were wondering how you look naked. Well, they don't have the right to see. I do." He paused a second, watching her levelly.

She stood trembling, rooted to the floor in outrage. *I'm a thing, a possession to him, just as I was to Rice!*

"I said, take off that virginal little gown *now*." Miguel's voice was growing increasingly menacing. He took another long, pantherlike stride toward her, trapping her between himself and the bed.

This was the final indignity! Ellie fumed. He may have consorted with countless whores, but he would not treat Ellie St. Clair like a common strumpet! Her own fierce temper and St. Clair pride overrode her judgment. She slapped him, her small hand leaving a red mark on his dark cheek.

Before she could evade him, his long arm reached around her tiny waist, pulling her tightly against his body. She kicked, clawed and bit, but he held on, ignoring the little soft-slippered feet which did little damage at such close quarters. He quickly secured both slim wrists and held them in one hand behind her back while he pressed her to him. Then, using his free hand, he pulled her waist-length hair down, forcing her to look up into his face.

Ellie could feel him trembling as much as she was. She scanned his face in fright, but also in curiosity. There was something hidden behind the harshly set features. His dark blue eyes reflected youth and vulnerability for a fleeting instant before coldness veiled them once more.

As her small, upthrust breasts heaved against his chest, he looked down at their pearly perfection. The words were involuntarily torn from him. "God, you are beautiful!"

Easing his hand from her hair, he traced a delicate path

across her slender throat, over her collarbone, then softly teased a breast as she leaned away from him. Time seemed suspended for a moment as the pale pink tip hardened. He smiled knowingly. The trespassing hand moved to the other nipple, eliciting a similar response. *Her body responds to me, even if her heart belongs elsewhere*, he thought in satisfaction.

Feeling the strange tingling sensation his skilled fingers evoked, Ellie was startled at the pleasure. Hesitantly, she raised her eyes, quivering with some primitive, unnamed need. The superior smirk she saw on his face devastated her. Disgusted with her body's humiliating betrayal, she stiffened and jerked away from his hand with a gasp. *Damn, I'll die before I let him know how he stirs me!*

He sucked in his breath. *So, she still tries to reject me, does she?* He released her angrily and stepped back, determined to end the miserable game quickly. Methodically, he unbuttoned his tight pants, now grown alarmingly tighter, peeling them off to stand in the center of the room, quite naked. "You see, *mi esposa*, I'm quite willing to undress in front of you. Pity you don't want to return the compliment."

Ellie stood rooted to the ground, pulling the shredded remnants of her peignoir around her trembling body as she watched him move with feline grace. She stared in fascination at his lean, muscular physique, unable to tear her eyes from his virile beauty. Such arrogance! He knew full well that he was pleasing for women to look upon. Then her gaze lowered to the rigid member that had pressed into her when he held her. Now freed and standing upright, it looked huge and menacing to her virginal eyes. All Aunt Bea's tales came back to her now, not so absurd as she had first thought.

Miguel, mistaking her crouched, fearful mien for a coy act played by a harlot, became increasingly disgusted and furious. He had tried so hard to hold his hurt and anger in check. "Why prolong the torture for both of us? Have done with it! You're no innocent maiden with virginal sensibilities!"

When he reached for her she twisted away with surprising strength while doggedly holding the torn nightrail across her breasts. Muttering a curse, he scooped her up with lightning speed and threw her onto the bed. Before she could roll off the other side, he followed her onto its soft surface. She thrashed and writhed frantically as he attempted to pull the tangled shreds of clothing from her body. She knew a few pretty good oaths, too!

He felt his control splintering as her silky skin brushed against his heated flesh. When she clawed at his face, narrowly missing his eyes, he feared she might blind him. When she kicked upward with her knee, he feared she might do even greater damage! They thrashed back and forth across the big bed as her hysterical frenzy continued unabated.

She had drawn blood, damn her! A long weal ran down his right arm, another along his temple, and her teeth had sunk into his hand and shoulder. His jaw ached abominably from where her elbow had connected with surprising force.

Finally he succeeded in rolling on top of her, virtually forcing the breath from her as he secured her dangerous hands by their slim wrists and carefully put his thigh over her flailing legs. He pinned her hands over her head and held them fast with his left hand. Then he took his right hand and ran it over her torso, feeling the velvety soft skin, now slick with perspiration and flushed red from exertion. Never had he felt such an intense surge of pure sexual energy. Held fast, she ceased her struggling, breathless as a young doe brought to bay by a large hound.

Quickly, he raised one knee between her thighs and separated them, thankful she was finally acquiescing. He entered her in one sudden thrust. Aching and desperate for the relief of climax, he did not feel her tearing maidenhead. As anger and pleasure mixed, blotting out everything around him, he worked himself toward a swift, mindless release.

Ellie writhed in furious silence, willing herself not to cry out as she fought him. The bruising pressure of his hands held her securely as he labored above her. She could smell the male scent of him, musk and sweat. This was even worse than Aunt Bea had described, but Aunt Bea had assumed she would be a dutiful martyr, submitting supinely, not fighting for her pride and honor like a cornered wildcat! The more she twisted away from him, the more her actions seemed to inflame him. Abruptly, he gave several long, convulsive shudders. His shaft seemed to swell inside her even more. Then he withdrew and rolled from her in one quick movement. She lay still, afraid to move.

Gradually, the enormity of what he had done washed over Miguel. He sat up in a daze and forced himself to look at his wife, lying rigidly in the center of the big bed. *Holy Mother of God!* He could see the smears of blood on her slim thighs. When he looked down at himself, the corroborating evidence was unmistakable. *She had been a virgin!*

"Why? Why did you lie to me? Christ! I could have killed you!" The words came out in a low, fierce rush of bewildered anger.

After all this, he's mad at me! But her indignation was short-lived. Abject humiliation overwhelmed all else. She refused to meet his dark accusing eyes as he sat beside her, glaring down. Ellie rolled on her side, pulling the sheet over herself, turning her back to him so he could not witness the scalding tears building up to overflow.

Miguel quickly got up and pulled on his pants. "I'll send Luz and Rita to you," he choked out, then retreated from the room in silence.

Alone. She felt so desolately alone. *Damn him!* Ellie struggled to remember every swearword she had ever heard the cowhands use. She forced her tears to subside, concentrating on her righteous anger.

Miguel fled downstairs and roused Luz, telling the sleepy and astonished girl to attend her mistress and to get Rita to assist her. His agitated manner and half-clothed body were mystery enough, but being summoned back to Doña Ellie's room in the middle of the wedding night was an even greater puzzlement.

When Luz awakened Rita, the cook was at once alert and inquisitive. "What do you mean, he was angry?" she questioned the young maid as they quickly climbed the back stairs.

Luz was hesitant. "Well, he was scowling and scarcely spoke, and . . . his face and arms were scratched. He was dressed only in pants, no shirt or shoes."

She reddened as Rita's shrewd gaze turned on her while they climbed the steps. "Where is he now?" the older woman asked.

"In Don Alex's study, I think," came the whispered reply.

Rita snorted, "Probably at the brandy bottle. Men! Bah! One slip of a girl undoes him." She laughed.

Laughter quickly turned to shock when the two women entered the bedroom and found it in a shambles. A candelabra—fortunately unlit—had been overturned and Ellie's beautiful bridal peignoir lay in shreds, tossed across a chair. Bedcovers were everywhere, pillows strewn around the room and quilts on the floor.

Ellie sat in the center of the bed, facing them with a sheet clutched tightly around her. Despite her tangled hair and pale, tear-stained face, she looked defiantly angry, as if daring the Kane servants to say anything in defense of their *patrón*.

"I want to bathe," she said with surprising calm. "Please heat some water."

Rita nodded to Luz, who quickly headed downstairs to comply. "I will bring fresh linens for the bed, Doña Ellie," Rita said, then added, "but first a fresh gown and robe for you." She turned to the armoire and selected a plain nightrail and robe.

Ellie flushed scarlet in embarrassment as she slipped from the bed and quickly slid the concealing folds of the robe over her nakedness. Rita threw back the tangled sheets and saw the smears of blood on them. She expected that, but her nod of calm acceptance ignited the girl's checked fury.

"I trust my virgin's blood meets with everyone's approval," she said scathingly, turning to stare out the window into the darkness.

Rita continued stripping the linens calmly, saying nothing. After she had remade the bed, she turned to the proud girl by the window.

"I am going to help Luz with the bath, señora. We will not be long."

"She is bruised on her wrists and hips. He must have held her down," Rita said in bafflement.

"But why would any woman fight Don Miguel?" Luz asked as they entered the kitchen, then blushed furiously and quickly turned to pour hot water from the cauldron into the carrying buckets.

Rita scoffed. "I may be old, but I'm not stupid. I've heard of Don Miguel's prowess as a lover. But the little silver Yankee did not give him a chance to show her, that is clear. He was always a gentle boy, tending wounded animals, kind to servants. . ." She shrugged in perplexity, thinking there was far more to this marriage than Don Adrian and Don Alesandro knew when they arranged it.

Miguel paced in the study like a caged animal. *Is she seriously injured?* he wanted to go ask, but dared not. He felt the guilt pressing down on him like suffocation. *What have I done?* That he had caused such hurt to one so small, so defenseless a woman, his own wife—shamed him beyond thought. *But she goaded me with her lies. So pure-looking, so beautiful. Her temper's as rotten as mine.* He continued pacing as his conscience lashed him. No woman deserved what he had done, even if she had lied.

But why would any woman tell the man she was to marry that she'd had a lover? He thought back over their conversation that fateful day in the garden. His own clumsy words about wanting to be a priest came back to him. He had unwittingly scorned her. Her pride had been just as fiercely stung as his own. Once again he damned Alex for the marriage neither of them had wanted. She was reckless and spoiled, he vile-tempered and jealous. They should not have been forced into the mess they were trapped in now. Still, the maddening desire he had felt for her nagged at him. He repressed it with a fresh surge of guilt.

Unable to bear the confines of the house any longer, and knowing that if he kept pacing the room drinking brandy he would soon be drunk, he put down his glass and went upstairs to finish dressing.

Dominican had been rubbed down and fed after his long, hard ride from Los Angeles. Miguel did not want to tire the big horse any further, so he chose a fresh one. Mounting, he set out into the night at a hard gallop.

Rosalie was closing the place down. It was past four A.M. and the last drunken customer, a rich old ranchero from up north, was saying good-bye to her. Just as she gently shoved him out and moved to slip the bolt, she heard Mike's voice.

"I need to talk to you, Rose."

"What in tarnation are you doing here? It's your wedding night, for God's sake!" Quickly, she reopened the door and a disheveled Mike walked in, clad only in a loose white cotton shirt and riding pants, hatless and without a jacket, although the late night air was decidedly cool.

"Jesus! You look awful. Drink?" He followed her into the parlor where she poured them each a snifter of her best brandy, then looked at his haggard unshaven face.

He paced back and forth, guilt-stricken and caged, taking the drink and downing it in a couple of fierce gulps as he distractedly ran a hand through his dark hair. Rosalie sat down at the table in one corner and patted the lace tablecloth, indicating that he should join her. He sat woodenly. She had never seen a man in such anguish.

She waited until he gathered his thoughts to talk about it. In a ragged voice he described the disastrous wedding night, not sparing himself at all. Then he looked up at Rosalie and finished brokenly, "There's nothing you can call me that I haven't already called myself."

Seeing the abject pain and shame written across his face, Rosalie knew he spoke the truth. Quietly she began, "So, your wife wasn't what she said she was. I wondered how the hell you knew that about her when I'd never heard a whisper in town. Fool thing for a girl to do, makin' up a story, pride be damned. But then everyone does a dumb thing now and then. Question is, what are you going to do now?'' Her hazel green eyes were level and calm, not castigating, just accepting.

''Hell, Rose, I don't know.'' He made a helpless gesture with his hands, spreading them on the table. ''How long will it take her to heal?''

Rosalie's lips quirked as she replied, ''I expect as long as it'll take you.''

He ignored her attempt at levity, feeling his superficial injuries were only more evidence of his bestial behavior. ''Oh, damn, why should I ask? She'll never let me near her. I know I'll never force her again. Oh, Rose, I'm so ashamed.'' He put his head down on the table, cradling it on his arms.

''Every woman is different, as I might have said once or twice. Some bleed a lot their first time, some don't bleed at all. In a week or so she'll heal, physically. It's her spirit I'd be worrying about, Mike.''

He looked up bleakly. ''What can I do?''

''You're married, honey, for the rest of your lives—and sure as shootin'—the marriage has been consummated. You have to talk to her, be patient, go slow, try and figure her out. You made a good start just now, realizing your priest talk set her off to make up that story about Brighton.'' She grimaced at the name and continued, ''He's been a customer from time to time and he's a real slippery bastard. The girl is well rid of him. Point is, she's been given a free rein all her life by her daddy and she's got pride and temper to match yours. Looks like she put up one hell of a fight.'' Rosalie inspected the bites and scratches on his person with a grin. ''Maybe she's got more feelings for you than her pride would let her show. Now that ain't all bad, if you can learn what makes her tick. She's bright and beautiful. You both could've picked worse, Mike. You can make it up to her, if you want to. Lordy, you could charm a jackass out of a cornfield.''

He shrugged in helpless resignation. ''I don't know,

Rose. We may be married in name, but despite my father's single-minded desire for grandchildren, he'll never get his wish."

Rosalie's reply was to snort a good-natured Anglo-Saxon obscenity.

CHAPTER
11

April 1853, San Francisco

It was a balmy spring day. The fog lifted in mid-morning, leaving a stunning blaze of bright azure sky dotted with fleecy puffs of clouds. Kate sighed and let the front door curtain fall. It was real Irish lace, imported from Dublin. "Lace curtain Irish." She smiled at the irony of it. For a saloon girl, a Belfast teamster's daughter, she had come a long way. David had not lied about buying her a mansion.

They lived in a huge three-story brick edifice, Georgian colonial in style, elegant to a fault, with sculptured gardens, a circular driveway, real French crystal chandeliers and Brussels carpets. Every room was filled with the best rosewood and mahogany furniture. "Luck of the Irish" was still producing at an incredible rate and David had invested in several other successful mines as well as banks and shipping businesses. He was now one of the richest men in the gold rush city, and his house reflected his achievement.

Just as she turned from the front door, David came

bounding up the steps with a legal document in his hand and a bright gleam in his eye. He handed Kate the stock certificate with a flourish and a kiss of greeting. Thank God she could now read papers when he brought them home!

He had bought a sizable chunk of Kane Connecticut, his father's shipping line. It was up for sale on the open market at premium rates, but despite paying more than he normally would for an investment, he snapped it up. Just wait until Alex's broker told him who had bought the largest single offering of the stock put up for their expansion!

"I'll let the old dog know I'm still alive and kicking, damn if I won't!" He laughed exultantly as she scanned the papers quickly.

"It means a great deal to you, doesn't it, David? Having his respect, making it on your own?"

He sobered and considered, then answered slowly, "Yes, more than I ever realized. At first I thought just this," he gestured around the magnificent room they were standing in, "all the trappings, the way of life, would be enough. But when I saw that name on the exchange lists, I knew I had to buy it, to let him know."

"Won't you ever go home?" Even as she asked the question, Kate dreaded the answer. Go home with his Irish mistress? No, he'd never let the fine Kanes meet Kate Muldoon to scorn her, or embarrass him.

"No, Irish, I won't go home. What would be the point? My dear mother certainly won't miss me. My brother is busy running the ranch, maybe even raising a family by now. I'm not sure he'd welcome me back after the way I ran out on him. Alex would probably take a horsewhip to me. Just so he *knows* I did it."

Kate breathed a sigh of relief, but at the same time felt a pang of sorrow. He should not be cut off from his family while they were all alive and well. She still remembered the pain when her parents and Aunt Tess had died. She had no one, but he had a mother, father and brother. Yet she knew if he ever went back to them, it would be without her.

"I think you should at least write your parents and let them know you're doing so well," she said. "Surely, your mother worries—"

Kate could say no more before David gave a snort of disgust and snapped, "My dearest *mamacita*. She detests me, Kate. She always did."

Kate gasped in shock. Although her memories of her mother were hazy, they were loving and warm. "You must be wrong, David! Why ever would you think such a thing?"

He laughed harshly. "If you'd ever seen Alex you'd know. I'm his spitting image, Kate. I grew up with the stamp of the old man all over me. Miguel, on the other hand, was an Alvarez. Mama took him and Papa took me."

At Kate's bewildered look, he added, "It goes back before either of us was born, I guess. Alex Kane and Maria Teresa Alvarez did not exactly make a love match, if there is such a thing in any marriage. They made a business arrangement in the best Californio or New England tradition. Her old, prestigious name and vast land grant for his money. You see, my father made a fortune in whaling and the hide and tallow business. By the time he was twenty-five, he had taken a modest New England shipping line and built it into an empire. But that wasn't enough for Alex Kane. He wanted to be landed gentry, to put down roots in California. In those days, when Mexico ruled California, that meant becoming Catholic and marrying a woman whose family owned land. Grandfather Alvarez was land poor and had only one child who survived to adulthood—my mother. Father wanted land and had money to build up the depleted stock and restore Cien Robles to its former grandeur. Grandfather and Father made a deal. No one asked Mother how she felt about it. And truthfully, Alex hasn't given a damn how she felt about anything since. They hate one another."

He poured a drink and took a sip of it, thinking painfully back to so long ago. "I was a born hell-raiser, took to betting on cockfights and racing the fastest horses on the ranch. Alex took me to my first bordello when I was fourteen, just to spite Mama. He tried to make me into an exact replica of himself. In some ways I am—all the bad, wild ways. But he failed to make me a proper ranchero, one who would sacrifice everything for the land, work and marry for Cien Robles. I don't want the land and all its ties, and I don't want to sire heirs to perpetuate all the old hatreds. God! How those two hate each other! Marriage is one long, miserable war, only unlike other wars, it lasts your whole lifetime and blights the very children you married to produce."

A few weeks later Kate stood in the front foyer adjusting her new hat in the mirror as she mulled over David's strange relationship with his family. She realized now that the desperately unhappy situation between his father and mother was in large part responsible for his fervent desire never to marry.

Just then a sharp rap on the lead-paned glass of the front door jolted her from her reverie. Taking two steps from the mirror to the door, she opened it. The butler, Ashley, hurried from the back, only to find the lady of the house already greeting her friend.

"Why Kate, you must have been waiting for me. Am I late?" Leah Wilcox looked only mildly abashed. Her plump, pretty face with its pale China blue eyes was surrounded by bouncing chestnut curls. She had become very dear to Kate since the two women had met last fall.

"You look deep in thought. Did David tease you about your hat again? Franklin always pretends he can't tell mine apart."

"No, no, Leah, David isn't home. He's at his office. I, I guess I was just thinking about him."

"Then why so glum-looking? Every unattached woman in San Francisco would kill to be in your shoes." Leah chuckled. "And a lot of ones who *are* attached, too, since their men aren't as handsome or rich as your Mr. Kane."

Watching Kate's unconscious flinch, her friend went on, "Oh, so I struck a nerve again. The great Kane name. Honestly, Kate, you're too sensitive by half. This is a city

of newly rich people and precious few of them are pedigreed like the illustrious Kanes. And you know what? No
one cares! Not even David. He isn't trading on the Kane
name. Why should you be so concerned about it? In San
Francisco, being a Muldoon is just as good as being a
Kane.'' To emphasize her point, Leah drove the sharp tip
of her stylish parasol into the thick Turkish carpet on the
foyer floor and placed both plump, gloved hands over the
handle.

Kate smiled weakly in spite of herself. ''Being a Muldoon
may be perfectly all right, but being a woman living with a
man to whom she's not married is quite another matter.
And besides, I think you're wrong about David's not
caring about his family name.'' Kate told her friend about
the stock purchase he made recently and the desire he had
to let his father know of his success.

''He'll never break the ties with his family, no matter
how hard he tries. And he shouldn't, even though they hurt
him terribly.''

Leah's eyes clouded with puzzlement. As the two wom-
en slowly walked outside and down the stairs to enter the
waiting carriage, she said, ''What do you mean, 'even if
they hurt him'? You've alluded to that several times.''
Then, seeing Kate's expression, Leah stopped short. ''Forgive my rude curiosity, dear. Franklin says I'm too impulsive and forthright for my own good and he's right. I'm
sorry to pry.''

''No, Leah, maybe I should talk to someone about it
and you're my very dearest friend. I was just thinking
about why David is so set against ever marrying.'' As she
spoke, Kate's eyes blinked back tears and her voice was
haunted. She recounted the conversation she had had with
David when he purchased the Kane Connecticut stock.

Reconstructing that conversation was very difficult for
Kate. She looked grimly across the carriage at Leah. ''So,
you see, nothing would be worse for David than marriage,
even to a real lady, much less to the likes of me.''

The jouncing carriage stopped in front of the most

fashionable modiste in San Francisco where Kate and Leah planned to shop.

"So, that's why he never married, the rascal! I never understood how he could leave a wonderful girl like you free, Kate." Leah burst out with this before she saw Kate's look of intense embarrassment. She was instantly contrite. "Oh, I'm such an impulsive fool! I didn't mean anything against you, Kate. You know I was another man's mistress before I married Franklin. I'm certainly not condemning you for David's mistakes. It's just that it's so distressingly obvious you adore him and he's so—so cavalier about you, showing you off like a shiny toy without considering your feelings."

Kate leaped to defend her lover. "Oh, Leah, that's not fair! David has done so much for me. He risked his life to rescue me from my uncle's place. He even taught me to read and write, how to dress, he's showered me with beautiful things."

"Yes, he's given you everything but what you want most of all, a proposal of marriage and a declaration of love," Leah responded dryly.

"I just explained to you why he's so set against marriage. His parents hurt him terribly with their perpetual fighting. He thinks that's what all marriages are like."

"That's hardly flattering after all the times he's seen Franklin and me together. I thought we were tolerably happy all these years." Leah's blue eyes were impish, trying to cajole her friend into a better humor.

Kate smiled and sighed. "I'm afraid it's all too complicated. Franklin came out west and made his own fortune. He has no long illustrious list of forebears to haunt him. He could marry the woman he chose and have to answer to no one. David is stuck with being a Kane, even if he denies his birthright. He is a Californio, an aristocrat. I'm an Irish saloon girl. Kanes don't marry Muldoons—if he ever considers marrying at all."

"Bunk! There's no reason on earth David Kane can't marry you. You are beautiful, bright and good, as fine-

mannered as any lady in this city. He just wants to have his
freedom and still keep you to himself at the same time.''

Kate shrugged sadly. ''I don't know, Leah. Perhaps, in
time, as he sees how truly happy you and your husband
are, he may reconsider.'' Even as she mouthed the words,
Kate did not believe them.

''What you really need to do, my dear, is to give David
a good shaking up. Kind of hurry him along, and Denton
Randolph is just the fellow to do it!''

Denton Randolph was a mutual friend, another wealthy
banker with business interests in San Francisco. He was
also attractive and most interested in Kate. At various
social gatherings he'd paid her a good deal of attention,
always circumspect and polite, but decidedly embarrassing
to Kate. So Leah had noticed, too. David did not seem to
be jealous, but he had no reason to be, for Kate was cool
and formal with Randolph.

''I couldn't lead a man on just to try and make David
jealous, Leah. It would be dishonest.''

Leah snorted as they took their seats in the front parlor
of the modiste's. They had walked from the carriage into
the shop, lost in conversation, oblivious to all the lovely
gowns, swatches of gorgeous fabric and elegant accesso-
ries that filled the beautiful room. The ritual of looking at
pattern drawings, material samples, matching slippers,
reticules and wraps went on as usual. Kate put Leah's
crazy scheme from her mind.

But that evening as she sat across from David in an
elegant French restaurant, Kate's thoughts kept returning
to what Leah had said. She hardly paid any attention to the
beautifully prepared meal on her plate, nor to David's
conversation about investing in a new gold claim near
''Luck of the Irish.''

In mid-sentence, David finally realized his usually alert
and sharply inquisitive Kate was completely absorbed
elsewhere. ''Irish, you still in the room or has your spirit
departed?'' His grin was infectious.

Returning it, she flushed over her calculating thoughts.
''I'm sorry, David. I was just thinking about Mrs. Talbot,''

Kate improvised, resurrecting an incident of several days past when a socially prominent matron snubbed her at the opera that they had attended with the Wilcoxes.

"Now, Katie, I thought you had more sense and Irish pride than to let that old crone get to you. Frank and Leah didn't give her the time of day."

"I know. It's just that I worry about them being seen with me. Oh, David, good people in San Francisco society don't mix with . . . the likes of me," she concluded lamely.

"You mean with a man who takes his mistress openly to all the social events in town, don't you?" David's eyes darkened from blue to black in controlled anger. His own uneasy feelings about Kate's tenuous position as his flaunted mistress bothered him quite a bit. The ugly incident with that hypocritical old harridan last week brought it into sharp focus. At the time Kate had reacted with her usual feisty pride and he had forced it from his mind. Now, here it was brought to surface again.

Kate placed one slim hand on his coat-sleeve placatingly. "No, that is *not* what I meant. I only worry for Leah. She's a lady and the wife of a banker. It could hurt her if she's seen too much with me in such obvious places. David, I never had a woman friend before in my whole life. Oh, I had Aunt Tess, but never another woman to talk to like Leah. I don't want her to be hurt."

He relented at her earnest entreaty, realizing again what a bleak, isolated existence she had, growing up with Will Bolton. "Leah *is* your friend, Kate. She went out of her way to befriend you because she genuinely likes you for who you are. If she's not worried about the Lucille Talbots of this city, you shouldn't be either."

Just as Kate was about to reply, she looked up and caught sight of Dent Randolph over David's shoulder. She blushed darkly as he came up with a dapper smile and bow, clasping David on the back and then kissing her hand gallantly in greeting.

"Miss Muldoon, you grow lovelier each time we meet. I was just about to dine with some businessmen over at the corner table when I caught sight of that fiery hair and had to pay my respects." He lingered overly long with her fingers and fixed her with his penetrating gaze.

At age forty, Dent was a millionaire several times over, first in the gold mines, then in real estate and banking. He was of medium height, muscular and well-proportioned with clear gray eyes, a dense thatch of iron-gray hair, thin elegant brows and a well-trimmed mustache. In his expensively tailored pearl gray suit, replete with gold watch and diamond stickpin, he certainly looked the part of a dashing entrepreneur. Most women considered him quite handsome, but his charm and Continental gallantry had always put Kate on edge. She sensed a ruthless cunning in Randolph and she did not want to be the object of his interest.

"Glad you stopped by, Dent, but don't let us keep you from your banker friends there. I smell a big deal in the offing." Did David's voice hold just the faintest hint of a warning, or was it her imagination?

As Randolph released Kate's hand and nodded to him, Kate watched David's eyes. They were as opaque and expressionless as if he were sitting in a high stakes poker game. So he was aware of Randolph's special attention to her!

Before Dent departed, he paused and said, "You still holding that game next week, David?" At the curt, affirmative nod, he left with a suggestive, "See you both Tuesday," but his eyes never moved from Kate's face until he turned and walked across the room.

"You hardly had to encourage him with girlish blushes and flutters, Irish. It isn't your style at all." The clipped, icy words were as unexpected as a splash of cold water in her face.

Kate sputtered furiously, her own guilty conscience and his unfairness combining to render her speechless for a moment. Then, throwing down her dinner napkin on the tablecloth, she rose abruptly. "I suddenly feel a loss of appetite. If you'll excuse me . . ."

He was up and by her chair in an instant, crisply

motioning to a waiter for a check. "Yes. Let's go home, Kate."

The rest of the week was a misery for them both, especially after Dent Randolph ran into Kate at lunch the following day. She was with Leah and another acquaintance, Martha Colter, a shy, giggling young woman who was married to Franklin's junior partner. The same lingering hand-kissing sequence was reenacted. After Dent left, Leah looked at her friend archly, wordlessly reminding her about their earlier conversation.

If Leah was silent, Martha was quite the opposite. "Isn't he just the most dashing man! Oh, if only he'd kiss my hand the same way he does yours, Kathleen. If I were single, I'd set my cap for him. Rumor has it he's looking for a wife. After all, he's of an age where he needs heirs to all that wealth and it's time he settled down. You know, when he first came out here . . ." Martha prattled on about Randolph's life history.

Later that afternoon they met David when they left Kate off at her house. Before either Kate or Leah could silence the loquacious Martha, she burst into an ecstatic description of their encounter with Dent. David merely nodded tersely, tipped his hat to the two women and ushered Kate brusquely upstairs into their house.

David was confused and angry. He was furious at his own unexpected jealousy over Randolph. Rationally, he knew Kate had not encouraged the banker yet he was incensed that the man was so persistent. Also, he was naggingly aware that Randolph was rich, attractive and in the market for a wife. Damn, he felt threatened and caged in. He had never cared for a woman before. They came easily and he let them go just as easily. But he wanted to be the one to do the letting go, and he was far from ready to release his Irish. However, he would not marry her just to hold on to her. If she had to have a man signed, sealed and delivered, she could go and Dent was welcome to her!

For two nights he went out on the town and partook of the fleshpots of the gold city. Pretty, practiced whores only served to convince him how much he preferred Kate's passion to their sophisticated reactions. The casual sexual encounters so frequent in his youth no longer satisfied him, yet he refused to acknowledge the reason.

When he returned home the third night, it was quite late. He hadn't even gone to a brothel. He simply went to a cheap bar near Sydneytown, got roaring drunk, picked a fight with several tars and was easily obliged. In the ensuing melee, he received a split lip and some badly bruised ribs, but at least he worked off some of the tension that had been festering inside him.

David knew Kate was aware of what he had been doing and that added to his guilt, which in turn further fueled his anger. He would be beholden to no woman. By the time the Tuesday card game arrived, both of them were like caged tigers, restless and ready to swipe at anyone or anything.

The poker game was a monthly event which David had made into a tradition of sorts since coming to San Francisco nearly a year ago. He no longer gambled for a living, but still enjoyed the relaxation of the game. The men with whom he played were all well-connected in business and finance in the Bay Area. The game was as much an opportunity to hear the latest information on stocks and other investments as it was a form of recreation.

Kate always acted as David's hostess. In a room full of men, she was readily accepted as his mistress and treated respectfully by all. In other social settings with their wives and daughters present, those same rich men were often forced to avoid greeting David and Kate because of her status as a kept woman. The hypocrisy of the city infuriated David, but his resolve was firm to remain free of the shackles that held Alex.

David dressed for the card game as he mulled over the past miserable week. Dent was a regular. There was no way to exclude him without causing a serious rift in the group. David hardly wanted to appear jealous or insecure. Kate would just have to choose. If she preferred Denton Randolph to him, so be it. He took particular care with his appearance that night, wearing a rich, dark brown suit of lightweight wool, tailored to fit his tall, slim frame like a glove. A cream silk shirt winked with diamond shirt studs and his thick, dark gold hair was freshly barbered and brushed back, emphasizing his cleanly chiseled features and gleaming white smile in a darkly tanned face.

Just as he put down his hairbrush and turned to leave the dressing room, Kate came in unexpectedly, still in her wrapper, obviously flushed from a hot, scented bath. The delicate aroma of fresh lemon wafted over to him as he watched her move toward her closet, unaware of his presence in the alcove off their bedroom. She had just washed and towel-dried her dark hair. It glowed like cherry fire in the flickering gaslights of the room. He felt a sudden tightening in his loins and a mad rush of desire to tangle his hands in the still damp, curling mane that fell to her waist, to kiss her and press her to him, to feel her coltishly slim body that fit so perfectly against his own. He shook himself free of the fantasy and once more became the gambler, in cool control. Reaching over to the dressing stand behind him, he picked up a cigar from the case and struck a match to light it.

Kate whirled at the hiss of the match. "Ooh, David, I thought you were already downstairs." In truth she delayed coming into the bedroom until she was sure he was through dressing. It was getting harder to watch that bronzed frame gleaming naked in the light, to see his muscles rippling as he donned his pants and shirt. Watching him shave had become slow torture for her. More than once in the past week she had fought down the impulse to throw herself at him and beg him to make love to her. But her bitterly stung pride held her aloof. *Let him go to prostitutes if that's what he wants—a different one each night!*

Seeing her nervous stiffening as he approached brought out the predator in David. *She's not as indifferent as she tries to pretend.* He flashed a blinding white grin, cigar still clenched in his teeth, then removed it to say, "I was just going down to see if Chin has everything set up, cards, liquor, whatever..."

As he spoke he trailed one hand, feather light, up her arm. It was like a burning brand through the thin silk of the wrapper. His gaze seemed to scorch her also, dwelling on the deep cleft between her breasts where the robe gaped open. Just coming from her bath, she wore nothing beneath it. He could tell. His eyes raised to her face where a telltale pink was staining her cheeks and neck. As he bent over to give her a light brushing kiss on the lips, she caught the scent of leather, tobacco and male musk. She stood still, hands clenched at her sides. He smiled, letting his hand drop from her chin, and then sauntered to the bedroom door.

"Don't be long dressing, Irish. The men will be here soon."

CHAPTER
12

April 1853, San Francisco

Dent Randolph stood in the foyer of the Kane mansion, transfixed at the vision of Kate Muldoon coming down the stairs. She was dressed in deep moss green silk that exactly matched the color of her eyes. The gown clung sensuously to every sleek curve of her willowy frame, seeming to float with her light tread as she moved to greet him. That fantastic darkest mahogany hair was piled in artfully placed curls high on top of her head, adding inches to her already considerable height. However, the effect was one of great delicacy. The lush swell of her breasts was starkly revealed as his eye traveled from the high coiffure down the slim neck to the beauty below. The gown was not only cut scandalously at the bust, but was also quite clinging below the waist. Its thin silky folds hugged her hips gently without a hint of petticoats. Each step she took revealed her long legs with shocking clarity.

Kate had been unsure of this dress when Madame Fourier urged her to try it on. Madame insisted it was the very latest thing from Paris and perfectly suited to her tall, slim build. But Kate had hesitated. Even in the dressing room of the shop with no one but the modiste present, she had felt wantonly naked. She bought it, thinking that she would wear it only when she and David dined alone at home. Tonight she felt a perverse desire to get even with David for his infidelities and to placate her own fierce hunger for attention. After he so cavalierly walked from their bedroom, she had pulled the dress out of the closet. Now seeing Dent Randolph's eyes light up, she experienced mixed emotions, delight at the blaze of passion written across his face, yet fear about what might come of an evening fraught with sexual tension. What would David's reaction be?

She did not have long to wait before she found out. Randolph clasped her hand just as David walked through the big arched doorway from the parlor. He took in Kate's dress in one sweeping appraisal, his eyes steady and cool, revealing nothing. Nevertheless, he sauntered to her side, slipping an arm possessively around her small waist in what appeared to be a careless gesture. Only she could feel the pressure of his corded biceps as he squeezed her with considerable force. Dent released her hand.

"Ready to lose some money, David? I feel lucky tonight." He smiled at Kane, but quickly returned his gaze to Kate. Then he nodded and ambled into the parlor where several other men were drinking and talking business.

David's dark blue eyes bored into her green ones for one quick instant before he gallantly offered her his arm and they entered the parlor. There was a new man present tonight, one Kate had never seen before. He was tall and gawky-looking with expensive yet poorly tailored clothing that hung on his spare frame. His sandy hair was thinning and cut too short to be stylish. The gold watch and diamond ring he sported, although genuine, looked garish and out of place on his person.

Randolph brought the stranger over and made introductions. "Miss Muldoon, may I present Walt Seavers from down south a ways. He's in the cattle business—in San Francisco for a short business trip. David, you and Walt met last week at the bank, I believe?"

David nodded in acknowledgment, shaking Seavers's hand, all the while noting the strange way the man darted glances at Kate. She had simply smiled and politely nodded at the fellow, giving him no particular encouragement. Seavers was not looking at her with the lustful abandon that Randolph had earlier, but with great curiosity. As a natural gambler, David was usually adept at sizing up people but Seavers's behavior puzzled him.

The game began as usual with moderate betting and lots of casual banter. Kate absented herself from the table, only entering the room when the men took an occasional break to load up plates at the elaborate buffet table next to the bar. Two houseboys served drinks while the game was in progress. When the players stopped to eat, Kate mingled with them, exchanging bits of gossip, listening to the details of their business deals and mildly flirting with several of the older, well-meaning men. She had always been standoffish around Dent, unsure of how to react to his more earnest attentions.

Dent and Walt Seavers were in one corner, plates in hand, while Kate helped old Jeb Turner to an ample selection of rare beef slices and smoked oysters, his particular favorites. As she and the elderly dry goods merchant chatted pleasantly, Kate was aware of a prickling along the base of her neck, as if she were being stared at. She glanced up and saw David instructing Chin Lee to bring ice for the bar. He was paying no attention to her. Then her gaze traveled past Randolph's broad back. Over his shoulder the piercing pale eyes of Seavers skewered

her like a butterfly to a velvet pad. She shivered and
looked away with a premonition that something very ugly
was going to happen that night.

For several hours it seemed Kate was wrong. Then she
heard loud voices coming from the card table at the far end
of the game room. Something started her heart hammering
in her chest, even before she could make out the words.

Seavers's harsh East Texas accent was strident and
carried clearly. "Yew won 'er in a card game. Don't see
why yew cain't bet 'er yerself, 'less o' course, yew don't
have th' cards, or mebbe the nerve."

Several shocked gasps—among them Kate's own—were
heard across the room. Against her will she was slowly
drawn the carpeted length of the room, her dragging footsteps bringing her closer to the table as the scene was played
out before her horrified eyes.

David's voice was icy and uninflected, in his best poker
form. "A man never bets his woman, Seavers, not if he's
any kind of a man. As to my nerve," he paused dangerously, "why not call my bet and see if I have the cards?
I'm betting ten thousand I do."

Seavers scoffed, ignoring the apparent danger that all the
other men in the room knew was charging the air. "I got
me plenty cash money already, Kane. Win or lose, I don't
give a shit. I heerd talk 'bout yore redhead down Los
Angeles way. Seems a friend o' mine an' his foreman sat
in th' game whar yew won 'er. Yew even shot thet feller
who lost." He paused, sizing up David Kane, deciding
that his own tough Texas background made him more than
a match for the pretty dude. "I got me ten—no," he
reconsidered and shoved out another stack of chips, "twenty
thousand here says I kin beat yew if'n yore bet's thet
redhead in return." He sat on the edge of his seat now,
diamond ring winking garishly as his clawlike hands lay
half curled on the table's edge.

The men around the table were all quite wealthy and
high stakes games were not uncommon, but the wager of a
woman—even a gambler's mistress—was unheard of. Only
Chinese prostitutes and African slaves could be treated so.

"See here, Seavers, you can't come in here and—" Jeb Turner tried remonstrating to no avail.

David cut in, "I'll handle this, Jeb." He made a placating gesture across the table to silence the indignant outbursts of all the men. Only Denton Randolph sat stone silent in his chair, waiting. David caught sight of Kate's chalk-white face from the corner of his eye, but centered his attention on Seavers, praying she would leave quickly and silently before she was hurt further.

"I'll see your twenty thousand and raise you another twenty, Seavers. Kate is not on the block. Maybe you're the one who's so unsure of his cards or his nerve that he has to bluff. You know I won't gamble her."

Seavers swore several obscene expletives relating to David's familial sexual practices, and then shoved out a marker for one hundred thousand. "Yew know I'm good fer hit, Kane. Hit jest proves what she's worth, I reckon." As if sensing Kate's presence, he turned and looked her up and down, then said in a softer voice, "Yep, I reckon she is worth it. Mebbe after I collect yore cash I'll jest offer fer the little lady direct, Kane."

David silently slid his own marker for eighty thousand onto the table. "Call."

Petulant, yet grinning in anticipation of victory, Seavers spread out a full house, kings over queens. Several men gasped. It was a hard hand to beat.

Still expressionless, David put down his hand. Four aces!

"Damn! What are the odds on seeing two hands like this in a game, eh, boys!" Brad Streeter burst out, vainly attempting to ease the tension. The other men surged up to congratulate David. He calmly raked in Seavers's marker and all the chips, but his eyes never left the loser.

Seavers sat still, his hands clenching and unclenching in clawlike impotence. To lose with such a hand! And, worse yet, to fail in his attempt to win the woman! Ever since he had found out they were here, he wanted to see the man who won old Bolton's niece in a card game. More than that, he wanted to see the girl herself. When he mentioned the story to Dent Randolph, a business acquaintance in San Francisco, the banker was at first dumbstruck, then fascinated. He arranged for Seavers to meet Kane and wangled an invitation to the monthly card game for him.

Randolph fully intended for Seavers to make the revelation about Kate's past at the game. All Denton Randolph's hopes were pinned on a desperate and humiliated Kate being catapulted into his arms. If he were really lucky, Seavers and Kane might even kill one another. Stranger things had happened in the violent gold rush city.

Now, as the two antagonists sat facing one another and the other men lamely milled about, Randolph moved with alacrity.

"Kate, please wait." He caught up with a fleeing dark green blur of rustling silk in the back hall. A side door opened to the patio and formal rose garden. Blindly, Kate twisted the knob and rushed out into the cool night air, her eyes streaming bitter, salty tears. He followed her out into the moonlight.

"Kate, I don't know what to say. I'm so abominably sorry I ever met the man or transacted business with him, much less brought him here. Where he ever got such a disgusting tale and had the nerve to spread it, I'll never know. Please—"

"It's true," Kate cut in. Her voice was flat. "It's all true. David won me in a game of showdown poker. My uncle was selling me to a killer, a rustler named Hank Clune. David offered him a chance to win a fortune if he'd wager me. Clune lost and died for his trouble. I'm saloon trash, a gambler's whore. Lucille Talbot and all her friends are quite right to snub me." Her voice finally broke and she began to sob as he took her gently in his arms.

"Oh, Kate, Kate, you are none of those things. You've been through hell and yet survived. You're a beautiful, warm woman. Any man would be proud to have you for a wife."

At that she flinched in his arms. "Kane's a fool!" He ground out the words. "He'll lose you, Kate. There are precious few women of your beauty and brains anywhere, much less in San Francisco. Oh, hell, I'm going about this badly, I know. What I mean to say is you don't ever again have to be subjected to a scene like that. If you marry me I'll honor you and love you, Kate.'' Slowly, he released her and forced her to look at him by raising her chin in one hand. ''Will you marry me, Kate? I'll take you away from this tawdry arrangement and give you the protection of my name and my fortune.''

She smiled wistfully as the tears continued to roll down her cheeks. ''It is a handsome offer, Dent. I thank you for it, especially considering you know the truth about me.''

''Then say yes, darling! Oh, Kate, I've waited a long time, made a great deal of money and at last I've found the woman I want to spend the rest of my life with. I realize I'm not as young a man as Kane, but I'll love you and give you everything you wish.'' He waited, still holding her trembling form.

It was so tempting. Security. Respectability. She could be like Leah. San Francisco society would admit her to its ranks if she were Mrs. Denton Randolph.

''Well, Irish, what *do* you say? I really don't own you, you know. I can't hold you against your will.'' David's voice was very soft, but it carried in the still night air. He stood in the doorway, also waiting.

Kate felt torn in two. Part of her so desperately longed to accept the upright proposal of Dent Randolph, yet she knew she could never love him.

How could she ever leave David? David, who had initiated her into the magic rites of passion, David who teased her, taught her to read, brought her flowers. David, who was her love. He stood there, awaiting her reply to Randolph, yet not offering to marry her himself. Always it would be on his terms, but she knew in her heart of hearts what her answer would be just the same.

With a small, shuddering sob she replied in a voice so low Randolph had to strain to hear it, ''I'm sorry, Dent, I just can't. You deserve a woman who will love you and that I cannot do.''

When Kate shook her head and withdrew from Randolph's

embrace, David felt a great band of steel loosen from his heart. He took a deep breath and began to walk toward Kate when a voice stopped him.

"Kane, yew half-breed bastard, no one's that shittin' lucky, not at cards 'er women!" Seavers hissed furiously. He had obviously added to his already considerable consumption of bourbon and was well on his way to being a mean drunk, and a dangerous one. He quickly pulled a .44 from where it was stuffed in his belt. Obviously, he hid it in the coat he left with the butler and had just retrieved it. Several men who had moved to silence him now froze in their tracks as he raised the gun on David.

Kane stood still, a perfectly silhouetted target in the moonlight. "You'll never make it down the street, Seavers. I have friends in San Francisco. Somehow I doubt you do."

Kane's calm demeanor seemed to infuriate the drunken man even further. With a snarled oath, he cocked the gun and sighted it in. What happened next occurred so fast it all seemed to blur together. Seavers fired as David lunged to his left into a flower bed. As he hit the soft blossoms he reached inside his jacket and came out with his Manton pistol in his right hand. His shot seemed to coincide with Seavers's, so swiftly did he move. Seavers missed his mark. Kane did not.

Kate broke free of Randolph's protective embrace and raced to David as he slowly rose, dusting himself off and looking at the sprawled form of Walt Seavers, crumpled on the flagstones.

Throwing her arms around him, she quickly ran her hands all over his body in a frantic search for injuries. "Are you hurt? Oh, David!" Kate flung her arms around his neck and hung on frantically as he returned her embrace. He softly caressed her head and back. Her elaborate coiffure now tumbled down in dark splendor, gleaming in the moonlight.

"I'm fine, Irish, just fine, now," he replied, brushing her tear-stained cheeks with his lips. As they walked arm in arm to the house, David called over his shoulder to Jeb Turner, "Send someone to get the marshal—and tell everyone to wait in the study. He'll want to question them as witnesses. I want to take Kate upstairs.''

After all the witnesses and lawmen left, David returned to find Kate changed into a filmy nightgown, curled up on a sofa in their bedroom with a book on her lap. With her hair brushed to a mahogany luster and a frown of concentration on her brow, Kate looked like a lovely waif.

Without a word, he went to her, taking the book from her trembling hands as she let out a startled little ''Oh,'' and looked up at him. Then he pulled her into his embrace and kissed her slowly, savoringly, running his hands up and down her back and buttocks through the thin fabric of the nightrail, pressing her to him intimately.

Kate was lost as she looked up into those compelling midnight eyes. She came eagerly into his embrace, running her fingers through the shock of his hair and down his shoulders which rippled with hard muscles. She opened her mouth to him and twined her tongue with his, tasting him joyously.

Still without speaking, he reached for the hem of her gown, lifting it to slip it over her head as she raised her hair to free it, helping him. She stood before him naked and drunk with desire. All shame left her as she arched her rosy-nippled breasts against his shirtfront, feeling them harden to points. She began to pull the diamond studs from his shirt, tossing them carelessly on a nearby table, then peeled the shirt from his body. She rubbed her face back and forth on his tawny-furred chest and licked and nipped at it as he held her, kissing her temples and stroking her hair.

Suddenly, he scooped her up and strode to the bed where he plopped her down, bending over to kiss her again, then suckle fiercely at her breasts. Kate moaned, pleading for him to join them together, reaching for his fly and unbuttoning it with trembling fingers. He stood to complete the job she had begun, tugging the pants off with one quick twist, then lying beside her on the big bed. With luxurious thoroughness, they kissed and caressed up and down one another's bodies. Kate again reached boldly for his shaft, eager for completion, but he held back, stilling her hand and slid slowly down her body so that his face rested on the dark curly mound between her legs. Gently, he opened her thighs and began to nuzzle and kiss her as she gasped with the hot, unexpected pleasure of it, her eyes first flying wide open in amazement, then closing in bliss. He teased, stroked and sucked with his tongue, teeth and lips, gently and steadily, until she arched up in a sharp cry of ecstasy. Her thrashing contractions told him of her release.

Slowly, he again moved up beside her on the bed, enfolding her once more in his arms as she shivered in the aftershock of the climax. He continued kissing her softly while Kate came out of her drugged satiation to realize that his hard penis still pressed her abdomen. Experimentally, she levered herself down as she stroked its velvety hard length with one hand. Kate had never done this before and looked up to David for direction. He gently guided her head with his hand, lightly, until she took the shaft into her mouth. Then he gasped in sharp pleasure and sank back onto the pillows, thrusting with his hips in an involuntary movement as she began to reciprocate his lovemaking. His ragged moans of passion convinced her she must be doing things right. It seemed so natural to love him this way. She continued, intensifying the sucking pressure of her lips until he exploded in a pulsing wave of orgasm, crying out her name over and over as his hands tangled in her hair.

When his breathing slowed, he reached down and gently pulled her up to lie beside him, stroking her back and kissing her. Kate let out a small half giggle, half sigh.

Quizzically, David's blue eyes regarded her. "Irish?"

Kate snuggled against him. Then, impudently, she looked up into the face that she would always adore and asked brazenly, "Can a man taste a woman as much as a woman can taste a man? I mean, there's so much more . . . with a man . . ."

When his laughter erupted, shaking the bed, her speech faltered into an embarrassed splutter and she blushed as dark as her hair.

When he could get his breath, David replied, "Oh, Kate, my Irish love, you never cease to amaze me, or please me!'' He kissed her savoringly on the lips, then went on. ''And in answer to your forthright question, yes, I could taste you and you were very, very good.''

''Mmm,'' she nuzzled his neck, ''so were you.''

Despite their reconciliation, Kate became more dejected in the following weeks as the notoriety of the shooting and the outrageous wager proposed by Seavers made her even more of a social outcast and object of amazement. A woman won on a hand of poker! Imagine that!

David, of course, was exonerated of any guilt in the killing of Seavers because all the witnesses vouched that the drunken cattleman had pulled a lethal weapon on Kane first. However, his newly enhanced reputation as a gambler and gunman bothered Kate. It seemed to her that everywhere they went people stared and whispered. David laughed and ignored them, telling her to do the same, but she found it impossible.

The only thing David failed to be blasé about was Dent Randolph. Ever since Dent's proposal, Kate had detected a decided coolness on David's part whenever the banker's name came up in conversation. Because he was a friend of the Wilcoxes, social situations became awkward. Kate and David frequently ran into him at restaurants and theaters as well as at Frank and Leah's home. Kate could not call David's reaction obvious jealousy, for he would never rail at her about talking with Randolph or in any way act the wounded swain. Yet she sensed a wariness on his part whenever he was faced with his rival.

When they were not confronted with Denton Randolph, David reverted to his usual teasing, charming self, casually accepting her decision to stay with him as his right and due. It rankled her, but she knew better than to fight it for he would never change.

Spring turned to summer and summer slowly warmed the foggy air of San Francisco. The scandal of Kate Muldoon became stale gossip, replaced by other events. Kate became used to the stares and snubs and shrugged them off just as David and Leah had always told her to do. Her life seemed to settle into a glamorous pattern she would have been amazed at a few years earlier when her work as a barmaid and cook was daily drudgery. Now she had maids and cooks of her own, a whole house full of servants to command. Her closet was full of beautiful gowns and her dresser was crowded with jewels. She was well-read, spoke with an educated accent and was in all ways a polished, sophisticated lady living in a cosmopolitan city. She ate in the finest restaurants, saw the best plays and had every divertissement imaginable at her fingertips. Her every dream had come true. All but one.

Her continued uncertainty about David sometimes drove her to the brink of despair. Then Leah would take her in hand and remind her that if she had no spoken or written vows, she had his fidelity and his laughter, his companionship and his concern. It should all amount to the same thing—love.

Kate never told David that she loved him. She was afraid to, for fear of what he might do or say. He was not a man to force or trap. Considering the marriage of his parents, it was hardly surprising that he was cynical. His scars were deep and usually well-hidden under a casual, charming air of indifference. But Kate knew the truth and his pain hurt her as much as it did him. So the summer passed as they enjoyed one another's companionship, loving, teasing, fighting and making up.

Then, without warning, Kate's world crumbled one hot day while she was out with Leah and Martha. They stopped for a mid-morning coffee and brioche at a small patisserie Leah favored. Kate suddenly became dizzy and began to slip into darkness, feeling the frantic grasp of her friends' hands as they assisted her to a chair in the outdoor cafe. They seated her in the shade of a tree where Leah fanned her and massaged her wrists while Martha brought a glass of cool water to revive her.

"I'm so embarrassed, I don't know what to say." Kate faltered as her vision cleared and the strange dizziness passed. "I've been skipping breakfast lately and I guess the heat was too much for me. My Aunt Tess was always stern about eating a good breakfast.''

"Why have you been skipping breakfast?'' Leah's eyes were concerned.

"Oh, just the heat. Queasy. No appetite. In the evenings I more than make up for it, believe me. Why several of my favorite dresses, including this one, are getting a bit tight . . .'' Kate's words trailed off as two pairs of sympathetic eyes fastened on her mutely.

"Kate,'' Leah began gently, "I—I know this is an indelicate thing to ask, but have you—that is, do you and David practice any kind of contraception?''

Martha's face was averted and for once she fell into a blessedly empathetic silence.

Kate was mute for a moment as she digested what her friend, several years older and more experienced, was asking. "No, that is, we never had to. I feared at first I might conceive, but after over two years, I just assumed I couldn't. Oh!'' Her thoughts raced backward, counting.

As if reading her mind, Leah asked, "When was your last time of the month?''

"Three months ago,'' Kate answered weakly, cursing herself for a fool. She had always been very irregular and assumed she was barren like her Aunt Tess.

Leah's eyes lit up with an unholy light. "Well, David's bachelor days are finally numbered!''

Martha let out a small nervous giggle and affectionately put her hand on Kate's arm in a reassuring pat. "You'll just love being a mother. I should know.'' She and her husband had four wild little boys that both parents doted on.

If her friends saw it as a solution to her unwed state, Kate certainly did not. What would David say? How could she tell him? After swearing her friends to silence, assuring them that she wanted to surprise David in her own good time, Kate took a hired carriage home to think alone.

At midday, David was at his office and the house was quiet. She had the cook brew her some weak tea and sat in her upstairs parlor worrying. Soon she would grow fat and unattractive, hardly a suitable way for a mistress to look!

What if he grew sick of the sight of her? Worse yet, what if he married her out of a sense of duty or pity? Kate shuddered, recalling David's words to her: *Marriage lasts your whole lifetime and blights the very children you married to produce!*

No, he never wanted ties to a wife or children. What they had shared was beautiful and good, but now it was over as she had always known it would one day be. But now she would not leave alone and bereft; she would take with her a part of her love to hold permanently.

Kate began to plan. All the glitter and frenzy of city life had been fun for a while, but deep in her soul lurked the Irish farm girl. She had been so happy for those brief months at the lovely little cabin outside Boomer Gulch where "Luck of the Irish" still yielded its golden bounty. She would return there, to a safe haven. After all, she owned half interest in the mine. The cabin was rightfully hers and the manager, Kurt Watchner, who had been left in charge, could assist her.

But what could she say to David to explain her sudden departure? To keep him from following? She had no heart to confront him with the truth and see dull resignation or anguished pity in those dark blue eyes. Carefully she worded a simple note:

David:

When you read this I'll be gone for good. Don't try to follow me. I will be well-provided for by your generous gift of half of "Luck." I can no longer go on living the way we do. You want freedom above all and I want permanence. I'm going to find a man who will marry me and put down roots with me. I know that is too ordinary and binding for you to consider. We were ever after different things and it is time our paths parted.

Good-bye,

Kate

There was no more to say, she sadly concluded, feeling vaguely dishonest when she wrote the part about finding a man to marry her. Of course she would have no other man. Not after lying with David, her beautiful golden love. Memories would serve her well. They would have to.

She packed her most treasured books, a few photographs and some simple dresses, riding clothes, underwear and a couple of sturdy nightgowns. All her magnificent jewelry she left behind. *It can go to my replacement,* she thought disdainfully, strangely untouched by the loss of the opulence of her San Francisco life. She had been far happier in a crude cabin and calico dress. But David had been with her then.

She resolutely forced the thought from her mind and went to the stables with her meager pack of belongings and enough food to last a couple of days. She'd take one good saddle mount, her mare, Featherweight. Although she was a poor rider, she needed a horse. If she pushed hard the rest of the day she could make one camp and be at the cabin by the following afternoon. It would be like old times . . . well, almost.

CHAPTER
13

June 1852, Cien Robles

Miguel left Rosalie's in the dim, gray light of predawn. By the time he arrived at the ranch, unshaven and exhausted, word of the wedding night disaster had spread through the big house. The groom who took his horse stared at him in mute condemnation. He went to his room and slept around the clock. For the next five days, he rose each morning at dawn and headed out to the range, working until he nearly dropped, coming in at dusk to fall into bed and sleep a dreamless sleep. He needed time to compose himself before he could overcome his shame and remorse. He was certain that she needed time to heal and regain her strength before she faced him.

When he rode in on the afternoon of the fifth day, he saw his mother's carriage in the stable yard. His parents had returned from the villa in town. Doña Maria was doubtless having a siesta and Alex would be in his study, washing down the trail dust with rum. The honeymoon couple had to be present at dinner. Miguel must face his wife tonight; there was no way to put it off any longer. He knew he had to talk with Ellie first before they greeted his parents and were both completely humiliated.

He bathed and shaved so that he felt somewhat refreshed physically, if still in emotional turmoil. As he dressed and prepared to confront Ellie, his conversation with Rosalie came back to him. Could he ever hope to charm his wife, to convince her to give the marriage another chance?

The thin voice on the other side of the door sounded strained and frightened in response to his knock.

"C-come in."

One look at her pale face and flushed cheeks grabbed at his vitals like a gut kick. He choked back his own self-loathing and entered the room hesitantly.

Ellie had heard him bathing and dressing, dreading his inevitable entrance through that adjacent door. Too soon, there he stood, dressed in tight tan breeches and high brown boots, his shirt open at the throat, exposing a hint of the black forest on his chest. With rising panic, she forced her thoughts away from that terrible night when he'd undressed before her. Ellie was still unwilling to confront her own conflicting emotions of fear and desire for this stranger who despised her. Staring into his dark

eyes, now veiled and fathomless, she simply waited for
him to speak.

"Ellie, we have to face my parents at dinner tonight.
They're back." He paused.

Did he seem unsure, nervous, even contrite? Ellie was
not certain, wrapped tightly in her own misery and righteous anger. "So, we must put on a proper front lest we
upset your beloved mother. No need to fear. I could hardly
cry rape against my own husband, could I?" She lashed
out at him, then stopped short, seeing his clenched fists
balled menacingly at his sides. When would she ever learn
to curb her foolish temper!

Slowly, he expelled his breath in a long, whistling sigh.
He had come to apologize and here she was clawing at him
before he could get his thoughts straight. Damn the little
cat, but she drove him to unreasoning fury!

"Will you give me a chance to talk for just a minute?"
He calmed his agitation and went on. "I am truly sorry for
what I did to you." He hesitated and took a deep, shaky
breath. "It was inexcusable, even if you did lie and
provoke me. But we are still married, Ellie. We have to
make the best of it." He watched her carefully, attempting
to gauge the effect his words had on her. She stood still, a
hand poised on the narrow-backed chair next to her dressing table.

After what seemed an eternity, she nodded, speaking
almost numbly, "Make the best of it. Yes, I suppose that's
true. God knows, I don't want them to find out what
happened either!" Shame coursed through her and flushed
her cheeks.

Seeing the angry red blush, watching her fingers tighten
whitely on the back of the chair, he again felt the waves of
remorse and humiliation wash over him. It was too late.
Rosalie was wrong. He could never undo that night and
he certainly would never again force her. Hoarsely, he
repeated, "I'm sorry, Ellie. I won't come into this room
again."

"Let us just put on the facade of a happily married
couple for our families?" She supplied the rest of the

bargain glibly, with a false smile pasted on her lips that did not reach the depths of her turquoise eyes.

He nodded in defeat, then turned to leave through the door adjoining their bedrooms, the door he had promised never again to enter. Unaccountably, she felt a swift stab of loss as she watched his retreating back.

Dinner that night was a strained horror. Ellie wore a plain, long-sleeved dress that covered her bruises. If either parent noticed the half-healed scratches on Miguel's face, neither commented. Miguel and Ellie were painfully polite to each other. Alex tried to attribute it to his and Maria's return to the house. Maria sensed their tension and was pleased to see the little Americana withdrawn and quiet, flinching when Miguel pulled out her chair or came near her for the simplest courtesy. She would remain in command of Cien Robles, its sole mistress, unchallenged by this rude, outspoken foreigner.

After a few days, Ellie's assiduous avoidance of her husband became evident to Alex, who also took note of his son's overlong hours in the saddle. Finally, one evening before dinner, he summoned Miguel to the study.

Never one to waste words, Alex plunged in, "That girl never leaves her room except to eat dinner with us or to walk on the patio after you've left in the morning. She was spunky and lively, but no more. What the hell did you do? She quakes whenever you come in the same room with her!"

Miguel turned away from his father's intense scrutiny and paced back and forth trying to gather his thoughts. He should have known the old man would figure out that things weren't right between them.

Alex's voice shook. "My God, I didn't want to credit the servants' gossip about your actually abusing her. It's true, isn't it?"

Nauseated as images of that horrible night replayed before his eyes once again, Miguel stopped and grabbed the back of a big oak chair on the opposite side of the room. "I only went to her that first night," he rasped out.

Before he could say more, Alex shouted a choice string

of expletives and whirled furiously on his son. "You young fool! Don't you know the difference between a whore from Rosalie's and a good girl like Ellie? You can't just take her like a serving wench!"

The irony of the remark and the slur against Rosalie stung Miguel. Rosalie had been such a gentle, patient teacher, had showed him how to be a careful, skilled lover. She did not deserve Alex's hypocritical scorn. As to what passed between Miguel and his wife, well, it was no one's business but their own. He would be damned if he justified himself to the old man or made excuses.

"You're a fine one to talk about how to treat a lady! Don't you think I know how you treat your wife? How much tenderness, love or respect have you ever given her?"

Two pairs of dark blue eyes locked in fiery combat. Then, surprisingly, Alex relented, his anger suddenly spent. He walked over to the bar and poured himself another rum. Downing it, he spoke softly. "Your mother was never like Ellie. Oh, she was beautiful when she was Ellie's age, but cold, so cold."

"Perhaps that was your fault, Papa. You stand too ready to condemn me for your own sins, I think."

Alex made a deprecating wave with one hand, seeming older and sadder. His shoulders slumped in defeat, aging him greatly before Miguel's very eyes. "Leave that be, son, leave that be. It's all over now, too late for us. But you're young and your wife is fiery and lovely. Don't let that damn Alvarez pride spoil it for you. She's worth fighting for, worth winning."

Miguel smiled in a cryptic, haunted way. "Strange you should say that. A friend of mine gave me the same advice." He paused a minute as if pondering. "But I don't know if I can do it. Anyway, it's between Ellie and me, Papa. We have to work it out, no one else. Just leave it be for now."

After more than two weeks of staying close to her room, Ellie was restless. For the first few days she was sore and terrified, but as her young body healed, her strong spirit reasserted itself.

When Miguel had confronted her the day Alex and Maria returned, just having him stand in her room made her breathless and pale. She cursed her cowardice, but assured herself it was only fear, nothing more. At least he was superficially apologetic, but she would never trust his fierce Latin temper, she resolved.

Ellie realized she had to learn how to survive in this strange household full of old hates. Until she knew the rules, she was helpless and one thing the spoiled, willful daughter of Adrian St. Clair had never been was helpless. Her first decision was to deal with Doña Maria, who had pounced on her earlier vulnerability and subtly needled her about all manner of petty things. Ellie never went to daily mass at home. Indeed, the St. Clairs' had no chapel on their own ranch and certainly no resident confessor! They had always been content with Sunday attendance and she would not become a nun like her mother-in-law, living on her knees in the chapel. Doña Maria's barbs about Ellie's friendliness with Luz would be settled as well, she decided grimly. She was used to much less formality at Twin Rivers in dealing with Mattie and the other workers. Luz, her young personal maid, had been kind in attending her on her wedding night and she was grateful. Ellie would never deal with servants like the imperious grand dame did.

She took perverse delight in doing anything she could to emphasize being American to the Hispanically rigid Doña Maria. Well, today she would shock the corset stays off that proper lady. She would go riding—astride, and she would wear one of her divided skirts! Let all the high-and-mighty Kanes be damned! She began to dress, grimly fastening the belt on her most tightly cut blue riding skirt as if girding herself for combat.

Combat it was. When she came downstairs, Miguel had already ridden out many hours past, and she secretly had to admit she was glad of that. However, Doña Maria was just returning from her morning prayers and ran into Ellie in the front hall. The shocked gasp she emitted fairly cracked the plaster on the thick stucco walls.

"What is that—that *garment* you are wearing?" Maria's tone was at its most icy and disdainful as she brought her initial outrage under control. Actually, such costumes, although rare, were occasionally worn by rancheros' wives. She *knew* what it was. She merely refused to consider that her son's wife would wear such a scandalous thing, much less ride astride!

Smiling sweetly, with a childishly innocent expression on her face, Ellie replied brightly, "Why, Mother Kane, it's my riding habit. I've asked Rafael to saddle Moonlight for me. I think it's time I began to see something of my new home, don't you?"

"Not in those shameful harlot's pants, you will not! If you must ride, it will be sidesaddle and you will be suitably accompanied by a groom and a maid as befits your station." The glitter in her jet eyes brooked no opposition, but there was nothing to set Ellie off more than a downright dare. Adrian had learned over years of bitter experience; it was Maria's turn now.

With sweet reasonableness, Ellie responded in feigned hurt, "Why, I can't imagine why you would think this skirt is improper. All the best ladies' academies back east allow their students to wear riding skirts. As to my riding sidesaddle," she shrugged helplessly, "you see, I don't own a sidesaddle and even if I did, Moonlight was broken to be ridden astride. I'd hate to predict what would happen if I even *thought* of trying to put one of those contraptions on her and mount. Why, I'd probably break my neck." As she said it she looked Doña Maria squarely in the eye, catching a glimmer of hope.

Doña Maria stared her down. Only the grinding of one high-heeled slipper gave away her agitation. "Go to your room and change at once." The voice was level and cold. No one disobeyed her except Alex, David and lately, she was loathe to admit, Miguel. But this chit of a girl certainly would not get the best of her!

Ellie returned the glare, all coy pretense at innocence dropped. She gave her quirt a vicious slap against her skirts. "I think not." With that, she brushed past her immobilized mother-in-law and out the front door.

For a minute, the older woman actually believed she would faint with the shock of such absolutely naked defiance from a girl she thought already beaten into submission. Much of the chit's willfulness had been subdued when she and Alex came back from Los Angeles last week. Something had passed between Ellie and Miguel. Since Maria never shared the confidence of any of the servants, she had not heard the stories circulating about the wedding night, but the frigid antagonism so thick in the air at dinner and the girl's small, flinching movements around Miguel had quickly indicated to Maria's shrewd eye that Ellie was as repulsed by men and their base cravings as she had been. Maria could almost have sympathized with Ellie if the girl had been anyone else but her son's wife and a Yankee, handpicked by Alex. But this defiance was insufferable!

Ellie walked determinedly toward the stables. Maria indignantly decided against making a scene and calling after the brat, or forbidding the vaqueros to saddle her mount. No, she would bide her time until Miguel came home. That would be the right moment. Perhaps he might even catch her riding about shamelessly astride. Serenely, she began to smile and turned back into the *sala*.

Ellie had her ride and was safely back in her room, soaking in a big tin hipbath when Miguel came home, bone weary and dust covered from a long day of riding from line camp to line camp. It seemed spring rodeo was scarcely past and already the fall one was nearing. He was at the foot of the big front stairs, about to make his long-legged sprint up to his room for a refreshing bath when the angry voices of his parents caught his ear. They were in the study and the door was ajar.

Suddenly, a tear-stricken Maria came flying out, a lace handkerchief clenched in her hands. She virtually collided with her tall son in the hallway. "Oh, Miguel, you simply must do something! She's your wife, after all. Your papa refused to say a word, not a word!" She sobbed fiercely.

Looking helplessly over his mother's petite shoulder at Alex, Miguel held the crying woman in his arms, attempting to soothe her. "What the devil's going on?"

Alex barked a sharp laugh. "Oh, a very big tempest in a very small teapot. It seems your wife took a rather unorthodox ride this afternoon, at least by proper Californio standards."

Miguel looked even more perplexed. He was sweaty, saddlesore and fast running out of patience with both of them. "Will one of you please speak English—or Spanish! Just explain."

Maria straightened up from his awkwardly comforting embrace. She never lost her timing. "It was her indecent dress, oh not even a dress! Miguel—she actually rode astride her horse like a man." Maria could not bring herself to use the words "dressed like a man."

"In men's breeches?" Miguel's voice fairly croaked.

Alex broke in with a deprecating laugh. "I think your mama exaggerates her case just a bit. It was a lady's riding skirt, but she did ride astride. Seems practical to me."

"Ladies do not ride astride." Miguel's face darkened like a thunderhead.

"My God, son, it's the girl's first outing since she's been here. Leave her some peace. Her father allowed it, even bought her the saddle and horse."

"It seems to me her father allowed her a few too many things." Miguel's eyes darkened in remembrance of her time with Rice Brighton. *They probably rode together.*

Maria calmed her sobbing and waited.

Alex shrugged, realizing again his helplessness in the thorny relationship between young husband and wife. Strictly speaking, what she had done was not acceptable, but damn, he liked her spunk and was glad to see her defy Maria. If only Miguel wasn't so much more Californio than Yankee. He chuckled to himself, considering what David would have thought of a woman riding astride in a split skirt—he'd love it!

Miguel slowly disengaged his mother's embrace and turned stiffly to walk upstairs. "I'll handle it," was all he said.

He knocked at the hall door to her room and Luz answered, indicating the young *patrona* was in her bath. He still felt damnably uncomfortable with the maid because she'd been one of his bedmates before his marriage. Now she was firmly aligned with her new mistress and looked at him as if he were some kind of monster. He retreated and scoured off his own trail dust, allowing himself time to cool down before talking to Ellie.

Small difference that breather made. When he repeated the knock an hour later, Ellie opened the door, dressed for dinner in a soft, clinging, rose silk gown. She looked incredibly lovely, big turquoise eyes shining and that mass of silvery curls piled high on her head. She was wearing a dress cut low enough to reveal the slight swell of those delectable breasts to his wandering eye. Awkwardly, he stood in the hall, realizing he could not break his word and trespass in her room again.

Wanting to have done with it, he began levelly, "I just talked with my parents about your little escapade this afternoon. My mother found your riding costume shocking. No wife of mine will dress that way or ride like a man. Go to the seamstress in town and have all the new habits you want made up. There are several sidesaddles in the tack room you can use until I have one made for you." He paused in the midst of his magnanimous declaration to see how she was taking it. That was his first mistake.

She stood frozen like a lovely pink and white statue, tiny fists clenched at her sides, fighting back furious, burning tears, quivering with anger. After a moment, she turned her back on him, dashing away the telltale evidence of her weakness, and then faced him squarely.

"I have always ridden astride. I was raised on Twin Rivers, on horseback. I don't know how to ride sidesaddle.

Besides, it's stupid. If you must keep me a prisoner in the house, so be it. Your mother wins another round, I suppose.'' The glitter in her eyes belied the quietly measured way she spoke.

"Fine. Sit inside until you wither.'' Feeling a cad and a fool, despite being in the right about forbidding her such a scandalous way to ride, he turned stiffly in the hall and stalked downstairs. Grimly, he repressed all the surges of guilt he felt. *Shit! I hate being married. Women should be a convenience, not an encumbrance.*

Ellie made him feel damnably responsible for her self-imposed solitude. She kept to her word in the following weeks, staying around the house, working at small chores about the flower beds and in the kitchens. She performed menial tasks that appalled his mother, but familiar things that she'd done as a girl in the smaller, less formal Twin Rivers household where a girl without a mother was left to her own devices.

One day he came upon her out in the courtyard gardens, dressed in an old calico gown, her hair knotted on top of her head with small tendrils falling across her face. She had just clipped a big basket full of purple and blue asters for the dining room. Smudged with dirt, she stood, obviously embarrassed and expecting a tirade from him. She had frequently endured such from his mother for her servant's penchant toward being dirty. However, Miguel surprised her. The picture of a little girl caught making mud pies and ashamed of herself was simply too endearing. He gallantly took the basket, complimented her on her work and escorted her inside. Even then, he noticed the way she flinched from taking his arm and walked a step ahead of him as if fearful of contamination. Well, she had no need to fear he would ever force himself on her again, he thought angrily.

As the weeks passed and Ellie continued to keep her distance, Miguel felt desperately in need of a release from the terrible sexual tension wound so tightly in him. Occasionally he thought of Sarita. He felt strangely unwilling to go to Rosalie anymore, at least for sex. That long night of confession after his wedding had changed their relationship in some subtle way. She had moved from lover to confidante. He grinned wryly, wondering how she would feel about that thought, little realizing Rosalie already had reached a similar conclusion.

Still, he needed a woman and could not touch his wife. Sarita was convenient, if unpredictable and clinging. He might go to town and visit some of the other girls at Rosalie's when he had the time. In the past, Rose had encouraged his experimentation with several of the young women who worked for her. She was professionally unselfish. He'd avail himself of them, he decided. But for now, Sarita would serve.

"I didn't come here for conversation, Sarita."

Grimly, Miguel began stripping off his clothes, brushing aside the beautiful woman's petulant questions. "Why do you not go to your gringa wife?" Sarita's eyes flashed. "Is she so cold in bed you must rape her?"

His eyes darkened in fury and he paused, half naked, like a lean jungle cat.

Sensing that she had made him dangerously angry, Sarita quickly let the subject drop and kissed him.

The story of the disastrous wedding night had spread covertly from the house servants to the rest of the ranch workers within a few days. Luz confided in horrified whispers to her cousin Sarita that the young *patrona* was bruised and Don Miguel fled the house as if chased by demons after the marriage was consummated. Now, almost two months later, here he was barging into her cabin before dawn, expecting her to simply fall into bed with him again. Did he want Sarita once more? Well, if he found cold comfort in his pale little gringa, good, but he would treat Sarita right from now on. Her eyes became calculating as she slowly slipped her thin cotton chemise over one heavy, dark-nippled breast, then the other, freeing them to the cool night air.

He scarcely seemed to notice her exotic posturing as he finished pulling off his pants, then grabbed a handful of thick black hair and pulled her half-clad body to his hard

naked length and sank back on her narrow, lumpy mattress. God, she was big-boned and fleshy, so coarse compared to his delicate, tiny wife, Miguel thought. He cursed
and gave himself up to pure animal instinct, blotting out
all the painful memories.

As he rode her hard, Sarita reveled in it. He was
splendid, all lean and hawkish, his beautifully sculpted
face rigid in concentration as he sweated above her. He
would be hers, she vowed fiercely. She would become his
favored mistress, no longer having to work for that proud,
imperious Doña Maria. She, Sarita, would have the grand
dame's son in her bed! Clawing, she pulled him even
closer to lock him in their ancient embrace.

Afterward, Miguel rose immediately and began to dress,
as laconic as he had been upon entering the cabin. Realizing that her hold upon him was purely physical and over
now, Sarita's mercurial nature flashed from ecstasy to fury.
All her earlier plans to ensnare him were abandoned. He
could not just come and go, using her mindlessly, caring
for her not at all!

"Did I not please you, Miguelito? I know I have fire,
querido, not like that frozen little stick you married. Why
do you treat me so coldly?" Kittenishly, she put a hand on
his forearm, kneeling up on the bed, a sheet clutched
artlessly over half her body. She poised midway between
pleading and wrath.

Miguel sighed. "What do you want, Sarita? My undying love?" He smiled sardonically. "Will you settle for
this instead?" Carelessly, he shrugged off her hand and
reached in his pants pocket. He tossed a five-dollar banknote
on the bed. "That's the going rate at the best brothel in
Los Angeles, Sarita. I'm afraid it's all I can do."

As he left the cabin with its leather door hinges creaking,
he heard the crash of a clay pot that Sarita hurled at his
retreating form. Bitch. He'd overpaid her, but then he
needed the quick oblivion of willing female flesh.

He silently let himself in the back door. It was daylight
and soon everyone would be stirring. Before anyone saw

that he had been in Sarita's bed, he would eat breakfast and vanish for the day.

However, someone had seen him. Bored and confined, Ellie had been sleeping fitfully for weeks. She had awakened before dawn at a faint noise from the adjacent room. Miguel always left early, but it was still quite dark outside. She rose and paced to the window, not questioning why she needed to watch his departure. He did not emerge from the inside courtyard. Ellie was mystified, for that would be the logical way to go to the stables. She walked across her large bedroom and looked out the other window facing toward the orchards and the servants' cabins in back.

There she saw Miguel striding purposefully toward Sarita's cabin behind a copse of oaks. Ellie knew enough backstairs gossip about that one. She had watched the sleekly beautiful woman eye her husband with a predatory air. And now, he was going to that cheap, calculating strumpot!

Ellie's pride was stung to the core, but she realized the absurdity of her feelings. They had agreed he would not visit her bed ever again. She could not reasonably expect him to remain as celibate as if he had indeed taken holy orders. He was even being discreet. It was early and no one but he and Sarita would know. Of course, how far that slut could be trusted to remain silent was another matter. It would be just like Sarita to spread word of Miguel's infidelity and his wife's inadequacy all over the estate!

Scarcely a quarter hour later, Ellie watched him return silently to the kitchen. All the while he was gone, she had paced, alternating between hurt misery and raging anger. She could not understand her own emotions. She certainly did not want him, nor did she want to be subject to public humiliation as a scorned wife like Doña Maria. *She is cold. Are you?* Or *do you still want him yourself?* An inner voice taunted her.

Shivering in the early morning cool, she pushed that disquieting thought out of her mind, allowing her wrath to take over. She would show him, damn him! She would show them all, Doña Maria especially. Resolutely, she walked over to the armoire.

Miguel went to the stables and mounted Dominican. Soon he was heading toward the west trace. After a few minutes he spotted a figure riding well ahead of him toward an isolated ravine, a shortcut where no one rode very often. Before he could make out the diminutive rider, he recognized the beautiful little silver-white filly. Moonlight was being ridden hard, fast and astride.

Furiously, he swore and gave Dominican a solid nudge with his heels, sending the big stallion into a ground-devouring gallop. Ellie heard him coming up on her and turned in the saddle only long enough to see who it was. Then she urged the fast little horse to surprisingly greater speed.

The little fool will break her neck! This time he let out a long string of choice Spanish epithets. Even old Rafael would be proud of his proficiency at swearing now! As he gradually closed the distance between them with his larger, stronger mount, he had to admire the little hellcat's horsemanship in spite of himself. Few men could ride so well over rough ground, dodging rocks and sharp, prickly bushes in such hilly terrain. To a Californio, raised from infancy in the saddle, horsemanship was a primary skill, to be prized above all others.

The beautiful little bitch rode superbly. Her small, fragile appearance was quite deceptive. By the time he'd considered that, he was alongside her, his big black towering menacingly next to her small white. He leaned over and gradually pulled the filly to a halt while Dominican pranced nervously.

His eyes raked the divided skirt, but despite his best resolve to stay angry, he found the costume not nearly as scandalously indecent as his mother had indicated. It was full like a skirt. The sight of her delectable little rump perched on top of the small saddle was provocative, however.

"I thought I made it clear to you about riding astride!" He found it difficult to keep his eyes off her heaving breasts beneath the silk blouse and open jacket.

Still winded from her furious flight, she gasped out, "I

needed some air, this morning of all mornings!'' The minute the words were out she could have bitten her tongue off. He'd know that she had spied on him! He'd think she was jealous!

Caught off guard, he cast a startled glance at her that broke his fierce scowl. Quickly, lest he give away his guilt, he resumed the black look while he wondered fleetingly if somehow she knew where he'd been this morning. Impossible. Or was it?

He took the offensive. ''I don't want you out in that costume riding like a hellion.''

''I've been riding like a hellion for fifteen years,'' she retorted.

''You could have broken your fool neck!''

''And I would have, if I had to ride with a sidesaddle and long gown trailing out beside me.'' Pressing her advantage, for she could see he'd been amazed at her skill, she went on, ''Admit it, Miguel, if I rode sidesaddle you'd have caught me in a trice. I couldn't have given that big brute such a run for his money.'' She gestured at Dominican, remembering him none too fondly from their wedding night. ''Is that how you want to win your races, taking unfair advantage of the competition, handicapping your opponent?''

He quirked one black brow. ''Strange, until now, I'd never thought of a wife as an opponent. And, *mi esposa,* I'd *never* consider you handicapped!'' His bold perusal of her slipped from her startled face to her breasts, down her slim leg to her little booted foot and back up.

Hating herself for it, she felt the flush stain her cheeks and creep down her throat and across her open blousefront. ''Oooh!''

She attempted to pull Moonlight free and dash off, but he was too quick, hauling her off the filly by her slim waist. God, she was so tiny, so light as he whisked her flailing frame hard against him. The sharp stab of desire he felt was so intense it was painful. Her face was only inches from his own and he could feel her writhing little body as it rubbed against his thigh and chest, inciting him to lose the last vestiges of control. Holding her with one arm, he tangled his fingers in her hair and brought her face up to his, branding her with a fierce kiss.

Miguel came to his senses quickly when he felt the stiffness in her body. Her lips remained tightly sealed and she pushed with all her strength against his chest. He looked into her eyes, darkened almost green in terror. With a sinking sensation he realized the extent of her loathing. What had he done to this warm-blooded, spirited girl? *She'll be afraid of me for the rest of her life.*

Slowly, gently, he put her down on the ground and dismounted quickly. "I'm sorry, Ellie. Dammit, it seems all I do is apologize to you! But you can't go riding all alone this far from the house. Believe it or not, there are some men out here even more despicable than I am. Ride your horse the way you like, just don't run off so far. Stay near the ranch house where my vaqueros are working, so they can look out for you." He hesitated a moment as she stood against Moonlight, using one arm to steady herself against the trembling in her legs. "Agreed, *pequeña*?" He waited, unsure of her response.

She nodded silently in assent, realizing what a concession it was for him to allow her riding astride. Quickly, before he could help her, she swung herself onto the little horse. Without a word they parted. She headed back down the ravine, toward the house at a much slower pace than earlier, without a backward glance.

Pequeña. Little one. A wave of desolation swept over him while he watched her ride away.

Ellie arrived home shaken and fled to her room. She looked in the mirror and rubbed her lips with her fingertips to feel where he had kissed her. Her face was ashen and her eyes looked twice their normal size. She began to undress with trembling hands, preparing for the bath she had asked Luz to fill.

Still in front of the mirror, she felt compelled to run her hands down her naked body. *How did it feel to him when he held me so tightly?* She was small and pale, yet she knew she was well-formed. Had he found her pleasing, or

wanting in comparison to Sarita? She looked at her pink
and white skin and silver-gilt curls falling in a tangle down
her back. Her scalp throbbed from where his hand bit in
and pulled the pins free when he kissed her. *Why does he
always hurt me?* Ellie was frightened of the nameless ache
buried deep inside her. She felt her throat tighten in a
wrenching sob and gave way to tears. *What do I want,
anyway?* She refused to accept the answer.

The next day when Miguel told his mother that he
would permit Ellie to ride astride, she was furious. Then,
seeing that hard, closed look in his eyes, she quickly
recognized that again she had trespassed into a place where
he would brook no opposition. That did not mean, however, that she would keep quiet around Ellie when Miguel
was not there. How had the girl ever gotten him to relent?
Maria considered it and did not like the possibilities.

For several weeks Ellie rode about the ranch, staying
near the main house, not racing off down isolated, rocky
ravines. But she wore her riding skirts like a banner,
proudly defying Maria, who scorched her with hate-filled
jet eyes. When the men were out, Maria's mute fury
turned to sickly sweet nagging about propriety and duty.
She rekindled all the arguments about daily attendance at
mass, something Ellie found abhorrent. The very thought
of being shut up for an hour a day in that small chapel with
her mother-in-law's venom goaded her into arising early
and escaping on Moonlight before mass. It was not always
easy since she had been sleeping poorly, but it was
worth it.

Ellie's sleepless nights were telling on her. Alex observed this, as well as noting Maria's continual, carefully
orchestrated needling. Short of straight homicide, he could
see little to do about his wife. However, he could befriend
his lovely daughter-in-law. She and Miguel remained stiff,
polite strangers and he was sure, from servants' gossip,
that they had not slept together since that first night.

Alex encountered her one day in the stable at mid-
morning. She had just come back from her daily ride when
he strolled down to meet her, taking in her jaunty taupe-

colored outfit and shining, flushed face. Looking at her clean young beauty, he cursed his son for a fool.

Ellie was startled at seeing Alex bearing down on her. Obviously, he wanted to talk to her, despite the careless manner he assumed. He had been kind and kept Maria from doing her worst on several occasions, but she was still in awe of her arrogant, handsome father-in-law.

"Good morning. I trust you enjoyed your ride?" His smile was dazzling and warmed the austere planes of his face.

"Why yes, it was beautiful. Moonlight loves the run and I need it, too. I mean, I've always ridden daily since I was a little girl. I've missed it . . ." she finished weakly.

Gently he waved her protests aside and guided her up the pathway to the gardens behind the big house. There was a copse of oak trees and a small bench there. "What you need, I think, is someone to talk to. Your father perhaps, except he isn't here, so I'm afraid, my child, you're stuck with me." He smiled again and she returned it, sensing his genuine concern. Lord knew she did need a friend.

They sat down beneath the trees on the old iron lattice-work bench. It was cool and peaceful. "It's lovely here. I've always liked to come out here to sit and look across Cien Robles," Alex said in a voice rich with remembrance.

It was a breathtaking view from the small knoll, overlooking a profusion of flower beds and vegetable gardens, all lovingly tended. The big house, with its massive white walls, red tile roofs and black wrought-iron grills, stood in majesty at the base of the hillocks. In one direction stretched a big stand of oaks behind which the neat array of cabins were situated. In the other direction the stables and corrals were set up, sprawling yet functional. In the distance the winery was dimly visible.

"And this is my husband's birthright," she said quietly, taking it all in.

"His, yours and, I hope, your children's." His eyes were that same unnerving dark blue, so like Miguel's. But framed with the graying blond hair, his seemed infinitely less menacing, more kind, almost wistful. Yes, she guessed that was the right word—wistful—a man with one last hope for grandchildren. And here she sat, part of that hope, knowing it would be forever denied him.

She looked suddenly at her hands folded in her lap, contemplating the heavy gold and ruby ring on her finger. Its weight troubled her.

"Ellie, I know things aren't right between you and my son. I feel it's partly my fault for forcing the marriage on both of you."

She stopped him. "My father had as much to do with it as you, Father Kane." She still felt awkward with the traditional form of his name.

As if sensing this, he said, "Why not just call me Alex? Father Kane makes me feel like a priest, and I assure you I could never qualify as one." His eyes sparkled.

In spite of herself, Ellie let out a small chuckle. "No, I'm sure that's true, Alex." All his scandalous reputation seemed insignificant in the face of his kindness and gentle good humor.

"Despite what Father Sebastian and my wife have tried to convince Miguel of, he couldn't either. I wasn't wrong to drag him out of that seminary, Ellie. He was born to run Cien Robles. I can see that now. And I think, in time, he will be a good husband to you."

At this, she once again lowered her head, unable to meet his eyes.

He felt her anguish and simply said, "I know he's not an easy man, Ellie. Part of that's my fault, too. I just want you to believe you have a friend in me. If ever you need to talk or want help, child, come to me, please. I know how Maria can be. Nothing will ever change that, but I can divert her from you some of the time. I'll do my best."

His sincerity and her loneliness overwhelmed Ellie. Adrian had spent the past month in San Francisco meeting politicians and conducting banking business. He would not return until fall. She had not spoken to him since her wedding night. Of course, she would never be able to confess the horrors of that to him or anyone. Pride forbade her. She could not admit her own lies about Rice either. All of it was useless, anyway, because she was committed and what was done was done. But she did desperately need a friend. It was an unlikely surprise that her father-in-law would turn out to be her ally.

She reached out and squeezed his hand, her face alight with its first real smile since coming to Cien Robles.

CHAPTER
14

September 1852, Cien Robles

The summer passed and fall came, gentle and golden. There was a bountiful harvest of grapes and olives and the fall rodeos were underway. Ellie rode Moonlight, worked in the gardens and occasionally shared a congenial conversation with her father-in-law. If Miguel was surprised at the strange alliance between his father and his wife, he did not show it. Indeed, except for polite conversation at dinner, he and Ellie never spoke and rarely saw one another.

Miguel went to Rosalie's place whenever he was not exhausted, but avoided Sarita and the other servant girls at the ranch. As the fall wore on his frustration became acute. He slept a door away from the woman he desired but could never have. Nothing lessened his obsession for Ellie. Each night he broodingly watched her as he sat at the big dining room table. Even when he could force his wayward eyes from the feast of her silvery beauty, he felt her presence and smelled her faint lilac perfume.

Maria and Ellie fought continuously, adding to Miguel's troubles. It never occurred to him that his mother provoked his wife as much as his wife provoked his mother. He only knew that the little vixen shocked Maria with her split riding skirts and free American ways. He owned that guilt also, for if he had not lost control that day in the ravine, he would never have allowed her to ride astride.

Ellie often went for solitary rides. To assuage her loneliness, she stopped at the corrals to talk with the vaqueros and watch them train the horses. She loved to feed the foals. Chaco, the stray dog adopted by old Rafael, followed her around adoringly and Ellie took to bringing him tidbits of meat from the kitchen.

Sarita, bitter over Miguel's desertion, observed the actions of his lonely wife, thinking it laughable that he and Ellie shared a foolish weakness for useless animals and did not know it. If the haughty kitchen maid was jealous because she had lost the *patrón*'s attentions, she was overjoyed that the *patrona* did not receive them either. But, try as she might, Sarita was unsuccessful in luring him back to her bed. She still remembered that last humiliating encounter when he had insulted her with a cash payment. No one scorned Sarita without reprisal.

She waited and she plotted. If Miguel believed his wife was a Jezebel, a temptress flirting with lower-class hirelings, he might send her packing, even have the marriage annulled. Sarita finally came up with a scheme that involved one of her lovers, Juan Morales.

The vaquero had only worked at Cien Robles for a year. He was handsome in a rough-edged way, with deep-set black eyes and a thick handlebar mustache. At six foot three, he was a brute of a man whom many of the serving wenches fancied. Sarita had cultivated him and found him to be a crude, selfish lover, but a useful man if handled right.

She seduced him in her cabin one warm fall evening, then set her plan in motion. ''But Juanito, it would be so

easy for a great stallion like you. I tell you, she looks at
you with hungry eyes. She's Yankee and was raised
without a *dueña*. I know she came to Don Miguel soiled.
He only married her to save the land. He does not touch
her. Everyone at the hacienda knows this.''

He considered. "I do not know, Sarita. I admit you
caught me staring at her. It is only that strange moonlit
hair that I like. I don't really want her." For the life of
him, Juan couldn't imagine why Sarita was encouraging
him to make advances to the *patrón*'s beautiful wife!

But Juan did have a bitter grudge against Don Miguel.
Ever since the younger man had taken over Cien Robles,
he had been adamant about the way horses were treated
and Juan's job was breaking horses. On numerous occasions the *patrón* had reprimanded him for being overly
rough. Last week Don Miguel threatened to fire him if he
ever again used a sharp Spanish bit. What sweet revenge it
would be to ride his little silver *patrona*!

Juan was suspicious when Sarita told him she would set
up a tryst between him and the *patrona,* but his own vanity
led him to credit her smooth talk. After all, had not Doña
Ellie watched him break horses?

Ellie did like to watch the horsebreaking, although she
had never paid attention to Juan Morales. She was simply
lonely and bored. It was natural for her to hang around
where the daily chores of ranch life took place. Adrian had
frequently taken her along to watch the branding of calves
with the *fierro* and *señal,* the hip and earmark that proclaimed
them Twin Rivers property. One of her fondest childhood
memories occurred the first time she was allowed to carve
the notches on a tally stick. This ingenuous Californio
recording device was a long wooden stick on which each
notch represented ten branded animals. Despite blisters on
her nine-year-old fingers from wielding the knife, she had
been triumphantly proud.

The fall sun was golden and the breeze rustled through
stands of wild mustard. Ellie smelled the clean scent of
wildflowers, horseflesh and leather, loving all three equally
well. She was glad she had defied Miguel and ridden out

to see one of the small rodeos. The sudden sound of a rider cantering up to Moonlight brought her from her reverie.

Juan Morales's face was wreathed in smiles. There she was, just as Sarita promised she would be! He did not work at the rodeo, yet it provided a perfect chance for him to meet Ellie in a secluded place away from the ranch buildings. Sarita had arranged it, assuring him Ellie was aware that he would meet her.

Grinning broadly, he greeted her, "Ah, Señora Kane, you are so far from the rancho. Are you lost?" He had been warned by Sarita about not being too obvious with the proud Americana. Seduce her gradually.

Ellie recognized Juan vaguely as one of the horsebreakers. What the devil was he doing out here near the rodeo? His job was back at the corrals. "I'm not lost, thank you. I'm going to the rodeo on the Ramirez property line. Aren't you one of the horsebreakers?" Her turquoise eyes were frankly baffled.

"*Sí*, Señora. I gentle beautiful fillies with great skill." As he spoke he rode closer, his big bay nudging Moonlight's flank, causing the little horse to shy.

Ellie felt a prickle of unease ripple over her and pulled on the reins to back off. Juan continued smiling, but did not edge his larger mount quite so near again.

"It is such a glorious day I took off from the horse corral. You will not tell Don Miguel, I hope?"

"It's not my job to report on the hours of the men, of course," she replied evenly, wondering what he was getting at.

"Ah, then I can perhaps convince you to take off a day from hot dusty rodeos, too? Come for a ride with me. I know a beautiful clear stream, Doña Eleanora."

Perhaps it was his overly familiar manner and suggestion, perhaps the Hispanicizing of her name that caused Ellie to bristle. "Thank you, no. I'm going to the branding. Please excuse me."

Her cold speech angered him. Who did she think she was to trifle with Juan Morales? When she jerked Moonlight back, he said angrily, "Not so fast, my little silver one! I know you desired this meeting as much as I did. I have watched your eyes on me in the corral. Do not play games with Juan. I do not like it!''

Ellie looked at him as if he'd taken leave of his senses. She was too angry to be afraid or to wonder where his bizarre notion came from. She whirled Moonlight. ''You're mad! Get out of my way.''

He spurred the bay forward and lunged for her reins, but Ellie was quick and so was her little horse. Gracefully, she dodged him and plunged down the road pell-mell toward the campsite.

It took every ounce of skill she possessed as a rider to outmaneuver him as he stuck doggedly half a length behind the little white filly. By the time she heard the bawl of calves and smelled the seared hair at the rodeo, she was nearing the end of her endurance and Moonlight was tiring fast. She had concentrated so hard on outdistancing Juan that it never occurred to her to yell for help. She only knew she must get to the vaqueros.

Suddenly, a rider appeared on the trail in front of her, just cresting the hill. Ellie reined up sharply, realizing that her insane pursuer was doing the same.

Miguel had just completed an early morning check on the small job here and was on his way back to the ranch house to arrange details for the big rodeo next week. Ellie was coming at him, riding like she had ridden that day in the ravine. Only this time another man was chasing her! Morales.

One look at Juan's furious scowl and Ellie's white-faced terror told him that his wife was fleeing grave harm. He helped her steady the heaving, snorting mare, grasping the reins in his hands after she had stopped Moonlight's headlong race.

''Ellie, are you all right, *pequeña*? What the hell's going on?'' He saw her shivering, sweat-soaked body and noticed the rip on the right sleeve of her blouse where Juan had tried to grab her arm and missed, tearing fabric instead.

Before she could answer, he turned his fury on Juan.

"You put your filthy hands on my wife!" His eyes were cold, but his voice was incredulous.

Enraged at the confusing turn of events, Juan realized Don Miguel would fire him because of the capricious whim of this *gringa* bitch. He decided he might at least get the satisfaction of beating the pretty face of her husband before he took off. With a snarl, he lunged the bay toward Dominican.

Both men fell to the ground, locked in a welter of thrashing arms and legs. They landed with a sickening thud. Ellie screamed as the two terrified horses shied away. Their sharp hooves narrowly missed the riders, who were now standing to confront one another.

Juan was three inches taller and substantially heavier than the rapier-lean Miguel. It looked as though it would be an uneven contest and Ellie's first impulse was to race for help, but before she could do so, help arrived. Hearing the commotion, one vaquero had called to his companions. In no time half the camp was there. However, Miguel did not call for help.

Indeed, when Pedro and Rafael moved to intercede, Miguel waved them back. "I fight my own battles. He came after my wife. I'll settle it my way."

Juan let out an ugly laugh. "You, pretty boy? You mean I'll settle it for you!"

With that, Morales swung a powerful roundhouse right that Miguel avoided with graceful agility. Juan was bigger and heavier, but his bulk slowed him down. Also, years of breaking horses had left him with more than a few souvenirs from being thrown. Broken bones and ruptured tendons healed stiffly.

Miguel had always possessed lightning-quick reflexes and his many months on horseback had toughened him considerably since he'd left his books. Anticipating just such a confrontation with a hired hand at some point— although certainly not over his wife—Miguel had been taking lessons in fighting from two tough, older vaqueros. One was a Yankee and the other a Mexican. They'd both survived by using their fists and brains in brawls. Now Miguel let their advice run through his mind.

Lesson: Always let the other fellow make the first move. Lesson: Keep out of his reach until you figure out his moves. Lesson: Stay cool and look for an opening. Lesson: Goad him into acting too fast so he gets careless.

Miguel danced and sidestepped like a matador, all the while watching the way Juan swung. At each missed punch or glancing blow, he taunted the big vaquero.

"You're slow and clumsy, Juan."

"All those horses you mistreated are taking their revenge."

"For each fall, another broken bone, torn knee, sprained shoulder."

"Too slow, Morales."

While he dodged and spoke in a low, staccato voice, Miguel jabbed with quick lefts, connecting with jaw and midsection. His Yankee coach, Blackie McGuire, had been a bare-knuckle boxer back east before seeking his fortune on the cattle trails to California.

The strange lightning-quick punches were not that punishing at first. But Juan wanted a traditional roundhouse fight, not a child's game, and grew increasingly angry at Miguel's taunts and jabs. Gradually, he got tired and careless. The punches, now in right and left combinations, started to hurt him more. For every glancing blow he could land, his younger, leaner opponent landed three solid ones.

Finally, throwing caution to the winds, he rushed in for a bear hug and the two men went crashing back onto the ground, rolling in the thick red dust, choking and coughing. By now, both were bruised and bloody, their shirts soaked with sweat.

All the vaqueros were spread in a wide circle around the two thrashing men, cheering them on, even betting on the outcome. Don Miguel had held his own far better than most expected. Californios were inveterate gamblers and the Yankee hands were lured into sharing the vice.

Ellie was frozen in horror, clinging to Moonlight for support. Reaching out a small hand to clutch Rafael's sleeve, she pleaded, "Oh, stop it! He'll kill Miguel! He's so much bigger and he's crazy!"

Rafael shook his head and grinned at Ellie, exposing four crooked, widely spaced teeth. "Ah, no, Señora, I do not think so. See how much faster and cleaner Don Miguel punches? Anyway, if we stepped in he'd lose face and be so angry he'd fire us all. Do not fear."

But she did fear! Her heart was in her throat and her blood was rushing through her head.

Just then, Juan rolled on top and got his big meaty hands around Miguel's neck. Realizing he'd be unconscious in seconds, maybe with a crushed larynx, Miguel grabbed a handful of the red dust and threw it hard into Juan's face. As the big man gasped for air and blinked at the burning pain in his eyes, Miguel pushed him off and rolled to the left. Without breaking the motion, he kneed Juan in the groin. The vaquero doubled over on his right side, immobilized in a fetal position. One hard punch to Juan's clenched jaw caused a resounding snap as the bone broke. He lay unconscious in the dusty road. Lesson: When you're losing, fight dirty.

Miguel got up, brushing off his clothes and moving slowly to see if all parts of his body were still functioning. His right fist throbbed wickedly, his throat was still burning from the chokehold, and he ached all over, but nothing seemed permanently damaged. Amid the shouted congratulations, he shrugged his way over to where Rafael stood with Dominican. He took the reins and mounted the big black. He cantered to where Ellie stood and grabbed her, depositing her roughly on the saddle in front of him. As she shrieked and kicked, the men laughed and made raucous comments about what to do with her. He rode hard toward the hacienda, ignoring her protests and their advice.

It was very much like their wedding night's furious gallop. When they got to the house he reined up sharply at the side of the big courtyard. After the hard ride he was hot, dehydrated and very sore. He let her slip down and followed in a stiff, painful motion, then threw her over his shoulder and proceeded inside the house. Sheer fury gave him strength to climb the back staircase to their rooms, ignoring her curses and blows.

Inside his bedroom door, he dropped her unceremoniously. As she struggled to stay on her feet, clutching at the doorknob, he said, "That big son of a bitch could have broken my neck, all because of you! Frankly, *mí esposa*, you aren't worth it. You stay home, out of harm's way. No more riding out to the campsites. Cowhands and you don't mix. *Comprendes?*"

She returned his fierce glare, hurt and humiliated, gasping for breath. "How dare you, you brute! I did nothing. That madman accosted me and chased me. You act as if I encouraged him!"

"That's what my mother and I have both been trying to tell you, you damn little fool! A beautiful woman can't go riding around by herself without inviting men like Morales to assume she's looking for some fun. That skirt and the way you ride only make it worse. You're acting like a tramp and I'm the one who's responsible for you. I value my neck, even if you don't. Stay away from the vaqueros!"

Tears stung her eyes and rage suffused her small body. She must not be returned to the limbo of her early days at Cien Robles, wandering around the house and gardens!

"I was raised on horseback, working at rodeos, notching tally sticks since I was nine years old! I can't sit in a carriage and ride with a *dueña*. I'm not like your mother!"

He snorted in derision. "That's obvious!"

"Yes, it certainly is! I'm not an aristocratic lady. I like being with working people."

"Like Rice Brighton? Did you meet him at the corrals or the rodeos?" The voice was ice cold now as he ground out the hated name.

She flinched from the bitter memory of Rice's betrayal and said, "My father never treated me this way!"

"I'm *not* your father, in case you forgot. I'm supposed to be your husband and if any other man puts his hands on you ever again, I'll kill you both, so help me God!"

* * *

Rosalie heard Mike's low murmuring voice coming from the front parlor and Suzie's cheerful, giggling reply as she led him to her room. After his marriage, Miguel had continued to frequent Rosalie's place and bedded Suzie and Lita, two of her best young girls. He and Rosalie, however, had not been lovers since that long conversation they'd had about his wife on his wedding night. Ellie had dramatically changed the tenor of their relationship. Rosalie was good-naturedly resigned to that. Indeed, it was inevitable that sooner or later Mike would turn to women his own age. "It was great while it lasted," she sighed. Damn if there was much more she could teach him about making love, but Rosalie still valued their friendship. She had watched him over the past months and worried about his haggard, driven appearance.

Discreetly, she entered the parlor and poured herself a glass of brandy, regretfully declining to take one of her best paying regulars to her room because she wanted to talk to Mike. The minutes ticked by as the ornate clock on the mantel kept its late night vigil. Finally, she heard the door to Suzie's room open and familiar footfalls came down the hall. As his long stride carried him to the parlor, she rose and walked to the bar to pour him a brandy. Without a word she turned and handed him the glass.

He took a sip and grimaced as it burned a path down his throat. Then he sat down and stretched his long legs over a brown velvet ottoman.

Rosalie appraised him, raising one neatly plucked eyebrow. "You look like you've been poleaxed, darlin'." She noted the deep hollows beneath haunted eyes as well as the bruised cheekbone and split lip that obviously came from a fight.

He smiled thinly. "You should see Morales. At least I'm still able to talk."

"You *want* to talk? I've been watching you and it's a lot more than a few scrapes and bruises hurting you, Mike."

Her cool hazel eyes were shrewd, missing nothing. It suddenly popped into his head how much better she understood him than his own mother. Then he grinned ruefully, realizing how much either woman would like the comparison!

"Yes, Rose, I'd like to talk, only I don't know where to begin or how to explain." He stared bleakly into his glass, swirling the contents in a circle.

"You've been working too hard and not sleeping near enough. I can see that for openers. How'd you get in a brawl? You're not the barroom type, babe."

He shrugged. "How else? Ellie." His fingers tightened on the heavy glass and he raised it to take another gulp of brandy, then reached over to the lace-covered table where several of Rosalie's custom-blended cigarillos lay. He lit two of them and handed her one. After a few deep puffs, he went on, "She nearly got us both killed. She insists on riding alone to the rodeos and hanging around the stock corrals, mixing with the hands. Well, one of them finally got the idea she was available and came after her. Jesus! If I hadn't been there, he'd have dragged her off her horse and . . ." He started to say "raped her" but choked on his own words.

Sensing the direction of his thoughts, Rosalie interrupted, "But you stopped him and saved her. She ought to be grateful."

He scoffed derisively. "That spoiled little bitch doesn't know the meaning of the word. Damn her! Why does she have to do everything in her power to rub me the wrong way, to endanger herself? If someone like Morales doesn't tear her apart, she'll break her neck riding like a man, hell-bent."

Rosalie chuckled. "I heard about the skirts a long time ago when she rode into town, right up to the dressmaker's shop, cool as you please. I bet she looks great on horseback all decked out in one of those specially made outfits." She eyed him speculatively to watch his reaction.

Miguel squirmed. "Yes, dammit, she looks great— beautiful! Is that what you want me to say? Yes, damn her soul, I want her! I lie in the next room every night, listening to her bathe and get ready for bed. I sit across from her at the dinner table and smell her perfume. Look, but don't touch, Miguel. After all, you're a man of honor and you gave your word!'' He slammed his fist down on the padded arm of the velvet chair with a muffled thud and swore a string of Spanish oaths.

Rosalie looked straight into his dark blue eyes and said quietly, ''Might it be, Mike, you're in love with your own wife? Worse things could happen, you know.''

He let out a laugh, half bark, half gasp. Incredulously, he dismissed the idea. ''I'm the young one who's supposed to be idealistic, remember? You're the woman of the world. Don't confuse love and lust. I certainly won't make that mistake. I've made enough others already, God knows.''

''So, you don't love her,'' Rosalie stated hypothetically, ''but you do want her. How do you think she feels—oh, I don't mean the front she puts up when you yell at her or scold her. I mean deep down inside, how does she feel? She might just want another chance with you, too. For all that rotten Mex temper, darlin', you're one good-looking stud and you damn well know it.''

He dismissed the idea immediately, inwardly cringing in remembrance. ''God, Rose, she flinches If I even come near her. Whenever I touch her she acts frozen, like a porcelain doll.'' He leaned forward in the chair, elbows on his knees, running his fingers through his hair and then sliding his hands over his face as if trying to squeeze back the memories.

Gently, Rosalie prodded, ''Is that how you want it to go on? Her with her hurt pride, never knowing how good it can be between a man and a woman? If she's ever going to learn, Mike, you're the one who's got to teach her.''

He sighed raggedly. ''All I ever do is hurt her. I can't seem to keep my temper when she's around.''

''Might be an itch there only she can scratch for you, not any other woman.''

The next afternoon Ellie rode to Los Angeles with the cook and two houseboys. She did not really go on the supply trip because she was interested in how the big kitchens of Cien Robles were run. Her real motive stemmed from deeply repressed jealousy, although Ellie would not admit it. *It's just curiosity, pure and simple,* she kept assuring herself. *I only want a look at Rosalie Parker.*

Mingling freely with the household staff, Ellie listened to servants gossip. More than once she had overheard the tales about where Don Miguel went late at night since he had quit Sarita's bed. She had been shocked when she found out that her own loyal maid Luz had been a paramour of his. However, that had been before their marriage and the girl was devoted to her now. Ellie did not bear a grudge. Luz was the past; Rosalie was the present.

From seamstress's helpers to kitchen maids, everyone had heard of the beautiful older woman who held Miguel's passion. Some perverse self-punishing instinct led Ellie to seek her out. She hoped the prostitute was cheap and aging. She feared the woman was lovely and sophisticated. She had to know.

When the cook and houseboys were busily occupied at the Mulcahey Emporium, Ellie went for a walk. She wore a simple lilac muslin day dress and carried a parasol trimmed in dark purple ribbons that blended with the gown. Her outfit was girlish and pretty, but, she hoped, not a costume to attract attention. Idly, she strolled in the afternoon warmth of October until she came to the quiet, shady street where she knew that place was situated. The building was unremarkable from the outside. What to do now? She could hardly debase her own pride by knocking on the door and asking to see the lady of the house!

She did possess one bit of information gleaned from the unlikely source of her seamstress. When Ellie was picking up several new dresses at the shop in September, Señora Valdez mentioned to one of her employees that Miss Parker would be in for her regular appointment that afternoon at two. It seemed the first of each month Rosalie made a shopping trip. Today was October first and Ellie hoped the madam would not change her routine.

She was in luck. From her secluded spot on the far side of the street, she saw a fancy gig pull up in front of the house. A woman emerged and stepped into the open carriage. She rode toward the seamstress shop, passing Ellie in a flurry of dust, but not before the girl had a clear view from behind her parasol.

The woman in the carriage was beautiful, no argument there. She was older than Ellie, although how much so it was difficult for Ellie to gauge. Not as old as Doña Maria, yet definitely on the far side of thirty. That was small consolation, however. Her gown was elegant, a beige silk that hugged a wasp-waisted, full-busted figure. She was a bit on the tall side, with a striking face and wide, hazel-green eyes under perfectly arched brows. Her hair was a lustrous chestnut brown, softly piled in curls on top of her head where a tiny hat perched.

Ellie felt a wrenching pain begin deep inside her. This was no brainless, pretty servant wench, but an older, sophisticated woman of the world. How much better could she hold Miguel's attention with all her skills and wiles than an inexperienced girl? Fiercely, Ellie reminded herself, *I don't want his attention! Rosalie Parker can have him and welcome!* She walked slowly back to the emporium.

Dinner that evening was a misery for Ellie, who kept her eyes downcast, feeling incredibly foolish and guilty. She had always been so vain of her silvery hair and beautiful face, but now she was brought low by a common harlot! She had actually been spying on her husband and could not meet his piercing blue gaze.

Late that night Miguel poured himself a third glass of Alex's best brandy and continued his restless pacing across the study floor. His conversation with Rosalie the other night still weighed heavily on him. Ellie's shuttered, flinching avoidance of him at dinner had only intensified his misery. She could not even meet his eyes! Then he forced his thoughts elsewhere, ruminating about his brawl with Morales.

Doña Maria had fretfully interrogated him about it, but feeling it was a matter between Ellie and himself, he refused to discuss the matter with her. Alex, of course, had heard everything from the vaqueros and was bursting with pride that his son had whipped a man twice his size.

Miguel had calculated since the day he took over Cien

Robles that he must fight more than one man who would challenge him. Both his age and the fact that he had been in seminary would make some think him an easy mark. Although he was relieved that he acquitted himself so well and that Simon's and Blackie's months of training had not been wasted, he was bitterly unhappy with Ellie for causing the fight. However, his conscience nagged him—he had manhandled her again. *She'll never forgive me.* He stared aimlessly out the window at the starry autumn night, standing very quietly in the little alcove off the side of his father's study. Suddenly, he heard the door open and close, followed by soft, light footfalls muffled in the thick rug.

Ellie had been unable to sleep and was sure Miguel was in town again. To take her frazzled nerves off feverish visions of him and Rosalie locked in a passionate embrace, she had come to Alex's study. It was a favorite refuge of hers, not only because of his kindly conversation, but also because it was the family library. She felt in need of a book for diversion on this seemingly endless night.

Ellie padded silently in her bare feet to the big oak shelves full of books. She did not see her husband standing in the alcove window, his figure outlined against the moonlit sky.

"It's late, *pequeña*. Good little girls are in bed."

She gasped and dropped a book from nerveless fingers, whirling to confront him, unconsciously pulling the lapels of her thin, silk robe tightly closed.

"You're drunk!" She could smell the fumes of brandy and glared at the glass held indolently in one hand as he leaned against the sashing.

"Yes, I am, or at least I'm giving it my damnedest effort." His eyes roamed hungrily over her slim, shivering form. She looked vulnerable and lovely in her pale pink silk robe, tiny bare feet peeking out from beneath the lacy hem of her nightgown. Her shimmering hair tumbled around her shoulders. She began to back away from him as her eyes grew into fearful turquoise pools framed by brushy, dark golden lashes.

Suddenly, he stood up straight. His facial expression

changed from the frank lust of a moment earlier to bleak desolation. "I'm not going to hurt you, *pequeña*. I gave you my word."

A flash of fire lit her eyes as she spat, "You don't live up to it very well! Or have you conveniently forgotten that day in the ravine or our wonderful ride back from the rodeo?" She was afraid and angry at the same time, but most of all she was bitterly hurt by his liaison with Rosalie.

He held the glass tightly in his hand until he realized he was about to crush it. After regaining his composure he set it quietly on the small window table and then leaned both hands against the wall, resting his head against his arm. "Oh, Ellie, what do you want me to do? I see the rest of our lives stretching out in front of us, living and sleeping in separate rooms, so near yet so far. I can't ever touch you. You loathe the very sight of me." He raised his head and looked over his arm at her, his eyes black with pain.

It hit her with jarring force! He desired her—Ellie— unsophisticated, inexperienced girl that she was, small and pale next to the voluptuous fire of Rosalie. All his anger and rough impulsive actions stemmed from sexual frustration! She could scarcely believe it!

Miguel rested his head on his arm once again. When he looked up, the study door was ajar and she was gone. He could hear no sound except the beat of his own heart.

Ellie had no one to confide in, not even Alex, especially not Alex. Although her father-in-law had become a good companion and sympathetic listener, she could not describe her present feelings to him. Indeed, she could not really understand them herself. She turned the dilemma over in her mind on a brisk fall morning as she ambled toward the stable. She did not know how to deal with the revelations of the other night. Miguel went to other women but wanted her. He was miserable at the thought of spending the rest of his life chained to a woman who hated him. *But I don't hate him.* She feared his violent, uncertain temper, yet was still drawn to him in the same inexplicable way she had been since the day they met. What did it mean? What kept her tossing night after night, sleeplessly? What gave her those feverish dreams in which he held Rosalie, then her? She would awaken, sweating and moaning.

"You are up early, Doña Ellie." Rafael gave her a gap-toothed grin as he emerged from the stable. His greasy shoulder-length hair bobbed as he bowed to her. "You wish to ride? I will saddle your pretty girl."

Ellie smiled, glad to have her disturbing reverie interrupted. Pretty girl was Rafael's pet name for Moonlight. Just as he turned to go back inside, a piercing scream erupted from the big barn about a hundred yards behind the stables. It was a cry of fierce pain, an animal's cry.

"Chaco!" Rafael's old arthritic legs creaked as he half ran toward the source. "*Dios! Los toros!*" he gasped.

Ellie was right behind him, her high-heeled riding boots slipping on the loose, rocky ground.

The bulls, those prize breeding bulls just arrived from the Mormons, were in the pens at the side of the barn. The cries came from there. When Ellie and Rafael came upon the scene, Miguel was climbing the fence of one pen. Inside, Ellie could see the small, shaggy, gray form of their mongrel dog, Chaco, lying in the dust with blood oozing from a deep gash in his side. He was panting heavily and no longer crying. Just behind him, in the center of the high-railed, heavily reinforced fences, stood the bull. He snorted loudly and pawed the ground, his fierce eyes now diverted from the dog to the man on the fence.

"Don Miguel, do not go in!" Rafael shouted.

The bulls were vicious and uncontrollable. Nobody went near one unless mounted on a well-trained horse with a tight set of ropes around the bull's neck to immobilize him. The dog must have blundered in the pen. The bull most likely trampled him with his sharp hooves, since there was little room to run at such a small target and gore it. To gore a tall man, however, was distinctly possible.

Miguel sat perched high on the fence. "Get me a couple of *reatas*."

Two more vaqueros had arrived by this time and were giving Miguel the same advice Rafael had, but they volunteered ropes. Ellie watched, heart in her throat, as Miguel sat on the precarious perch, diverting the bull's attention from the dog while he carefully coiled one lasso. Another vaquero did the same from the safety of the ground across the other side of the pen. Ellie perceived their plan. Both men threw in sync, each capturing the bull by his neck from opposite sides, quickly securing the ropes to the fence posts.

Held quasi-immobile, the bull bellowed and pawed, straining at the ropes, but could not reach Miguel as he dropped into the pen. Quickly, he scooped the dog up to hand him to Rafael through the narrow openings between the horizontal logs of the pen. Ellie didn't breathe until Miguel was up and over the fence himself.

The dog was covered in blood by now, a small, pathetic mass of raggy gray hair and thick red gore. Miguel looked intently at Ellie. "Run and get a bucket of clean water, some thread, a needle and a bottle of whiskey from the bunkhouse. Manuel should be there. He'll know where everything is. Bring it to the stable." With that, he took the small burden gently from the old man and walked steadily to the stable as Ellie raced toward the bunkhouse.

Ellie helped Rafael hold the little dog, placing its head in her lap and soothing it with her hands. Miguel worked carefully, cleansing the wound with water and then whiskey, cutting the thick shaggy hair away from the wound with a sharp knife and then suturing the gaping opening together.

"Easy, *perro*, easy." Miguel's voice was silky and hypnotic as he stitched. The little animal's frantic pain seemed to abate, as if the sure, gentle hands sewing up its injury were transmitting a balm of themselves. For all his fierce pride and vile fits of temper, his sarcasm and brutality, here was a side of her husband that Ellie had never seen. He'd risked his life for a cur dog, Rafael's pet, valueless except to the old man and her.

She stroked the dog's ears as she watched Miguel's hands complete the task. Such beautiful, strong hands. How would they feel stroking her with such gentle persuasion, sensuously caressing bare flesh? Her cheeks flamed and she glanced up at his dark head, bent in concentration. Then, as if sensing her thoughts, he looked up and their eyes met and held. She was reminded of their encounter at the betrothal dinner. One of his hands reached over to brush hers where it lay on Chaco's head. It was a fleeting caress, but she felt it as intensely as a direct hit by summer lightning. Ellie wanted to reach out and brush a stray black curl off his forehead, but she shyly looked down at Chaco instead.

His task completed, Miguel stood up. "He's lost a lot of blood but no organs seem to be punctured. If we can keep him quiet until those stitches heal, he should be good as new, Rafael."

"Muchas gracias, patrón."

The two men talked rapidly in Spanish then, something about using an old Indian herb that would work as a sleeping potion on the dog so he could rest easily, but Ellie wasn't paying attention. She sat bemused on the stable floor with the little dog resting in her lap. Her mind was far away.

In the following weeks Miguel and Ellie established a strange, uneasy truce. It seemed as if the incident with Chaco had drawn them both into a more receptive frame of mind. The next morning, Miguel stopped by the stables to find her hand-feeding the little mutt bits of chicken filched from the previous night's dinner.

"You'll have him so spoiled he'll be too lazy to chew the bones." He grinned down at her as she flung a great mass of silvery hair across her shoulder and looked up at him, like a child caught stealing candies.

"Oh! He will not," she replied spiritedly. "Besides, Chaco is too weak to wrestle a bone, at least for a few days. I do believe you saved his life. I add my thanks to

Rafael's.'' Her clear turquoise gaze was dazzling and innocent.

Miguel felt his pulse speed up. ''Rafael adores you, you know. He told me how often you come to the stables to watch him work with leather and to pet Chaco and feed him treats, like this.'' He smiled at the chicken scraps. ''An old man gets lonely when he's consigned to repairing tack and making saddles. I'm glad you befriended him.''

''He's a dear man and he never tires of telling me about the young *patrón*. Were you really such a paragon as a child?'' She dimpled.

''Rafael taught me how to ride, how to gentle a horse without cruelty or force,'' he said in remembrance. Then, returning to the present, he laughingly added, ''Lately he's even taught me how to roll cigarillos and to swear. So much for my saintliness!'' Then looking at the dog, he changed the subject. ''You really are taken with the little rascal, aren't you?'' It was a side of her he never thought about before.

''I play with him each morning before I ride. He's always here waiting for me with that fluffy little tail wagging.'' Fondly she stroked Chaco's head. He was still too weak to sit up, but the tail was thumping noisily on the ground where he lay.

Miguel walked over and knelt down beside her, stroking the little raggedy dog who licked his hand. ''If you like, and Chaco can spare your company for a while, I'll take you to see the rodeo camp.''

He had forbidden her to ride out to the campsites since the day he fought Juan Morales. She had complied, confining her rides to the immediate area, bored and angry.

Her eyes lit up in undisguised pleasure at his offer. ''Oh, do you mean it—I mean—I'd love to see the big one on the Twin Rivers line!''

''Then let's go,'' he replied, a smile dazzling her with its slash of whiteness across his dark, handsome face.

So, they had come to take occasional rides together. If both were guarded in their movements and careful when they touched, it was at least a beginning, as if each could sense a change in the other but was uncertain of how to proceed further.

CHAPTER
15

October 1852, Cien Robles

The chill night air bespoke the ending of October and the coming of winter. It was a clear, sparkling night with stars sprinkled across the vault of the heavens like winking diamonds. The courtyard was filled with people and a mariachi group played a haunting, lovely melody that wafted to Ellie on the second floor balcony.

The courtyard was ablaze with braziers giving off rich golden light and heat in the cool night. White tablecloths were set with gleaming silver candlesticks, the flames of the candles winking softly. Huge sprays of bright, fall flowers made a riot of colors—rust, gold and orange. Food was abundant: huge haunches of beef resting in spicy sauces, earthern bowls of hot green chilies, plump chickens and pheasants stuffed with sweet apple dressing, cutglass trays of succulent olives, mounds of tart-sweet oranges and the finest wines. All the largess of the groaning board, including the wine, was produced at Cien Robles.

Now, as Ellie stood on the balcony, waiting for her husband to arrive, she took inventory of her careful toilette for the hundredth time. Her dress was a deep turquoise silk, shot with silver threads, with a rounded neckline that she felt was shockingly low. Nonetheless, Señora Valdez

assured her it was quite the height of fashion and very
becoming on one with a small, high bustline. The sleeves
were long and fitted closely to just below the elbows where
they spilled loosely down to her tiny wrists in a froth of
fine-spun silver lace. She wore aquamarine earrings and a
square-cut aquamarine pendant at her throat. Her hair was
arranged in an artful display of curls, half of it piled high
on her head, half trailing down her back and over her
shoulders, held in place by several combs set with matching
aquamarine gemstones.

*I look fine. Why am I so nervous? I've been to lots of
fiestas before,* Ellie scolded herself, but knew in her heart
the reason this one was special. She must look perfect for
him. She must exceed Rosalie in cool, sophisticated beauty. Clasping the little silver fan tightly in her fingers, she
sighed.

Miguel came out on the balcony, leaving his bedroom by
the outside door, and stood behind her. He thought Ellie
looked like a sea nymph, all aqua and silver. She glittered
in the moonlight. All he could think of was to take her in
his arms and hold her to him in fierce, protective passion.
She was so delicate, lovely and small, so perfect A sweet
ache of desire throbbed through every fiber of his body.
Forcing himself to calm down, he cleared his throat and
stepped beside her.

"Good evening, *pequeña.*" He took her fingertips and
kissed them lightly, trusting himself to do no more. At
least she did not draw away flinching anymore, thank God!
"You are so very beautiful."

The earnest way he accented each word touched her
more than she could say. *It* is *true,* her heart fairly sang; *he
wants me more than Rosalie!* Radiantly, she smiled up at
him. "Thank you, Miguel. You look splendid."

It was certainly true. He was dressed in a formal black
charro suit with a white silk shirt and red sash. The
tailored lines of the fitted short jacket and hip-hugging
pants flattered his tall, lean body and the silver studs
trimming the suit added a dash of glitter in contrast to his
black hair and midnight blue eyes.

He gallantly offered her his arm and they went downstairs into the babble of sounds and kaleidoscope of colors in the courtyard.

Alex and Maria were standing with Adrian near the fountain, where the young couple had been instructed to present themselves for a formal fanfare and introduction to the assembly. Maria saw them smiling, arm in arm, and her eyes narrowed in a swift stab of jealousy before she suppressed it.

"Here are our children, Alex," she said with acid sweetness.

If her tone of voice put him on his guard, the picture of Miguel and Ellie coming toward him drove her antagonism from his mind. What a splendid pair they made! Adrian voiced the same opinion.

The evening progressed in a blur of music and laughter. Indeed, it seemed the only one not enjoying herself was the hostess, Doña Maria. As soon as Miguel took Ellie for the first dance, Alex excused himself and his wife from Adrian and guided her into the study, an iron grip on her elbow.

Once inside, she whirled furiously on him. "What is the meaning of this?" She spat the words at him, rubbing her tender arm where he had bruised the flesh.

Alex smiled chillingly, the way only he could, and walked slowly over to the bar to select and light a long black cigar. Blowing a ring of smoke, he looked across the distance between them and then spoke glacially. "I want to make one thing graphically clear. Our son and daughter-in-law are having a good time tonight, enjoying one another's company. Nothing, I repeat, *nothing*, will disturb them. Do you quite understand?"

Maria felt frozen by his icy blue eyes. She shivered in spite of the warmth of the room, then spoke. "I do believe you'd actually kill me if you thought I came between them! Never fear. They are married and I will hold my peace."

When she turned to leave, he could see anguish reflected

in every line of her body. Alex poured a stiff rum and downed it in one fiery gulp.

As Miguel put his arm around Ellie's waist and led her to the open courtyard for the first dance, he could feel the tension between them like the flexing of a taut wire. He knew they would have to dance at the fiesta—it was obligatory for the guests of honor—and he dreaded it. They had not danced since their wedding and now he felt raw and vulnerable as he took her very carefully in his arms. Could she sense the stiff, disciplined holding back that he practiced? He prayed not. He had already revealed more of himself in that half-drunken moment of weakness in the library than he wanted her to see. He did not trust Ellie and he feared for her to know the power she held in her small hands.

Ellie had never been so confused as she was when he drew her into his embrace. They began to follow the slow cadence of the music. She, too, felt the tension between them, that strange magnetic pull that took her out of herself and drew her to this man who held her. She had been terrified of him, of his touch, yet perversely she still sought it. All the times she had watched him in rapt fascination flashed before her eyes. She could see him as he knelt in the church during their wedding, as he gently ministered to the wounded Chaco and as he worked at the roundup camp fire, with sweat running in rivulets down his dark furry chest while he branded calves in the heat and dust. Thinking of how she'd imagined him caressing her body, how she wanted to run her hands over his lean muscles, she blushed heatedly. How could she want a man who had done nothing but hurt her and scorn her?

They danced in silence for several moments, each lost in thoughts painful and private. Gradually, the tempo of the music picked up, swelling to a sensual, wild and primitive rhythm. As she had the night of their wedding, Ellie again felt herself pulled into its hypnotic web. She had danced for him that night, but it did not please him because he believed she belonged to Rice. Would she please him now? Some force beyond her conscious volition seemed to take over as she swayed in and out of his molten embrace, hips undulating to the beat, feet keeping the close rhythmic pattern. Her cheeks were brightly flushed as he responded, moving with her in the intricate weaving of the dance.

More than a few envious caballeros looked at Miguel's little silver Americana, in awe of her delicate, sensuous beauty. Many women who vaguely remembered David's bookish younger brother gone to be a priest were fascinated by this dark, handsome stranger who danced with such virile intensity.

The music stopped abruptly and there was applause from the ring of spectators. It was obvious that the young couple were enamored of each other. They stood for that brief moment, oblivious of the onlookers, dark blue and light turquoise eyes telling more than they dared speak.

Once again the music resumed, this time in a slow, traditional melody. Confused by the swift end of the frenetic first dance with its aftermath of attention, Miguel and Ellie were eager to continue. Both wanted time to marshal their emotions. He reached for her and she flowed into his arms. Gradually, as more couples filtered into the open courtyard and the noise rose, Miguel and Ellie had privacy to talk and the camouflage of a crowd in which to move without being the center of attention. She felt the hardness of his body as he held her to him and he inhaled the sweet lilac fragrance that drifted up from her hair.

"You dance like a wild little silver gypsy." His voice was low and hoarse.

Ellie couldn't tell whether it was a compliment or a condemnation. Fearfully, she raised her eyes to meet his. Feeling the flush steal up her throat and across her cheeks, she gathered her courage and asked, "Did it displease you?"

The breathless, frightened quality of her voice cut him to the quick. She, too, remembered the last time they had danced and his brutal treatment of her afterward. He swallowed over the tightening in his throat and replied, "No, *pequeña*, it didn't displease me. I meant what I said as a compliment." At her startled look of relief, he smiled, forcing his voice into a teasing tone. "And you have my solemn word of honor not to carry you off, slung across my shoulder like a sack of potatoes!"

She strove to match his lightness. "Or ever to put me up on that devil horse again? The ground never looked so far away."

Now his smile broadened into a grin. "Dominican is gentle as a lamb. I can't understand why everyone on Cien Robles is afraid of him."

"Everyone but you and Rafael. He told me all about how you raised the black from a colt and reclaimed him when you came home. Do all wild things respond to your touch so readily?"

He looked straight into her clear, aquamarine eyes. "No, not all wild things, *pequeña*."

They danced in silence for a few moments then, she with her head close to his chest, feeling his heartbeat while he held her like fragile china.

From the edge of the glittering crowd of revelers, a pair of black eyes slitted in hate, watching the laughing exchange between the young *patrón* and his wife. Sarita was pouring chilled wine at one of the tables when she saw them. They certainly did not dance or talk like cold antagonists. Their every movement suggested far more that they were lovers. Oh, she had watched the little gringa's eyes devour Miguel from a distance when he was not aware. She had seen it several times when she followed the *patrona* to the stables, but Miguel did not seem to return his wife's ardor. At least, Sarita had convinced herself of it until now. However, confronted with the scene unfolding before her, she could no longer deny her worst fears. She swore as she spilled some wine, and received a swift rebuke from Manolo, the chief steward, who sent her immediately back to the kitchen.

Alex was elated as he watched Miguel and Ellie.

Adrian stood next to him smiling. "I must say, Alex, I was concerned over some rumors I heard earlier about those two not getting on. Eleanor seemed remote and nervous when I was here last, but now, well, things are working themselves out. I must confess I was uncertain when Miguel took his brother's place. Perhaps we made the best bargain all the way around.''

He raised his glass in a salute to his taller friend who joined him in the toast. Yes, indeed, things were working out even better than Alex had dared hope.

As she relaxed in her husband's arms, Ellie began to feel better about the evening, soaking up his gentle nearness. The music, the soft warm glow of braziers and winking candles, the cool, starry night all cast a benediction.

Miguel felt her contentment and responded to it with a gladness of heart, but he also felt anguish. Now she danced in his arms, surrounded by the noise and laughter of the crowd. But what of later when he escorted her up those long stairs to their separate rooms? He ached with wanting her, yet was afraid to upset the delicate balance of truce they had been living. The very thought of her numb rejection stopped him from pursuing the thought. He must wait, but a voice nagged him: *how long can you wait?*

Ellie became increasingly aware of his pensive mood as he grew silent. She sensed the carefully controlled way he held her, gentle, yet under restraint. She was uncertain of what it meant.

Finally, after several more turns around the courtyard, he broke the silence. "Let's stop for a while and investigate those tables groaning with food and wine. Hungry?"

She nodded in assent although she was far too confused and excited to want food. But they did drink rich, red wine and dance late into the night. The wine seemed to relax his tenseness. Unused to drinking, Ellie became almost giddy. She could not say if it was the wine, the lovely night or her husband's embrace that caused her lightheadedness.

All too soon, the last of the revelers departed or retired to guest rooms. The fiesta was ending. Miguel and Ellie bid Alex, Maria and Adrian good night. Arm in arm, they walked inside and began to ascend the stairs toward their quarters, each lost in a maelstrom of confusion. More than anything, he wanted to carry her to his room, to that big, lonely bed, and make love to her, yet his pride forbade him. He had given his word. She was content in his arms tonight, just dancing, laughing and talking. He could ask for no more.

The hallway was long and dimly lit by flickering candles set in recessed wall sconces. The polished oak floor gave off a soft luster and echoed the click of his boots and her high-heeled slippers. They had not spoken since they left their parents below, as if each dreaded or anticipated what lay beyond the bedroom door. When they reached her door, he stopped.

Gently, he raised her hand to his lips and kissed it. "Sleep well, *pequeña.*"

With that he turned and swiftly walked to his room, never glancing back to see her standing in the hallway with her hand on the doorknob, her hair and dress flickering with molten silver in the candlelight. She listened to the echo of his footsteps as the night swallowed them up, then slowly entered her room. Luz was asleep on a chair by the bedside, waiting for her mistress to return. Wanting no questions or conversation, Ellie awakened the girl and sent her to her quarters, assuring the maid she could manage by herself.

She undressed, carelessly laying the beautiful silver-aqua gown over a chair. Then she pulled the pins and combs from her hair and let it flow down her bare back, brushing it until it glowed and crackled around her shoulders. A thin, cream silk nightgown embroidered with tiny pink rosebuds was laid out for her. As she slithered into its whispering folds, feeling it caress her body, Ellie felt an emptiness such as she had never known. She climbed into bed and closed her eyes.

"Sleep well, indeed!" Ellie gritted her teeth and rolled over for what seemed the hundredth time, but sleep would not come, despite the dancing and wine. She pounded the pillow and listened, afraid to hear sounds from next door. If he went out tonight, to one of his women, Ellie knew she would not be able to bear the pain.

After over an hour of tossing, she threw off the covers and rolled out of bed in one violent, angry motion. *You're a coward*, one part of her mind accused. *No, no, he should come to me*, she answered herself in a wail of anguish. *But he never will*, the night whispered.

Miguel lay stretched across his big bed, flat on his back, arms crossed behind his head, staring at the ceiling. He thought about getting dressed and heading to town. Even if Rosalie's place was closed, she'd let him in.

"Who am I deceiving?" he muttered hopelessly under his breath and reached to the bedside table for tobacco and paper. Carefully, he rolled a narrow cigarillo and then lit it, lying back to resume his sleepless vigil. Suddenly, he heard a slight creak as the door adjoining his room to Ellie's opened. She stood framed in a halo of light from the candle in the room behind her, a tiny, vulnerable figure. Very slowly, hesitating with each step, she moved across the distance between them. She was trembling and she was lovely. The thin silk of her gown seemed to melt into the curves and hollows of her delicate body.

He rolled up on one side and ground out the cigarillo in a crystal dish on the table, never taking his eyes off her, never saying a word. Ellie looked at him in the soft light issuing from the open window where the moon beamed. His hairy chest was bare, and from the way the sheet was draped over his long frame, it was obvious that he was naked underneath its scant cover. God! What had she done? Her fear began to war with her need and she almost turned to flee when he finally spoke.

"Come here, *pequeña*." His voice was whisper soft and low in the stillness of the night.

She was very near the bed now, yet afraid to take that last, irreversible step. Then he sat up and his hands slowly reached out to her. Her arms stetched toward him and his strong dark hands closed over her tiny pale ones, drawing her to sit on the edge of the bed. She looked so tense, like a frail silver bird, poised for flight.

He took her chin in his fingers, raising it so she had to meet his midnight blue gaze. Willing her to look into his eyes, he kissed her very softly, barely brushing her lips.

"Are you sure, *pequeña*?" The question seemed wrenched

from him as he struggled not to hold her little hand too tightly.

The kiss and the gentle pressure of his hands felt warm and good to her. Her eyes glowed like the gemstones she had worn that night. "Yes, Miguel, I'm sure."

"Then let me love you, Ellie. I promise I won't hurt you."

He drew her down on top of his chest as he reclined back on the bed, holding her lightly and raining soft, butterfly kisses over her face. All the while his hands ran up and down her spine, around the curves of her small buttocks. Unsure of what to do, but loving the delicate caresses, Ellie lay with her breasts pressed into the hardness of his chest and let her hands grasp the flexing muscles of his shoulders.

Slowly he sat up again, continuing the kisses, then trailing them down her throat and across her shoulders. As he moved, he pulled the drawstring at the front of her nightrail, loosing the neckline so he could slip it down her arms, baring her pert, high breasts to his gaze. He groaned as he felt the silky perfection of first one, then the other, cupped in his hands. The night air was cool on her bare skin, but his hands were warm and the sensations they evoked caused her nipples to harden and contract. She let out a small whimper of shocked pleasure and thrust them against his palms. Then he moved his head to take one in his mouth and suckle it. She writhed with the wild, sweet tingling, her hands eagerly tracing random patterns across his shoulders and arms.

His breathing was erratic as he whispered, "Stand up, Ellie." Gently, he eased her nightrail off. It fell in a whisper to the floor.

He drank in her loveliness, taking time now to appreciate the porcelain delicacy and perfect proportions of her small exquisite body, without the heat of anger to obscure his vision. He let his eyes rake her from head to toe and back up again, gently holding her by her hips. She was glorious, with small, pink-tipped breasts thrust up proudly. The hollows on the sides of her tiny waist seemed to gleam while the flair of her slim legs enticed his eye to the silvery curls at their center.

Ellie watched his face as he took inventory of her body. She felt embarrassed standing so wantonly naked before him, but at the same time, a queer little thrill began to grow deep inside her, replacing the modesty with a surge of pride. He hungered for her body and thought her beautiful. It was written in every line of his face as he kicked the covers from his own hot, naked flesh and swung his long legs to the floor to stand next to her.

She returned the compliment shyly, looking at his tall dark frame, so beautiful, hard and male. He was splendid-looking, like a sleek black panther. He took her breath away.

"Touch me, Ellie." It was as much a plea as a command.

She complied, her eyes glowing with wonder as she ran her flattened little palms up his lean, hard-muscled arms and across his furry chest. She came barely to his shoulders. He groaned and pulled her to him in a fierce, possessive kiss. Feeling her stiffen in fright, he brought himself under iron control, softening the kiss, tipping her head back and trailing delicate nips and licks down her throat and over her breasts. After he was sure she was no longer frightened by his passion, he placed one arm behind her knees and lifted her onto the middle of the bed. He followed, lying on his side to continue the soft caresses, pulling her closer to the length of him so their bodies were touching.

Ellie was drugged by the sensations overwhelming her, so sweet and so intensely exciting. Inexperienced as she was, she let her instincts guide her, pressing her body closer to his, savoring the hard, hairy feel of his lean body, holding him fast with her hands. Then she lightly raked his shoulders and back with her nails.

Feeling the heat of her response, Miguel was elated but also fearful of his own passion. He must go slow and control himself so as to give her time. Carefully, he held her, stilling them both until he could regain his composure. Even without entering her he was ready to explode!

"Oh, *pequeña*, it's never been this impossible to go slow before," he breathed in her ear as he kissed it, then her temple and eyelids.

Ellie didn't understand the exact meaning of his words, but she did sense that his holding back reflected his gentleness and concern for her. When he once again kissed her lips, she gasped in pleasure, opening her mouth. She was shocked, then delighted, when his tongue plundered inside. It felt wonderful. Gingerly, she returned the caress, letting her tongue dart into his mouth as he growled in pleasure and intensified the kiss. She writhed in an ecstasy of new sensations, kissing him back fiercely, arching her hips as she clung to him.

Miguel knew she was ready. Gradually, he moved one of her hands down between them to grasp his aching shaft. Her little fingers closed about it before she realized what he was doing. He felt her stiffen for a second, the well-remembered fear returning.

"Easy, *pequeña*. I won't hurt you. This time it won't hurt," he whispered between kisses as he continued to hold her gently.

What else could she do? It had been so wonderful until now. She felt some indefinable, persistent ache growing deep inside her belly. Might he assuage it this way? She let him position himself above her and spread her legs with his own. All the while, he kept her hand on his hard, pulsing phallus. Very slowly, he rotated the tip across the wet opening to her core, still guiding her hand to move it. She let out a small moan of surprised pleasure and then he pulled her hand away, sinking in full length.

Involuntarily, she arched to receive him and they both gasped in delight. Far from the pain of the first time, the entry was smooth and slick.

After a few slow, long thrusts, he stopped, holding still inside her while he struggled to keep from spilling his seed. Sensing he was holding back to please her, she lay still, feeling his trembling and the frantic hammering of his heartbeat. When he resumed the stroking, she moved with him, reveling in the hunger of her own body to merge with his; to feel him filling her. Gradually, the core of heat inside her began to widen and she was afire with the joy of it, wanting it never to stop, yet wanting some unknown completion. Several times he stilled their frantic movements and held her tightly as he struggled for control. Now she was beginning to understand his pain, his need. Then it burst upon her in dazzling, aching, sweet contractions. When he felt them, he raised up over her to watch. It was like an atonement for Miguel. With each flushed wave of pleasure that suffused her, he made up for some small part of the earlier hurt he had inflicted on his wife.

In a haze of ecstasy, she opened her eyes to look up into his face as he, too, climaxed. Ellie could feel the pulsating emission of his seed into her body, adding to her own sense of fulfillment. He collapsed on her, trembling, and she held him tightly to her, legs and arms locked fiercely around his body.

After they caught their breaths, he carefully rolled them to lie on their sides. Her pale, silvery body was still tinged with dark pink splotches from the intensity of her orgasm. He traced his fingertips softly across her belly, breasts and collarbone, then up her neck, wondering at the sight, as the marks gradually faded. Never with the dark-complexioned girls at the ranch, or even with the fairer women at Rosalie's, had he seen this. Miguel realized he had just shared something unique and wondrous with his wife, but he was unable to find the words to tell her how he felt.

As her body calmed and relaxed into a warm, lethargic satiety, Ellie knew it was beyond her wildest imaginings, but having nothing else to compare it with, she also lay mute.

Finally, he broke the silence, saying simply, "This is how it should be, *pequeña*."

Her whispered "yes" was a soft breath.

He reached down to pull the covers over them and she snuggled into his embrace as if she had been custom-made to fit there for the rest of his life.

Ellie awoke just after daybreak, feeling something was different. She was in Miguel's room, in Miguel's bed and he was sleeping next to her with one arm possessively drapped across her belly! They were both naked and Ellie had never slept unclothed in her life. Miguel lay on his stomach, head turned facing her with one long leg caught over hers. Unable to move without waking him, Ellie took the moment to study her husband in the bright sunlight filtering in the window. She felt the heat of a dark blush as she remembered how bold she had been to come to him last night. What would he think of her wanton behavior in the clear light of morning? For all he was half American, he was still a traditional Californio. Yet he had seemed so pleased with her last night, so hungry to make love to her, so gentle in doing it.

As she drank in his features in repose, Ellie realized with a sudden shock that she loved him, this arrogant Californio, this stranger. Yet no more a stranger. His face was not so hard in sleep, but rather looked boyish despite the dark bristle of whiskers across his jawline. The dense brows and curly black hair invited her caress, as did the beautiful lips and dark lashes veiling those midnight eyes, eyes that had been dilated in passion last night.

When had she fallen in love with him? Her mind flitted back across the months, seeing the unhappy seminarian at the betrothal meeting, the cold stranger in the church, the angry brigand lifting her onto Dominican, the outraged husband on their wedding night. Yet she also remembered the superb horseman who admired her riding, the brave man who risked his life to save Rafael's dog, the sweating ranchero who worked side by side with his men and the charming dance partner at the fiesta. There were many sides to this complex man. Maybe she had always loved him, and only now realized it. *For better, for worse,* she smiled to herself.

Whisper soft, she traced her fingertips across his brow and lips, then down the lean muscles of his shoulder and across the dark hair on his forearm where it lay over her own much lighter flesh.

He stirred and opened his eyes, catching her in hungry perusal of his half-covered body. The arm she caressed tightened and drew her to him.

"Ooh!" Ellie gasped in surprise as her aqua eyes met his dark ones at very close range.

"Good morning, *pequeña*. You see, you did sleep well." His eyes glittered with infectious mirth.

"Vain man!" She blushed furiously, uncertain of how to act with him now. How much of her own feelings should she reveal?

She lowered her lashes when he kissed her good morning, feeling his lips lightly brushing hers, then moving down as he ran his scratchy beard over her delicate throat and shoulders. It felt wonderfully male, and she tingled. One little hand ran up and down his shoulder while the other buried itself in the thick black hair on his head.

"I can't seem to get enough of you, little one," he half-growled as he rolled on top of her, careful to support his weight on his elbows. He kissed her long and thoroughly. Quickly this time, he probed between her legs with his shaft to find her wet and eager, opening to him. He sighed as he slid inside, now welcome and familiar. Ellie tightened her legs around his hips and moved with him to a fast, hard completion that surprised them both with its suddenness.

Her silver-gilt hair was spread across the sheets and tangled beneath his arms. Freeing a coil of springy silk curls, he raised its fragrance to his lips and ran it across his cheek.

Ellie looked up at him in joy, touched by the tender gesture. They lay still, locked together in that most intimate embrace. Each was unwilling to disturb the communion of the moment when a sharp knock sounded. Luz entered the young *patrona*'s room carrying a tray with hot chocolate and fresh bread.

"Doña Ellie, here is . . ." The girl looked at the empty bed before blundering to the open door to Miguel's room, which Ellie had forgotten to close in her nervousness last night. "Ooh! A thousand pardons, *patrón, patrona*!"

Miguel had quickly pulled the sheet up over them as Ellie burrowed beneath him, trying to sink into the mattress. Before he could subdue his laughter and call after the retreating Luz to return later, the girl had vanished, leaving a trail of sloshed cocoa.

"It could have been worse, you know," he got out between chuckles. "If she'd arrived a few minutes earlier, we'd never have known she was watching!"

"Ooh, it's not funny!" Ellie's face was flaming. She could not meet those laughing blue eyes.

He tipped her chin up and kissed her nose. "It's all right, you know, *pequeña*. We *are* married."

She bit her lip, still mortified. "It's different for you. You're ... men are supposed to ... oh, darn!" She spluttered as he watched her, his lips twitching. "If we go downstairs now everyone will know." How could she explain her mortification?

With a straight face, he replied, "Well, we'll just have to be very grave and serious. Keep them guessing."

She smiled weakly at that and he went on, "Don't you think my parents will be happy to know we have a real marriage now?"

Nodding in assent, she felt sure Alex would, but as to Doña Maria—well, she was not deceived where her mother-in-law was concerned. Nor did she think the host of serving girls he'd bedded would be exactly overjoyed either, not to mention Rosalie Parker!

CHAPTER
16

November 1852, Cien Robles

Everyone at Cien Robles could see the young *patrón* and his lady were in love. They rode together frequently, he on

that big, black devil, she on her small, white filly. They
laughed and touched often, caressing each other with their
eyes. She brought basket lunches to where he worked in
the cool November air. The two would excuse themselves,
going off alone to share the repast as the vaqueros called
good-naturedly after them.

Ellie loved her young husband with all her heart. In
fact, she had never been so happy as she was in the past
month, laughing and making love with him. Yet never in
all their light, teasing banter or fierce, sweet passion had
he said that he loved her. *It was a forced marriage,* she
reminded herself. *He didn't choose me.* She should be
grateful that they were compatible, that he found her
sexually attractive, but Ellie wanted more. Perhaps that
would come in time. She would just have to be patient and
hope, trying valiantly to hide the naked love locked deep
in her soul. Nothing could be worse than seeing embarrassed
tolerance or, worse yet, pity, reflected in those midnight
eyes.

Miguel, too, was confused by his feelings. He had
steadfastly told himself for months that he simply wanted
Ellie, that it was pure lust, nothing more. But when she
had come to him, their joining was beyond any feeling he
had ever imagined. Yet he feared to put the name of love
to it. For all his expert tutoring and practice in physical
relations with women during the past year, Miguel had
little experience with them in any other context. He'd
grown up in the shadow of his glib, charming father and
brother, shyly avoiding women. His only female contact
had been with his mother. Maria's religious devotion and
rigid propriety were his only models for female behavior
until he was befriended by Rosalie. Obviously, his wife
was neither a Maria nor a Rosalie.

In addition, the rankling wound of Rice Brighton kept
eating at him like a cancer. Ellie had thought she loved the
foreman even though she had not given herself to him. Her
unchaperoned American upbringing was alien to Miguel.
All the strict religious and cultural mores of his youth still

bound him. Nevertheless, despite his mother's dislike of Ellie and Alex's championing of her, Miguel was helplessly drawn closer to a truth he did not want to confront.

Adrian made an overnight visit the first week in November and expressed his regret to Ellie that he could not be there for her birthday at the end of the month. Miguel overheard the brief conversation and realized how little he still knew about his wife. She would be nineteen on November 27th. If he had not found this out by accident, Ellie's birthday would not have been celebrated.

Miguel made a special request of old Rafael. He also asked his mother to arrange a party. Reluctantly, she agreed, stating they should begin with a special mass and that it was his duty as Ellie's husband to discuss it with Father Sebastian.

Ellie's birthday morning dawned and the house bustled with preparations for a feast, but Miguel and Ellie slept late. It was chilly, although a dim winter sun had made its appearance, casting frail rays in their big bedroom window. Ellie snuggled down into the covers, half-awake, feeling the soft caresses of her husband's fingertips grow more insistent as they stroked her back, then moved over the curve of her buttocks and down the sensitive inside of her thighs. The warm, hard length of his naked flesh rolled next to her, grabbing her from behind to gently squeeze and tease her breasts as he kissed her neck.

"Happy birthday, *pequeña*. Are you ready to face the day?"

"Umm." She arched back into his embrace, feeling his whiskers scratch the tender flesh of her neck. "I guess so. Another year older."

He laughed. "So old, nineteen. You still have a few good years left."

Before they could go further in the playful prelude to making love, a sharp knock at the door caught them unaware.

"What is it?" Miguel said impatiently in Spanish,

knowing it must be a servant and wondering who would dare to interrupt.

In his native language, an embarrassed Manolo replied, "Don Miguel, your mother and Father Sebastian are waiting . . . the family mass in honor of your lady's birthday . . . it is time."

Ellie lurched up in horror, peering at the small wood-encased clock on the mantel across the room. "Miguel! It's almost nine! Why did we oversleep?"

He dismissed Manolo with assurances they'd be down shortly, then sat up, chuckling at her frantic haste. "Why indeed? I seem to recall staying up rather late last night to please this silver witch who—"

She cut him off by throwing a pillow at his dark, tousled head to silence his teasing. Then shivering in the cold, she donned a wrapper and poured water in the basin for her morning ablutions. A discarded lavender silk nightgown lay on the floor beside the bed where it had been carelessly tossed last night. She stepped over it, watching him smile in silent delight.

Like two conspirators they sped down the main stairs and crossed the courtyard to Maria's chapel. Ellie had left her hair simply brushed down her back and Miguel was nicked from a speedy shave. Despite the haste, they were half an hour late.

Alex stood in the door of the chapel, unwilling to spend one minute more within its sanctuary than absolutely necessary. He saluted them with a silent but warm smile, ushering them inside. Doña Maria was kneeling at the front of the small room, deep in prayer. Father Sebastian gently rebuked the tardy ones with sad obsidi-an eyes.

Miguel felt himself squirm as he genuflected, then relaxed a bit. *Damn, I still feel guilty, just like the time when I was ten years old and missed catechism because I was so busy fishing with David.* Ellie, now sensitive to his moods, looked from the sorrowful priest to her husband and sensed something was amiss between them.

The chapel was ornate, with an altar of dark pink marble brought all the way from Mexico. The candlesticks and crucifix were made of the purest gold, elaborately wrought in Spanish rococo style. The air was suffocating with scented candles and their dim amber lights flickered all around. The room gave Alex claustrophobia. Miguel, who had always found it comforting as he grew up, for the first time unwittingly shared the sensation of discomfort with his father. The mass was mercifully brief. Once over, the family adjourned to the dining room for a sumptuous breakfast and the opening of Ellie's birthday gifts.

Just as they sat down at the table, the sound of hoofbeats outside interrupted them. Manolo admitted a visitor to the front hall, a beaming Adrian St. Clair.

"Surprise for the birthday girl!" He gave his delighted daughter a warm bear hug as she squealed excitedly.

"You said you couldn't get back in time, Dad!"

"Well, I decided to make a concerted effort, especially considering what I found in San Francisco for you." He produced a small elaborately wrapped box from his pocket with a wink to Alex, who shared a conspiratorial grin.

Doña Maria, always exquisitely polite, ordered the servants to set a place for Ellie's father. Ham fried with green chilies, *huevos rancheros* swimming in red sauce, stacks of crisp corn tortillas and bowls of brandied fruit were quickly eaten so they could adjourn to the main *sala* where Ellie's presents were waiting.

Doña Maria's gifts were a beautiful rosary and leatherbound prayer book for which Ellie gave her sincere thanks and a warm hug. Her mother-in-law accepted the gratitude graciously, but Ellie could still feel Maria stiffen when she kissed the older woman's cheek. *She'll never accept me no matter what I do,* she thought in well-hidden dismay. Then, as Alex presented a large package to her with a flourish, she put aside her misgivings, refusing to let his wife spoil the day.

When she pulled off the satin ribbons and lay open the

box, the sight took her breath away. It was brocade—the most magnificent weave she had ever seen—yards and yards of it, a dress length for a ball gown. The background was a deep clear violet shot through with patterns of delicately sprigged lavender flowers, creating a shimmering tapestry of silvery purple that changed from pale to dark with the light's reflection.

"Your dressmaker in Los Angeles assures me it will go with your coloring and has a selection of patterns for you to choose from."

"Oh, thank you, Alex!" Ellie gave him a joyous hug and kiss, then picked up the fabric again. "I've never seen anything like it before in any shop."

"I sincerely hope not! It just came off my ship from Canton. It's all the latest rage in San Francisco," Alex added dryly, with a sharp look at Adrian.

Beaming, her father presented his small package to Ellie. She tore into it with the same willful spirit she'd shown at birthdays since she was a small child, much to Adrian's delight.

Again her gasp was audible. Nestled in the satin interior of the case was the most exquisite amethyst jewelry Ellie had ever seen: delicate, prismed earrings and a necklace with the square-cut gemstones set in graduated sizes so that the largest one would nestle just at the top of her breasts. The winking lavender stones were held together by filigreed silver of the most intricate workmanship.

"It matches the material! But how did you two know?" She looked from Adrian to Alex and back.

Alex laughed. "Last month when your father was visiting, we went to the dock to watch cargo being unloaded from my China run. I spied the fancy brocade and took it to Mrs. Valdez for her approval. Adrian took his cue and found a bargain in San Francisco." His friend nodded like a schoolboy set at the head of the class after winning a spelling bee.

Miguel moved forward at this point to gently take the jewelry from Ellie and set it beside the brocade. "Enough of this finery. For my gift you'll have to come to the stable.'' He took her arm and ushered her to the door, gathering wraps from Manolo for her and his mother.

A sudden dread that he might have bought her a sidesaddle flitted through her mind, but she repressed it as the small group walked to the stables. Alex and Adrian chatted, while Adrian graciously included Doña Maria in the conversation, telling her about several old Californio ranchers outside San Francisco who were well-known to the Alvarez family.

Miguel and Ellie, far ahead of the older adults, entered the musty interior of the stable. Ellie blinked her eyes, adjusting to the change in light. Then she saw it, hanging across the rough, oaken bars of Moonlight's stall. Laughing with pleasure, she ran her hands lovingly across the intricately tooled leather and beaten silver trim of the saddle. It was small, custom-made for a woman, but a real western saddle, not a sidesaddle!

''The old one Adrian had made for you is wearing out from all your hellion riding. I thought you might like a new one. It is a bit gawdy, but Rafael gets carried away when he works.''

Her eyes glistened with unshed tears and she was too moved to speak as she flung herself into his arms, holding on to his neck in a deathlock of love. Of any gift he could have given her, he had chosen the most touching way of telling her that he accepted her American ways and felt pride and pleasure in her as his wife.

Miguel, too, felt the emotion that the gift triggered, drawing them closer together. He held her tightly, lifting her feet off the ground and stroking the silky, silver hair that fell below her waist. He understood for the first time what it meant to her, having his approval, and he understood why he gave it.

''Happy birthday, *pequeña*. I love you.'' He breathed the words into her hair and buried his face in its lilac fragrance.

Slowly, she raised her head and looked at him, seeing in those midnight eyes what she'd dreamed of for so long. Her eyes looked like huge aquamarine pools, shimmering with unspoken love and her lips trembled as she placed a small hand on each side of his beloved face, reaching up to kiss him softly and deliberately.

"And I love you, *mí esposo*, more than life I do!" She felt her heart would burst with joy.

The tender moment was interrupted as their parents came noisily into the stable. Maria stiffened as much at seeing them in such intimate communion as at seeing the hated saddle she knew her son had perversely ordered for his wife. She forced a neutral smile as Adrian and Alex admired the workmanship of the little saddle with Ellie and Miguel. He explained that he'd commissioned Rafael. The tooling and silver trim were the old man's artistic genius coming out. It was truly beautiful and Ellie vowed to thank Rafael for his special pains in doing the job so handsomely.

Miguel and Ellie went for a long ride that afternoon, leaving their parents to visit and rest. She took special care with her appearance, dressing in her best deep blue riding skirt and wearing a cream silk shirt open at the throat and clinging to her breasts, covered only to the point of scant propriety with a matching short blue jacket, worn open. They were gone well into the early fall evening. When they came in, flushed and laughing, Maria had already had the cook hold dinner for nearly an hour. Quickly, they changed and joined the family for the meal, then made their excuses to walk in the countyard.

They ambled to the fountain and sat on one of the big stone slabs that edged it, listening to the soft, tinkling music of the water in the still cool night. The air was brisk. Despite the shawl she wore, Ellie was chilled and shivered. Miguel placed an arm around her shoulder and drew her tightly to his side.

"Better? Your dress is too thin for the November air."

She nodded, snuggling into his embrace. "You give off such wonderful heat. I felt it the night we danced at the fiesta. It was cool then, too."

His eyes were merry. "The weather was cool, but you, wild little gypsy, were decidedly not cool. In fact, speaking of heat, you gave off quite a bit, as I recall!"

She reddened in remembrance, then looked up into his face. "I danced to please you."

"And you did, *pequeña,* you did." He stood up, pulling her with him. "Dance with me now!"

Silently, with only the music of the fountain, they locked in a slow, sensuous embrace, scarcely moving their feet. Ellie clung to him in wanton abandon, twining her fingers in his hair, pulling his head down and opening her mouth to give him a fierce, sealing kiss.

Maria left Alex and Adrian to their cigars and brandy. She decided to return to her chapel and pray for surcease from the burning anger that filled her every time she watched her son and his wife. How, oh how, she wanted old Adrian St. Clair to take that scheming minx home to Twin Rivers!

She walked silently from the dining room into the courtyard, to cut across to the chapel. Just then, she caught sight of Ellie pulling Miguel to her in a lewd kiss, molding her little body against his like a practiced harlot, perpetrating an obscene seduction right out in the open courtyard where servants or family could witness it!

"Shameless little bitch," she spat involuntarily. Even as she whispered the words to herself, Maria flinched at her indelicate use of language. She must confess to Father Sebastian and seek his guidance!

Ellie fairly floated downstairs the next morning, still rapturously happy after the most wonderful birthday of her life. Her husband loved her! His words alone were more precious than all the silks and jewels on earth. Before he rode out that morning, he had reaffirmed his declaration of love. Ellie hurried around the corner into the dining room for a light breakfast and collided with Maria.

"Oh, I'm sorry, Mother Kane! How clumsy of me. I wasn't watching where I was going." Effusive in her new happiness, Ellie was willing to be charitable even to her mother-in-law.

Doña Maria, however, was having none of it. "You frequently don't watch what you are doing, or where, I'm afraid, my daughter. I meant to discuss a matter with you today. Perhaps this would be a good time, over breakfast, while the men are occupied?'' It was not a request. Grimly, she ushered Ellie into the breakfast room and over to the sideboard. Silently, they each filled a plate with hot crusty bread, honey and preserved peaches, then moved to one corner of the long oak table. Maria gave thanks for the food and began to eat.

Ellie pushed the fruit around her plate and dipped a crust in the honey. When she tried to swallow it, she nearly choked and quickly took a gulp of the strong black coffee by her plate. She desperately did not want to antagonize Miguel's mother. Now that she and her husband were in love and their marriage was so splendidly happy, she promised herself that she would be patient, but Maria's deep-seated animosity fairly radiated across the table.

Finally, Ellie could stand it no longer. ''You wanted to discuss something with me?'' She struggled to keep the tone of her voice light.

Maria now seemed ill at ease, sensing that Ellie's direct approach meant the girl would not be cowed. ''I don't know how to put this delicately.'' The older woman stopped and primly daubed at her lips with a napkin, then went on in an aggrieved voice. ''For some time now I've noticed the rather open, indeed careless, displays of intimacy you indulge in with my son. Men are, well, quite lax about such matters, but a lady cannot allow herself to act with so little dignity.''

Ellie began to color, anger starting to churn deep in the pit of her empty stomach, burning like the hot black coffee. Before she could speak, however, Maria continued.

''I realize there is a conjugal duty that the Holy Church sanctions, which must be performed for the procreation of children, but that should be left behind closed doors—''

''Where I'm sure you'd be happy to consign it. Behind closed doors and in the dark of night!'' Ellie interrupted furiously. ''I'm sure you considered your duty a horrible penance every time you were forced to do it. Well, I don't share your unnatural revulsion!''

''That is obvious!'' Maria shot back, all pretense at

delicacy dropped. "I saw you playing the harlot by the fountain last night! Right in the midst of my home, in the open courtyard where any and all could watch you entwine yourself with Miguel! It was cheap and vulgar, an offense to any woman who reveres the teachings of the holy faith."

Furiously, Ellie stood up and threw her napkin on the table. "That is not true and you had no right to spy on us!" The very idea made her ill, those cold, black eyes watching something she considered so private, so beautiful.

As she watched Ellie's fury grow, Maria felt herself regaining control. "Before you leave, consider this. I confessed to Father Sebastian this morning. He requests you go see him at once. Your sins of the flesh are beyond countenance. You need spiritual guidance."

"We'll see whose sins are paramount, mine of love or yours of jealousy!" With that, Ellie almost ran to the chapel. The old priest had presided at their marriage. He could not castigate her for loving her own husband, not when Ellie explained the truth. Heaven only knew what the old harridan had told him!

Her interview with Father Sebastian left Ellie shaken. His faith in his saintly *patrona* was unshakable. If Doña Maria felt her daughter-in-law was acting in a lascivious manner, then Ellie must examine her own conscience. Perhaps she did dwell too much on the physical side of her marriage, he chided in a kindly but firm manner. Sins of the flesh were more serious in women than men. She was the young *patrona* who must set an example for others on Cien Robles. The old priest gave her time for prayer and self-reflection, but told her to be ready to make a full confession before Sunday mass.

With trembling fingers she buttoned her blouse and pulled on her heavy riding skirt. She must clear her head by taking a good hard gallop on Moonlight, to work off the worst of her ire before she saw Miguel, lest she tell him harshly what she thought of his mother and his mentor. "Jealous old biddy. If she can't have him, no one can. And as for that blind old priest, he believes every word she says as if she was the Blessed Virgin herself!'' She slammed the door as she left the room.

Ellie had intended to ride out alone to an isolated stretch of land where she could gather her thoughts before she talked to Miguel. But as luck would have it, he was at the corrals when she led Moonlight from the stable. He had come back to speak with the new horsebreaker, hired upon the abrupt departure of Juan Morales.

Seeing Ellie from afar, he walked toward her and the small filly. He could sense something was wrong at once. Her anger, seething below the surface, fairly vibrated off her, even causing the calm little Moonlight to shy and prance.

''*Pequeña*, what's the matter?'' His dazzling smile was warm and infinitely comforting.

Without meaning to, she flew into his arms and began to hiccup her sobbing, furious tale of humiliation, beginning with being upbraided for what Doña Maria saw in the courtyard last night and ending with the whiff of hellfire delivered by Father Sebastian.

Miguel let her get it all out, walking her slowly across the open land between the corral and stable to a copse of oaks on a small knoll. There he drew her down to sit beside him, leaning against one of the big trees. The rich brown leaves blew in the dry November wind.

He sat for a minute, looking at the sky, letting the breeze clear his thoughts, as if struggling for a way to explain to her. ''Ellie, I'm sorry you're caught up in this. It really has nothing to do with you. Oh, little one, how can I explain it to you?''

''Then you don't think I'm a wanton Jezebel who's leading you down the path of damnation!'' It was as if a great weight was lifted from her shoulders. A small part of her feared, once she'd blurted out everything, that Miguel might still align himself with his mother.

He smiled sadly and touched her cheek. ''If you are wanton, you're just the way I want you, and if I'm on my way to perdition, it'll be on my own conscience, not yours, *pequeña*. I'll speak to Father Sebastian tonight and see he gives you some peace. All you have to confess is love. I know that."

"Oh, Miguel, hold me." Ellie turned quickly into his arms and he held her securely, soothing her hurt and fright.

As he stroked her hair, he went on. "Father Sebastian is upset because he wanted a different life for me. He still suffers under the delusion that I could have been a priest. He hoped for it for so long, ever since I was a boy, I guess."

Ellie stirred in his arms. "Did you really want to be a priest, Miguel?" The question still bothered her when she thought of the role she had played in changing his life.

He smiled at her devilishly. "And do you think I'd have made a good one?"

She shook her head.

"Why not?" The question was now one of mock gravity.

"Ah, I fear you'd spend much of your life doing penance for the mortal sin of concupiscence. You'd scarcely have time for anything else!"

He laughed out loud now, tickling her and rolling them both to the ground to nestle in the leaves. "You know me too well, *pequeña*. So, you see why the good father despairs. You're a woman and therefore to blame. After all, it was Eve who tempted Adam in the garden."

She made a little sputter of disgust at that bit of theology, then sat up to run her hand through his hair. "In that case, I'd better do what's expected of me." And with that, she lowered her head and kissed him ardently.

They lay still in their warm, sunlit bower of rustling leaves for several minutes, just holding one another. Ellie felt a profound sense of gratitude for his support and acceptance. She had been foolish to doubt, but there was still his mother.

Slowly, tentatively, she began, "Miguel, I understand about Father Sebastian, but I'm afraid, well, I don't understand about your mother. I've tried to please her—oh, not at first. I know I was horrid, but this past month, since we've, we've been..."

"Lovers," he supplied gently, allowing her to go on.

She flushed, holding on to him tightly and continued,

"Yes, well, it seems instead of being pleased that our marriage is so good now, she's angry with me, as if she blames me for something. I don't know what to do." She shrugged helplessly and forced herself to meet his dark blue gaze.

He sighed and took a deep breath. "I'm afraid I haven't been exactly fair to you about Mama either. I'd hoped in time she'd come to accept us, maybe she will someday, if there are children."

"Well, I'll be happy to work on that if you think it'll help," she whispered, snuggling deeper in his arms.

He smiled and kissed the top of her nose. "Yes, so will I, believe me! But I can't promise even grandchildren will make Mama change her mind about you."

"Because I'm a Yankee, not a true Californio from an old Mexican family?"

Now it was his turn to shrug. "In some part, I'm afraid it's true, but it's more complicated than that. You see, she wanted me to be a priest, too. It was her dearest wish. All her life, the church has been her haven, her only solace and defense against my father. He's tyrannized her and made her life hell. Her father forced her to marry Papa. There was no love, only greed. Grandfather Alvarez sold her to him. It took a fortune to restore Cien Robles. Papa never lets her forget whose money kept the land grant for her.

"That was only the beginning. He's always been arrogant and cruel, flaunting his mistresses in front of her, ridiculing her traditional ways and making it clear that she was good for only one purpose—to provide the future Kane heirs to Cien Robles. She's never known a husband's love, Ellie. Try to understand. After all I've put you through, you must know what bastards we Kane men really are."

Vehemently, she shook her head. "That's not fair! If we had a bad beginning, it was my fault, too, and we've succeeded together. You seem to hate the part of you that's like your father. Is the resemblance so dreadful?"

"Yes! It is. I'm like him, like David, so much more than I ever guessed, but I'm not proud of it." His face was set in tight, bitter lines.

"That's wrong, unfair, not only to you but to Alex. Oh, Miguel, he's not all bad. I know about his reputation in town." She thought to herself, *And yours, too, my love.* But she said aloud, "There's another side to him that's kind. He does love the land and maybe he sacrificed too much for it, I don't know. I do know it takes two people to make a marriage fail. You see only one side of it. He wants to—"

"Don't ever defend my father to me, Ellie!" He cut her off, getting up in an abrupt, catlike roll. He began to pace back and forth in the leaves, grinding them beneath his boots. "You don't understand how he really is and what he's done to my mother. I can't begin to tell it all. I don't want to. You'll just have to make the best of it around here and I'll try to get her to do the same."

Slowly, Ellie stood up, brushing the leaves from her clothes. As she watched him speak and pace, she could feel the anguish burning deeply within him. There was much more here than she understood. All she knew was that she had hurt him terribly with her attempt to act as mediator between him and Alex.

"I'm sorry, my love. I don't understand, but I will try. Please, be patient with me and I will be kind to your mother." She added under her breath, "If it kills me."

He strode across the distance separating them and they embraced once again. There was confusion and doubt, but there was also love.

"Why does your son hate you?" Ellie stood just inside the door to Alex's study, addressing him in a low, intense voice as she closed the door silently behind her.

The tall old man behind the desk paused in pouring his usual before-dinner rum and looked over at his determined little daughter-in-law.

He grinned crookedly and downed a gulp of the fiery liquid. "You don't believe in sugaring a question any, do you, girl?"

"I—I think I have a right to know. I'm caught in the crossfire between Miguel, Maria and you and I don't understand why you all tear at each other so. Your wife

certainly won't tell me and my husband can't. It—it hurts
him too much to talk about. I inadvertently caused him
more pain this afternoon. You said you'd be my friend,
Alex, and you have been. I'm grateful, more than I can
express, but I have to understand—"

He held up his hand as a gesture of surrender, then sat
down in his big high-backed chair by the window, motioning
her into another one across from it. "It's true, you do have
a right to know, but it will tarnish me in your sight, my
dear, so I hate to be the bearer of painful truth. Yet so be
it. I suppose you've gathered that Maria and I never
exactly had a felicitous marriage?"

Ellie nodded. "Miguel told me about his grandfather
accepting a large cash settlement from you in return for her
unwilling hand in marriage. That you wanted Cien Robles,
not her. I understand about her dislike of Americans.
That's part of why she resents me. But her own sons are
half-Yankee and she loves Miguel . . ." Her voice trailed
off into puzzled silence.

"Yes, she loves Miguel. He's the Alvarez, you see, the
dark one who bears the resemblance to his blueblooded
Californio progenitors, not to me."

"But that's not true, he does resemble you! His eyes,
his mannerisms, his build, there's as much Kane as Alvarez
in him."

He smiled with such wistful sadness that she was reminded
of that day on the knoll when he spoke to her of his forlorn
hope for grandchildren. "Yes, I see that now, and so does
his mother, but as a boy, well, both of us were blind. Did
you ever meet David?"

The question startled her, but she nodded uncertainly.
"Yes, once or twice when you came to visit Dad. I was
just a girl and didn't take much notice."

"David is my mirror image," he said with bitter irony.
"As I watched him grow up with his blond hair and wild
Yankee daring, it was as if I was looking at myself as a
youth. I've old portraits, quite good likenesses of me
as a child. David's are interchangeable with them. He was
my adored son, the one I lavished everything on, took with

me everywhere I went, tried to mold into a replica of me in mind and spirit as well as body. Even took him to his first whorehouse when he was just fourteen. That shock you, girl?'' He looked across at her, taking his eyes off the window and fixing his level midnight gaze on her.

"No, but I think I begin to understand. If you lavished everything on David, there wasn't much left for Miguel.''

Grimly, he nodded. "Oh, I wanted another heir, another son. One's too chancy, you know, for an arrogant young landholder, a phony grandee, if you wish. I had to have a backup. But after two daughters were stillborn, Maria swore I'd never come near her again.''

At Ellie's look of shocked surprise, he went on, "Neither David nor Miguel knows about them. You're the first person I've told. David was only three when the second girl was born. I never wanted to talk about it. Maria felt it was God's judgment on our unholy wedlock. She detested David for being alive and healthy, looking exactly like the man who caused her such pain. She—well, to put it bluntly, Ellie—she hated sex. At first I thought it was me, the way I forced her to marry me, because I was American, but that wasn't really it. I don't think she could ever...'' His voice faded and he gazed at the window in embarrassment. "Hell, needless to say, I found other diversions and left her alone. You can't imagine what it does to a man's ego, Ellie, to have his own wife shrink from his touch with revulsion, to submit herself in tight-lipped misery, saying her rosary all the while. I swore I'd never go near her again. Then, as I got a little older and richer and thought on it more, I decided pride be damned, I needed another heir.'' He chuckled mirthlessly here. "Even recruited the bishop to talk to her about her duty and what the church requires a wife to do. So, she suffered my attentions briefly and Miguel was the result. It was as if she had been waiting for him—another Alvarez to ally with her against me. Since she nearly died when he was born and was so overjoyed to have a live, healthy child who didn't look like his sire, well, I let her have him.'' He sighed and gazed out the window.

When he resumed speaking, his voice was raw with pain. "We had an agreement, unspoken and gradually arrived at, but binding nonetheless. I had David, she had Miguel. How little we really know of other people, Ellie. How vain and stupid and wasteful we can be. David was like me in many ways. He defied my every command, never wanted to be tied down as a youth. Just like me. I left my father and ran off to sea. He ran off to war, then..."

She smiled weakly and said, "He ran off to escape marrying me."

"Oh, it wasn't really you, child. It was all the responsibilities to the land. Ironic, don't you see? I sold my soul and sacrificed Miguel to hold this land for David, who never wanted it! By the time I realized that Miguel loved the land, that he was the one born to run Cien Robles, the one the inheritance belonged to..."

"He is the one you loved too late and could never tell?" Her aqua eyes were glistening with unshed tears. Now she understood.

"You're a fine, perceptive lass and you love him. I'm the one who should be grateful, Eleanor. Love my son for me. He'll accept it from you, not me. Never from me..."

CHAPTER
17

February 1853, Cien Robles

Through the wet months of winter, Miguel worked almost as hard as he had during spring and fall rodeos. It was the season to ride to the line camps and see how the isolated herds of cattle were faring, to check on the remuda, the spare cowponies the vaqueros drew from when a mount was injured or killed. All Cien Robles matériel had to be mended and new things ordered—food staples, seed for spring crops, barrel staves for wine casks, a new olive press—the list was endless.

Ellie watched her husband and father-in-law work closely together. Increasingly, she could see the resemblances between them, but she also sensed the undercurrent of animosity. Alex was too proud to offer peace and admit his love for his son; Miguel was too stubborn to accept it. The stalemate continued. She would stand at the window of the big *sala* on winter days and look out toward the corrals where the two tall, lean men conferred. "They are so alike even if one is fair and the other dark," she mused. Miguel would issue a withering reprimand to a vaquero treating a horse roughly or throw back his head to laugh at a jest and look just like his father. He was Alex's alter ego, those same flashing blue eyes, that wonderful smile.

She often observed Alex gazing sadly at his son's retreating figure. Only she knew the pain that he suffered and saw it etched in his face. But at least father and son were running Cien Robles together. Alex had delegated almost everything to Miguel, acting only as advisor. He spent most of his time overseeing his shipping business in Los Angeles. They were civil at meals, both making the effort for Ellie's sake, she was sure, although she knew they argued in private. Alex even curbed his acerbic tongue when he spoke to Maria—no small feat. Ellie knew he did it out of a desire to please Miguel, not because of any feelings for his wife.

Maria had realized she could not win her son's affection by attacking his wife. Indeed, Ellie was irritatingly eager to make her peace with her mother-in-law and was supported by Miguel at every opportunity. Although he was unfailingly kind to her, Maria could see his first loyalty was now to his wife. Grudgingly, she relented, not wanting to risk an open confrontation with her son.

For all the tensions and sorrows seething beneath the surface, Miguel and Ellie were happy in their newfound love, experiencing a closeness with another human being that neither of them had known before. Both were learning how to trust after childhoods of loneliness and isolation. With each other, they were whole.

Eighteen fifty-three came quickly and soon the warm hints of an early California spring followed. Before the frantic work of rodeos again absorbed them, Adrian St. Clair decided to celebrate his sixty-fifth birthday at the end of February with a big fiesta at Twin Rivers. He would use the occasion to officially announce the merger of the two largest spreads in Southern California. After all, he was older than Alex and before long, he'd be gone. Twin Rivers would pass to his daughter and son-in-law.

Ellie was nervous. It felt so strange being back at Twin Rivers after living for eight months at Cien Robles. She felt as though she was dreaming as she dressed the first morning after her arrival. She was in the master bedroom of the Twin Rivers ranch house, which Adrian had not used since his wife died. It was large with big windows facing south and west, admitting the brilliant colors of the Pacific sunset through small, beveled panes of glass. The hardwood floors were waxed to a high luster and braided rugs in deep blues and browns were scattered about. The mahogany furniture, polished every week, still glowed like new.

Looking around, Ellie felt like an intruder. "I never really knew you," she said softly, touching the gilt-edged frame of the daguerreotype of a frail blonde woman with delicate features. It was taken the year she died. Aside from her silver-gilt hair and small bone structure, Ellie felt she had not taken after the Waggoners. Squirrel-tough and fiery-tempered, she was every inch old Adrian's daughter.

Ellie had come to Twin Rivers five days early to prepare for the huge celebration. Several Cien Robles servants, including the redoubtable butler Manolo, and a number of maids, Sarita among them, came with her. Ellie would not have chosen the sullen girl, considering her past relationship with Miguel, but Doña Maria was still in charge of the household and made the selection. Ellie acceded to her mother-in-law's wishes. She could hardly voice the real reason for her objections and offend the old lady's delicate sensibilities.

Miguel would not arrive at Twin Rivers until the evening of the fiesta and Ellie missed him terribly. Each night spent alone in the big four-poster bed was successively harder to bear.

The third afternoon of her visit she encountered Rice Brighton in the kitchen. Ever since she planned the trip to Twin Rivers, Ellie had dreaded the possibility of a chance meeting with him. Rice stood by the big oak chopping table in the middle of the room, leaning indolently against it while he drank some cool cider just poured by Sarita. Before Ellie could turn to leave, he straightened and looked her up and down in the familiar fashion that had been exciting when she was a green girl. Now it was repellent to her.

"Howdy, Miss Ellie, or I guess it's Doña Eleanora now?" He grinned boyishly, using all his charm.

Ellie smiled stiffly. She remembered the last time she had seen him in the line shack. "Mrs. Kane will do nicely."

He stopped smiling.

Ellie had never told anyone that he'd attempted to rape her. Indeed, she tried hard to blot it from her mind. All her girlhood romantic dreams had been ground under the heel of this handsome, crafty schemer. Looking at him now, she was appalled at her own gullibility. Small wonder her dad forbade her to marry the fortune hunter! As she compared him to her husband, she could not believe that she had ever fancied herself in love with Rice Brighton.

He obviously had not given up on her, however. As she issued crisp orders to Sarita she could feel his hot, lascivious gaze on her.

He leaned back and sipped his cider. "Being lady of two manors seems to agree with you, *Mrs*. Kane." He stressed the title almost insultingly. "You look in the bloom of health."

Gritting her teeth at his studied testing of her, she turned and smiled oversweetly. "Perhaps I'm just in love, Mr. Brighton."

He raked her again with those cold gray eyes and quiried softly, "With your husband or with Cien Robles?"

Remembering her lurid confession to him about her impending marriage, she flushed in embarrassment as well as anger at his presumption. She shot back, "Unlike some crude individuals, I consider a human being of infinitely more worth than material possessions."

He smiled that slow, infuriating grin once more and excused himself to go back to work. In a corner, washing baking tins, Sarita noticed the exchange and vowed to find out what had gone on between the *patrona* and the St. Clair foreman.

Finally, the afternoon of the fiesta arrived. Ellie ordered a huge tub of hot water and put her favorite lilac bath salts in it. Just as she eased beneath the surface of the water and began to inhale the fragrance, the door opened into the bedroom. Eyes closed in luxuriation, she assumed it was Luz, bringing her ball gown.

"Just put it on the bed and leave, please. I want to be by myself for a while."

"Some welcome after five days of sleeping alone!" Miguel strode to the tub.

Ellie stood, heedless of the water sloshing from the tub, and threw her arms around his neck, kissing him exuberantly. "Oh, darling! I didn't expect you for hours yet. I've missed you so much."

Smelling the warm, floral sweetness of his wife's naked body, Miguel groaned, leaning over to embrace her more closely, running his hand up and down her wet back, slick with lilac perfume. "*Pequeña*, five days without you was hell, not to mention the nights." He ran his palm over one small, silvery breast, then cupped it in his hand as she arched against him, gasping in pleasure and surprise.

"Oh, I've gotten you soaking wet!"

It was true. The whole front of his shirt and vest were drenched, as was the back of his neck and his shoulders. He laughed. "I smell like a mixture of horse sweat and lilacs. I'll get some strange looks tonight if I don't bathe. For now, though, I'll just watch you while I undress. They're bringing more hot water—unscented, I trust—for my bath."

As she sponged herself slowly, she never took her eyes off him as he stripped shirt and vest, boots and pants. And while he undressed, he watched her bathe. When he was naked, he reached over for the big white linen bath towel and held it, waiting to dry her. She stepped dripping from the tub, incredibly beautiful as the water ran in delicate patterns across the sleek curves of her pointed breasts and slim hips. One drop hung suspended in her navel. He reached out a fingertip to dislodge it, tracing its descent into the silver-gilt patch of fur below as she gasped in soft pleasure. Her eyes feasted on him, on his splendid male nakedness, staring at dense black chest hair that tapered below his lean waist toward the erect shaft protruding from a thick black bush. His legs were long and hard, like the rest of his body, taut with muscle that rippled beneath the skin. She reached up and softly raked her dripping nails along his arms and down his chest, down further to gently enfold his pulsing phallus in her wet little hands. It was his turn to gasp.

"If we don't wait until I get a bath, *pequeña*, you'll smell like horse sweat and have to bathe all over again."

"I don't care. As you said, *mí esposo*, it's been five days and five nights." On tiptoe she arched her hips against him and he growled deep in his throat as he scooped her up in the towel, tossing the small bundle effortlessly on the big four-poster just across from the tub.

Quickly, he followed her onto the bed, unwrapping her like a gift. He rolled her across the big bed, pulled the linen towel away and threw it to the floor. Then he stretched out beside her, his long dark body enveloping her slight pale one, to begin a long searing kiss. She opened her mouth eagerly. When she began to buck and arch against him, he held her slender hips in his hands, quieting her with soft Spanish endearments. Then very slowly, he spread her thighs and slid inside her with an anguished groan of pleasure. Ellie held on to his shoulders, raising up to sheath him, letting him set a calmer pace so that he could hold off and bring her to pleasure first. It did not take long until she gasped in surprise at the suddenness and intensity of her orgasm. Miguel felt the shuddering of her slight frame and quickly let go of his own iron control to join her. As they lay in the chilled room, panting from the exertion, sweating and satiated, he glanced over to the fireplace. The low fire set to warm her as she bathed had burned out, but they had not noticed.

Gently, he nuzzled her neck. "I was right. You smell like horse sweat now, just like me. Back in the tub with you, *pequeña.*"

She let out a low, seductive chuckle. "No, I smell like *man* sweat, which I happen to prefer." She rubbed a drop of perspiration off his chest and purred.

The sounds of laughter and music drifted upstairs as Ellie was finishing her toilette. The dress of lavender brocade glittered and gleamed, throwing off dark and light patterns as she moved. Its skirt was very full with a tightly fitted waist that emphasized her slenderness. The deep V of the princess waist was repeated in the décolletage. Her amethyst necklace nestled in her cleavage. Luz piled her hair high on her head and used a curling iron to create a welter of soft ringlets, with several sleek long curls falling over her right shoulder. Nervously, she put the dangling prisms of amethyst in her ears and tilted her head to watch them reflect the light.

"All silver and lilac, even your eyes look smokey and mysterious." Miguel came silently across the braided rug. He had entered the room and found her posing in front of the floor-length oval mirror in the alcove. God, but she was a vision! Alex's and Adrian's gifts were a perfect foil for her hair and coloring. The aquamarine depths of her eyes looked darker, almost silver-gray. She would, without doubt, be the most beautiful woman at the celebration and she belonged to him. Miguel still did not trust the depth of emotion he felt for his wife. At times like this, it scared him. "You're breathtaking, Ellie."

She turned with a radiant smile to inspect his dark gray suit, studded with silver. His shirt front was stark white and elaborately ruffled as were the shirt cuffs. A severe black sash and intricately tooled black dress boots completed the look of masculine elegance.

"You look magnificent," she said simply, gliding over to caress his dark cheek, freshly shaven and smooth, knowing by the time the party was over it would again be scratchy with the growth of black beard she loved.

When they came downstairs arm in arm, many of Adrian's friends commented on what a superb couple they were. A brilliant match made by two wily old rancheros. Small wonder Kane and St. Clair were the two largest landholders in Southern California. They were the sharpest businessmen.

The house was lit from attic to cellar. Throngs of people spilled onto the patio and into the flower gardens at the side of the house. The night was starry and warm, promising an early spring. There were several bands, as Adrian had hired a group of Yankee fiddle and banjo players, as well as the Mexican mariachis who played at all the fiestas. A pianist played melodies on the antique piano so prized by Ellie's mother. Tables of food were set throughout the house and grounds. Whiskey, wine and homebrewed beer from Adrian's cellar flowed freely.

Miguel's early arrival, their lovemaking and the rush to get ready had taken Ellie's mind off any possible confrontation with Rice Brighton, but as they mingled with the guests, wealthy neighbors and common cowhands alike, Ellie was once again reminded that everyone in the county had been invited. Rice would doubtless be present. At least in the press of such a crowd, she could hope to avoid him.

Midway through the evening, Adrian called for attention in the enormous living room and people crowded around him. When the din lowered, his big voice boomed out. "I have an announcement to make. In fact, I have several, some surprises, some not. First of all, I want to present our children, the heirs of Twin Rivers and Cien Robles."

A boisterous round of applause and cheers accompanied his introduction of Miguel and Ellie. Then Adrian proudly explained that the two ranches were to be merged and that he and Alex were going to step down from direct control in the next few years. Miguel Kane would be running both places.

From the time of the betrothal agreement Miguel had realized this would ultimately happen, but his father-in-law's words, nevertheless, caused him some consternation. The responsibility was awesome, yet Adrian and Alex stood there beaming, placing their trust in him. God! He wasn't even twenty-four years old yet! Sensing the direction of his thoughts, Ellie squeezed his hand in a brief gesture of reassurance. He smiled down at her with a look of love and pride shining in his eyes.

Alex spoke up then. "Adrian and I decided if the places would become united, as have our offspring, then a new name and a new brand were in order. And tonight, as a surprise, we're unveiling it. Twin Rivers and Cien Robles will one day put this *fierro* on every steer hip—Oak River." He unfurled a piece of steer hide with the new brand burned on it.

The two men had decided to combine elements from both ranch names for the new brand. They took the mark for the river from Adrian's brand, and added an "O" for the oaks of Cien Robles.

In the forefront of the crowd, the whole family was gathered, including Maria. Ellie was immediately delighted with Alex's surprise, realizing how hard he and her father must have worked on the new brand. She felt Miguel stiffen as she proudly placed her hand on his arm during the unveiling. A look of black fury flashed over his face and passed between him and his mother, who was standing across from them. Questioningly, Ellie pressed his arm again and he turned his attention from his mother.

She whispered, "What is it, what's wrong?"

Looking down at her with his haughtiest Californio air, a look strangely reminiscent of his Yankee father, he said, "Did you know about this?"

Ellie was taken aback at his sudden accusatory manner. "No, it was their surprise for us, but I don't understand. Surely you don't object to the brands being combined, since both ranches will be ours someday?"

Seeing her look of baffled hurt, he softened slightly. "I'll explain later."

Ellie was not mollified. She knew Miguel's angry mood had something to do with Doña Maria, who stood ashen and shaking as everyone in the crowd offered congratulations. When would the merger take place? So exciting and such a great challenge for a young man! Miguel stiffly but politely responded to the well-wishers and left the question of when his father and father-in-law would retire to be answered by them. Shortly, the music struck up again and Miguel cut through the press to take his mother's arm and walk with her toward the hallway leading upstairs. Ellie smiled at well-meaning friends and expressed her excitement and pleasure to Adrian and Alex. Gradually, the crowd thinned and everyone went back to dancing and feasting.

Adrian was bubbling over with good humor and was oblivious to Miguel's displeasure. "Where'd that young man of yours go, Ellie? I need to arrange a time for him to meet my men."

At this, Ellie blanched. "Dad, about the men, will Rice be working under Miguel directly?" The thought of *that* had not occurred to her until this minute.

He patted her hand in dismissal, laughing. "Now, don't fret, honey. I have no doubt Miguel could handle him, but there'll be no need." He lowered his voice, walking her into a small alcove by the French doors leading to the patio. "By the time we get things set up, Brighton won't be a foreman here anymore, or likely anyplace else."

At this cryptic remark she looked up sharply. She had suspected Rice's unscrupulous nature ever since that day at the line shack when he'd hinted at murder, but she'd dismissed it as the brag of a man who simply wanted to seduce and live off a married woman. Was he really dangerous? She paled, thinking he might actually try to kill Miguel.

Again, Adrian assured her, "Don't look so frightened. I'm not going to shoot the varmint, although I don't doubt he deserves it. Ellie, I know you sort of worshipped him as a kid, but I've been doing some quiet checking on missing cattle over the past year or so, and it seems my suspicions are finally beginning to be confirmed. Rice is involved. I don't know the details for sure yet, but I think I'll have him in a few weeks."

"Rustling?" She whispered it in a gasp.

He nodded, adding, "This isn't the time or place to discuss it. I know you're fond of him, honey—"

She interrupted sharply, "No! I—I mean that was over before I married Miguel. I've known he was no good since—well, never mind, I just found out. But rustling! Oh, Dad, be careful!"

"I've lived sixty-five years and no one's done for me yet, so you don't need to fret. When I'm sure of all the facts, I'll sit down with Alex and Miguel and tell them the whole story. In the meanwhile, my foreman might just be looking at the wrong end of a rope. For now, though, I don't want you to say a word to anyone, especially not to the servants. You know how things get out."

For over an hour Ellie mingled with guests and danced, searching in vain for Miguel. Well, damn him, if he chose to spend the whole evening with his mother, there was nothing she could do about it. The thought of going upstairs and interrupting their private conversation made her stiffen her chin resolutely. She'd not stoop to search him out.

As she danced with Dan Mather, one of Adrian's banker friends, she considered her husband's strange behavior. Suddenly, someone cut in on Mather. Before she regained her wits, Rice Brighton was smiling as he whirled her around the floor. Damnation, the last thing she needed!

Just as she was about to make an acerbic request to leave the floor, she saw Miguel standing just outside the patio door. That witch Sarita was hanging on his coat-sleeve, pouting prettily. He was hardly rebuffing her, either. Ellie looked back at Rice and smiled archly.

"You having a good time, Mrs. Kane? You're certainly the belle of the ball. I've never seen such a beautiful woman as you look tonight." His gray eyes were glowing with passion.

Although she was immune to his flattery and distrusted his motives, Ellie needed some balm for her wounded female vanity. She'd just spent an hour foisted from man to man while her own husband thought it better to hide with his mother, then reappeared with his doxy!

"Yes, thank you, Mr. Brighton. I'm having a splendid evening. My father always could throw a wonderful party." The dance was a waltz and it made her slightly giddy and breathless.

Rice whirled her about expertly, enjoying the flushed, exquisite beauty she radiated. Once again he cursed Adrian St. Clair and all the Kane clan, vowing he'd claim this lovely girl for himself, one way or another. Then he'd take her down a peg from her high-and-mighty airs.

"Your husband will have a man-sized job cut out for him pretty soon. Twin Rivers men won't take kindly to working for a Kane, especially one who's half-Mex."

Ellie stiffened and replied, smiling through gritted teeth, "That would be peculiar since half Dad's men are of Mexican ancestry themselves. Even those who aren't— why ever should they object to my husband? He does speak English, Rice!" Her anger had caused her to slip back into the old habit of using his first name. She could have bitten her tongue.

As if sensing her discomfiture, he chuckled. "I was wondering how long we'd be so formal, Ellie. Seeing how I watched you grow up and, ah, other things, I don't think we need to use last names, do you, Ellie?"

His galling familiarity and allusions to their past relationship infuriated her. Levelly, she looked at him and said, "Since I'll probably never speak to you again, it's a matter of supreme indifference to me. Will you escort me from the floor or shall I just go, leaving you looking most unchivalrous?"

His face darkened, the faint reddish veins beneath his eyes standing out in repressed fury. "Whatever your ladyship desires."

Before Rice sought Ellie out to dance, he had arranged to have Sarita waylay Miguel. That gave Brighton time to hold the beautiful woman he'd almost snared for his own, and for Miguel to see his wife in her old sweetheart's arms.

"Who is that man Ellie's dancing with, Sarita?" Miguel had been trying to get free of the wench, but now he decided she could be a useful source of information.

"Oh, him." She made the "him" sound both ominous and sensual at the same time. Quickly, she saw Miguel's jealousy and knew she could fuel it. "That is Don Adrian's foreman. Rice Brighton is his name. You have never met him? How strange, since he is such a good friend of Doña Ellie's."

"What do you mean by that?" His face was a thundercloud now.

"Oh, only that they talked in the kitchen the other day about old times. Cook said they were *novios* once. Oh, but that was long ago, I am sure, Don Miguel."

Her protestation obviously did nothing to soothe him. Just as he was about to burst in the room and drag Ellie away, he reconsidered. Damn if he'd be a fool, making a jealous spectacle of himself in front of the guests. He chatted amicably with Sarita, all the while covertly studying his rival.

The man was older, probably thirty, he guessed. Miguel felt young and unsophisticated as he watched the big, handsome Americano and Ellie waltzing across the floor while carrying on a laughing conversation. He was holding her closely and often glanced at her breasts, partly revealed by the low-cut gown. Brighton had watched her grow up since girlhood, had a lifetime's worth of experiences with her on

Twin Rivers. He was attractive in that fair, Yankee way so many women admired, with heavy bones and bulging muscles. His light tan hair was wavy and well barbered. Yes, he'd be quite appealing to a young girl.

While Miguel was tallying up Brighton's assets and growing depressed, the couple abruptly left the floor, heading toward the hall doorway where Alex and Adrian stood. Miguel extricated himself from a grinning Sarita and walked straight across the crowded room. By the time he reached the door, Brighton had vanished into the crowd and Ellie's petite form was almost obscured by her father and Alex. With little more than a curt nod to them both, he whisked her onto the dance floor.

"I see you've been well taken care of in my absence, *pequeña*. Brighton is a very good dancer. I wonder what else he's good at." His voice was low and crackled with repressed fury.

She reacted as if he had slapped her, missing a step in the slow, easy cadence of the dance. "Why, you—you jealous, petty tyrant," she hissed. "First you go off for an hour with your mother, leaving me alone to dance with any passing stranger, then you reappear with one of your paramours hanging all over you, and you have the unmitigated gall to lecture me when all I did was dance for a couple of minutes with my father's foreman! He cut in on Dan Mather. What was I supposed to do? Run to my husband for protection? You were otherwise occupied!" By this time she was out of breath with anger and her voice was rising dangerously loud.

They were near the door to the back hallway which led upstairs. He quickly shoved her through the passage and followed. When they were in the hall, he headed for the stairs, fairly dragging her along until they reached their room.

"Calm down, Ellie. You're the one creating a scene now. You were afraid I would earlier, remember?" His voice softened as he watched her gulp for air, her face no longer flushed but ashen. "Damn, two shaking women in one night's just more than I can handle, *pequeña*. I'm sorry." He stepped toward her and enfolded her in his arms, confessing, "You're right, I was jealous. And I had no right to listen to Sarita's gossip and storm after you. Forgive me?"

Ellie tightened her arms about his waist and stilled her trembling as he stroked her back. His touch was soothing and so were his words. "Yes, yes, of course. I'm sorry I got so hysterical, too. I—I don't like Rice Brighton and I didn't want to dance with him." She added darkly, "I only did it to make you jealous when I saw Sarita. Oh, Miguel, why do we hurt each other?"

As she looked up in earnest entreaty, he took her small beautiful face in his hands and studied the glistening unshed tears in her eyes. Then he lightly brushed each eyelid with a kiss, causing the droplets to fall in silvery trails down her cheeks. As he wiped them away with his fingertips, he said, "Maybe because we love each other too much?"

"Never that, there can't ever be too much love, my darling." She reached up and kissed him back. "Hold me, just hold me."

"I'll never let you go, *pequeña*."

From the curve of his shoulder where her head nestled, she spoke in a muffled voice. "Miguel, what happened to your mother? You were both so angry earlier. She was shaken. What was it?"

He let out a low, whistling breath, then drew her to a big overstuffed chair next to the unlit fireplace. He sat down and pulled her onto his lap. "Ellie, did you ever think about what Cien Robles means to us?"

She looked blank a second, then said, "How do you mean that? It's your inheritance, your family's land, just as Twin Rivers is mine. Now they're ours."

"With an English name and brand," he said bitterly. "Cien Robles is a Spanish name. The land has been in the Alvarez family for three generations—four, counting me. Ellie, my mother has watched her whole heritage trampled underfoot. Her customs, her flag, now even her language. The new name must be American. Alex did it as another slap at her, another vindictive way to show her that he's won.''

''But that's not fair! Oh, don't you see, how can he win and she lose if *you* are in charge? Besides, my father, who never thought of hurting your mother, helped plan this. He may even have thought of the name. You let your hate for Alex blind you to reason. They meant well, Miguel. I'm sorry about the way things are changing for the Californios. I grew up in Mexican California. I didn't want a war, neither did my father or yours, but things are what they are and no one can change them. California is a part of the United States now and you're half-American by birth.''

He grimaced in disgust at that

''That's the root of it, still the real issue, isn't it, Miguel? You don't hate Yankees in general, you just hate your father.''

''Leave it alone, Ellie. I told you how I feel, how my mother feels. We're losing our inheritance. Even if I keep it in name, it's the Kane name and every trace of the customs, language, the way of life she and I grew up with will be obliterated in time.''

She sighed helplessly. ''What can we do? What would you like to call our land, Miguel? It will be ours, and our children's, but they'll be three-fourths Yankee.'' She looked at him with a question in her eyes.

He smiled sadly at her. ''I'm not blaming you, my lovely little gringa. Come here.'' He drew her closely against his chest and tipped her head back to kiss her slowly, savoringly. ''We'll have beautiful children, like their mother.''

''Well, I'm glad that's all right. I do want to start a family,'' she murmured dreamily as she rubbed her silky little chin against his cheek. Already, she could feel the faint scratch of a beard. ''But what about a new name? You could choose one. I know Dad and Alex would be willing.''

''As a matter of fact, for a long time I've thought about the two places, and a simple brand. Double *R*.''

She looked quizzically at him.

"Rio del Robles. Two *R*'s. Easier for a smith to make the irons and it means the same thing as Oak River. If all that'll be left in California is a few Spanish place names, at least I want to keep that."

"Then tell Dad and Alex tonight!" Her eyes were bright.

He shook his head. "No, let it go for now. Nothing's been done or will be for quite a while. Neither your father nor mine is exactly in his dotage, and I need to get to know Twin Rivers, the people and the land first. That's plenty to do."

Thinking about Rice and the rustling, she silently agreed.

CHAPTER
18

April 1853, Cien Robles

The shadowy figure of Rice Brighton slunk between the trees, vanishing into their black embrace to wait and watch. He was sweating in the cool April twilight as he watched the big hacienda of Cien Robles. Sarita was late, damn the bitch! She had been useful ever since he'd met her several months ago at the Twin Rivers fiesta. She was Miguel Kane's cast-off mistress, jealous and embittered. Sarita wanted Miguel and Rice wanted Miguel's wife. They were natural allies.

Sarita had her uses. When she had boasted to him that she was Ellie's personal maid he was pleased. She would be a first-rate source of information. She had told him

Ellie had a fortune in jewelry kept in her bedroom, the bedroom she shared with that greaser bastard she married! He ground his teeth in rage as he looked at the lighted windows where Ellie was doubtlessly preparing to bed with him. *Where is Sarita?*

Rice had turned on his charm, flattering her and telling her how stupid Miguel was to desert her for his pale gringa wife. Sarita was a good piece in bed, passionate and experienced, but he found her possessive and bad-tempered. He would be glad to be rid of her. First, however, he needed her to steal the jewels.

He cursed his rotten luck. Adrian St. Clair had trapped him, nearly caught him, too. That last herd he'd set up for the bunch to steal had been watched. His crew of rustlers were routed and several captured. Billy Malley, a panicky boy, had talked, telling Adrian about Rice's part in the operation. If Sam Mars had not escaped and come to warn him, he would have ridden back to Twin Rivers last night, right into the waiting arms of the sheriff and Adrian.

Now he was on the run, hiding out, in need of a stake to get him east into the Mormon territory where he had connections with the organization who bought his stolen cattle. He had dealt with them directly for over a year, since the Clune brothers died. Now he could lead raids on the vast cattle and horse herds. He knew the lay of the land and how the herds were dispersed and patrolled. Yes, they would be willing to cut him in, especially since he brought two clever partners with him: Sam Mars, an old companion from Twin Rivers, and Juan Morales, the embittered horsebreaker from Cien Robles, who had joined him a few months ago.

However, before Rice joined the outlaws he had a couple of scores to settle, one with Adrian St. Clair for trapping him and one with his high-and-mighty daughter for throwing him over for the damned half-breed Mex! He'd get his revenge by kidnapping Ellie Kane and having his fill of her, then sending her back to her father and husband when he was damn good and tired of her. If only Sarita would hurry with Ellie's jewels. She was stealing them now and with each passing minute he was more sure she had been caught.

Sarita had just spent the most terrifying moments of her life. Oh, why had she let Rice talk her into this? He was smooth and clever and not a bad lover, although she still preferred Miguel. Well, if Miguel would rather go to that pale stick of a wife Sarita would have revenge on them both.

Rice had come to her cabin early that morning, explaining that he was fleeing Adrian St. Clair. He needed Ellie's jewels. Sarita's first impulse was to refuse his request for help. But when he told her he planned to kidnap Ellie and use her as a hostage, she agreed to aid him. As she had with Juan Morales, Sarita had lied to Rice, bragging that she was a lady's maid. In truth she was assigned to the kitchens and her cousin Luz was Ellie's maid. But Sarita would do anything to get rid of Ellie and lying was the least of it.

At lunch that day she had casually questioned Luz to learn where Ellie's jewel box was kept. While Luz was occupied downstairs and Ellie was in the flower garden, Sarita stole into the bedroom. Quickly, she moved to the big oak bureau next to the outside window and opened the third drawer. Tossing aside the silk slips and lacy pantalets, she found what she sought. Her hands clawed at the box and opened its clasp to see the winking opulence of amethysts, rubies and aquamarines. Just as she reached in to touch the fiery beauty beckoning her, an icy voice broke the hypnotic spell, speaking in clipped Spanish.

"I thought I heard someone in here. Explain yourself, girl." Doña Maria's haughty tone rang through the room. She knew this sneaky, worthless chit had been one of Miguel's lightskirts in days past, although she would never deign to acknowledge that. Stealing, however, was an overt and grave offense with which she must deal.

Sarita froze in terror. Then she began to calculate. The old *patrona* hated her gringa daughter-in-law. They were in complete agreement on the matter! Perhaps something could be worked out. A sly, secretive smile began with her lips, never moving to her eyes. It was a desperate gamble, but she would bet on the old woman's hate.

"I think, *patrona,* you might wish to see these gone," she paused to run the glittering gems through her fingers, "if it meant your son's wife vanished with them, no?"

Doña Maria said nothing but continued to stare at the young woman. Her silence was eloquent.

Sarita took the cue. "Rice Brighton, from Twin Rivers, waits for these. He is fleeing east, to one of the outlaws' strongholds. These would help him escape from Don Adrian. Rice wishes to take his old sweetheart along with him . . ."

Doña Maria scoffed, "She will not go with a hunted outlaw and leave all this." She gestured around the elegant room, but the implication included all Cien Robles.

Sarita's smile now became genuinely malevolent. "Who said, my lady, that the American woman goes willingly? She often rides alone when her husband is too busy to go with her. After Don Miguel leaves at daybreak tomorrow, you could give her a message that he wants to meet her in the *arroyo* at the big cottonwood stand. Rice will surprise her there. If she is gone and her jewelry with her, who is to say she did not flee with her old lover?" Almost afraid to breathe, Sarita waited. Was the old woman's piety greater than her jealousy?

The girl could not discern what emotions warred behind those obsidian eyes. Maria's face was as impassive and haughty as ever.

Doña Maria finally broke the silence. "Take the jewels. My daughter-in-law will go riding to the *arroyo* in the early morning." With no more ado she turned and swept through the door as silently as she had entered.

Sarita closed the cask with a final click and let out a long, ragged breath of relief. It had worked! She had been unsure that Rice could catch Ellie's fast little filly if he had to ride her down on the trail. But if she was sent to that densely overgrown stand of trees expecting Miguel, she'd dismount and Rice could easily trap her. Sarita began to smile. Doña Maria was now as guilty as she in this abduction. The old harridan could never again browbeat her. Sarita would have the whip hand, for the great lady had stooped to be her accomplice.

The day was beautiful. Cattle grazed in the stands of mustard. Wildflowers bloomed in profusion and the morning sky was blindingly azure with small fingers of white clouds rippling on the horizon. Ellie rode Moonlight at a slow pace, savoring the day and her secret. For the past weeks she was increasingly certain of it. Since last October she had prayed for this and feared it was not going to happen. Now, at last, she was sure. Her courses for the second month in a row had not come, and for the past three weeks her breasts and waist had grown slightly. In December she would have Miguel's child.

For over six months, as they made love with such frequency and intensity, she waited anxiously, praying to conceive. Cien Robles—no, Rio del Robles must have its heir. But far more than that, she wanted to give the husband she adored a child born of their love. Now, at last, it would happen. Even Doña Maria's grim face at breakfast could not daunt her spirits. Miguel had ridden out very early and Ellie had been so tired of late that she scarcely heard him leave their bed. When she came down to eat, it was nearly nine, a scandalously late hour. Then she saw the note from Miguel beside her breakfast plate saying he wanted her to meet him and bring a lunch. Today she would tell him! It would be their own special sharing, just the two of them.

Rice was nervous as he sat with the warm morning sun filtering down on his shoulders through the cottonwood leaves. He was well-hidden. All he had to do was wait. If only Sarita was right and the old lady wanted to get rid of her daughter-in-law enough to send her into the trap. Well, she had let Sarita go with the jewelry, hadn't she? He smiled grimly and patted his saddlebag filled with a fortune in gemstones, gold and silver. Now all he needed was his little silver Ellie. By the time he finished with her—no, he reconsidered; maybe he'd keep her. She had adored him as a girl. In his limitless vanity he refused to believe that she couldn't be won back. He thought of what he'd do with her, how he'd make her beg him. She was no blushing, prim virgin anymore. Maybe he should thank that damn Mex for that. When a more experienced man plied her with skill, she would fall into his arms. He could hardly wait to get her to the camp in Aguas Calientes. Just thinking about it made him harden. Of course, he would have the devil's own time keeping the other men away from her. But with Mars and Morales behind him, he would make it clear to the outlaws that he was running the operation. His plans were interrupted by the sound of Ellie's approaching horse.

She rode into the clearing near his hiding place and dismounted by the edge of the meandering stream. After tying Moonlight's reins to one end of a fallen log, she sat down on the log and stretched languorously, revealing to Rice the lush outline of her breasts straining against the thin silk of her shirt. Her hair was down, caught in back with a simple green ribbon that matched her jacket. She took off her hat and put one small booted foot on the log.

Rice silently dismounted and walked from the trees, stalking her. "Well, my lady, fancy meeting you so far from your castle, and all alone, too."

At the sound of his drawling voice, Ellie whirled, nearly unseating herself. "What are you doing on Cien Robles?" She tried to keep the fear from crackling through her voice, but little icy prickles began to run and down her spine as she realized how isolated the place was and how menacing he looked, standing over her. Quickly she stood up, only to realize she was at even more of a disadvantage. Rice towered over her and his barrel chest filled her line of vision. Whe he reached out and quickly grabbed her slender shoulders in an iron grip, a shudder of terror washed over her.

"Let me go. My husband—"

"Isn't coming. He sent me in his place."

He laughed as she shrieked a denial and struggled ineffectually to get free. With one fast movement he slapped her across the face as his good humor faded.

"Keep it up, little bird, and you might get a broken wing. Or," he considered, stroking her jaw where he'd just hit her, "if you're real nice, I just might make you sing."

When he lowered his head, intent on kissing her, she twisted away, frantic in her loathing. "You're mad! Miguel will kill you." She could remember Juan Morales's broken body lying unconscious on the ground and was sure her husband's jealous rage would exact a terrible penalty from Brighton for this.

"Yeah, honey. Well, he'll have to catch me first! Maybe when I get through with you, he won't want you back. Maybe you won't want to go back." His old, greasy arrogance surfaced again.

"You vain, stupid thief, you common rustler, how dare you even think I'd let you—"

Before she could go any further the look on his face stopped her. "How did you know I'm a rustler? Your old man tell you?" When he referred to Adrian, his face was a mask of twisted hate.

Suddenly the enormity of her danger hit Ellie. She had been sent on a fool's errand. Miguel had not written that note. Indeed, she realized, except for signing their betrothal agreement and marriage lines, she'd never seen his handwriting. Who wrote the note? Who lured her into a trap so Rice could kidnap her? Miguel wasn't coming here and this man, a thief and probably a killer, had her at his mercy! Her and her baby!

He shook her. "Well, did Adrian tell you?"

"Yes, he told me. Why, Rice? Why steal when you had such a good job?"

He sneered at her attempted reasoning. "Good job! Shit! Work for your old man, then for your greaser husband, for pocket money while they get even richer? I should have married you, not him! I should own Twin Rivers. Well, if I can't have the ranch, at least I'll get the rancher's daughter. I've got plans for you, lady. You're coming with me to a little rendezvous. Meet some interesting gents. Yessir, we'll have quite a time of it before we're through. You got away from me once. Not this time."

With that, he scooped her up and threw her across his shoulder like a small stick doll. When he approached a nervous, shying Moonlight, he grabbed the reins in one hand and tossed her to the ground with his other arm.

"Now, I'm only going to say it once. You mount up and ride like a good little girl or I'll knock you out and tie you across the saddle like a sack of cornhusks!"

Thinking of the new life she carried within her, Ellie blanched. He could hurt her and kill the baby. *Oh, please God, please Holy Mother, no*, she prayed silently. Realizing how useless it was to argue with the implacable hate she saw etched in his criminal's face, Ellie nodded in agreement.

They rode for several hours without stopping or talking. He kept his rangy bay near Moonlight and gave Ellie no chance to flee. She was a superb horsewoman, but she realized how useless and dangerous it was to try and outrun him, especially in her condition. She must think of some means of escape, trick him when his guard was down, but she must not anger him so he would attack her and endanger her baby.

Finally, in late afternoon they stopped at a small stream to water and rest the lathered horses. He took the picnic basket from her saddle, a canteen from his saddle and approached her as she sat frantically eyeing the terrain and looking for a weapon.

"Pretty fancy," he said, looking in the basket at fried chicken, canned peaches, crusty bread and dark yellow cheese. "I'd advise you to eat, Ellie." He offered some cheese and a hunk of bread, then the canteen. Realizing that she needed her strength to keep her wits, she choked down the food, and after carefully wiping it off, she even drank from his canteen.

Rice smirked. "After I spend a few nights loving you, you'll be glad to share anything my mouth's been on." His voice was lewd and it made her skin crawl. He took the canteen back and drank long from it, all the while watching her.

"You used to like me rather well, Ellie. What happened, baby? I never figured you'd be one to choose money and position."

Her cheeks flamed and before she thought, she blurted out, "You're a thief and hypocrite, Rice! You didn't want me. You wanted Twin Rivers. You're the one who chose money, not me."

He leered at her. "And what did you choose, baby? That fancy Mex boy, green from a seminary! Only because his daddy owned Cien Robles."

"My husband is more man than you'll ever be! He works daybreak till nightfall, right alongside his men. You'd never be able to run a big ranch that way. You'd have married me for Twin Rivers and then lived it up while others did the work for you, until the place went under!"

He tossed the canteen down and stood over her menacingly. "So, he's a real ramrod, huh? We'll just see how he compares in other ways."

She scooted back, her ire turning to fear. He laughed a low, ugly guffaw and turned to pick up the bay's reins. "First, let's make that outpost camp. Then, when we're safe and comfortable, I'll give you some lessons. Mount up."

It was almost twilight when they reached the camp. Ellie was thoroughly disoriented, thinking they had been moving east and vaguely north across wild hilly country that she had never seen before, far from Cien Robles land. The stronghold was at the mouth of a narrow canyon with a steep rock outcropping at its opening. Rice called a password, then swore when he received no response.

The nearer they came to the camp, the greater her terror. Her mind twisted desperately, but no means of escape occurred to her. Rice was six feet tall, she scarcely over five; he was beefy and barrel-chested, she fine-boned and slim. She could think of no other plan than to seize a weapon and hit him from behind, but he did not give her the slightest opening.

They entered the interior of the hidden canyon, quickly climbing to the clearing beyond a dense stand of alder. The campsite could hold at least half a dozen men, Ellie guessed, judging by the size of the crude lean-to and number of cornhusk mattresses in it. A big fire pit with a spit rigged over it for roasting stolen cattle was in the center of the clearing.

There was no one there, but the camp looked as if it had recently been occupied. Rice dismounted and then pulled Ellie down. Quickly, he tied up the two horses and then dragged her to the fire pit. He roughly shoved her onto a big log that served as a bench in front of the fire. Then he knelt and poked at the coals which still smoldered when stirred.

"They must be on a raid somewhere. Be back by dark probably. I'd guess they left late morning judging by these coals." He added a few more pieces of dry wood until there was a small fire burning. Scowling at her, he said, "Got an old friend of your husband's riding with us. Greaser fellow name of Morales. He's got a real grudge against the *patrón* for firing him."

Ellie blanched. *My God! That madman who attacked me!*

Rice watched Ellie's reaction with curiosity and pleasure. He grinned. "Yep, he's a mean hombre, that horsebreaker. Maybe I'll give you to him for taming if you don't please me."

She steeled herself and said as levelly as she could, "Him or you, I see little difference, Rice. Miguel will kill you both."

He swore and stood up, looming over her. "You think you're so high-and-mighty, the great lady of the rancho? Think your husband's on his way to save you? Well, sweetheart, let me show you something that may set you straight. Forget about ever seeing your greaser lover again. From now on, you please me! You better, or I'll trade you to the Mormons when my gang finishes with you. They buy women, you know. Put them in harems."

As he spoke he pulled the saddlebags off his bay and

opened one. When he took her enameled jewel cask out
and opened it, spilling the contents on the ground, she
gasped in shock.

"How did you get my jewelry? *You* wrote that note and
let me think it was Miguel!"

"Why, Ellie baby, you got it all wrong." His voice
became soft and smooth, almost like he was soothing a
dim-witted child. "There was no note. You took your
jewels and sneaked off this morning to meet me, don't you
remember? We're running away together, my love." Then
his voice hardened. "And your jealous, high-minded husband will believe it. You and your jewelry gone just when
I had to cut and run from your old man at Twin Rivers.
You think your husband will follow and rescue you? Don't
make me laugh! By the time he gets in tonight and finds
you gone, word of my flight should reach Cien Robles.
He'll put it all together, sugar." He laughed evilly and
stepped over the pile of gems to grab her.

Her heart gave an aching lurch as she realized how the
situation would look. Her body felt leaden and woozy as
she desperately fought to regain her equilibrium. He grabbed
her roughly and pulled her hard against him, squeezing the
breath from her lungs.

"Now, baby, it seems to me we have some unfinished
business from that day at the line shack." He began to
unbutton her blouse.

Ellie's lethargy turned to fierce resistance as she felt his
defiling, rough hands on her body. "No!" She kicked at
him and twisted out of his grasp. He swore when her boot
connected with a shin. Her blouse had come open and she
was shaking, her breasts heaving in fury and fear. She
backed away, her eyes scanning the camp desperately in
search of a weapon.

He advanced on her relentlessly. "I'll break you like a
ripe melon if I have to, Ellie. I can please you or hurt
you. Either way, I'll enjoy it."

His clenched fists, so big and brawny, caused a wave of
terror to wash over her. The baby! Instinctively, as he
stepped closer, her hands went around her midsection to

protect the new life there. He couldn't hit her and cause her to lose Miguel's baby!

Rice stopped in his tracks, his eyes narrowing as he watched her. She looked different, her breasts and hips fuller than he remembered. He swore a string of choice epithets. She was breeding! That greaser bastard's kid would soon make her big and useless to him!

Ellie watched him with a sick, sinking instinct, realizing that he knew she was pregnant. "Please, don't hurt me." Her voice was calm in spite of her fear.

Slowly he relaxed. Well, no help for it, at least for now. She was so desperate to protect her child, she'd do whatever he asked. He could make her cooperative and that might be enjoyable, yes, very enjoyable indeed. He grinned.

"Well, hell, little bird. I think you're about to hatch, huh? Thought you looked a little bigger in the tits." His grin faded, replaced by a reptilian menace that made her shudder. "You do what I tell you, *everything* I tell you and you'll keep that baby. Fight me, talk back to me, give me any trouble, and all I have to do is give you one hard punch right in that delectable little belly . . ." He let his words trail off as she blanched, trembling before his looming body. "You understand me?"

Numbly, she nodded.

"Good. Now, come here and let me show you what a real man feels like, what you've been missing."

Following his directions, she came slowly, shakily into his embrace, shivering in revulsion as he enveloped her, yet standing passively in his arms.

"You used to have more fire, baby. I remember when you and I would sneak off from your pa and you'd melt in my arms. Put your arms around me and act like you did then, my fancy silver-haired piece. Do it!"

Her eyes glittered in terror and fury, but Ellie put her arms around his neck and held on to him.

"Now, kiss me," he ground out in a hoarse whisper.

Forcing down the bile rising in her throat, she complied, lips closed tightly. He forced them open and pillaged inside with his tongue. Just when she thought she'd faint from the degradation of this charade, a cold voice interrupted them.

"I hate to break up such a touching scene, but I've come to reclaim something that belongs to me. At least, she used to belong to me. Now I'm not so sure I want her back." Miguel stood across the clearing by the wooded entrance to the campsite. His face looked as if it were chiseled from granite in the dim twilight. His eyes were black with hurt fury.

Rice swore and whirled, pushing Ellie to the ground as he confronted his unexpected antagonist.

"How the hell—"

"One of the vaqueros saw my wife ride toward the *arroyo* with a basket. Then, quite unexpectedly, he encountered me and wondered why I wasn't with her. Of course, it never entered his mind that the señora would meet someone else." As he spoke, his voice was laced with scorn, covering up his desperate pain and confusion. "The ground's soft from the rain. It was easy to trail you." He held his rifle pointed at Brighton as he walked closer to them, then motioned for Rice to drop his gunbelt.

Grudgingly, Rice did so, all the while waiting his chance. As soon as he saw Miguel's eyes catch sight of the jewel cask lying beside Ellie, he knew what he would do. "Ah, so you see our getaway loot. Inventive of her to think of it, but then Ellie's always been a clever little girl." As Brighton expected, Miguel's whole body stiffened. The full implication of her taking the jewelry hit him. Not enough, however, to cause his aim at Rice's midriff to slip. Suddenly, the outlaw became frightened. One slug from that Patterson and he was a goner. He looked at the slim young man before him whose infuriated eyes and clenched jaw radiated hate.

Ellie was afraid to move for fear of distracting Miguel's aim, yet desperate to defend herself from Rice's lies. When her husband stood directly in front of them, she slowly picked herself up and sat on the log, scooting away from Brighton. "Miguel, more of them are coming back!

Morales is with them! We have to get away from here. I—"

"Save it!" He cut her off savagely. "You can't help your lover. I'm going to kill him." With that, he kicked Rice's gunbelt behind him and threw his rifle after it.

Rice's face split into a big grin as he sized up the younger man. They were of equal height, but Brighton was heavier with thicker bones and a beefy frame in contrast to Miguel's whipcord leanness.

If he was deceived, Ellie was not. She'd seen how fast and deadly her husband could be in a fight. But Rice's cohorts could return at any moment and there was always the chance that Rice would land a lucky blow. The guns were on the other side of the two circling men. She stood up, waiting her opportunity.

Miguel forced himself into calmness after Rice landed several hard, swift blows. At first, he was too angry to think straight, only wanting to beat Ellie's lover senseless, but Brighton was not as clumsy as Morales. As Simon and Blackie had often said, mad is careless and careless is losing; Miguel began to watch for an opening. He jabbed and weaved, landing telling combinations of punches that dazed Brighton. His leaner, slighter frame helped him now. Brighton carried excess weight that slowed him down and left his poorer reflexes exposed to the lightning jabs of the younger man.

Finally, they went down when Brighton lunged and catapulted them to the flat, packed earth near the glowing coals of the fire. As they rolled, Ellie seized her chance and raced around the thrashing men to the guns across the clearing. By the time she reached the rifle, Miguel had come up on top of Rice and was raining punishing blows on the other's face. Miguel was unaware that his jacket and arm had been burned in their earlier roll across the clearing. Oblivious to pain or anything else, he bludgeoned Brighton's inert form mercilessly.

Rice looked so limp and broken that Ellie thought he was dead. Then she heard the sound the hoofbeats—at least a half-dozen horses. Frantically, she leaned down toward Miguel, saying, "I hear the rest of them coming back!"

He did not acknowledge her, so fixed was he on Brighton. She screamed at him, now frantic that the outlaws would catch them and kill them both. "Miguel, his friends are coming—Morales and a half-dozen armed men!" As she yelled, she pulled at his shoulders. Finally, her frantic voice penetrated and he stopped, seeming to come to himself out of some dark, primitive well of vengeance.

His voice hissed in the darkness as he spoke through gritted teeth. "Get Moonlight." While Ellie turned and raced to mount, Miguel scooped up her jewels, then hurried to Dominican. They hid in the dense foliage inside the canyon passage. Shortly the outlaws approached, loud and careless, obviously secure in the wilderness fastness of their hideout. They laughed and joked, completely unaware of the intruders. Once the six had galloped by, Miguel took Moonlight's reins from Ellie and led them silently out in the darkness. He increased the pace as a pale moon began to rise and they could see. For several hours they rode in silence.

He finally slowed the horses' headlong gallop and stopped by a tree-enshrouded water hole. "Get down and rest Moonlight." His voice was stiff, almost emotionless, as he helped her dismount. He let go of her quickly, almost causing her to fall before she had oriented herself to being off the careening horse.

"Miguel, I—I'm dizzy," she said in supplication, reaching out for his arm. She touched the burned one and he flinched in agony. "Oh, I'm sorry! You're hurt. Let me see—"

He turned from her and walked swiftly to the stream where he knelt and drank, washing his face in the cold water to revive himself and clean away the dried blood from the fight.

Ellie came to his side and sat down on the bank. "You *are* hurt." She had a silk neckerchief in her hand that she dipped in the water and wrung out. "Let me clean your face. Oh, Miguel!" Her breath caught at the swelling on one cheekbone and the cut above his right eye. Gingerly, she daubed at the injuries until he caught one small wrist and stopped her.

"Tend to yourself first, my dear wife!" The sarcasm in his voice registered on her as did his penetrating gaze. Her blouse was still half unbuttoned where Rice had opened it. Miguel glared accusingly at the bare flesh.

As she gulped and reached to refasten it, she sobbed out in desperation, "You act as though I went with him willingly, as though I stole the jewelry. Oh, Miguel, how could you believe Rice's lies?"

He arched one thick black brow sardonically. "How, indeed, my little silver witch? What did he need to say? If Pedro hadn't seen you and told me, you'd have been free and clear. No one would have trailed you or known where you went, only that you and a fortune in jewelry had vanished, along with Rice Brighton."

"Couldn't you at least hear me out?" Her voice began to rise in hysteria and fury. "I found a note by my breakfast plate from you—or at least it was signed with your name—asking me to ride with a lunch basket to the *arroyo*. When I got there Rice was waiting. He sneaked up on me. Miguel, he had the jewels. I don't know how—"

He looked at her scornfully. "Someone as wily as you can do better than that, surely. There's no way in hell he could have put a note in the breakfast room or stolen your jewel cask." He sighed raggedly, hurt and anger etched in the planes of his face. "What kind of a fool do you take me for, Ellie?" Then he laughed. "On second thought, I guess a pretty big one, besotted with my beautiful silver goddess. Alex and Adrian may have forced you to marry me, but not to stay, eh?"

As he spoke, her bewilderment grew. So did her pain at his lack of trust. She was exhausted and frightened, wanting nothing more than the comfort of his arms. Big, shiny tears began to slip from the corners of her aqua eyes. Furiously, she brushed at them with small fists, shaking her head in denial of all he said. "I don't know who helped him, but someone must have. My God, I'd never go with him! I loathe him!"

He sneered, "I could see how much you 'loathed him,' remember? You weren't exactly fighting off an attack. I ought to know how you can fight, little hellcat."

Her head flew up at that cruel taunt. She stuck her chin out and took a deep breath. "You're right, I didn't fight him. I did exactly what he said." Her voice sounded surprisingly calm now as she suppressed her pain. "He said if I didn't, he'd hurt the baby."

At that his eyes glittered in the darkness like black sapphires. He riveted them on her small, trembling face. "You're pregnant—and he knew?"

"He guessed. When he threatened to hit me, I—I must have . . ." Her voice faded away into choked, humiliated silence. This was certainly not the way she had envisioned telling him he was to be a father!

Ellie was not prepared for his next question. "Whose is it?"

Her anguish cut like a knife. "How—how could you ask?" was all she could say before she felt the nausea rising in her throat. .

"I guess it's most likely mine," he replied grimly. "After all, I was with you every night. You only had your trysts with Brighton a few days a week when I was too busy to ride with you. Was that why you fled, Ellie, fear of a chance that the child would favor him?"

Goaded beyond endurance, through a haze of hurt and bone weariness, she slapped him. Realizing almost at once that she had hit his bruised cheek and cut lip, she relented, "Oh, my love, I'm sorry! I didn't mean to—"

She reached up to caress his face, but he silently stopped her, grasping her slim wrist in a viselike grip and throwing it from him as if it were a rattler. He stood up and stalked to Dominican, mounting in a jerky motion, his anger showing in the way he rode.

"Get on Moonlight and follow me, or so help me God, I'll leave you for those brigands to tear apart now that your lover's dead!"

With shaking legs she limped to the little filly and struggled to mount. They completed the ride to Cien

Robles in silence. Just as they rode up to the corral and he dismounted, she began to slip from her horse, too exhausted to awaken and break her own fall. Miguel was there at once. Wincing at the pain in his burned arm when he grabbed her, he lifted her from the horse and carried her, semiconscious, to the house. It must have been well after midnight when a stunned Maria and agitated Alex greeted him in the front entry.

Alex shouted for Luz and Rita to attend the unconscious girl. "God, is she hurt? What happened to her? Where did you find her? I've had men out searching everywhere for both of you for hours!"

"She's just exhausted, Papa. I found her in a canyon northeast of here in the foothills, with Rice Brighton."

With that, he strode quickly up the stairs to their quarters, with Luz and Rita following. He kicked open the door to her old bedroom and walked in, dropping her on the bed. Then he turned to the two women and said, "Just undress her and put her to bed now. Forget the bath." He turned on his heel and left the gaping women.

Downstairs, Maria stood riveted in shock at the rear of the hall. When she heard that Miguel had ridden after Ellie and Brighton, she was terrified that the outlaw might shoot her son, but never had it occurred to her that he would bring his wife home unharmed. Thank God she had found the note she'd forged that morning and destroyed it before anyone saw it! There was nothing to connect her to the abduction except Sarita. She must watch the servant most carefully. But who would believe the word of a tramp over that of the *patrona*? Taking a deep breath, she waited for Miguel.

"You can't be serious! Ellie would never do such an insane thing!" Alex roared at a grim, tight-lipped Miguel.

With a scowl, his son tossed the enameled jewel cask onto Alex's desk, spilling its glittering contents across the dark oak surface like a bursting meteor. "She had these with her. What do you make of that?"

Alex looked levelly at Miguel, seeing the pain behind the tightly held anger. He ran one long-fingered hand

across the gems and quietly said, ''Why not wait and ask
her in the morning when she's not in a state of collapse?''

Maria, who watched the whole exchange in the study
from her chair by the window, now rose and stepped
toward Miguel. ''What did she tell you, *mí hijo*? There
must be some explanation.'' She was quiet reasonableness
personified.

Sadly, Miguel looked at her. All her earlier warnings
about Ellie were right and now she asked for excuses just
like Alex. ''No, Mama, there's no believable explanation,
just a fairy tale about a note from me luring her to the
arroyo. She offered no reason for the jewelry being there.
No, she took it and went with Brighton. He was her first
love, when she was a girl at Twin Rivers.''

''Bullshit! I don't believe it,'' Alex exploded. Then he
said more quietly, ''This wouldn't have anything to do
with the trouble between you and Ellie earlier?''

''That's between me and my wife. You can talk to her in
the morning. Let her tell you whatever she wants.'' With
that, he walked out of the room, after grabbing a bottle of
brandy from the bar next to Alex's desk.

Maria turned her venom on her husband after Miguel
was gone. ''So, your splendid little Americana is just what
I always said she was, a faithless harlot! A thief! And
you've saddled Miguel with her for life. I'll never forgive
you, Alex!''

He looked at her with surprising calm and sadness in his
dark blue eyes. ''You never have, my dear, you never
have.''

CHAPTER
19

Ellie lay in her lonely bed, awash in misery as tears trickled from the sides of her eyes, dampening her temples and hair. She felt too tired to cry anymore, but the silent torrent of salty water kept on of its own volition.

When she heard Miguel's tread on the floor in the next room, *their* room, she shakily got out of bed and wrapped herself in a blue robe. Silently, she opened the door and stepped into the bedroom to see him upending a bottle and taking a long pull at the contents. Catching sight of her from the corner of his eye, he turned and walked to where she stood, small and vulnerable. Wiping his mouth with the back of his hand, he said, "Hell, Ellie, go to bed. You're exhausted and so am I."

She swallowed and gathered her courage to ask, "Why did you put me in that old room?" Before he could reply, she reached out and threw her arms around his waist. "Please, hold me, oh, please, my love. You must still love me as I love you. You must!"

Gently but firmly, he pulled free of her embrace and held her at arm's length.

"It won't work, Ellie. It's finished. From now on, that's your room and that's where you'll sleep—alone."

"While you sleep where? In Rosalie Parker's bed? In Sarita's?" She spat the accusation at him in a frenzy of jealous rejection. How could she have abased herself so, to crawl to him when he didn't want her, didn't trust her, didn't love her? Her heart tore.

At the mention of Rosalie's name, Miguel was caught off guard. "How the hell do you know Rose?" Sarita or any of the ranch girls he'd believe she could have found out about, but Rosalie?

Ellie felt the heat of the flush, as much from anger as embarrassment. "You think I'm so stupid, so naïve? You're every bit as famous a whoremaster as your father, who you're always so ready to condemn!"

He smirked at her. "Well, I guess you're right. I am at that, considering who I married."

She would have flown at him with nails out if he hadn't caught her wrists and scooped her up in his arms. He walked back through the door to the other bedroom where he tossed her on the bed.

"This is where you sleep until the child is born. Then we'll see if it's mine or Brighton's. He's fair like you. If it's dark like me, I'll know it's mine."

She sat bolt upright in the bed. "That's monstrous! Your own father—half your family is blond. Your child could easily be, too."

He grimaced and cocked one brow. "As I recall you saying more than once, there's a strong resemblance between me and my father." His expression became fixed and grim. "If it's a Kane, I'll know."

He walked back to the door, then paused and said softly, "And Ellie, if it's Brighton's get, you and your bastard go back to Twin Rivers the next day!"

Blindly, she reached for the nearest object at hand, a small vase on the bedside table, and hurled it at his back. It hit the closed door with splintering force, leaving shards and petals strewn across the floor. The vase had been half-full of water and now the glistening droplets reflected in the candlelight, like a bright string of tears trailing from her bed to that closed door between them.

Ellie woke with an aching head, swollen eyes and a dry, sour taste in her mouth. When she sat up, her stomach gave a violent lurch and she was forced to bend over the side of the bed, retching in violent, dry heaves, for she'd had nothing to eat since mid-afternoon the day before. Shakily, she rolled back over onto the sheets, pale and spent. *Well, my first morning sickness*, she thought grimly.

Just then a timid knock sounded and Luz's voice softly asked to be admitted. Fleetingly, Ellie wondered if all the servants had heard the tale of her flight with an outlaw.

"Come in, Luz."

The girl entered hesitantly, unsure of how to act or what to expect. Taking one look at her small, silver-haired mistress and then at the wreckage in the room, she let out a shocked gasp. "Oh, señora, let me get you some water and then clean this up."

Doña Ellie was as white as the bedsheets with a tear-ravaged, puffy face. Broken glass was all around the left side of the bed. Luz had been confused about the wild stories she heard concerning her mistress and that *cerdo*, Rice Brighton, but now she was certain how bereft and alone her lady was. It wrung her heart to see the little one in such condition. Surely Doña Ellie loved Don Miguel. She would never leave him for trash like that outlaw.

Efficiently, she sent word to Rita to bring breakfast and bathwater, then cleaned up the shattered vase. If Ellie had any doubts about the servants' feelings for her, they were quickly dispelled when Rita came to assist Luz with the bath.

Taking one look at the white, trembling form immersed in the hot tub, Rita asked, "When is the child to come, Doña Ellie?"

Ellie stiffened in surprise and turned to look into warm, kind eyes, solicitous, not condemning. Rita knew whose child it was, even if the child's own father did not!

"In—in December, I think, but how did you—?"

Rita smiled, glancing at the untouched breakfast tray and then back to the small figure in the tub. "You are pale and do not like the looks of *huevos rancheros* and tortillas. Also, you begin to grow in some places. It is natural, eh?"

Ellie colored at the remarks, but was grateful for the

rapport she still retained with these women. Pray God they held fast to their faith in her!

Luz, who had taken the broken porcelain downstairs to dispose of it, returned while Rita was helping the *patrona* dress and brush her tangled hair. "Don Alesandro wishes to see you, señora, when you feel well enough to come downstairs."

Ellie blanched. *Oh, please, don't let him desert me,* she prayed.

Rita smiled reassuringly and said, "You need something to calm your nerves and settle your stomach so you can eat and gain strength. Then things will look better."

When Ellie drank several cups of Rita's herbal tea and ate some biscuits, she did indeed feel better. After a bath and a cold compress to clear her ravaged face, she felt nearly human.

Alex opened the study door and ushered Ellie in. "Sit down, child. Are you recovered from the ordeal enough to talk?" At her nod as she sat down, he went on in his abrupt, straightforward manner. "Good. My damn fool son gave us some insane story about you taking your jewelry and running off with Adrian's foreman."

"Did you believe him?" She fixed him with a clear, aquamarine gaze, needing to know where she stood, trying to match his candor.

He snorted in disgust. "Hell, no, but Maria sure latched on to it! Little wonder."

He pulled up a chair across from hers and very gently took her hand. "Only you know the truth, Eleanor. Tell me, so we can figure a way out of this tangle."

Her eyes filled with crystalline tears and she began to sob, then forced herself to stop. She said helplessly, "I—I don't know everything that happened, that's the trouble. I can't explain how Rice got my jewelry or who wrote that note. If my husband has no faith in me, I can't prove I'm innocent."

At his urging, she went through the whole series of incidents: her ugly encounter with Brighton the week of the party at Twin Rivers, Adrian's suspicions about the rustling, the note she assumed was from Miguel, the violent abduction and the startling appearance of the jewelry. When she got to the humiliating scene in the camp, she had to tell Alex why she did what Rice demanded.

"I couldn't fight him after he threatened to hurt the child."

Alex's eyes blazed in triumph when she paused. "Oh, Ellie, you've made me so happy! Thank God Miguel got there as soon as he did!"

She shook her head. "No, it was too late, he saw me d-do what Rice wanted—kiss him and let him, let him . . ." She broke down in sobs of such wrenching misery, Alex shot up from his chair, moving around to put his arms about her shoulders protectively.

"And like the hotheaded young fool he is, he believed the worst. Oh, Ellie, he's young and has more than a little of my foul, jealous temper in him. It's taken me years to learn to curb it and I still often fail, even when I don't mean to explode."

"In a way, I can't blame him. It looked so terrible. The jewelry was there, I went to the *arroyo*, I was embracing Rice. If only— only he trusted me . . ." she finished wanly.

Alex's face darkened considerably at this. "Yes, the whole thing smacks of a trap with someone in this house in collusion wih Brighton. Someone who had easy access to your room and knew where you kept things."

Ellie's head snapped up at this. "You—you mean one of the servants? Oh, but they've all been so kind, so loyal."

"Not necessarily a house servant." He paused and began to pace. "It could have been someone else, someone who can read and write to have forged that note from Miguel, someone who hates you and wants you gone and disgraced."

Ellie's blood chilled to ice water as she considered this. The black look on Alex's face did nothing to reassure her. "No," she whispered like a litany. "Please God, no! She could not hate me that much."

Alex gave her a look of pity. "Yes, my dear, she could. The only other candidate in the household is Father Sebastian, who may indeed hold a grudge against you, but I hardly think he's capable of this. His priestly office wouldn't allow it," he finished scornfully.

"But—but how could Maria know Rice? She's never met him, would never associate with him. It's impossible to imagine."

"Have you ever seen Brighton's handwriting? Can he write? Could he have forged the note and had someone smuggle it in?"

Ellie nodded hopefully. "He's had some education, I know, although I've never seen his handwriting." Eagerly, she seized upon the idea. The very thought that her mother-in-law hated her so badly as to wish her dead, or worse than dead, was too horrible to contemplate.

Alex was still unconvinced. "It is possible, but the other is more likely."

Ellie looked at him with misery etched across her face. "Oh, Alex! We can't prove anything. The note's gone, Rice is dead or hiding in bandit country. And you know what would happen if either of us accused Maria! It would drive Miguel further away from me and you than ever."

He sighed and ran his fingers through his graying hair. "Yes, yes, of course, you're right. And, if I try to get the truth from her in a direct confrontation, she'll run straight to him with tears and righteous indignation." He swore a string of epithets, then walked back to the small, forlorn girl swallowed up in the big chair. "I'm sorry I'm no more help, but we'll straighten this out, I swear it, Ellie."

"Alex, you are a help and a comfort. If you didn't trust me, I—I don't know what I'd do."

"Well, for now, just take care of that grandchild of mine and try not to let Miguel keep hurting you. Time changes things a great deal. Holding his child in his arms may do more than all the evidence in any law court, you know."

At this she stiffened, remembering Miguel's threats about the baby, but she said nothing. It would only infuriate Alex and drive a wedge deeper between him and his son.

A frantic Adrian came to Cien Robles the next day, terrified that Rice had endangered his only child. When Ellie assured him she was fine and then told him about her pregnancy, he was elated. Then, realizing something was amiss, he asked her why she was so distraught. It was

Alex who took him aside and briefly glossed over the ruse and subsequent estrangement between husband and wife. Adrian wanted to take her home with him, but she assured her father that she would rather remain at Cien Robles.

In the months that followed, the distance between Miguel and Ellie was far greater than it had ever been in the first few months of their marriage. Both were aware of what they once shared and had now lost. Each was absorbed with private pain so intense that even speaking of it was impossible.

By the end of summer Ellie was swollen with the baby, suffering from the heat, persistent nausea and backaches, but most of all from never ending depression. Every night she'd look in the mirror at her naked body before crawling into her lonely bed. Her arms and legs, even her hollow-eyed face, grew thinner as the child in her belly grew larger. "No wonder he finds it so easy to avoid me. I'm ugly!"

Doctor Lawson worried about her frailty and listlessness. Ellie had always been strong and healthy despite her delicate coloring and fine bones. He feared her unhappiness was undermining her health.

Alex was Ellie's only crutch, supporting her through the long agonizing days. He expressed concern about her thinness and poor health one afternoon as she sat forlornly on the cool stone bench in the flower garden under a big oak tree.

"I'm scarcely thin, Alex! Look at me!" She placed two tiny hands over her protruding abdomen and smiled wanly at him.

"Yes, but look at the rest of you. My grandson doesn't need to grow fat at the expense of his mother's health. You've got to eat, girl!"

She smiled a bit more. "Oh, so now you've sure it's a boy, huh? Well, he or she will continue to grow regardless. I try to eat, but so little seems to agree with me or appeal to me."

"I know how unhappy you are about Miguel and lord knows, you've reasons, child, but don't let your sorrow harm you or the baby."

"I'll try harder to eat, I promise. The doctor left some medicine and Rita's brewing her herbal tea for me again. With cool weather I'll feel some respite. Now that rodeo is almost over, things will quiet down and I'll get more rest."

Both of them knew that once rodeo's sixteen-hour days were over, Miguel would resume his forays into town, spending nights at Rosalie Parker's. There might be less noise and confusion after fall rodeo ended, but the nights would be even lonelier, with her husband in the arms of another, instead of sleeping exhaustedly in the adjacent bedroom.

"Damn him for doing this to you! I'd hoped the young fool would come to his senses by now. He's just inflicting more pain on you." At his agitated outburst, Alex whitened for a split second, interrupting his pacing to take a steadying breath. Then he casually walked over to the bench and sat down beside her.

"I'm not the only one Dr. Lawson is worried about, am I, Alex?" Her clear, blue-green gaze leveled on his features. She had noticed his occasional shortness of breath and pallor for many months, indeed for nearly a year. He was very good at covering this, presenting a strong, arrogant facade to the family.

Only Ellie, who had become so attuned to him, realized that he was hiding a serious illness. Since he never volunteered to discuss it, she had not brought it up. He had been pushing himself too hard lately, going to town to work at the shipping office and then making the long ride back at night to afford her some company at the dinner table. Otherwise, she was caught between the polite veneer of Miguel and the barely repressed venom of Maria.

He smiled at her and the lines in his hawkish face seemed more deeply furrowed than ever before. "It seems, little one, that you are becoming entirely too observant for your own good." He sighed. "I've had a heart problem for years. The past year it's gotten worse. The doctor wants me to quit working and stop drinking rum and, er, abstain from some other things. Frankly, I can't think of any way to kill myself quicker!"

She smiled sadly at that, then put her hand over his arm and squeezed. "Just heed a bit of your *own* advice. Try to get more rest and don't push so much. Maybe an occasional night in town might be a real benefit to your health, Dr. Lawson notwithstanding."

He laughed and looked at her with great fondness. "Oh, Eleanor, how I wish I had been able to watch a daughter of mine grow up like you."

"You have, Alex, you have," was her soft reply as tears glistened in her eyes.

Miguel drove himself until he dropped. For the first few days after he brought Ellie back to Cien Robles, he worked dawn to dark, falling in bed too exhausted to think. He supplemented the toil with generous doses of brandy each night. After a couple of weeks, however, nothing could keep his thoughts from straying to the adjacent room where his lovely little silver-haired wife slept. He lay awake, his mind unable to stop picturing her slim body bathed in dim moonlight, as he'd seen it so often when she lay beside him. Then he could reach out so easily and . . .

Miguel tossed fitfully and swore. Finally, after he'd almost gone to the closed door, almost broken his word to her and given in to his own hunger, he dressed hastily and went downstairs. *God, I had my hand on the doorknob—I came so close to opening it.* His palms were sweating. *Damn the bitch! I need a drink.* Silently, he went to Alex's study and poured a generous slug of brandy, then stretched out in the big chair behind the desk to sip it. He'd been up since four that morning and spent most of the day on horseback. It was past midnight and still he couldn't sleep. The brandy burned a fiery trail down his throat, but did not soothe his anguish. He knew any of the maids in the back cabins would welcome him, yet it would not satisfy him. Indeed, as he sat contemplating it, the act seemed cheap, an open advertisement of his estrangement from his wife. Servants gossip. He did not want some mindless, romantic peasant girl giggling and bragging to her friends, or a calculating, wheedling bitch like Sarita hanging on him. No.

When Dominican's hoofbeats sounded in the distance, Ellie heard her husband ride toward Los Angeles. She, too, lay awake thinking about the bed next door. She knew where he had gone.

By the time he arrived at Rosalie's, she was closed for the night, but his insistent knocking finally roused her. Swearing, Rosalie walked to the door and peered through the narrow side windowpane before opening it.

"Crap, Mike, this is a hell of a time to come calling. I just got to sleep an hour ago. Haven't seen you in so damn long, thought the hogs ate you, baby."

Sighing, she ushered the silent man into her room, adjacent to the back door. He looked disheveled, naturally in need of a shave at this hour of the morning. "Dammit, Mike, you're drunk!"

He grinned crookedly. "Just a little, Rose, just a little, but not so much that..." He tossed his hat on the nightstand and moved toward her, taking her in his arms.

This was a surprise! She passively let him embrace her; he remembered all the soft, special places and pleasures of her body. It had been so long, ever since he'd married Ellie St. Clair. Oh, he'd come back for months afterward but only to talk or to go to Suzie or Lita. Rosalie had begun to think of herself as a surrogate for Father Sebastian. Then last October, his nocturnal visits stopped altogether and Rosalie figured he'd finally followed her advice and fixed things up with his wife. Now here he was in the middle of the night again, drunk and obviously randy as a polecat. She ought to take a flatiron to him. She ought to, but she didn't.

"Oh, damn you—ooh, Mike—you're too good, even if you are—aah—drunk..." He interrupted her with a deep, bruising kiss, hungry and arousing.

"Suzie's next door, Lita's even here. You usually—"

Before she could say more, he growled, "I don't want them or I'd have gotten them. I want you, teacher, you. Teach me something new."

She returned his embrace ardently now, chuckling softly. "Now why is it, darlin', that I don't think I can anymore. But... never let it be said I'm not a woman to try."

Feverishly, they undressed one another and fell, amid a welter of thrown clothing, onto her bed. For all the brandy and lack of sleep, his weeks of enforced celibacy demanded a fierce release. As he plunged into her, Rosalie realized with a sudden shock that she was as eager, as desperate as he. Quickly, she took her pleasure, achingly sweet and sharp for all its unexpectedness, just before he shuddered and collapsed on her, rolling them to their sides to pant in sated unison.

He was asleep before they disentangled arms and legs. Silently, she rose and picked up her discarded wrapper from the floor. After putting it on, she moved to the small cabinet where she kept a bottle of good whiskey and poured herself a drink. As she sipped it, she looked at the dark figure whose long limbs sprawled across the bed. God, he looked haggard and exhausted. She almost laughed aloud. *Maternal instincts, Rosie, old girl? I hardly think they'd fit considering how he affects you.* Her silent thoughts were bittersweet. *In my own way, I guess I love him.* Rosalie swore to herself. *I'm old enough to be his mother, for Christ's sake!* No, it definitely wasn't a maternal instinct, but it was a fascination that could not last. He had not been here for nearly a year. Surely he had been sleeping with his wife. Something terrible brought him back to her for solace; she was sure of that.

"What's wrong, Mike?" Rosalie's level, hazel-green eyes demanded a straight answer the next morning at breakfast. She let him sleep off his exhaustion and brandy until nearly noon, then woke him for coffee, eggs and tortillas.

He sat across from her, remembering his first morning in this room, so long ago. He ran a hand through his unruly black hair. Miguel guessed he'd known even before he came here that he'd have to tell her the whole sordid tale. He did, from the beautiful beginning that warm October night of the fiesta to the shattering aftermath in the rustler camp when he beat Rice Brighton senseless and reclaimed his wife.

"She's pregnant, Rose. And I don't even know if it's

mine," he concluded, choking on the last words, unable to say more.

She let out a low, whistling breath, scarcely able to take all of it in. Why would any woman leave him for scum like Brighton? It was pure insanity. Of course, there was no accounting for women's tastes, but knowing what she did of Mike's wife, it just didn't fit.

"I know it looks bad, babe, but—oh, hell, I just don't believe it. No woman'd leave you for Brighton. I ought to know!" She looked into his face speculatively. "Yeah, you pleased her well enough, I'd bet this place on *that*!"

He managed a weak smile that ended in a cynical, hurt shrug. "You're flattering, teacher, but maybe a little bit prejudiced? Hell, who knows what goes through that little hellcat's head? I, for sure, don't. She and Brighton knew each other for years while she was growing up. I don't know . . ." His voice trailed off and he leaned his head on the back of the chair, eyes closed, long body taut with pain and uncertainty.

He's so young. They both are. Fool kids, both crazy in love and don't know how to act. Her train of thought as she watched him led her to say aloud, "I don't pretend to know your wife, but what she did last summer just doesn't fit with this."

He opened his eyes and jerked his head forward, cutting in quizzically, "What do you mean, what she did last summer?"

"Well, I never told you, figured it was her business and, well, call it women's pride or something. I kept her secret. She came here to Alavera Street one day when I had a regular appointment with the seamstress. Oh, she stood out all right, even though she tried to act like she was just passin' by. With all that silver-blonde hair and those dainty manners, even dressed plain, she was a beauty and a lady. Now why do you suppose your wife of three months would come to stroll back and forth across the street from this place and then hide behind a parasol when I drove right by her?"

Miguel looked at Rosalie incredulously, as if she'd lost her mind. "What the hell are you talking about?"

"Just think on it, honey. You never went back to her bed after that first night. You came here. Word does get out, even to good women. Think your ma doesn't know about Lorry? Well, she may not care, but I think Ellie did. She came to see me. Oh, not face me or make a scene and belittle herself, but a young girl who's inexperienced and jealous might just want to check out the competition, if she's got gumption. See if I was a cheap old floozy or a high-toned whore." She grinned wickedly for a flash. "Don't rightly know what she concluded, but the fact she came to see means a lot. Hell, Mike, it ain't the thing a girl in love with an old boyfriend does! It's what an unsure, lovestruck wife does, a woman who wants her man back. If she loved Brighton, why'd she give a horse's ass who you slept with?"

He considered her words in silence for a few moments, wanting desperately to believe, shaken by the revelation. Then he stood up and stretched, trying to relieve the merciless tension that had him drawn taut as parched rawhide. He paced to the window and said, "I just can't erase the picture of her and Brighton at that camp, Rose. Dammit, I can't! She had her arms around him, kissing him. Her blouse was unbuttoned. He wasn't raping her—they were lovers!" The blaze in his eyes turned opaque as he covered up his anguish and stopped short. "I—I have to go. Don't let me bring you down, Rose. Seems all I do is come here to pull myself together."

As he walked over to the washstand and picked up his hat, she stood and placed a gentle hand on his arm. "Just give things a chance, baby, let them sort out. I have a hunch it'll be all right."

He nodded as he gave her a fleeting kiss on the cheek and walked out the door, but she knew he didn't believe her.

CHAPTER
20

Alex sat in the small *sala* of his Los Angeles villa, holding a sheath of papers in his hand numbly. Dolores came into the room carrying a glass of his best rum and set it on the side table next to his chair.

"*Querido*, you look so strange. Is it the pains again?" Her dark round face expressed worry. She was a pretty, plump young Chilean girl whose thick black hair was coiled at the back of her neck in a gleaming cluster of interwoven braids. Her shiny brown eyes were warm, framed by expressive brows and thick black lashes. She was not beautiful in a classic sense, but rather Madonna-like, radiating gentleness and kindness.

Alex smiled fondly at her. "No, dear heart, no pains, just surprise—maybe chagrin." He took a generous swig from the glass at his side, then turned back to the documents.

"My elder son, it seems, has come into a great deal of money. Since I doubt he's taken up robbing stagecoaches, or married a rich woman, he must have made a fortune honestly. He said he might strike it rich in the goldfields up north. Damned if he hasn't!"

Dolores looked quizzically at him. "How do you know he has so much money? Has he written you?"

Alex grinned sardonically. "In a sense, yes. These," he waved the papers in his hand, "indicate a purchase of stock, interest in my shipping line, put up for sale last month by my San Francisco brokers. We're expanding the China trade and wanted some short-term capital. I never expected we'd sell as much as we did at the rates I offered. I didn't need the cash that much, so I just sent out feelers. And here it comes back. That young rascal owns almost twenty percent of Kane Connecticut! I figured half a dozen cautious speculators would take small shares. But David has bought up the whole damnblasted works! Just to show me he's alive and kicking—no, make that *rich* and kicking!''

''You are pleased?'' She could see by the gleam in his eyes that Alex was excited, but beyond that, she was not sure what it meant.

He sobered as he thought on it. ''Well, let's just say, *querida*, I'm relieved to know he is alive. But I'm still damn well ready to horsewhip him for his arrogance. He always defied me. Running away from the ranch . . .'' He shrugged helplessly at this point. ''Well, that was a blessing in a way. God knows it turned Miguel's life around. He was the one for Cien Robles, not David. But, hang it all, Lorry, the gall of the braggart! He had to rub my nose in it! To let me know he was making it his own way without me, he bought a lion's share of my shipping lines! He stowed away on one of those ships when he was a lad, barely twelve as I recall.'' He laughed almost wistfully.

''Some things never change. Ah, Lorry, I have two sons, and I have no sons at all . . .''

David raced up the marble steps of their house, perspiring heavily. August in San Francisco was always hot, but the summer of 1853 was a scorcher. He carried a large box tied with gold silk ribbons. Banging the door open noisily, he grinned like a schoolboy and called out an exuberant greeting. ''Anybody home?''

The prim butler Ashley took the box from David. ''Good afternoon, Mr. Kane.''

David cast his eyes at the long, winding staircase to the second floor and handed his hat to the servant. ''Where's Miss Muldoon, Ash? I have a present for her.''

Before the bewildered man could reply, David took back
the box and began to ascend the stairs in ungentlemanly
haste. He couldn't wait to see her face. That was why he
was late this evening. He'd been passing by LaRochelle,
the finest modiste shop in San Franciso, when he saw the
emerald green silk cape in the window. He knew it was
perfect for Kate. As green as her Irish eyes it was, cut in
long, straight lines, the lushness of the color and shimmer
of the silk its only adornments. He loved to buy clothes for
Kate. She had grown up without lovely things, so starved
for beauty. As he opened the bedroom door, David was
already boyishly excited, anticipating her delight.

"Irish? Where are you, love?"

The room was ominously still, as was the whole house,
considering it was well past the dinner hour. Suddenly,
David felt a chill of premonition.

Then he saw an envelope, addressed with only his first
name, sitting on her dressing table. Slowly, he dropped the
box on the bed and moved toward the message, feeling an
inexpressible dread. He tore the heavy cream paper open
and read the brief farewell Kate had written hours earlier.

Without realizing it, he sank onto the chair in front of
the table, his eyes still fastened on the spidery, uneven
script of her writing. She had mastered grammar but never
penmanship. He read and reread the terse lines, trying
desperately to make sense of them. Why, without any
warning, would she suddenly decide to "find a man who
will marry me and put down roots"? They had been so
happy of late and lord knew, after the affair with Denton
Randolph, she realized she could pick and choose if she
wanted a husband. She could have had Dent or a dozen
other rich men. Kate had never indicated any interest.
Why now?

Crumpling the note in his pocket, he rose and strode
downstairs with determination. A scant half hour later, a
distraught, hatless David Kane interrupted the Wilcoxes'
dinner.

"David, what's happened?" Franklin Wilcox waved
their butler away as soon as David had been ushered

hurriedly into the dining room. It took only a cursory look at his friend to see how upset he was.

Without a word to Franklin, David turned to Leah and said, "Is she here, Leah? I don't know where else she'd go in San Francisco, unless she's already picked out her new husband." He added the last as a bitter afterthought.

Leah Wilcox stood up, whitening visibly. What had that fool girl done? She dropped a spotless white linen napkin into a bowl of consommé without noticing and went to take David's hand.

"You'd better begin by explaining what's happened, David. I haven't seen Kate since we went shopping early this morning."

"She left this." He fished the crumpled note from his pocket and handed it to Leah, then began to pace. "Will someone please tell me what the hell's going on? When I left this morning, she was fine. Now this! I came home around six and found it waiting for me." He ran his fingers through his thick gold hair, pushing it roughly off his forehead in agitation.

Franklin approached him with a shot glass of amber liquid and urged him to drink it and sit down. They all returned to the table where both men turned expectantly to Leah.

Her China blue eyes were filled with concern, pain and a trace of righteous anger. "So now you want her back, now that she's gone and left you," she said, tossing the scrap of paper onto the table.

Angrily, David leaned forward. "Of course I want her! She's my woman. I thought I'd made her happy. She's had plenty of chances to marry." He said those final words with scorn. "Why now, Leah, why all of a sudden, without saying a word to me? Oh, damn it all, where's she gone if she's not here?" Now his anger faded to bewilderment and fright.

Calmly, Leah interrupted, "She's not run off to marry anyone, David. You can set your mind at rest on that score, no matter what the note says. Kate has too high a sense of honor to do that, I know."

At his honestly confused look, she sighed. "I should have known she'd take it this way, not be practical."

"What the shit are you talking about?" David's patience was fast reaching the breaking point. All the easy calm of the gaming tables deserted him as swiftly as his Irish luck had.

"Kate is pregnant, David." The flat statement hit him with deadening impact. He sat dumbly as Leah went on. "We just found out this morning, or at least Martha and I convinced her that all the symptoms she's been ignoring are real. I hoped she'd tell you so you'd have to marry her, but I guess I forgot about that stubborn Irish pride. She told me once that you were against marriage. She also said, 'Kanes don't marry Muldoons.'"

As a guilty flush stole over his face, David remembered the various times in the past years he'd considered Kate's place in his life, arrogantly dismissing any thought of marriage, especially between a Californio and a saloon girl.

Leah took in the painful discomfort of the elegant-looking man in front of her without pity. "She was right, wasn't she? More fool you, David Kane! Kate's worth all the fine pedigreed ladies in this state, your mother's blue-blooded relations included!"

"Where is she, Leah? Where would she go? She took almost nothing, only her horse and a few changes of riding clothes, not her jewels, nothing."

"Did you think you could buy her like a pot in a poker game? Is that why you think she stayed with you? For the jewelry?" Leah's voice dripped scorn.

David stood up abruptly, angrily knocking over his half-finished whiskey glass onto the linen tablecloth. "I never meant to buy her, Leah. I only wanted her to have all the fine things she never had before."

"You wanted her to have everything but your name, a name for your child. My young friend, that is the only thing she would ever place real value on, that and your love, if you have any to give."

Ignoring the cutting tone of her voice, David remembered how happy Kate had been in that simple, rude cabin at the Luck. No, she never wanted wealth and its trappings. She only wanted him to love her and share his life with her.

"She's gone back to the cabin, of course! I've been a fool!" At Leah's look of disdainful agreement, he quickly continued, "I'm going after her and I'll bring her back, tied to my saddle if need be."

Swiftly, before he could leave, Leah urgently placed a restraining hand on his arm. "David, please, understand. She doesn't want your pity or for you to marry her out of some misguided sense of honor. Don't force her back into what she considers a shameful existence as your kept woman, or as a shotgun bride. You'll break her spirit if you do either one."

He replied stiffly, "I won't break her spirit, Leah. I do have some sensitivity, even if you seem to think I'm made of ice. What's between Kate and me we'll settle ourselves."

Kate had ridden until late and then made camp, sleeping uneasily and awakening before daybreak. She felt that same queasy lightheadedness she'd felt for so many weeks as she ate a cold biscuit and drank from her canteen. By early afternoon she would arrive at the mine. As she rode through the warm morning sunshine, she was lost in thought about the coming baby and how she would care for it.

Immediately, Kate had decided she'd assume a false name, a married name, Mrs. Kate Montgomery, newly widowed, from San Francisco. Let those in the camp who remembered her as Kane's woman make of it what they would; no child of hers would carry the stigma of bastardy if she could help it. She thought of baby names. Would it be Teresa, a girl named after her beloved aunt, or Sean, a boy after her father? She hugged herself in joyous anticipation and rode ahead swiftly, resolutely pushing all thoughts of the child's father from her mind.

Shortly after noon she sighted the familiar shallow valley and then the cabin. It looked forlorn and forsaken. They had not returned since that sad departure a year earlier and no one had tended the little house with her loving attention. Kate squared her back as she rode up, determined to set things right in this humble place she had grown to love so much.

She dismounted and began to walk up the path slowly through waist-high grass, toward the closed door. It was midday and Mr. Watchner must be at the Luck, overseeing the work. Something about the cabin did not feel right. As she placed her hand on the wooden latch and raised it, the hairs on the back on her neck prickled. Telling herself to stop being silly, she opened the door and walked into the main room.

The sight that greeted her was disheartening. Greasy filth coated the once spotless oak floorboards. Tin dishes encrusted with unidentified food were strewn across the trestle table and randomly scattered on the other furniture. The fireplace was sooty and overflowing with ashes spilling over onto the hearth.

Kate swore sharply as she entered. Kurt Watchner would answer for this! She stomped furiously into the center of the room and let fly one arm, clearing the debris from the table in a sweeping gesture.

"Ya still got thet temper, ain't ya, Irish missie?" The voice was terrifyingly familiar even before she whirled to confront the speaker, who stood behind the front door. Stoker Lawrey's shambling bulk loomed in front of her as he slammed the door. Visions of her rifle resting in the saddle scabbard flashed through her head. Quick as a fox she turned and put the table between them, then backed toward the bedroom door.

"I do not think, *leibchen,* you will escape so easy, *nein.*" The voice was as silky as it had been in the Civic Center that fateful day when Streicker lost "Luck of the Irish" to David. The small, dark man stood in the door frame, a knife in his hand, solemnly taking in her frozen terror.

"You do not expect ever to see me or Herr Lawrey again. *Nein,* I am certain." Now he smiled, a slow crooked half-grimace. "Where is your gambler, Herr Kane?

Is he not come with his beautiful fräulein? We watch the trail as you approach, all alone. No man.'' He shook his head in mock reproval as he closed in on her.

Caught between two loathsome menaces, Kate's eyes took a lightning inventory of the room, desperately searching for a weapon. There was a paring knife half-hidden under one plate on the floor by the hearth. *I have to stall and edge toward it!*

''What are you doing here? You lost this land in an honest game. When Mr. Watchner returns, he'll bring the law down on you.'' She spoke to Streicker in the strongest voice she could muster, amazed at its forcefulness, despite her dry throat.

From behind her, Lawrey snorted a laugh of derision. ''Ya jist better not be pinin' away fer old man Watchner, nope. He be pushin' up daisies out back.''

Kate released an involuntary gasp, but refused to face the foul-smelling miner who had assaulted her last year in the very garden where they probably buried poor Kurt Watchner.

''You see, *leibchen,* we have taken quickly the hidden vein of gold from the east side of this claim.''

''Ya'd a niver got all thet gold pickaxed up so fast if'n it weren't fer me, Streicker, n' ya know it. An' I was th' one what done fer Watchner, too. He'd a split yer skull like mush if'n I hadn't a hit 'em with thet shovel.''

''Yes, yes, Stoker, mein own true comrade. I was fortunate to have your aid. But not to forget,'' he wagged his finger deprecatingly, ''I find you half-dead of gunshot and knife wounds in the woods last year. Our partnership has been good for both, *ja*?''

As the two men talked, Streicker caressed the narrow blade of his knife. Then Stoker moved toward Kate.

''Now, missie, yew 'n me, we got us some unfinished bizness, with no damn Chink ta bother us.''

As he lunged, Kate rolled across the floor. Just as he knelt on one knee and reached for her thigh, she got a grip on the hidden knife and swung at him. She grazed his hand, drawing blood and a roar of fury.

Before she could strike again, the wiry German was between them, viciously kicking the knife from her hand and stepping on her wrist. He stood over her, looking down at the redheaded giant who was on his knees, nursing his bleeding knuckles and cursing vociferously.

"I think, mein comrade, the fräulein and I first have business. If I did not lose this claim to her gambler, never would you meet her at all, *ja*?"

His voice was so soft, it amazed Kate that the infuriated brute before her listened, much less retreated. With a queer thrill of nausea, she began to fear the little German even more than the filthy miner. Streicker was evil incarnate and he seemed to have some bizarre hypnotic power over Lawrey.

Ever so slowly, the German removed his boot from her throbbing wrist and stepped back to survey her. Then in mock gallantry he reached down, took the injured hand and carefully pulled her up beside him. She was almost as tall as he. Looking into his cold gray eyes levelly and suppressing a shudder, Kate stared back at him.

"Still so proud, still you belong only with winners, *ja*? Well, we will see, *leibchen*. Now it is I who am winning. We see how you like—" She broke his hypnotic, sibilant hold by spitting in his sadistic face.

Streicker hissed slightly, then smiled an evil grimace while he held her wrist in a bone-crushing grip. Suddenly, he released her, turned and tossed his knife with consummate skill at the wall behind him. It stuck with a sickening thunk. He removed a linen handkerchief from his pocket and calmly wiped his face, waiting to see what she'd do. Kate made a lightning plunge toward the knife, but just as she reached it, Stoker was on her.

"Nope, not that easy, missie." As if one cue, Lawrey shoved her back toward Streicker.

She tried to twist away from his steel-tight grip, but could not free herself. The German was amazingly strong for such a thin, slight man. Not allowing herself to look into his cold eyes, Kate bowed her head and went limp until she felt him loosen his hold just a fraction. Then she reared up, intending to give his midsection a mighty gouge with her elbow. But, as if reading her mind, he released her the instant before she could connect. She lost her balance and careened against the trestle table, bruising her hip. Gritting her teeth, she rounded the far side of the table, but she was not fast enough to elude Lawrey, who pulled her roughly against his ample girth. She suppressed her nausea when his enormous hand rubbed across her breast and down her side, over the aching hip.

They're playing with me, damn them!

The German issued a crisp order, interrupting her frantic thoughts. "Herr Lawrey, will you be so kind as to escort the fräulein to the bedroom for me? I find the filth of Herr Watchner's creation in this room distasteful. On the bed I have clean linen." Stoker knew the game was over. He left off his pawing and began to drag her toward the bedroom.

Kate saw her last chance. She wrenched her arm free from Lawrey's grip and broke for the outside door. *If only I can reach my rifle!* She swung the door free and felt the hot glare of sun as she raced down the path, only to be felled by Lawrey's bulk as he sent her crashing to the hard-packed earth, rolling them both into the tall, scratchy grass by the path. They kicked and thrashed until Kate hit her head on a rock hidden in the undergrowth. Everything faded to black.

In less time than it took him to get to the Wilcox place, David was back home, tearing off vest and silk shirt as he raced upstairs to change into riding gear for the long trek to the cabin.

As he furiously threw cold foodstuffs into a pair of saddlebags in the kitchen, Chin Lee entered the back door, arms laden with wood for the stove. In the past year, Chin's English had improved markedly. "Ah, Mister David, so glad see you. Missee not here. Nobody know where is she."

Throwing the saddlebags across his shoulder, David answered in agitation, "Kate's gone back to the cabin and I'm going after her, Chin. We'll be back in a few days."

Chin's pale yellow skin wrinkled into a worried frown.

"Bad place! Evil bear man maybe still there. Chin go with you, save Missee."

"I haven't got time, Chin. She's got at least five hours' start on me and I don't like the idea of her riding alone to a goddamn gold camp any more than you do."

By the time David arrived at the stable and saddled his chestnut, Chin Lee was behind him, laden with a motley but menacing assortment of knives as well as a small sack of provisions. He threw an old saddle on his mule while David checked his Dragoon Colts and Patterson rifle. By the time David had carefully loaded his extra ammunition into the saddlebags, Chin was ready. They set off down the road, the mule falling quickly behind the big chestnut. Never daunted, the Chinese knew the way to "Luck of the Irish" as well as David. He'd get there as fast as he could for his Missee.

David rode slowly but steadily through the night, picking up speed when the moon rose, slowing again in the predawn blackness. Around noon he approached the cabin, urging the exhausted chestnut to use its last spurt of energy.

He rounded the trail on the narrow valley floor, only a few hundred yards from the cabin. First he heard barking laughter and guttural grunts, then soft moans as he drew closer. He slowed his horse and quickly dismounted, rifle in hand. When he cleared the undergrowth, he saw Stoker Lawrey holding a semiconscious Kate while the little German, Streicker, hunched over her in the act of rape. Her clothes were torn off and she lay very still. They were so absorbed in their brutality that neither man heard David's approach until the sharp, deafening report of his rifle took the right side of Streicker's head off in one close-range shot. The small man's body slammed into the dirt. Lawrey looked up dumbly to face David's careful aim. Even a poor shot would have had difficulty missing the big brute. David fired, then kicked Stoker's body away and knelt by Kate.

She was dazed and shivering in the noonday warmth. He quickly carried her inside the filthy cabin, past the debris on the floor, into the bedroom. He laid her tenderly on the bed and freed her of the pitiful remnants of her clothing.

By the time he had gotten clean water from the creek and cleansed her cuts and abrasions, she was regaining consciousness.

"David?" Kate's voice was hoarse and weak, as if she had screamed loudly and long. "Is—is it you?"

He put a hand to her cheek, gently stroking it, avoiding the cut lip and bruises. "You'll be all right, Irish, just lie back."

"Those men, they—oh—they . . ." Her voice broke into rending sobs as he held her. Then suddenly, she doubled up, clutching her abdomen in a scream of agony. As she writhed and twisted, he tried to hold her and calm her violent thrashing. A large red stain spread across the thin sheet.

"The baby, oh God! The baby—no, no . . ." Her voice trailed away in soft, gasping wails as the contractions hit her.

Frantically, David realized what was happening. She needed a doctor, yet to move her or leave her to go for one were equally unthinkable. With trembling hands he tore clean sheets for packing to stop the bleeding. Then he held her tightly until the worst seemed over. How long that was, he could not say. All he could do was pray the Chinese was not too far behind.

As he held her in his arms, David knew real fear of the most gut-wrenching sort. He'd been scared in the storms at sea as a cabin boy, and he'd been sickened during the hand-to-hand fighting in Mexico during the war, but never had he felt the bottomless terror of this helplessness as he held Kate and felt the life slowly seeping from her body. He softly kissed and caressed her face and hands, soothing her with reassurances and endearments, trying desperately to comfort her as she shivered in shock.

He cursed his selfish stupidity. *I was furious with you for daring to leave me. I was going to drag you back to San Francisco! I wasn't even man enough to marry you! Oh, Katie, I need you! My Irish luck, my life, my soul!*

David shivered. Death held no terror for him, but life without Kate did.

By the time Chin arrived, Kate was chalky pale and had lost a great deal of blood. The Chinese ran into the cabin, passing the two slain men outside without a second glance. He was back from Boomer Gulch with the doctor in less than an hour, having beaten his already exhausted mule nearly to death in haste.

Dr. Jensen, a wizened man with keen blue eyes and an unruly shock of white hair, was a skillful surgeon and a compassionate man. David was grateful for both as the gentle old man examined Kate, treating the head injury and medicating the multiple cuts and bruises inflicted by Streicker and Lawrey. He, like Chin, had made no comment on the two bodies littering the front path.

"This salve should clean up all the marks on her skin without a trace. Indians up north make it. My colleagues don't much appreciate it, but I've seen how it heals. Keep applying it and she'll not be scarred, beautiful child."

"Will she live, then?" David could hardly force out the words. "There was so much blood . . ." His voice trailed off in horror.

"Well, son, she's lost the child, but she's a fighter. She's young and strong. I've had women lose this much blood and recover. Important thing is to keep her warm and get some nourishment in her and watch for fever." He hesitated, recalling the brutality of the rape, then went on to explain. "The dirt from the ground and even the tears in the birth canal, well, we don't really know why, but they seem to cause a fever in women sometimes. You did right with the packing. May have saved her life. Now I've going to have to take it out and cleanse the area. You better hold her. It isn't going to feel good."

Whitening, David complied, all the while keeping up a low, soothing stream of one-sided conversation with Kate to reassure her—if she could hear him. The bleeding had stopped and this seemed to satisfy the old doctor, who stitched the tears in her cruelly abused body and applied an herbal concoction.

"Shootin's too good. English got the right idea—draw and quarter 'em still alive," he muttered to himself as he worked.

Whenever she flinched and cried out in pain, it was as if someone were branding David with hot irons. Dr. Jensen finished, then stood up and covered Kate with a clean sheet and blanket. "I'll be back first thing in the morning. If we can keep the fever at bay, she'll be all right. The shock seems to be wearing off, but it's hard to say. Sometimes women take years to get over this kind of thing. She can have more children later. You tell her that when she comes around. It's usually the first thing any woman wants to know after a miscarriage."

The obvious kindness of the doctor touched David. He never once asked if the child were David's or if he and Kate were married. After the old man had gone, David left Chin busily cleaning up the filth of the cabin's main room, and took a long walk outside.

He realized achingly that he had wanted the child they just lost, perhaps as much as she had. It was Kate's child and his, created from their love. But it was too late now; the child had been killed in an act of unspeakable savagery and he was to blame. She loved him and he returned that love by taking it for granted, never stopping to think of the inevitable consequences of their lying together. She had tried to protect her child from shame in a society where her own name was already tarnished.

"I never cared, never even thought you had the same rights and feelings as any fine-born lady. Oh, Katie, what have I done to you?" The evening wind blowing through the pines gave him no answers. He turned and went back to the cabin.

Through the next three days David would have gone mad if it were not for Dr. Jensen and Chin Lee. Kate contracted a fever late that first night. The Chinese washed kettle after kettle of linens while David and the doctor took turns bathing her in cool wrappings to lower the deadly heat that suffused her pale body.

A thousand times David wished Streicker and Lawrey

resurrected. He'd seen things the Apache did in Mexico that he would have relished trying on those two, dead so quickly by necessity.

"She will live, David. Her body will heal, only give it time." Doc Jensen tried to assure him as he watched her toss and cry out in feverish anguish.

"Her body might heal, but can you say her mind and spirit ever will?" David's voice was rough and low with repressed tears.

"I expect, son, a whole lot of the answer to that question is up to you," was the laconic reply.

By the end of the fourth morning, the fever broke and Kate drifted into a deep, exhausted sleep. Dr. Jensen, who had been more afraid than he let David suspect, was immensely relieved.

In the weeks that followed, David and Chin shared the simple chores around the cabin, chopping wood and cooking, securing supplies and washing laundry. The town marshal came out the day after the shooting and disposed of Streicker's and Lawrey's bodies as well as locating Kurt Watchner's hidden grave. He found the cache of pilfered gold the thieves had buried near it.

David tended Kate with patience and devotion. He slept on a pallet on the floor by her bedside so he could hear if she called in the night. The fifth morning she regained consciousness.

Kate felt as if she were rising out of a pool of stagnant, warm water. She was hot and itchy, it was hard to breathe, and her mouth, lordy, it tasted like the settlings in the bottom of one of Will Bolton's spitoons. She coughed and tried to sit up, shaking her still woozy head to clear it.

David was standing by the bedroom window, watching the sunrise. When he heard her, he fairly flew to the bedside. "Irish? Katie, you're awake!"

"Jasus, and you look like a stampede of mules overran you," she rasped out, touching his sunken, stubbly cheek gingerly. He was haggard and hollow-eyed, with unkempt hair and a bristly gold beard.

He grinned that dazzling white smile and replied, "Some

greeting for your nurse! You don't look so great yourself, but the doc assures me you'll be beautiful as ever in a few weeks." He drank in her clear green eyes and delicate cheekbones, lovely even through the ravages of bruises and fever. "Oh, Katie, you're all right! I was so afraid and all the time the doc kept telling me what fighters you Irish are. I should have believed him, or put my faith in Chin's special tea."

She grimaced. "Is that the taste I have in my mouth? I remember how it smelled when he made it at home." Home. Back in San Francisco or here, home would always be wherever David was, she suddenly realized as he took her in his arms.

For the rest of the day she alternately ate the hot, nourishing tidbits Chin prepared and slept to regain her strength.

David was so overjoyed at her recovery that he gently cajoled her and teased her, never allowing their conversation to turn to serious matters. He was fearful of upsetting her or bringing on a relapse if she was upset in any way.

Finally, one evening after he had made a trip to town to hire a new supervisor for the mining operation, David returned to find Kate walking unsteadily around the bed.

"Dammit, it's too soon for you to be up doing that! You'll hurt yourself, you little headstrong fool." Quickly he rushed over, lifted her off her feet and deposited her in the center of the bed.

"I have to be up and about sometime. I can't lay abed the rest of me life. Besides, who better to know if I feel strong enough? You can't be stayin' here and waitin' on me hand and foot forever . . . ooh . . ." Her voice broke and she turned into the pillows, sobbing. The return of the brogue that she had suppressed over the past year indicated the state of her agitation.

David took her in his arms, forcing her to look at him as he tipped her chin up with one hand. "It's all right, Katie, everything's going to be all right," he crooned.

"No, no it's not. I've lost the baby. Oh, David, you warned me about this dangerous place and, like a fool, I came anyway, tryin' to recapture the past. Now I've lost the future, too. I wanted the baby so much, so much.''

As her voice subsided into silent, racking sobs, he fought desperately for a way to console her, to share their mutual pain. He began slowly, hesitantly, he who had aways been so cool, so glib with women. "Irish, Doc Jensen said you can have more children. We'll have another baby, all the babies you want—''

"You don't have to say that, David. Please, don't! I know how you feel about marriage and family ties. You owe me nothing." She bit off the last words through clenched teeth as she sat up rigidly in his arms.

"Kate, you're going to listen to me. We have to settle this. We're going to get married."

Again she interrupted with a shrill, "No! No, I won't! I can't marry you. Oh, you don't know, you can't even imagine what they did to me, how filthy and defiled I am!''

This time he took her by the shoulders and shook her. "Yes, my love, I do know. You told me."

She whitened and stilled at this, her eyes becoming enormous. She searched his face fearfully.

"I do know. In your dilirium, you relived it all. Oh, Irish, I would give anything to take that memory away from you. But we can leave it behind, if you'll just listen to me, trust me. I love you, Kate."

She was silent for a moment, hearing for the first time what she had wanted so desperately to hear for two years. Now the words barely registered; she was so intent on her shame, so fearful of his pity. "You only feel sorry for me—feel obligated. I'll not be havin' your pity, David Kane! You never wanted a wife, less an Irish saloon girl for one, least of all one who's been soiled by filth like those—those animals—''

He silenced her the only way he could, by kissing her, softly but firmly. "Stop wallowing in guilt that's not yours to own! What they did—it's past and dead. Together, Katie, we can bury it and go on. As for marriage . . ." He sighed, desperately searching for a way to put into words his newly discovered feelings. "Ever since I came flying after you, I think I realized what I'd always been afraid to admit.''

She watched him stand up and begin to pace, running his fingers through his hair, tossing it off his forehead, marshaling his thoughts. *He looks like a nervous schoolboy!* she thought in silent amazement.

He turned and grinned ruefully. "Leah gave me a real dressing down for my hypocrisy about pedigrees. Now I know my aversion to marriage had nothing to do with your social station. That was only a conventional excuse.''

She looked puzzled, then suggested, "You mean because your parents had such an unhappy marriage?''

"'That's part of it, but I've had lots of time these past days to think about it, Kate. It runs far deeper than that.'' He came over and sat down by her again, carefully intertwining her slim fingers with his larger ones.

"Katie, my wanting to marry you has nothing to do with pity, only love. Let me tell you about a boy growing up on Cien Robles.

"I don't think I was ever able to love anyone as a child, except for my kid brother, and I tried to love Alex—as much as he'd let me. He was always so damn set on making me into his image that he made it hard. I never loved a woman, though. You see, Kate, it wasn't just that my parents' marriage was bad—it was a *war* over us, Miguel and me. I always wondered why Mama didn't seem to want me around. Oh, she'd pray for me, light candles in chapel for my reckless, sinful wildness, but she always kept me at a distance. She was so beautfiul, *la patrona*. Other mothers held their children and loved them, but she never held me.

"Once I sneaked off from lessons and went fishing by myself at the pond near the big house. I was only six or seven. Caught the biggest bass I'd ever seen, must've gone six pounds at least. I thought it would please Mama, that she'd want it cooked for dinner. I raced into her *sala* and presented her with my fresh catch. Funny how you never forget some things.'' He paused here and his eyes darkened in pain. "She let out a shriek and slapped me, then put a lace kerchief to her nose, telling me to get that vile, smelly thing out of her sight and take my muddy body right along with it. My offering was not appreciated. I buried it with full honors in the backyard that night and was sent to bed without supper.

"I don't know when I quit trying to make her love me. I had a succession of nursemaids. I was especially fond of Naomi, but she left when I was five. Mama never kept the Yankee governesses Papa hired for very long. He insisted they be American so I'd learn English, but she had her ways of getting them to quit. By the time Miguel came along, she got Papa to hire a Mexican woman to care for him and a male tutor to teach us both English. Mama loved Miguel and lavished all her attention on him as he grew. Me she only prayed for!" He gave a sharp, bitter laugh.

"I should have been jealous of my brother, but hell, it was hard to hate a kid who fixes starling's broken wings and hand-feeds calves who lost their mamas. Besides, if Papa was hard on me, at least I got his attention. He totally ignored Miguel. I guess my brother and I formed a bond, sort of hanging together in self-defense. Mama smothered him with overprotective love and Papa was always whipping me into shape."

"Did your father love you?" Kate was reluctant to interrupt his reminiscence, but she thought it was unbelievable that his parents had treated him so cruelly.

"I guess in his own way he meant to, if only he could have let go—quit molding me to be like him. That is the ironic part, though. I *am* just like him—at least I look just like him and I'm bad-tempered and mulishly stubborn and inherently selfish. I guess I embodied everything my mother hated in him, right down to the way I looked from the day I was born."

"But—but that's monstrous! How could a mother not love her own child?" Kate could not imagine such coldness.

He smiled sadly. "How could a father ignore his own son? Yet Papa would never have given Miguel Cien Robles if I hadn't run out on him. Miguel's the one who loves the land. It's his birthright, not mine."

He was silent awhile and she let him ruminate. Then he spoke again, so low she had to lean close to hear. "I never told anyone what I've told you, Irish. I guess I never put it all together before. I never let myself love a woman, not after I failed with Mama. When I was barely fourteen, Papa took me to my first brothel in Los Angeles. I thought I'd finally figured out what to do with women after that. It was funny really. As I grew up, women got easier and easier for me. I could charm them, make them love me and I could leave them when I wanted. Enjoyment with no emotional ties. I loved their bodies, but not them. It was always so casual, so distant. No threat, no hurt. Then you, you . . ."

Whisper soft, he traced her facial planes with his finger-tips, searching in her eyes, pleading for her to understand. 'Kate, you were different, not like any woman ever before. The first time I saw you at Bolton's in that dingy room, I could tell you were special. All the time since, with your Irish temper, your humor, your unselfish love, your won-derful passion, you touched my heart, and I was afraid to face what was happening.

"When—when you lost the baby, I realized how much I wanted it, too. It was a part of us, binding us together. Oh, Katie, we can have another baby. I do love you, so much it still scares me. I guess it always will. Marry me, Irish? Please. I need you."

Throughout his long confession, Kate sat raptly as he bared his soul to her. When she looked into his face and saw the tears scalding hot rivulets down his cheeks, she knew she loved him even more than before.

She flung her arms around his neck with a fierce, joyous sob. "I never believed, I never dared hope before. You are sure . . ." She let her words trail off, but it was not a question; it was an affirmation of what he had just spoken. "I love you, David. I've wanted to say it for so long, but the time was never right until now, not until now."

Their tears and their kisses mingled as they sat on the bed together, holding one another, their love a bastion against the world's cruelties.

CHAPTER
21

Kate and David returned to San Francisco a month after her ordeal. Dr. Jensen was amazed at the strength of her recuperative powers. She had healed marvelously. The doc's vile-smelling Indian salve indeed left her free of external scars. Inside, her terror still lay buried deeply. She begged David to tell no one what had happened at the cabin, not even the Wilcoxes. He concocted a story about her suffering a miscarriage and having to spend a month regaining her health before they returned to San Francisco. It was partly true.

Chin rode ahead two weeks early to prepare the house and bring the message about the upcoming nuptials to all their friends. The wedding was set for the month after their return, a civil ceremony with no fanfare. Kate and David both realized that the whole city knew they had lived together for a year prior to their marriage. Even in a gold rush boomtown tolerant of flamboyant life-styles and loose morals, it was not in the best of taste for one of the city's richest tycoons to have a large formal wedding with his mistress. Only a few close friends were present for the occasion.

It was her wedding day and Kate was terrified as she looked into the mirror one last time, trying desperately to ignore Leah and Martha's chatter.

They're so happy, why am I not? God knows this is what I've always wanted, always dreamed of, ever since I first saw him, Kate thought to herself in silent desperation.

As she adjusted the delicate yellow roses in her head-piece and plumped a fiery curl back into place, Kate realized the ceremony was only minutes away. Her dress was the most elegant she had ever owned, made of yards and yards of pale green watered silk. The square-cut neckline and fitted long sleeves were severe with a full yet featherweight skirt, caught with more fresh roses at the train in the back.

Nervously, she fingered the exquisite jade necklace at her throat. It was a wedding gift from Chin Lee, given to her the day before. He had been so shy, yet determined when he brought it to her.

"What is it, Chin?" Kate had asked, motioning him into the sitting room.

Bowing, he had presented the tiny box to her. "For Missee Kane. Wedding present from this unworthy one."

When Kate opened the box she had gasped at the beauty of the necklace, intricately hand-wrought gold and sculptured jade, a perfect match for her wedding dress. "Oh, Chin, it's lovely beyond compare, but so expensive. You must have used a year's wages—"

Before she could go on, he shook his head and said, "Not so, not so. In my family, from China. I keep for bride."

"But then you should keep it for your own wife when you marry."

Again the determined gesture. "When first come to California, Chin marry. Give necklace to bride. Wife die of cholera. Never marry again. Missee have. Chin wish it so."

Kate was touched beyond words. Resorting to a most disquieting gesture, she had hugged the dignified Oriental.

"It's time, Kate. Lordy, but you do look a picture!" Leah came bustling back into the room, giving her charge another inspection, obviously satisfied with the results as she clucked like a mother hen over the flowered head-piece.

"This was a great idea, using fresh flowers for your hair. Who'd ever have thought of it."

Absently, Kate replied, "Oh, it's done in Ireland sometimes." She thought about other things, completely unconcerned with her appearance.

If Leah noticed Kate's nervousness, she did not mention it, but calmly ushered the bride from the bedroom into the main hall leading downstairs. Kate looked down the long, curving staircase at David, standing so tall, looking so elegant and handsome, all the pain and hurt of the past behind him. He looked up at her and his eyes glowed sapphire blue, shining with love. The warmth of his expression spanned the distance between them and brought a smile to her pale lips. God, she did love him, her splendid David! Slowly she began her descent.

Whispering shadows of twilight gripped the city while pale shafts of sunset filtered through the bedroom window. Kate held her left hand up to catch the soft light on her rings, the slim gold wedding band now nestled next to the larger engagement ring with its massive square-cut emerald, a beautiful, matched set. Nervously, she ran her right hand over the rings just as David came up behind her, taking her cold fingers in his warm hands and kissing them sensuously, lingering over her ring finger.

"I thought we'd never get them to leave. The whole point of a small ceremony is to get rid of the guests as soon as they've been fed. Your friend Martha does love to talk. Even Franklin was deviling me by staying late, I do believe." As he spoke, he nuzzled her neck and shoulders softly.

She gave a husky laugh. "You were awhile seeing them off."

"I see you put the time to good use, though." His eyes raked her approvingly as he held her shoulders cupped loosely in his hands, now inspecting the ivory silk gown and robe she had changed into while he saw to the departure of their wedding guests. The ivory lace and silk warmed her golden skin and set off her fiery hair, which fell to her waist in a riot of curls.

He took handfuls of her hair, raising it across her shoulders and burying his face in its fragrance, first on the left side, then the right. After he let it cascade down freely, he stepped back and began to carelessly shed his brown brocade vest, silk neckerchief and diamond stickpin. When he started to unfasten his gold shirt studs, he reached over and raised her hand, palm up. Then he placed the studs and cufflinks in it and shrugged out of the silk shirt.

Watching the play of muscles ripple across his furred chest and hearing the careless hiss of his shirt as it fell, Kate was reminded of that first time he'd undressed before her in the bleak upstairs room at Bolton's. It seemed an eternity since then.

He took the studs and cufflinks from her and stepped over to the bureau, quickly depositing them in a gleaming welter. When he embraced her, she could feel his heartbeat. He squeezed her gently but firmly, rubbing his hard, hairy chest against her soft, silk-clad breasts.

David picked her up and stepped over to the bed, slowly sliding her onto the silk sheets. He followed her down, sitting on the edge of the bed as he pulled off his boots and stockings, then stood and stripped off pants and undergarments in one swift movement. Without looking, Kate could envision his body, all lean and golden with that glistening arrow of fur narrowing from his flat belly down to meet his pulsing shaft as it stood proudly erect amid dark tawny pubic hair. One slim, hard leg flexed as he sank his knee onto the bed.

"Kate?" His voice held a hint of puzzlement, seeing her rigid, still form, eyes staring straight up at the ceiling, as frightened and shy as that first time. "You look a little warm with all that clothing on, wife. It's beautiful, but . . ." He slid beside her and deftly began to unfasten the silk frogs of the robe, baring the tops of her breasts where the low-cut neckline of the gown revealed her smooth skin. The single thickness of sheer silk showed her dark nipples. He brushed his hands across them lightly, then moved to ease both robe and gown off her by raising the hem and sliding the silky layers up her thighs, stopping to caress her long, sleek legs in the process. She lay very still, not turning into his embrace, not helping him remove the peignoir.

After he slipped the clothes over her head and tossed them to the floor, he looked down at her, making no further attempts to touch her. He lay on his side and propped his head up with one hand, elbow resting on the pillow.

"Look at me, Kate," he commanded softly. Mutely, she gazed up at his face. "It's been a long time since you've been so shy. In fact, not since the first time I made love to you." He paused a moment, waiting for her to respond, watching the tears gather in her eyes.

"Doc Jensen told me you might feel this way for a while. That's why I've slept across the hall the past month. Figured if I waited until I was your husband, it might make it all right." Her tears continued to fall silently as he spoke. "I was wrong, but you should have told me how you felt, my love. I'd have understood. I'll wait, as long as it takes, Irish, as long as it takes."

At this, Kate could hold in no more. Great racking sobs tore from her and she flung herself against his chest, burying her face in the warm furry expanse of it as he enfolded her in his arms, crooning soft endearments to her and stroking her hair.

When the worst of the weeping was over, she hiccupped between sobs. "I'm so sorry, David. I—I thought it would be all right, too, once we were married. I shouldn't have married you. I can't even be a wife! What's wrong with me? What have *they* done to me?"

The anguished whisper cut through him like a knife. Before he and Kate left the cabin, the doctor had explained to him the possible aftershocks of such a brutal attack, that she might be unable to respond to him physically, might actually be repelled by sex. He'd vowed to be patient, to let her mind heal as her body had. Now after almost two months he was finding his newly established celibacy to be more and more difficult. It had been naïve to assume that wedding vows could erase the ugly stain of Streicker and Lawrey.

He was sure she had talked to no one about the nightmare, not even Leah. "It's all locked up inside you, Kate. You have to let it out and then let go. We have the rest of our lives to work it out together. There's nothing wrong with you that time won't heal. Only remember I love you."

He continued stroking her hair, then went on, "Now, let's just sleep. It's been a long, exhausting day. We'll talk in the morning." He looked into her eyes for acquiescence, praying she could at least bear to lie by his side and sleep. It was a small beginning. "All right, Irish? If not, I'll let you sleep alone until—"

"No, no, please don't go," she interrupted, reaching out to hold him tightly. "Oh, David, this is so unfair to you!"

He kissed away the trickle of tears from beneath her thick, reddish lashes and shushed her softly, then pulled a sheet over them and held her protectively until she fell asleep.

In the following week, David realized the horrible fears his wife had hidden from everyone. She was having nightmares, terrible dreams that made her thrash and moan in her sleep. She would wake in a cold sweat, shivering uncontrollably. She had been afflicted for the past month since they returned to their big San Francisco home, but because he had slept with two heavy oak doors between them, he had not heard her.

Knowledge of her pain and knowledge of a cure proved to be two different things, however. He ached with longing to consummate the marriage, to hold her and feel her respond with sweet wild abandon as she had in the past. But she could not and he blamed his own blind selfishness for that. He prayed time would heal her.

Wanting Kate to have some fulfilling activity to take her mind off the tragedies of the past, David talked to Leah about charity work. As a pillar of the San Francisco community, Leah Wilcox was head of numerous fund-raising events for widows, orphans and old folks. When she told Kate about the organization of a free school for the indigent, Kate was at once interested in helping. Because she herself knew what it meant to be unable to read and write, she was especially sensitive to the children who came so full of hope and eager to learn. The school filled her days; the night were still taken with ugly, troubled dreams.

Several weeks later Kate came home tired after a day at the school to find David waiting for her in the foyer. "You look as if it was a busy day, Irish," he offered, giving her an affectionate peck on the neck.

"Yes, it was hectic. Enrique spilled a whole bottle of ink and Lorie hit Lars Knutsen, that new Norwegian boy! Honestly, as if the language differences weren't enough, they're hellions. Were you and your brother so hard to handle?"

He grinned. "Well, it depends. What did your precious Lars do to Lorie?"

"You *did* have to bring that up. He smeared her pigtails with the creamed herring he'd brought for lunch! Girls do retaliate, you know."

"I thought so. Well, Miguel and I were exemplary boys. We were absolutely never near any herring, creamed or otherwise, so I know we never did that. Now, the ink . . ." He put his arm around her shoulders as they walked slowly upstairs to get ready for dinner.

"Katie, I heard the strangest thing today. Seems for the past several years there's been a woman practicing medicine right here in San Francisco. She runs a clinic on Portsmouth Square and has fine credentials from back east, a bona fide physician." He awaited her response as they walked into their bedroom.

"And you think I should go talk to this female doctor, that maybe she could help me?" She said it low and tentatively.

"That's why I brought it up, darling. She has a fine reputation and since you don't want to talk to Leah—"

At this she shook her head and walked hurriedly across the room. "I just couldn't, not to anyone who knows me, please, David."

"Shh, it's all right. I understand. That's why I thought this Dr. Denton might be a possibility. She's a young woman, but a stranger, someone who you don't know, a professional." He finished the exposition almost on a questioning note.

Kate squared her shoulders doggedly after a minute's silence. "Well, why not? It's sure and we cannot go on like this forever..."

The waiting room at the small clinic on Portsmouth Square was crowded. Kate looked over the motley assortment that waited stoically, including several gristled miners in denim pants, an odorous old drunk, a prim-looking middle-aged spinster and several pregnant women. Some were well-dressed and apparently prosperous, but most appeared down-at-the heels poor, obviously unable to pay. Several ragged children tugging at their mothers' skirts touched Kate's heart. The women, mostly argonauts' wives, were hollow-eyed and exhausted, their dreams of quick riches in California goldfields long gone.

Just as she was about to take a seat from a shyly polite miner who rose and offered it, a strikingly beautiful young woman with burnished gold hair and eyes the same color as Kate's entered the room. Quickly, she took visual inventory of those waiting, apparently finding most familiar. When she saw Kate, however, she came over to her.

Lord, I do hope she's not the doctor! Kate thought silently with a start. She looked to be no more that eighteen or nineteen and was far more delicate than Kate had imagined the doctor would be.

"Are you a new patient?" The blonde smiled, but her deep green eyes were haunted.

"Are you Dr. Denton?" The minute the words were out Kate hated herself for the amazed squeak in her voice.

The vision laughed softly. "Heavens, no! I'm just her assistant. She's training me as a nurse. I'm Amanda. May I have your name for the records?"

Kate relaxed and smiled. The warmth of this sad young

woman was comforting. "Kate M—I mean, Kathleen Kane. Mrs. David Kane. We've only been married a few weeks and I'm afraid I'm not used to my new name yet."

Nodding, Amanda wrote it in the small ledger she carried. "Please have a seat. I hope you don't mind a bit of a wait, but there are so many." She shrugged helplessly, looking around her.

Smiling, Kate did as she was asked and Amanda called a name and checked it off the list. An old man with a heavy limp hobbled after her into the office.

Considering the number of people in the waiting room, they were seen with amazing efficiency. Kate passed the time playing with several little girls whose pregnant and tired mother was glad to have their energies directed elsewhere.

"Mrs. Kane?" The voice was musical and soft, but firm. The speaker had to be Dr. Elizabeth Denton. She was of medium height, slightly plump and dressed in a no-nonsense navy serge suit that fit rather haphazardly. Her straw-brown hair and level brown eyes were mild, but her facial planes exuded a quiet strength that immediately drew Kate.

Why, she reminds me of a younger Aunt Tess. With that surprising thought she followed the woman through the narrow doorway, feeling reassured.

Once seated in the small, cluttered office, Kate's nervousness returned. Where to begin? How to begin?

Dr. Denton helped her. "This is your first visit to me, Mrs. Kane. I've read about your husband on the financial page of the *Alta*. Why, may I ask, would the wife of a wealthy man come to an obscure clinic when she could go to my highest priced colleague?" She gave a slight, self-deprecating smile as she spoke. "Is it perhaps because you need a woman to talk to, not a man?"

That perceptive remark brought Kate's head up with an abrupt jerk. She flushed as she fidgeted. "Yes, you're right, at least part of the reason I came was because you're a woman and a doctor, too."

"Some people would disagree with you on the latter point, some on the former," Elizabeth put in dryly.

Kate gave a soft laugh, then plunged in determinedly. "I don't know how to explain this, but I will try." With that she gave a painful recounting of the rape and miscarriage, then her subsequent marriage and the awful frigidity that threatened her happiness with David.

Throughout the narration, the doctor was calm and sympathetic, nodding and urging her to continue when she hesitated in anguish several times. When she finally finished, Kate looked out the window. Never in all her life had she felt so drained.

Elizabeth's response was gentle. "You realize, don't you, that if what Olaf Jensen said is true, then your problem isn't physical, but a state of mind? In all the years I've known that old man, he's never made a misdiagnosis. I'd take his word your body is healed."

"I know that. I feel all right. Doc Jensen even said I could have more children and I do want that, very desperately."

"How did you feel about men and making love before you were attacked? Did you enjoy it or just do it because you had to?"

That blunt line of inquiry brought Kate up short! She could feel the heat in her cheeks even before she began to frame an answer. "I'd only been with David until . . . what happened to me." She paused, then looked the older woman squarely in the eye. "I was his mistress for nearly two years. No one forced me. I loved him and loved making love with him. That's why now, this—this is so awful. I prayed it would go away, but it goes on and on. I see *them* each time."

"That's not unusual under the circumstances. Does either one of them look anything like your husband?"

"God, no! One was a huge, filthy brute, the other a thin, dark little bastard. My husband is—"

Before Kate could describe him, Elizabeth smiled and interrupted, "I know what David Kane looks like. That he looks so different may be of some help. That and the fact that you want things to be as they were before your attack. I'm going to write an unorthodox prescription for you, Mrs. Kane, one I hope will work, given time and patience, on your part and on your husband's.''

Trembling, Kate poured the brandy, using both hands on the narrow-necked crystal decanter to steady her aim into the snifters. The candles were lit beside their big bed, which was turned back revealing creamy ivory silk sheets. She had taken special care with her bedtime toilette, beginning with a soak in a lemon-scented bath. She wore a nightgown of bronze satin edged in four inches of heavy ivory lace, plunging in a deep V between her breasts. It hugged every curve of her body and was slit up both sides, revealing the flair of her slender hips and shape of her long legs whenever she walked.

After her visit to Dr. Denton, Kate had purchased the new garment. David did not know that she had been to see the doctor and he had not seen the creation she wore tonight. In agitation, she checked her appearance for the hundredth time in the mirror. The color of the gown accented the dark, fiery highlights of her hair. When she moved the curves of her calves and slenderness of her angles were revealed.

She heard him ascending the stairs and said a brief, silent prayer. She had to manage to do this, simply had to.

"You ready for bed, Irish? It sure took you . . ." His voice faded into a long, agonized gasp when he looked at her, his body frozen in mid-motion. He had begun to remove his chocolate velvet smoking jacket when he caught sight of her, poised at the bedside table with a snifter of brandy in each hand, offering one to him.

Earlier, they had shared a light dinner and intended to retire by ten. Kate had planned the whole evening in advance, pleading tiredness and excusing herself from the dinner table to come upstairs and get everything ready.

"Kate?" His voice was very uncertain, reflecting grave confusion. When she had not mentioned Dr. Denton after he suggested Kate consult her, he had assumed his wife did not want to visit her. He had not mentioned the doctor again. But now, this. What did it mean?

"Come share a drink with me while I tell you about my visit to Dr. Elizabeth Denton's office. Did you know she's known Doc Jensen for years and places high stock in his Indian herbal remedies, too?"

Dumbly, he shook his head, taking the proffered snifter from her like a sleepwalker, waiting to see what she would do next. She sat down on the side of the bed and patted the spot next to her, indicating he should sit. The flickering candlelight cast flashing amber sparks in the brandy as they raised their glasses together in a toast. "To Dr. Denton," he managed weakly.

Kate smiled and clinked her glass against his lightly, then downed a fiery gulp of the warm liquid. "The doctor had a theory, a prescription, she called it, for me to try, if you'll let me. There is just one condition, however, my commanding love. You have to let me make all the moves and not try to take over. This is for you . . . and . . . in being for you . . . will also be . . . for me." As she spoke, she punctuated her words with small light kisses across his face, neck and ear.

"You're the doctor, Irish," he groaned, sitting very still, but his gaze roved over her, resting on the shadowed cleavage between her high, pointed breasts where the gown fell away. He took another swig of brandy.

Slowly, as they sipped their brandy, she began to undress him, bit by bit, starting with the smoking jacket. She gently slipped it from his right shoulder, then his left. Setting her brandy on the table, she knelt before him and pulled off one shoe, then the other while he half-reclined on the bed, resting on his elbows, watching those glorious bouncing breasts as she worked. By the time she finished with his hose and stood up to unfasten his shirt, he was breathing erratically. Quickly, he took one last gulp of the brandy and reached over to set his glass alongside hers on the table. As she bared his chest, she nipped and licked at it, using the flattened palms of her hands to trace soft, caressing patterns in the thick mat of tawny hair. She reached up and ran her hands over the curves of shoulder muscles and down the hardened biceps of his arms, all the while peeling off his shirt.

When she had the shirt off, she pulled him up with her to stand by the side of the bed, running her hands over him, eliciting gasps and groans of passion. Then she unbuckled his belt and unfastened his trousers. Just as she began to ease them down, he involuntarily reached for her to enfold her in his embrace.

"No, David, just let me." Her voice was whisper soft yet firm.

With fists clenched at his sides, he stepped out of his last garments to stand naked before her. She gently pushed him back across the bed, then sat alongside his reclining figure, tracing the contours of his body, beginning with his lean legs. She moved upward to lovingly caress the jagged scar on his right thigh where a Mexican musket ball had left its mark. She explored his arms, face and then moved down his chest, tracing the patterns in his body hair that all seemed to lead her back to that wonderful, inevitable hardness.

When she touched him there, he ground out between gasps, "I can barely stand it, you know, not being able to take you in my arms. Oh, Irish!"

She shook her head, her hair falling like a fiery curtain to tickle his belly as she stretched out on her stomach at a crossed angle to him on the big bed. "I have to stay in control. It's part of the cure. You'll just have to stand it!"

"I'm completely in your power, believe me! Oh—believe me." He shuddered, then forced himself to relax as she went on with the maddening seduction. It seemed to David that she was memorizing every part of his body with languorous, delightful skill, agonizing in her slow deliberation.

To Kate, it was a rediscovery of how splendid he was,

her beautiful golden man, her husband. "You are glorious, my darling, all of you." With that, she moved over the swollen shaft, straining for attention. It was effortless and natural to stroke it with her hand, then take it in her mouth. When she did so, he arched up, frantic in his need after his long abstinence. Sensing his quick surge of desperation, she held still for a moment, then moved ever so lightly and slowly. This was David, her love, and she was giving him pleasure, filling his need, being his wife. It felt good. Kate let that warm, gratifying sensation wash over her as she felt him stiffen and swell all too quickly in one final explosion of ecstasy. It was hot and sweet and utterly wonderful.

Slowly, she raised up, moving her body so she could lie beside him. "I know after so very long, it was too quick. We'll do it again, soon." She kissed him softly on the lips, eyes, temples, all across his face.

"I'm not greedy, just grateful," he responded, returning her butterfly kisses avidly. "Oh, Kate, I love you, I love you. Please, let me love you now?" He tried to lean up and take her in his arms, but she stopped him, placing a small palm on his chest, pressing him back onto the bed.

"Not just yet. For now, you don't realize what I've just gained. I need to rediscover your splendid body, my love, one step at a time. I'll tell you when I'm ready. After this, I know I soon will be. But now, we have all night and I think I detect—ah, yes." She ran experimental fingers down his trembling belly and took him in her hand once again.

As soft fall sunlight filtered in the room, David rose, careful not to awaken his sleeping wife. She lay on her side, her left arm draped outside the sheets, the slim, delicate fingers limp in repose with her wedding ring glinting as the light struck it. Her face was in profile as she slept. He could envision it as it had been last night, aglow with wonder.

Remembering her admonitions not to rush things, he

restrained an impulse to pull back the sheets and make love to her. There was apparently a need for her to take the initiative, gratifying him while she rediscovered her own passions gradually. He would bide his time gladly. *Didn't she say she would tell me when she was ready?*

Silently, he walked across the thick carpet and pulled open his armoire. Kate watched his lean, naked body move with such grace, muscles rippling as he slipped on a robe. A small core of heat was building deep within her, but she did not move, only watched until he retreated into the adjacent dressing room to ring for his valet. Dr. Denton had warned her not to go too fast, but to take her time and be sure she could be comfortable with every facet of his body before allowing herself to respond. Last night was gratifying beyond her wildest hopes. Not only did she please him and give him desperately needed release, but she enjoyed doing so. It felt good to give, to feel him respond, and, yes, just as the doctor had said, it felt good to be in control, to have him in her power. First she must be able to experience that, then feel free once more to give in and let him have the same power over her.

For the next weeks, they continued the newly established routine, she the seducer, he the seduced. Her nightmares became less and less frequent.

David considered this late one morning, realizing how glad he was that she was recovering from the past. *But, God, I can't keep my hands off her much longer!* A sudden gust of wind caught at his coat and sent his hat flying. It landed in the mud from the morning's rain. He laughed and let it go. He was meeting Kate for luncheon.

A sudden storm had blown up on the bay and was moving inland with amazing rapidity, soaking pedestrians in a torrential downpour. Quickly, he hailed a covered hack outside the exchange and directed the driver to the free school where his wife was working that morning. So much for a brisk walk! San Francisco streets, quagmires of mud even under optimum conditions, were at their worst when it stormed. Just as the laboring horses rounded the corner of Kearny Street, David looked out the window to see Kate in the yard of the big frame house that served as a school building. She was gathering up toys discarded by the children when she had them run indoors to escape the downpour. Struggling with several jump ropes, sticks and hoops, she tripped, sprawling in the slippery mud. Toys now forgotten, Kate angrily tried to untangle her sopping skirts and stand up.

There she was, hair plastered down her back, dress sticking to her heaving breasts, skirts and petticoats dragging her deeper into the mire as she slipped and swore. By the time he had instructed the hack to wait and had run to her rescue, he was overcome by the humor of the scene. And by the rain. David's fine broadcloth suitcoat and pants were drenched. His boots sunk in the mud as he reached down to help her up, only to find himself pulled down into the wallow with her.

"Laugh at my plight, will you!" Her smile was dazzling despite the dim light. She took one mud-soaked hand and ran her fingers through her hair, sending a great sopping mass flying with a resounding plop, audible even above the noise of the storm. Mud now trailed in rivulets down her face as he reached his own mud-covered hands up to cup her shoulders, pulling her over to his lap.

She traced a pattern with muddy fingers across his once beige coat and he returned the favor across her collarbone and down her breasts. Her soaked batiste dress was nearly transparent and even her fine linen camisole did little to hide the tautening nipples that rose at his touch. Both her hands moved to his hair. Taking a big hunk of sideburn in each fist, she pulled his face close to her own and kissed him. "I said I'd let you know when I was ready."

He gave an exultant laugh at the raging skies and scooped her up, struggling to rise on the slippery footing.

Kate and David forced themselves to hold back on the interminable hack ride home, sitting still in muddy misery, afraid that if they touched it would lead past the point of no return—right there in the rocking confines of the public coach! Once in their own house, David ordered Ashley to lay a fire in their bedroom and draw a hot bath in front of it. While that was being attended to, the mud-covered master and mistress drank brandy in the sitting room, oblivious to the trails of muck they deposited on fine Turkish carpets.

The fire in the grate crackled loudly, as if warning the storm outside to stay at bay. The flames warmed the bedroom and cast a rosy glow into every corner. A huge tin tub stood near the hearth, steaming with fragrant bathwater. The two wet figures in it were unconcerned with the elements as they soaped one another, sensuously washing away mud and grime while staring into each other's eyes.

Now, clean, warm and ready to dry off, David vowed to go slowly, to make it last for Kate, who had waited unfulfilled for so long. He knelt up in the tub, reached for a towel, and put it over her head, beginning to rub, kneading sensuously through her wet hair, gradually pulling her to kneel up facing him. Ever so softly he kissed her neck and trailed his lips lightly across her collarbone, down to one high, eagerly thrusting breast, then the other. She arched her back slowly, flexing forward to rub her body against him. He tossed the towel away and gripped her buttocks in his hands, cupping them and pressing them to him. With growing ardor he licked and suckled each breast, moving rapidly between them, back and forth.

Kate returned his caresses, twining her fingers in his hair, running her hands down his back and over his shoulders, until he could withstand the undulating entice-ment of her slim body no longer. Releasing her, he slipped quickly from the tub and then helped her stand beside him in the flickering firelight. He grabbed two more big white linen towels from the clean stack on the washstand and wrapped them together in a warm cocoon. Each rubbed the other with slow, circular motions, drying off while stoking passion to a frantic pitch.

"I think we're dry enough," David said hoarsely, shrug-ging off the towels and lifting her in his arms. He walked quickly to the bed and rolled them together on it.

Kate clung to him tightly, still lulled by the gentle, warming intensity of slow wooing by the fireside. However, pressed full length against him on the bed, a tiny flicker of the old terror began to play at the back of her consciousness. As if he could sense the first hints of her unease, he loosened his grip and forced himself to slow down once again, whispering low endearments as he lightly nipped, licked and kissed all over her body.

This is David, my beautiful golden David, my husband, an inner voice chided her in a rush of desperation. Then, forcing herself to be calm, she began to use her hands and mouth, as she had before, to feel his body, the texture of rippling lean muscles and crisp blond hair, to taste the clean muskiness that was only his. Gradually, the fear receded, replaced by the building heat until finally she was involuntarily writhing against him.

David reached down with one hand to test her readiness. As he caressed the place between her legs she moaned and gasped in expectant pleasure, wet and eager for him. Ever so slowly, giving her every opportunity to signal him if she was uncertain, he rolled her on her back and moved over her. When he entered her, she arched to meet him, crying raggedly, "At last! Oh, David, at last!"

Now that he had finally achieved what he had hungered for so long, he was in no hurry, easing her fast, frantic movements to slow, smooth ones, prolonging the pleasure for them both. Still, after so long a denial, Kate did not need much time. The spasms hit her in glorious waves of heady dizziness. He held back as she panted in abandon, alternately watching her and kissing her; then he resumed his sure, even stroking. It took longer the second time, and when he felt her peak again, he added the intensity of his own heaving orgasm to hers, expending one last anguished moan of exquisite pleasure when he exploded inside her.

Kate did not believe it had ever been this good before. Gasping, she tightened her knees around his waist and held him fiercely, wanting to keep their bodies joined forever. All the specters of rape, pain and terror were banished. She could feel the tears of joy and relief well up and overflow.

She feared David might misunderstand, but he did not. "Cry, Irish, my love. Get it all out. I know, I know, it's good to be free again," he whispered in her ear, kissing the salty trails from her eyes and sheltering her in his embrace.

It was so good to be free, truly to be David's wife, at last.

The next week, Dr. Elizabeth Denton received a lavish fee along with a note from Mrs. Kane.

> David and I wish you to do us the honor of delivering our first baby; we hope this will be within the year. Thank you with all my heart.
>
> Kate

CHAPTER
22

October 1853, San Francisco

David swore absently at the expensive gold watch that had stopped midmorning. He was meeting Franklin Wilcox and Denton Randolph for a business lunch at Ushers, their private club just off the square. As he hurriedly flagged down a hack and climbed in, he thought about the upcom-

ing meeting and smiled. As an investment banker, Dent
Randolph was shrewd and resourceful. Now that he was no
longer a rival for Kate, David found him a lot easier to
accept socially. For several weeks after their marriage,
Randolph had been dour and standoffish, but he had finally
offered David congratulations. They were presently involved in several business enterprises together.

Everything in David's life was settled now that he was
secure in Kate's love. He was making money, not only in
mining but in shipping and in lumber. It seemed everything
he touched turned to gold. Walking into the posh club, he
suppressed a sudden desire to whistle a bawdy seafarer's
tune. The rigid protocol of Ushers would frown on
that.

As David entered the back room where his associates
waited, Dent hailed him. He was standing beside a
shorter, portly man whose back was turned to David.
But David did not need to see the face to recognize the
man.

"David, I have a cattleman here from your old baili-
wick. You might know him. Up here for a big stock
auction." Dent grinned just a bit too broadly to suit David
as he made the introduction. "David Kane, meet Adrian
St. Clair."

If David had ever been more acutely mortified in his
life, he was damned if he could remember the time. No
help for it, he smiled automatically and shook Adrian's
hand. "We, er, have known one another since I was a
boy, Dent. Your guess was correct." He looked at St.
Clair to see how he was reacting to the man who had
jilted his daughter only months before their wedding
date.

Adrian's smile was decidedly thinner than David's as he
spoke. "David's father and I are neighbors. In fact, his
brother is now my son-in-law. So, gentlemen, in a manner
of speaking, we are related." If he was pleased with that
fact, Adrian was keeping it a secret.

Both Franklin and Dent could sense undercurrents of
emotion between the old man and the young one.

Franklin was quick to speak up with forced joviality. "Lucky thing then that Dent ran into Mr. St. Clair this morning at the bank and invited him to have lunch with us. Isn't it a coincidence, David, your brother and you both getting married at the same time?"

Oh, shit! David's silent expletive was so intense he almost voiced it aloud before he recovered himself.

At Adrian's look of shock, David quickly interjected, "My brother and Mr. St. Clair's daughter were married well over a year ago. Kate and I married just last month."

"Well, well, it seems congratulations are due as well then, David." Adrian's voice was almost gentle.

Nodding at Dent, Franklin Wilcox made a quick decision. "Dent, since these two obviously have a great deal of catching up to do, why don't we leave them to have luncheon in private? Our discussion of the timberland sale can wait until tomorrow, can't it, David?"

If there was any way David could have disappeared into the mahogany wall panels, he would willingly have done it. Oh, to be invisible! Feeling like a string puppet, he stumbled through good-byes to Wilcox and Randolph, making a mental note of how often Dent brought the damnedest people to meet him.

It was a dazed David Kane who entered the parlor of his home that afternoon, making straight for the liquor cabinet to pour himself a good stiff drink of rum.

"Darling, you're home early! I'm so glad—" Kate began, then broke off her greeting. He was home too soon and never drank in the afternoon. "What's wrong?"

He pondered for a few seconds while examining the cut-crystal glass in his fingers as if he had never seen it before. *How can I explain this to her? Damn it all, I hate to leave her alone just when we're finally so happy.*

Sighing, he placed the glass carefully on a table and walked over to take her hands in his, bidding her to sit on the small sofa next to the window. Bright autumn sunlight turned her dark hair fiery red and her green eyes almost golden.

"Kate, I have to go home for a visit, but I don't know how long it might be. Hell," he scoffed ruefully, "they might throw me out the front door as soon as I arrive, I don't know."

"Often I've told you to go, but why so suddenly, when you swore never to return?" Her voice was soft, puzzled and a bit hurt. He said he would go, but made no mention of taking her.

He stood up and began to pace agitatedly before he replied. "I ran into Adrian St. Clair this noon at the club. Damn if Dent Randolph doesn't find the worst possible people to drag in!"

"You mean the father of your . . ." She stammered to a stop, flushing in embarrassment.

"Yes, exactly my reaction, the father of the girl I practically left standing at the altar! Interesting luncheon partner, don't you agree?"

"But I thought your brother married her, that it was all worked out?"

He scowled and ran his fingers through his hair. "So did I, but according to old Adrian, and I quote, 'He treats his livestock a damn sight better than he treats his wife!' Miguel, if his father-in-law is right, has taken the leading madam of Los Angeles as his special paramour!"

"I can imagine what his wife thinks of his dallyings with a notorious prostitute!" Kate's indignation was fierce.

David barked a harsh laugh. "His wife isn't able to protest much due to her delicate condition."

"She's pregnant? But that's wonderful news!" To Kate, who so longed for a child, it seemed the solution to everything.

"Hell, that's the least of it! From what her father tells me, Miguel's probably got half the women in Los Angeles County pregnant!" He ran his hands through his hair again and shook his head to clear it. "How in the name of all his holy, sanctimonious seminary days can one man change so much?"

Kate quietly suggested, "Maybe he hasn't really changed at all, but finally become himself."

David grinned at her crookedly. "The Kane in him will out, you mean?"

"Something like that. You said your mother and that priest had such a hold on him as a boy. Well, maybe he's just making up for lost time."

At that he laughed out loud. "It might just take him a few years to catch up with Alex—and me." He added the latter to forestall her imminent protest. He knew what she was thinking.

Then sobering, he came over and sat down beside her. "Kate, whatever it means, something's seriously wrong at Cien Robles and my brother and his wife are unhappy. A good part of that is my fault—I forced the marriage on him by running out. I have to go back and see if Adrian's crazy. If not, well, Miguel and I were close as kids. Maybe I can help. God, who'd have ever imagined it! I bet Mama's livid. Miguel and Rosalie Parker! And I thought he'd have a hard enough time handling one young girl when he was forced to marry!"

"Oh, and you think a woman needs to be 'handled,' now do you?" She raised her eyebrows in mock indignation and her brogue returned as she cocked her head saucily at him.

"Well, Irish," he said, moving closer to her on the sofa, "I always thought you liked it when I handled you ... like ... this ..."

As they prepared for bed that evening, Kate was still troubled by a nagging whisper in the back of her mind. She sat at her dressing table and brushed her hair, deep in thought.

Noting her pensive mood, David took the brush from her hands. "Allow me?" With soft, slow strokes, he ran the bristles through her hair until it crackled in splendor. "Why so quiet, Irish? Are you missing me already? I shouldn't be gone that long, you know."

Kate glanced down, then squared her shoulders and swallowed. She turned and took the brush from him, gripping its ivory handle tightly in her slim fingers. "David, why can't you take me with you? It is because I *am* Irish, that I might disgrace you?" Her voice was very low, almost a childlike whisper.

He knelt beside her chair, pulling her hands into his grasp. The look in his sapphire eyes was piercing. "Don't talk crazy, Kate! I may have a crazy brother to deal with, but I'll be damned if I'll have a crazy wife, too! Look at you—you're beautiful, intelligent, refined. Not a woman in the state can compare to you. I love you. That's why I won't let them hurt you. My mother trots out family pedigrees like they were charro horses. Human beings are no more than blooded breeding stock to her. Alex isn't much better. He bought his way into that whole closed society and I defied him and ran away from it before it smothered me. He'll blame you because of what I did. No, Kate, you wouldn't have a chance. I don't even know how my brother or his wife would treat you."

Kate sat stiffly, unconvinced. "David, I don't need to be protected. You may be right about your parents, but you obviously still care for your brother or you wouldn't be going back. Maybe his wife could use a friend, a woman near her own age. I doubt you mother approves of her a great deal more than she would of me. After all, she's a Yankee." She waited.

He shrugged and sighed. "There you have a point, but it's too much to ask, Kate. I can't be sure we'll even be allowed inside the door."

"Or," she turned away in anger, "you can't be sure if you bring saloon trash with you that they'll let *you* in the door!"

He swore and gritted his teeth. She could be so blindly stubborn and this unfounded insistence on her inferiority hurt him most of all. Gently, he stroked her quivering jaw, then turned her face, forcing her to look at him. "You look like a wounded fawn." That brought forth a blaze of anger, as he hoped it would. Kate would never allow herself the luxury of self-pity.

"Wounded is it! Hardly that, David Kane. I can take

care of meself and if you're proud of me, no one, no one else on earth can hurt me! Let those high-and-mighty Kanes do their damnedest!''

It was settled. Kate went with her husband on the long, autumn journey into cattle country.

CHAPTER
23

October 1853, Cien Robles

Maria rose stiffly, gripping the altar rail with thin, blue-tinged fingers, cramped from clutching her rosary tightly. How long had it been? Hours? She was not sure, but her knees and back cried out in stiffened protest when she stood. It was no use. She had failed once again. Daily, often several times a day, she came to the chapel to pray. She had yet to feel her thoughts ascend heavenward. Since last spring when Miguel brought Ellie home after her abduction by Rice Brighton, Maria had been trapped in a hell of her own making.

Maria would never forget her stark terror as her furious son carried the dazed girl upstairs. Then to find out that Ellie carried a child—Maria's own grandchild! Maria had refused to consider that possibility until confronted with irrefutable proof. However, as the months passed, Ellie's body swelled, giving eloquent testimony to the growing life within her.

When Maria had allowed Sarita to take the jewels and then had forged the letter, she had not thought much about the consequences of her part in Ellie's kidnapping. She had forced herself to think only of how much better off Miguel would be once freed of the lascivious little creature he had married. It was for his benefit, after all, that the girl go off with her old lover. Maria convinced herself that once the cheap gringa was with Brighton she would revert to her old ways and gladly stay with him. Then Maria would go to Father Sebastian and confess her small part in what turned out to be a fortuitous accident. Miguel's travesty of a marriage could be annulled and all would be well.

However, once Ellie had been retrieved and the bitter grief between husband and wife emerged, Maria had been afraid to confess. What if Father Sebastian insisted she tell her son what she had done? Merciful Mother of God! Miguel would turn that implacable anger on her. Now he lavished it on his ill, despondent wife. No, Maria did not possess the courage to confess.

Desperately, she knelt again to ask for guidance. So intent was she on her prayers that she did not hear her daughter-in-law come into the sanctuary. Ellie was thin and haggard. She walked silently down the aisle to confront Maria, who gasped in shock.

"You should not creep up to people while they are in communion with God," she managed icily, her old haughty manner returning instinctively. "It is not proper."

"Instruct me, Mother Kane, just what is proper? Is it proper to steal? To lie? To help a madman kidnap your own son's wife? To risk Miguel's life as well as mine? Is that *proper*?" Ellie's voice was low and vibrant, cutting through the stale, incense-laden air of the small chapel like a rain-freshened wind.

"What insane accusations are these?" Maria drew herself up and tried to walk past her pale, furious daughter-in-law.

Ellie stopped her, one hand on her abdomen, the other grabbing Maria's beringed hand and thrusting it against the quivering life in her belly. "This is your grandchild and you know it! You know how I love your son. I've never been with another man. I loathe Rice Brighton.''

Maria withdrew her hand as if burned, whitening with shock at the truth of Ellie's words. She stood frozen in the chapel aisle.

''I know you hate me and want me gone, but how could you do this to *him*? How could you hurt your own son so terribly? You know he thinks I've been with Rice, that the child may not be his. This is your grandchild, your son's child and if it's half St. Clair, it's damn sure half Kane! It will be a boy and it will look like an Alvarez. I swear it! When you see your grandson, you think on what I've said. If you can live with the pain you've caused Miguel, you're no kind of mother!''

Before the horrified Maria could speak, Ellie vanished through the candle smoke. It was as if Maria's own guilty conscience had conjured Ellie's accusing form, then willed her away when the pain became too unbearable. Shaken and dizzy, Maria dropped onto a hard wooden bench to collect herself.

Ellie's accusations were true. Miguel worked from dawn to dusk like a man driven by the fires of hell, his face bleak and haunted. He seldom spoke and never smiled. He went to town frequently, openly betraying his marriage vows with harlots. The nights he stayed at home he drank himself to sleep. Yet for all of that, Maria could not confess and turn his bitterness with Ellie toward herself. She desperately hoped that the child would look like an Alvarez as Ellie had promised. Then Miguel would recognize his own and rejoice. She would wait.

The ensuing months were not easy. Ellie was desperately ill in the latter stages of pregnancy and the doctor blamed it on her sadness over Miguel's behavior. Alex snarled at both Maria and Miguel, hating them for Ellie's pain.

And still, Maria could not pray.

Alex crumpled the letter and threw it on the desk, then laughed sadly. ''You'd think nothing had happened these last two years. First David writes to tell me he's leaving. Now he writes that he's coming back." He muttered a long string of oaths and sat down, the sharp pains in his chest causing him to whiten and sit very still until his erratic heartbeat returned to normal.

As he concentrated on recovering his breath, he failed to notice Ellie steal into the study. She had hoped for a chat with Alex to ease her unhappy day, but immediately recognized that his pale, still reaction meant his heart was troubling him again.

"Alex, just sit back. I'll get some water." She spoke calmly, but in her condition, she moved awkwardly.

"Forget water. The rum." He made a quick gesture with his right hand toward the liquor cabinet.

Obediently, she filled a shot glass and offered it to him. "What's the matter? You've been caged up in here all afternoon, ever since that rider came."

He took a sip of the rum and leveled his dark blue gaze on her thin, pale face, its planes and hollows accentuated by fatigue and illness. "You look pretty rotten yourself, and you're a hell of a lot younger than me. You need this tot of rum more than I do."

Looking at those sapphire eyes, she was poignantly reminded of her husband's eyes when they had once been warmed by love for her. Pushing the pain to the back of her mind, Ellie chided him, "You're avoiding my question. Did that rider bring bad news?"

He shrugged. "Yes and no. Hell, I don't know. The prodigal returns. David's coming home, rich and successful and married."

Ellie's eyes narrowed in a sudden flash of anger. She abruptly sat down in the chair next to his and tried to collect her thoughts. What did this mean? "You—you wouldn't give Cien Robles back to him? Miguel's worked so hard—both ranches are doing so well since he's taken over—"

Alex shook his head vehemently, silencing her, then spoke gently. "Oh, Eleanor, child, you still love him so much, still fight for him after all the pain he's caused you." He sighed as she sat mute and miserable under his kind scrutiny. "No, of course I would not, and David would never ask to run Cien Robles. He never wanted it in the first place. He's not capable of doing what Miguel does and they both know it. So do I."

"Then why—why is he coming home? To show off a rich San Francisco wife? Some grand society dame, no doubt." Her delicate little face hardened in anger at her cavalier brother-in-law.

Alex gave a bitter bark of laughter. "Hardly that, my dear. He's married some damn Irish saloon whore from Bent Fork—the same girl who caused the shooting fracas two years ago. I'd hardly call her high society," he finished sarcastically.

Even though Ellie knew she never wanted to marry David, this still hurt her pride. She, a St. Clair, beautiful and accomplished, scorned for a saloon girl! What kind of spoiled, schoolboy was David Kane? To leave all the responsibility and backbreaking work to his brother? Just looking at Alex's face, ravaged with hurt and illness, made her even more furious. How could he do this to his own father most of all—the father who always loved him best? Ellie was well-prepared to dislike her brother-in-law.

Alex interrupted her angry reverie with his words. "To tell you the truth, I don't know why he's coming back. For all that we're so alike, we were never good at understanding one another. Maybe he wants to flaunt his self-made success. Maybe he actually hopes we'll welcome his bride." He shrugged. "He and Miguel were close as boys. Maybe his guilty conscience has finally brought him home to make peace with his brother. I guess we'll just have to wait and see."

Kate fidgeted with her reticule, pulling out a tiny hand mirror to check her hat and hair for the tenth time since the coach had come onto Cien Robles land over an hour ago.

"You're gorgeous, Irish. Quit fussing." Smiling his

most encouraging boyish grin, David put the mirror back in her bag and gently squeezed her hand.

Kate looked into those deep blue eyes, so full of warmth and assurance, finding her strength there as always. She would make him proud of her. She would act the part of a fine-born lady, as genteel as her mother-in-law or sister-in-law. Damn them, she would! Still, the old taunting thought danced around the corners of her mind: *Kanes don't marry Muldoons*. The Kanes and all their Californio relatives were Catholic. She and David had been married in a civil ceremony. Her new in-laws probably did not even consider them married. As her thoughts skittered about, veering her mood from mulish self-confidence to nervous agitation, the coach suddenly slowed. They rounded a bend and the dense stands of oaks gave way to a breathtaking sight, the hacienda of Cien Robles with its whitewashed adobe walls and red tile roof gleaming in the afternoon sun.

Kate gasped in shock. She had known the ranch was one of the largest in the state, but nothing had prepared her for the splendor of the huge complex of buildings, stables and corrals that spread before her.

"Why, it's a kingdom, something from a storybook," she breathed.

David smiled. "Don't let the size intimidate you, Kate. It's only a place—and believe me, it's not enchanted! The people are all mortals, all too human in fact," he finished darkly.

Ellie heard the commotion of the coach arriving. Slowly, hampered by her swollen belly, she rose from her bed. Padding silently to the window, she looked out but could not see them. Sighing, she rang for Luz to help her dress to meet the unwelcome visitors. Pray God they were only to be visitors, not permanent residents!

As she descended the stairs, clad in a plain lavender day dress, Ellie felt sure she would look drab indeed next to her brother-in-law's flashy wife. She fully expected to see a garish, expensively dressed woman with orange hair, dripping in diamonds, speaking with a crass Irish brogue.

But Kate was a surprise to Ellie. She wore a simply tailored elegant traveling suit of dark rust linen that complemented her hair. She was indeed a redhead, but it was obviously a natural shade, very dark and quite lovely, arranged in a coil at the back of her neck and covered with a small hat that matched her suit. Grudgingly, Ellie admitted she looked every inch a lady. As she reached the bottom of the stairs, she could hear Kate's voice, soft and well-modulated. David's bride appeared gracious as well as beautiful.

Kate caught her new sister-in-law's descent from the corner of her eye as she attempted to make stilted small talk with Alex, who had come out to greet them, none too heartily. She knew this must be Ellie, the delicate, silver-haired wife of David's younger brother. The poor girl was pale and thin, despite the fact she was large with child. She looked desperately unhappy. Alex greeted her warmly, taking her protectively on his arm.

At least she has a friend, Kate thought ruefully to herself, knowing full well the arrogant disapproval Alex held in check as he greeted her. He was polite to David and Kate, yet the warmth in those dark blue eyes now beaming at Ellie had not extended to his other daughter-in-law.

Kate had been startled at how much David resembled his father, even though her husband had told her often that it was so. Elegant and sleek, Alex Kane was slightly graying and his face lined, yet he was David a generation older. He had seemed colder, too, until he looked at Eleanor St. Clair Kane.

"Ellie, you remember David, and this is his new wife, Kathleen, er, Kate." His voice was clipped and impersonal as he completed the introductions.

David's blinding smile and winning charm turned on in full force. If he felt any unease at meeting the woman he had jilted two years earlier, he did not show it. Rather, he was gentle and almost teasing in his boyish appeal, trying to win the reticent girl over. "Your father told me about my pending status as an uncle while we were still in San

Francisco. Kate and I are both very happy about it, Ellie. One reason for the visit was to meet our new niece or nephew. My brother is a very fortunate man.''

"A great deal more than he deserves," Alex put in darkly.

Ellie quickly changed the subject, not wanting to air the terrible breach between her and Miguel before his brother. "I trust your trip wasn't too bad. It's still awfully warm for late October. Perhaps you want to freshen up and rest before dinner?" She wanted to show them that she was the young *patrona* of Cien Robles and they were only visitors.

As everyone was making small talk about the unusual fall weather and dusty coach rides, Maria's imperious voice cut across the foyer. Everyone halted their progress toward the stairs. "Why, David, finally we see you after so long, with your new wife." Her glittering black eyes raked over Kate insultingly. She pronounced the word *wife* like a malediction.

Ellie felt a faint stirring of empathy for Kate as she watched her sister-in-law flush under Maria's scrutiny. "They've had a long, hot coach trip and a bad steamer ride, Mother Kane. I was just going to show them to their rooms—"

Maria smiled witheringly at Ellie and moved purposefully to David, interrupting Ellie. "David, let me see how you have fared away from your family." She pulled his tall frame down for a perfunctory peck on the cheek.

He smiled measuringly at her. "Still lighting candles for me, Mamacita, or am I permanently damned?"

The small set lines around Maria's mouth tightened and her hands clenched before she recovered herself. "Of course not. God and his Holy Church never despair of anyone."

Alex and Ellie exchanged knowing glances. Both felt certain of Maria's complicity in the abduction and wondered how she saw the state of her own soul.

Kate watched, an isolated bystander. But the warm pressure of David's hand on her elbow gave her courage.

They all spoke of her more than to her, as if she were a child or an imbecile! Kate noted the way Maria had interrupted Ellie. Her guess about the girl's relationship with her mother-in-law was correct. Perhaps in time she could win Ellie over. It was useless to hope for Alex and Maria to like her.

Alex let Maria take charge, playing the grand *patrona* and issuing imperious orders for servants to show David and Kate to their suite. He solicitously urged Ellie to go back to her rest, adding for David's benefit that Miguel should be in from the east range in a couple of hours. If the brothers were to have a private reunion, their chance would be then.

As soon as Miguel rode up to the corral and tossed Dominican's reins to Rafael, he knew David had arrived. The whole place was abuzz. He looked at the old man, who nodded uncertainly.

"Yes, *patrón*. Don David and his wife are here." Rafael had always liked the sunny, easygoing David, but he knew who deserved Cien Robles and who loved it with his life's blood. It was Miguel's inheritance. He hoped the return of the runaway would not change that or destroy the formerly close bond between the brothers.

Miguel, too, mulled this over as he walked with long, ground-eating strides toward the big house. "So, *hermano,* you come back now. Into a mess you hadn't bargained for, I'll wager." He felt a faint misgiving. *Would his father turn Cien Robles over to the elder son?* The old man was certainly furious enough with the younger one. Since Miguel had brought Ellie back from the outlaw camp, father and son fought worse than ever. Alex obviously believed some absurd fabrication of hers about being tricked by servants in cohoots with Brighton.

As he thought of his nemesis, Miguel swore. Brighton, against Miguel's fondest hopes, was not dead, but alive. Now he rode with a large band of rustlers, including that bastard Morales.

Miguel forced his thoughts away from the bandits and focused on his brother once again. *If not Cien Robles, what the hell does David want?* That thought was still in his mind as he swung open the study door.

When David looked up to greet his brother, he was not prepared for the coldness in Miguel's eyes or the unsmiling, beard-stubbled face. *He's harder and older, so changed from the seminary boy I fed to the wolves two years ago,* David thought sadly to himself.

Without saying a word, Miguel carelessly tossed his dusty hat onto the desk and poured himself a stiff whiskey. He took a drink, then pulled out the makings for a cigarillo from his vest pocket and began to roll it.

Leaning indolently against the oak bar, he finally spoke. "You haven't changed. Remarkable after so long an absence."

David grinned crookedly, as he surveyed Miguel. "I sure as hell can't say the same for you, *hermano*." He gestured toward the whiskey and tobacco, then took out one of his black cigars and lit it. Raising his glass in mock salute, he said, "To corruption."

Both men drank as the silence thickened. Miguel casually sauntered across the room and slid into Alex's chair behind the desk, across from where David was sprawled on the leather couch. "Why did you come home, *hermano*?"

Gravely, David replied, "Not to take *that* away from you." He gestured toward the chair. "You can stake your life on it. I don't want the ranch, Miguel. I never did."

Two pairs of midnight blue eyes locked for an instant. Miguel bit off his words carefully. "What makes you think you could take it away from me, even if you did want it?"

David smiled then, surprised at Miguel's dare yet wanting to placate him. "I take your point. I also know Alex couldn't run the place without you. I couldn't do it either. I'm no good that way. That's one reason I ran out on you both. I'm a city boy, *hermano*."

"With a city wife." The rejoinder was a rebuke.

"No, as a matter of fact, Kate would probably be just as happy in a simple cabin with a good garden. All the money I'll ever make will never impress her. But we're not talking about Kate, are we? I ran out and left you with Ellie St. Clair as well as Cien Robles. I know you're not sorry about the ranch. I gather from all I've heard, you don't exactly shrink from women anymore, either.''

Miguel smiled for the first time, a hard cynical twist to his lips. *Just like Alex,* David thought in shocked recognition.

Very quietly, Miguel responded, ''No, I like women well enough. They seem to fancy me, too.''

''Even Rosalie Parker?''

''Especially Rose. Christ, you've only been here an hour. Who told you about her? I'm sure it wasn't my beloved wife. Her pride's too stung for that.'' His voice was low and rough, dripping scorn.

''It was her father, when he was in San Francisco. *That's* why I came home, *hermano.* Call it brotherly concern, call it guilt. You married Adrian's daughter in my place and now you're both miserable—hell, I guess I wanted to see if I could help,'' David finished lamely. As he sat across from the grim, tight-lipped man who was his only brother, he realized how useless it all sounded.

Miguel finished his drink and set the glass down on the desk, then stared levelly at his brother. ''Your whole trip was pointless. It's over and done, David. I married Ellie. Nothing can undo that, no matter how much either of us might want to.''

David looked helplessly into his glass, then back at Miguel. He had bungled things badly. Now was obviously not the time to discuss his brother's marital problems. What if the girl hated him and fought the match? He needed more information. First he must talk to Alex, some of the servants, find out about Ellie.

''Well, when the baby's born, you may both feel better about things.'' David strove for a positive note.

''Maybe, maybe not,'' was the enigmatic reply.

Kate smiled as she watched David undress slowly and thoughtfully. She had talked with Luz earlier and was sure

David would be interested in hearing about the women's conversation.

"You're thinking about Miguel and his wife?" she asked, but already knew the answer.

Absently, David nodded. "I really botched things this afternoon. God, Irish, he's so different, so cold, so . . ."

"Grown up," she supplied. "He couldn't stay a boy forever, not even for you, darling. You know, it's strange. I was struck by how much alike you and your father are, even though you'd warned me, but despite his darkness, Miguel's like him, too."

David smiled. "I grew up with them both and I never really saw it before today. I'm not sure it's so good. He seems to have all Alex's worst traits—he's arrogant, selfish, womanizing."

Kate's green eyes danced. "Of course, you're none of the above." As he shrugged, she giggled.

"You know I'm a reformed man . . . well, at least I've reformed my ways with the ladies."

"Speaking of ladies, what do you think of your brother's wife?" Kate looked serious now.

"She's a real beauty. I had visions of coming home and finding a spindly blond waif. I hadn't seen her since she was a kid. He sure can't object to how she looks."

Kate sighed and brushed his assessment of Ellie's physical appearance aside. "Men, always judging a woman by her looks! I meant *her*—her mind, her feelings. David, she adores her husband! Couldn't you see it? Oh, she tries hard enough to hide it, but I could tell. I watched her all evening. The minute Miguel came in the room, she couldn't take her eyes off him. She loves him and he treats her like dirt. It's a crying shame. I talked to her maid and got quite an earful tonight."

He looked up, startled. "How could you get one of the servants to talk to you?"

Kate smiled and answered, careful to use her brogue, "You forget, Davie, me love, I was a maid like Luz, and a far worse establishment it was, too. We speak the same language, we do.''

''And what did this fount of information have to say?''

Kate told him all the bits and pieces Luz had gleaned in the past months since Miguel had brought Ellie back from the outlaw camp—the fight, the separate bedrooms, her despondent illness, his drinking and whoring. The consensus of all the servants was that the little *patrona* loved her husband, but he condemned her.

David digested her information, then said, ''Well, I agree, she seems taken with him, but what's the hell's his problem?''

''I'll keep listening for servants' gossip. You might talk to some of the vaqueros you knew before you left. They're a good source of information, too.'' Abruptly changing the subject, Kate put down her brush and said, ''Was I right about your mother and Ellie or was I? They hate one another. Your father's the surprise, though.''

Nodding, David said, ''Well, he certainly favors Ellie, but then he arranged the match and would do anything to spite Mama, anyway.''

''No,'' Kate objected. ''He genuinely loves her like a daughter. I'd stake my life on it. Wish I could say the same about his feelings for me, but I expected no more.''

David took her in his arms and kissed her neck gently. ''Oh, Irish, I warned you how it would be, damn them all.''

''Just you love me, David, just you. It's enough, much, much more than enough.''

With meticulous care, he obliged her.

CHAPTER
24

October 1853, Cien Robles

David ran whistling downstairs, laughing as he thought of Kate and Luz. His wife never ceased to amaze him with her ingenuity. Enlisting the maids in their cause, indeed! He chuckled. Somehow they would mend this mysterious breach between Miguel and Ellie and then go home to San Francisco. He was a stranger at Cien Robles now.

His thoughts were suddenly interrupted as he came to the foot of the stairs and saw his father emerge from the room adjacent to the study. Through the open door he could see a bed. Apparently, the old man slept there. Why on earth?

Hearing the click of David's boots on the pink marble foyer, Alex looked up to greet his son. "Good morning. I trust you had a good night's rest after your long journey?" He shook his head, rubbing his temple with one slim hand. "Wish I had imbibed less last night and I might have slept easier."

David gestured in the direction of the room Alex had emerged from. "That where you sleep now? It was a parlor before."

Alex laughed easily. "I hardly need a big suite and I obviously don't want access to your mother's rooms. I gave Miguel the big bedroom when he came home. This is convenient and suits my needs. Breakfast?"

Briskly changing the subject, he ushered David down the hall to the sunny breakfast room. The sideboard was laid with eggs in rich, spicy hot sauce, crisply fried beefsteaks and mounds of hot biscuits.

As they poured thick black coffee and laced it with cream, David said, "I was thinking of going out with Miguel today. Just to see what he does to get so damn filthy every night. We need to talk, anyway."

Alex scoffed. "You've been a city boy too long. Your brother rode out two hours ago. He's usually the first to rise, often before the kitchen servants, and goes without breakfast. Of course, he's usually in no shape to want food anyway, or he's served breakfast elsewhere . . ."

"How does he manage to run two places as big as Twin Rivers and Cien Robles then?" David asked in amazement. When Adrian had informed him of the merger, he had grudgingly admitted how well Miguel oversaw both ranches.

Alex shrugged, half in disgust, half in admiration. "He's worked grinding sixteen-hour days ever since he came home from the seminary. Got the respect of the men right off, even studies new techniques in livestock breeding and modern cultivation of grapes and olives." Alex related the taming of Dominican and the purchase of the Mormon stud bulls. He took particular relish in describing the fight with Juan Morales when Miguel soundly whipped a man twice his size.

David sat back, sipping his coffee, watching his father's eyes glow as he talked about the second son he had always ignored. When they finished breakfast, David wiped his mouth with a napkin and pushed away the empty breakfast plate. "You sound like a proud father. I always told you Miguel was the one who loved the land, not me."

Alex fixed him with a baleful stare. "That your way of getting around your own shortcomings? You did run off just a bit irresponsibly, as I recall. Anyway, I'm paying for my sins, David. We all do, you know."

Before David could ask about that cryptic remark, old Rafael, hat in hand, was shown into the room by a kitchen maid. He was obviously uncomfortable at the intrusion.

"Don Alex, Don David," his voice broke in agitation, "Don Miguel asks that you come to the corral with me, *pronto. Por favor.*"

Alex snorted furiously. "Asks! Demands is more like it!" Throwing down his napkin, he stalked out of the room, with a rheumatic Rafael hobbling after him. Amazed, David followed.

Miguel and an older man, a small, wiry stranger who was expensively dressed, stood by the main corral nearest the house. They were in heated conversation.

Alex came upon them, overhearing Miguel's voice, "We'll see this settled, Carpenter. You can't have those steers—"

"Yes, he can, dammit!" Alex cut in sharply. "I sold them to him in Los Angeles last week. That herd is old longhorn stock, with none of the new bulls' get in it. It was a good price."

Miguel's face was ablaze with fury, held in check because of Lem Carpenter and David. "May we talk this over in private, Papa?" Miguel motioned for them to go into a nearby stable.

Alex, perverse and angry, would have none of it. With glittering midnight eyes he stood still, relishing the fight. "There's nothing more to discuss. I agreed to sell the herd on Friday."

"Well that's fuckin' lovely because I signed to sell it and some similar stock off Twin Rivers on Wednesday to John Schuler—for a better price!"

David almost dropped the cigar from his mouth. His prim, religious brother never used words like that, nor did he defy their father!

Alex whitened, realizing his blunder. "Why the hell didn't you tell me? Of course, I forget how busy you are traveling back and forth between here and town," he added scathingly.

"I spent the week between here and Twin Rivers working out the deal. You were the one gone to your townhouse in Los Angeles when I came back. How the hell was I supposed to know you'd start going behind my back again and interfering in livestock sales? Stay in town and shuffle papers for your shipping lines!''

''You could easily enough have ridden a scant dozen blocks from Rosalie Parker's to my place to tell me what you'd arranged,'' Alex cut in nastily. ''But I guess you were too tired, keeping a woman old enough to be your mother happy!''

Miguel let out a volley of fine Spanish oaths that would have done Rafael proud. ''Leave Rose out of it! You've no room to talk, keeping that Chilean tart in Mama's townhouse! She's young enough to be your daughter!'' He turned and stalked away, then stopped and threw back over his shoulder, ''Don't do this again. My sale is a prior claim and it's in writing. Your deal with Carpenter's off.'' With that he vaulted over a corral fence and vanished around the side of the stable.

Alex was visibly shaken. The barb about Lorry cut deeply, far more than he wanted David or anyone else to see. Well, Miguel wanted to argue in private and he chose public. Now he'd have to eat crow in front of Carpenter. Before he could do more than shrug and turn to offer Carpenter his apologies, a blinding pain lanced through his chest. Alex gripped the splintered wood of the railing and deepened his breathing, hoping to slow his erratic heartbeat.

The next thing he remembered, he was propped against the corral rails, sitting on the ground with David and Ellie beside him. Her pale face was smiling at him, but her lips trembled when she spoke.

''When I heard all the yelling I knew you and Miguel were at it again. What's he done now?'' As she spoke, she carefully rubbed Alex's temples and then took a glass of water from Rafael and offered it to him. David helped his father sit up.

''Oh, hell, Ellie, it was my fault this time. I pulled a boneheaded stunt. Thought I'd made a good deal and arranged a sale without consulting the man who runs the place. Where's Carpenter, anyway?''

''Gone,'' David supplied. ''He said he knew if Miguel sold to Schuler there was nothing he could do. Cussed some, though.''

Alex smiled thinly. "I bet." He began to rise, pulling himself upright on David's arm. "If you two worriers don't mind, I'd like to be alone for a while." He put up a hand to still Ellie's protest. "I'm fine now. Just can't seem to take losing a fight as gamely as I used to." Jauntily, he strode away toward the gardens in back of the big house. Ellie expected he would rest on his favorite bench.

"He's really ill, isn't he?" David gripped Ellie's arm. "I just realized the reason for that first-floor room and it isn't just to get further away from Mama. What's wrong? Why the hell doesn't Miguel—"

She whirled on him furiously, like a spitting wildcat, her aquamarine eyes glittering with unshed tears. "How dare you! How dare you come back after running away! Now you return and have the gall to condemn your brother who took his family obligations seriously! Miguel doesn't know Alex is ill. My husband works dawn to dusk, running both ranches, and doing an outstanding job of it, too. You have no right, no right at all to even *be* here!" She broke into sobs. "Alex loved you best, gave you everything and you repaid him by turning your back on all he held dear."

David was rocked by her fierce loyalty and the accuracy of her condemnation. "You're right. I seem to be butting in everywhere I'm not wanted, the guilty peacemaker come too late, trying to salve his own conscience." Sadly, he trudged toward the house, leaving her to regain her composure.

David entered the foyer just as Kate walked toward the front door. She was a vision in apple green muslin with her hair tumbling down her back. "Darling, I overslept and got an appropriate scolding from your early-rising mama." Conspiratorily, she added in a stage whisper, "She doesn't even know yet that I'm a heretic! She was two hours on her knees before breakfast while I slept the sleep of the damned!"

He smiled in spite of his morose turn of mind and kissed her lightly. "We won't tell her. Any more coffee out back? Don't bother the servants. Let's see if Rita has any in the kitchen."

"David, what's going on? I heard you and Alex race out

and then Ellie followed a few minutes later. I was just coming to see—''

He gave Kate a short version of the events at the corral, concluding with Ellie's impassioned attack on him. "She's right, you know. I've run out on my responsibilities all my life.''

"You're not fair to yourself, my love.''

He shrugged in dismissal and said, "Ellie's so damn torn, loving them both, knowing what Papa did to Miguel, yet loyal to the old man for being her only friend here. And I'm the one who betrayed them both.''

"I wondered why she seemed so angry with you ever since we arrived. I never thought for a moment she had designs on you as a suitor who spurned her. Not after I saw the way she followed her husband with such hungry eyes.''

"She loves him all right. But why's the man being such a jackass?''

"Well, one thing's for certain. You'll never get her to tell you, but maybe I can. At least I can try. Lord knows she needs friends.'' David's information, combined with what she had learned from Luz and Rita, gave Kate an idea. Praying it would work, she walked determinedly toward Rafael's tack room.

Ellie sat ungracefully on the floor. Chaco leaned against her legs. Ellie was now too large for the dog to sit comfortably on her lap.

"*Patrona*, you spoil him too much,'' Rafael scolded as Ellie fed the mutt another bit of last night's roast beef.

"Well, I have to do something since I can't ride. Oh, Rafael, you don't know how I long to take Moonlight out and run her legs off!''

"You're very lucky to be able to ride that well. Of course, you're also lucky to be having a child. Soon you'll be back on your filly. I've been admiring her in the stable.'' Kate stood in the door as she spoke.

Her sudden appearance caught Ellie unaware. Here she was looking like a silly child all covered with dirt and dog hair in front of David's beautiful, stylish wife. Awkwardly, she tried to stand.

"No, please, don't get up. Let me sit down." Before Ellie could stir the dog, Kate was on her knees in the dirt, careless of her lovely green dress, stroking Chaco.

He took a few experimental sniffs and then gave Kate's hand a hearty lick and went to sit in his new admirer's lap.

"Well, I've never seen him make friends so fast." Ellie was surprised.

"We had dogs at my aunt and uncle's cantina. They were strays really, but I fed them. I was a cook and maid in a tavern when David met me." Level green eyes met confused turquoise ones.

Ellie was taken aback by Kate's admission of such humble origins. Still, she had said cook and maid, not bar girl, or worse. Ellie itched to know the truth. "You grew up here? I mean, in Southern California? But Alex said you were Irish." Ellie blushed as she recalled the rest of what Alex had said.

Kate smiled ruefully. "I can imagine what Alex said, and not just that I was Irish, either, although to Kanes and Alvarezes I'm sure that's bad enough! Yes, I was born in Belfast, although I don't remember it. When I was two or so my parents and my father's sister came to New York. When I was four my mother coughed her life's blood out with tuberculosis in a cold tenement. My father worked in a foundry until he was killed in a forge accident when I was nine. Then my Aunt Tess married a man who brought us to Bent Fork and the cantina." Kate stopped petting Chaco as she mentioned Will Bolton.

Ellie did not know what to think of Kate's forthrightness. She was direct and honest when Ellie had expected the phony airs of a clever fortune hunter. Ellie's clear, blue-green eyes looked at the lovely woman sitting on the gound beside her. "You're right about Alex not liking you, but he isn't completely unreasonable. He's forgiven David for leaving home. Give him time."

Kate smiled gently, the gold flecks in her dark green eyes glinting. "Everyone needs time, I guess, even you." It was not a question but a simple statement of fact. "Ellie,

you have to understand about David and his father. I know
he was the favored one when he and Miguel were boys,
but things are always more complicated than they seem.
He never wanted to be a rancher and he could never live
up to Alex's very high standards. We all have to be who
we are, not who others want us to be.''

Ellie let out a bitter, hollow laugh and said, ''Well, I
can understand that. Who I am never pleased my mother-
in-law and never will. For a while I hoped—never mind.''
Shaking her head sadly, she lapsed into silence as Rafael
came into the room.

''That rascal. Now he has two beautful señoras to fuss
over him! I know how much Doña Ellie misses her
morning ride, but if you wish, Doña Kathleen, I can
saddle a horse for you. We have a fine sidesaddle, hardly
even used.'' As he said this, he grinned a crooked,
toothless smile at Ellie, who returned a conspiratorial
wink.

Kate fidgeted for a second, then said, ''That's all right,
thank you, but I had better not. I'd only break a leg and
probably injure the poor beast. You see, we never had a
horse, could never afford one for me to ride when I was
growing up in Bent Fork. David bought me a grand little
mare, Featherweight, but I'm still a terrible horsewoman.
They scare me to death! I only ride when I have to.''

Ellie, like all Californios, grew up on horseback and
could not imagine a life without riding. How deprived
Kate had been! ''There's nothing to be afraid of. Horses
are as easy to understand as dogs, only bigger.''

''A *lot* bigger,'' Kate interjected.

Ellie laughed and then on impulse said, ''If you'd like, I
can teach you about horses. Please. It would give me
something to do.''

Kate nodded brightly at the winsome note in her young
sister-in-law's voice. ''That would be wonderful.''

As they walked toward the corral the two headstrong
young women decided, over Rafael's halfhearted protests,
that a regular western saddle was more practical than a

sidesaddle. Kate would never please Doña Maria, so why even try?

In the following days, Ellie showed Kate how to talk to horses, how to select a well-trained riding mount, how to gentle a skittish animal with words and hands. After a week of simply getting acquainted with Saber, the beautiful bay gelding they had selected for her, Kate felt her confidence growing. By the time she actually began to walk and then trot the bay around the corral, all the stiffness that had marred her riding before seemed to vanish.

The friendship that grew between Ellie and Kate was a natural alliance. Neither one had ever had a woman friend her own age. Kate had a loving relationship with her aunt and was very close to Leah Wilcox, who was twelve years her senior, but never had she had a youthful confidant. Ellie, who was raised alone with only elderly servants and her father, had no female friends or relatives at all. Her years in finishing school had been a misery of friendless isolation. She had been a freak, the lone Westerner, far too pretty to be trusted by the plainer Eastern belles. For the first time in her life she had a woman friend.

The budding friendship was sealed a scant two weeks after Kate's arrival at Cien Robles. The first Sunday when Kate and David went to mass with the rest of the family Kate heeded David's advice and simply followed the motions everyone else went through. Neither she nor David took the sacrament. However, the first day in November was the feast of All Saints, a day of obligation, when all Catholics received the sacrament. That meant making a confession first. Before David had thought of this, Maria cornered both Ellie and Kate Saturday morning at breakfast.

Sternly clearing her throat, she interrupted their soft laughter. The growing friendship between them alarmed her. Two Yankee harlots allied against her! Now that Miguel had become such a stranger, she felt alone in her own ancestral home. They would at least go to mass and

set an example for the lax men, especially her younger
son.

"Father Sebastian is waiting to hear your confessions."
At Kate's blank stare, she added, "Tomorrow is the holy
feast of All Saints when we all partake of the blessed
sacrament. Had you forgotten?" Her tone made it clear
that such a lapse was to be expected from someone of
Kate's background.

Ellie rose, knowing full well it was an obligation to be
fulfilled. Kate nervously followed under Maria's baleful
stare. Waiting outside the small chapel for Ellie, Kate
skipped frantically over the fragmented bits of information
she had picked up from a smattering of Catholic friends.
What did you *do* in there?

It didn't take long until Ellie came out, looking none the
worse for the ordeal. Kate felt reassured. There couldn't
be that much to it. She would simply tell the priest about
her slips with profanity and uncharitable thoughts about
her in-laws, perhaps about that bit of steak she filched
from the kitchen on Friday morning after working up a
ravenous appetite while riding. Smiling confidently, she
entered the chapel, forcing aside her misgivings.

A scant ten minutes later Father Sebastian and Kate
stood before Maria in the main *sala*. He said gently in his
thickly accented English, "Tell her, Doña Katherina."

Swallowing very hard as Maria stared at her, Kate
squared her shoulders. "I am not Catholic. I was raised as
a Methodist by my aunt. I thought everyone here would be
happier if I just did what you all did."

"You failed, however, my child, to know a simple act
of contrition. I could not permit you to partake of the holy
sacrament under such pretense." He turned to placate
Maria's wrath. "I could not in conscience give her the
host tomorrow. It was her decision to tell you why she
would not be permitted to come to the rail." Then he
smiled consolingly at Kate and said, "I would be happy to
instruct you in the faith if you wish."

Watching Maria's grim, tight-lipped face, Kate managed

to stutter, "I—I'll discuss it with my husband, Father. If he wishes it—"

Maria interrupted, "Your husband, indeed! You were not married in the Church, were you?"

"No, we had a civil ceremony performed by David's friend, Judge Jameson." Kate's voice was calm, but her anger was igniting.

Maria continued, not recognizing the signs of Kate's Irish temper. "I thought not. Is there no end to the perfidy I must endure? Your union has not even been blessed by God. I might have expected as much from David."

That made Kate furious. David's cold, unloving mother would not blame him for her upbringing. "I was born Methodist. David had nothing to do with it. And, I might add, if the Methodist Church was good enough for my parents and my aunt, I see no reason to apologize for it or to castigate my husband. We didn't tell you to save your feelings. I'm sorry we even made the effort!" Kate stalked out of the room, almost colliding with Ellie, who had heard the shouting and had come to see what was happening.

Ellie took one look at Kate's stormy face and overheard the hissing whispers of Maria and the soothing consolation of Father Sebastian. She followed her friend upstairs.

Kate sat on the bed, shaking. *Lordy, what have I done, letting my temper overrun my mouth again! Thank God I didn't use any profanity! At least, I hope I didn't! I pray I didn't!* Groaning, Kate rubbed her temples feverishly with her fingertips.

"My grandparents weren't Catholic either, you know." Kate had left the door ajar, and Ellie entered. She was smiling as she sat down beside Kate. "I'm descended from a long line of French Huguenots. Grandpa St. Clair only converted so he could buy land from the Spanish government back in 1815 or thereabouts."

"Oh, Ellie, I'm sorry about this whole mess. David never takes religion seriously. I'm sure he never thought it would come to this! Now his mother will be even more furious with him. Thank you for understanding, though.''

''What are friends for?'' Spoken so simply, those were the most welcome words Kate had heard since she arrived at Cien Robles.

CHAPTER
25

October 1853, Cien Robles

Alex rubbed his hands in glee. ''Damn if I know when I've had such a good laugh! Confessed eating meat on Friday and uncharitable thoughts about her wretched old father-in-law, did she?'' He burst into gales of laughter. ''I can just see that old prune-faced priest when she couldn't make an act of contrition!'' He wiped the tears from his eyes.

David regarded his father levelly, seeing little humor in the situation. His stricken wife had met him in tears a scant hour ago. How stupid of him not to remember that tomorrow was a day of obligation and that she would have to make a confession! ''I'm glad you're so amused, Papa, but Kate had a miserable time with Mama.''

Alex looked at David's serious face, realizing for the first time how deeply attached his son was to that Irish hoyden. Well, damnation, he was beginning to like her better himself. ''Why is it I suspect your wife can give as good as she gets? Don't underestimate her. She's got spunk enough for Maria and a whole phalanx of priests, just like Ellie. And—even more important—she still has you to champion her." He paused, obviously thinking about Miguel and Ellie's estrangement. Then he continued. "I'll be honest with you, David. I was proud of you when I got that stock sale certificate. After that I had several contacts in San Francisco keep track of your exploits. But I did not approve your choice of a wife."

David's face darkened, but Alex motioned to him to be quiet. "Ellie took to Kate right off and your wife's certainly turned out to be very different from what I expected. I've watched Kate befriend Ellie and that puts her high in my book. And then this, this wonderful gaffe with Marla about her religion. And dressing her down! I love it, I positively love it! I plan to tell your lady she has a friend in her irascible old father-in-law if she wants him. Wouldn't doubt it a bit if she told me to go straight to hell, too." He sipped his rum. "And I wouldn't blame her!"

"To Kate!" Father and son toasted and downed their drinks.

After a strained dinner that evening, David watched Alex and Miguel exchange a few brief, hostile words. As Miguel turned and strode toward the front door, David observed Alex. His father stood staring after his younger son with a look of raw anguish on his face. Ellie had said Alex was paying the price for his earlier neglect of Miguel. David had been inclined to be philosophical, feeling after all the hurt of childhood years that his brother had a right to be unforgiving. Now he was not so sure.

He followed Miguel to the stable, but his thoughtful pace did not keep up with his brother's swift one. Miguel already had Dominican saddled and was just about to swing up on the great beast when David approached him.

"A little late for checking stock, eh, *mano*?" David

knew that, dressed in dinner clothes, Miguel had no intention of working but was headed for town.

"Want to ride along, *hermano*? Suzie or Lilly would be happy to oblige you. Oh, but I forget, you're a happily married man now. No more sins of the flesh?"

"I'll ride with you, but only to talk."

"Suit yourself. It's a long ride to get no reward at trail's end." Miguel leaned indolently against Dominican, waiting while David went inside the stable and saddled up.

As they rode in silence for several minutes, David racked his brain for some way to get his brother to talk, to explain the hateful anger toward the wife who so obviously adored him. What happened on the trail to make him so bitter when he brought Ellie back? Neither Ellie nor Alex would speak of it.

Finally, David decided he must break faith with Alex and tell Miguel about their father's illness. It was a place to begin, at least. His father's eyes still haunted him from dinner. "I know you have good reason to be bitter with Papa, Miguel. What he did was wrong."

"No more than what Mama did to you," Miguel said sadly. "It's over and done with, David. Let it lie."

"Easier said than done. He's so damn proud of you, of how you've handled the ranch, both ranches. You should have heard him tell me, *hermano*. He realizes his mistake. He finally understands us, why I don't belong and you do. He wants to love you, Miguel, only you won't let him."

Miguel let out an oath and increased Dominican's pace. "Now that I've proven myself in spite of him doing his damnedest to stop me! Hell, he'll never let go. You saw that stupid blunder with Carpenter. He still has to be '*Don* Alesandro.' Well, it won't work anymore." Miguel's face was set in harsh lines.

"Yes, I saw the scene at the corral and I also saw what happened after you stormed off. He collapsed, Miguel. He's had a bad heart condition for years and kept it from everyone. Ellie found out, but until last week no one else knew." David watched his brother's face. Something fleeting passed over its sculpted planes, but it was impossible to identify in the dim moonlight.

After a minute, Miguel said, "Why tell me? So I'll start caving in to him, letting him run over me like I was a green boy again? If he can dish it out, he can damn well take it."

David smiled sadly. "Funny, that's just what he said. You have to learn to forgive, Miguel. If you don't—if you leave things the way they are and he dies, you won't be able to live with it."

"I'll chance it," was the emotionless reply.

David sighed. This was going to be harder than he had ever thought. "When someone near to you almost dies, you realize how much you love him and, dammit, man, it scares holy hell out of you! I know!"

Miguel heard the note of anguish in his brother's voice, a sound remembered from long ago, one afternoon by the pool when a weary young soldier talked with his younger brother about the horrors of war. Not since then had David, the glib, charming older brother, unburdened himself to Miguel.

Now he did. Slowly, painfully, he told Miguel about his treatment of Kate, of her love and his casual indifference, of her flight and its tragic aftermath. "We lost the baby and I almost lost her. God, Miguel, if she'd died, never knowing I loved her . . ." He let his voice trail away in silence.

The only sounds in the still, cold night air were the rhythmic pounding of the horses' hooves and the piercing, mournful wail of a distant coyote.

Finally, Miguel broke the silence. "I'm sorry, David, for both of you, even for Alex, maybe. I don't know what I feel anymore. There's so much that's happened, I can't sort it out. Everything's changed so much. *I've* changed so much."

"It could all work out for the better. Even if Alex did force the match, you have a beautiful wife who adores you and soon you'll have a child—"

Before David could say more, Miguel whirled on him in
pained fury. "Yes, a child, only whose child will it
be—mine or Rice Brighton's?"

David sat as if riveted to the saddle, numbly riding
through the crisp November air as he listened to his
brother's anguished tale of betrayal. When Miguel had
finished, David said, "It couldn't be. There must be some
explanation. She loves you. Both Kate and I would gamble
our lives on it."

"Well, your luck would flat run out, so don't."

Kate paced furiously back and forth in front of the
window. It was nearly three hours since David and Miguel
left the ranch. From Ellie's stricken eyes and Alex's black
scowl, Kate knew where Miguel was headed, but why had
David gone with him? She trusted her husband, but worried about his brother's influence. Hearing hoofbeats, Kate
parted the curtain and peered out at the moonswept scene
below her. David was riding up to the stable. Quickly, she
threw on a heavy velvet wrapper and slipped from the
bedroom. On her way down the long hall of their wing,
she heard muffled sobbing coming from Ellie's room and
renewed her fury against men in general and two brothers
in particular.

David was still mulling over his brother's bitter, shocking story as he rubbed his horse down. The stable door
creaked and he turned, hoping he had not awakened
Rafael. "Irish, what are you doing up so late?"

Her eyes were glittering a dangerous dark green as she
stepped into the musty stall, shivering partly from cold,
partly from fury. "I might be askin' you the same. Where's
your brother? *His* wife's awake, too."

David appraised his wife's fierce stance, then grinned,
glad to see something of humor in what had been such an
unsettling night. "Why you little Irish hellcat! You're
actually jealous!" He moved to take her in his arms,
laughing as she stamped her foot and backed away.

"Katie, be reasonable. It takes a good two hours to ride
to Los Angeles and the same to ride back. If I'd gone with

Miguel, even for the briefest sampling, I could scarcely be back in under three hours.'' He took out a gold pocket watch and showed her the time. "Irish, even I can't fly, and neither can he.'' He gestured to the horse patiently waiting for its rubdown to be completed.

Seeing her lower lip begin to tremble, he reached out and pulled her into his embrace. "You're freezing. That robe isn't nearly warm enough.'' He nuzzled her neck as she snuggled against him like an obedient child.

Suddenly she wrenched her head up and glared into his face. "If you weren't with Miguel, where in hell were you?''

He chuckled mirthlessly. " 'In hell' is a good way of putting it. I rode with my brother for over an hour and he's in hell, sure enough.'' As he quickly finished rubbing down the palomino, David told Kate of his brother's agonized confession.

"I don't believe a word of it,'' was her staunch reply. "Ellie would never do anything like that. It's insane.''

Gravely, he nodded. "I agree, but the point is he's convinced and the evidence is damning, Irish!'' When they entered the house, still talking in hushed whispers, David pulled Kate toward the study. "You're freezing and I could use a drink to settle my nerves. It'll warm you up, too.''

When they entered the study and closed the door with a soft click, the still night air seemed to magnify the sound. A soft gasp came from the corner bookshelves before either David or Kate said a word.

"Oh, I'm sorry. I didn't mean to intrude. Please, I was just getting a book to take upstairs . . .'' Ellie's voice faded away in mute misery, her tear-ravaged face betraying her unhappiness.

"It's all right. We were just going to have a drink. Have one, too. It will help you sleep.'' Kate took her tiny sister-in-law by the shoulders and gently guided her into a chair while David poured them each a shot of brandy.

Bravely, Ellie took a sip, then whitened, choked and

went into a spasm of coughing. She sheepishly spoke up after recovering her breath. "I think I'd better stick to warm milk."

Kate said firmly, "You need some rest. Whenever my Aunt Tess couldn't sleep, she made a toddy of hot milk and whiskey. I'll make you one with brandy."

Each bearing a snifter of amber liquid, the trio headed for the kitchen in silent conspiracy. Ellie was still acutely uncomfortable around David, yet she had grown so fond of Kate that she could not be impolite to him.

When they reached the kitchen, Kate set about heating the milk and David seated Ellie at a large wooden work table, then took a chair directly across from her. "You know I rode with Miguel tonight. We talked, Ellie. He told me what he saw, or *thought* he saw in that camp."

She flushed furiously, then stiffened in anger. "I cannot discuss this with you! Miguel had no right—"

Kate interrupted sharply, "Here, drink this and stop to think. You and Miguel are tearing at each other, walled up in misery and pride. Someone has to sort this out, Ellie. You have a child to think of, not just yourselves."

Silently, Ellie sipped the hot, soothing concoction. It was far more palatable than straight brandy and helped calm her nerves. She did not want to trust David, but Kate was right about the ugly stalemate she and Miguel had lived the past months. It could not go on after their child was born. Slowly, in agonizing bits and pieces, she dredged up every detail of the nightmare that began that sunny morning last spring and ended with the humiliating, hate-filled exchange between them at Cien Robles that night. She even confessed her suspicions about her mother-in-law.

"She did it, I know she did! Alex is sure, too. Maria wrote that note and signed Miguel's name. I faced her with the truth months ago. She's guilty. I could tell, even though she denied it."

Kate and David exchanged incredulous looks. Neither had imagined Maria to be the culprit. Surely it was a servant or Brighton himself.

"Ellie, I'm the last one to defend my dear mamacita, believe me, but how could she even have met Brighton? Believe me, I know her. She wouldn't spit on his boots, much less deal with him." David's earnest words fell on deaf ears.

"I don't know how Rice got her to do it, but she had to be the one who wrote that note."

"How could she forge so well? I mean, to make it look like Miguel's handwriting, his signature?" Kate's careful practicing of penmanship made her acutely aware of the difficulty in writing legibly, much less like someone else!

Ellie flushed. "We hardly exchanged love notes before our wedding, Kate. I never saw my husband's handwriting before. I—I didn't even look at his signature on our wedding lines. I never thought to question the note, not then."

"I'd put my money on someone who was jealous, all right," Kate said thoughtfully. "What do you know about a pretty kitchen maid named Sarita?"

David, who had himself dallied with Sarita in years past, darkened perceptibly. He covered his discomfiture with a delicate cough. "Well, she'd be the type to have an affair with Brighton all right."

Ellie smiled grimly. "And with my husband. Yes, Kate, she was one of the women he used to visit. Maybe he still does. She would have wanted me gone, too, I suppose. I'm so tired." The milk and brandy had done their work.

Rising, David said, "Well, we'll never find out here. If either Sarita or my mother helped Brighton, the only logical place to begin is with the instigator of this whole damn mess, that rustler. I'll just have to find him and beat the truth out of him."

Ellie's head jerked up. "You'd do that? Go after him? But he's dangerous—a killer. I can't ask you to risk your life."

David grinned his most dazzling boyish smile. "Not to worry. I'm well-acquainted with Rice Brighton and all his tricks. Besides, I have an old score to settle with him myself." He and Kate exchanged knowing looks, recalling the grizzly scene in Bolton's Cantina on another dim winter's night.

"While you search for Rice, I'll do a bit of snooping here, David. I've heard some interesting rumors about Sarita. You know how well I can pry information from servants." As she spoke she helped Ellie up and they began to walk slowly toward the front hall and the stairs leading to their bedrooms.

Tired and preoccupied, none of the three saw Maria as she watched them leave the kitchen. Once she was sure they were gone, she emerged from the shadow of the black hallway. She had heard David's horse return and then Kate and Ellie go downstairs. Sleep eluded her most nights now, but no comings or goings escaped her notice. Maria sat down at the kitchen table, sinking weakly into the chair her son had just vacated. She had to think. She had to pray. If only she *could* pray.

Sarita hurried to the woodpile to gather a load of logs to start the morning cookfires. Soon everyone would be stirring and Rita would yell at her if the fire was not laid. Sarita had gotten up early in hopes of encountering Don Miguel on his return from town. He often stopped in the kitchen before daybreak to grab some cold food before heading out to work after a night's carousing at Rosalie Parker's. However, today she had not seen him. Sooner or later she would have him back in her bed. If he did not lie with his wife, he needed a woman at Cien Robles and Sarita was determined she would be that woman.

With that thought fixed in mind, she knelt at the woodpile and began to gather an armload of the jaggedly chopped hunks of oak. A snapping twig stopped her momentarily. Probably that accursed gringa wife of Don David's snooping around again. She bent over and resumed her work, then caught the gleam of a wickedly flashing blade out of the corner of her eye. It was too late. Before she could even drop the wood or raise a hand to shield herself, the knife had done its work, silently and effectively. Blood spurted from the deep slashes across her throat, soaking her heavy unbleached cotton serape. As the logs slipped from her dying fingers and fell in a dull clatter, she followed them onto the heap of the woodpile to lie broken, bloody and still.

Kate returned slowly to the house after seeing David off on his quest for Rice Brighton. It was a cold, evil morning, shrouded in fog. November, warm for so long, was finally turning to winter.

A scream cut through the morning quiet. Following the shrieks of terror, Kate ran across the side yard toward the kitchen. She found Rita bent over the blood-soaked body of Sarita.

By afternoon the ranch house had begun to settle down. The sheriff had come and gone. He was doubtful they would ever find out who did such a thing. Both Miguel and Alex knew Sarita had made enemies among the hands and the other servant women and they had told the lawman as much. Everyone went back to work and Father Sebastian made arrangements for a funeral mass the following morning. He was fearful for the state of her soul at the time of death, and began to pray for her at once.

"Who could do such a terrible thing, Doña Kathleen?" Luz was ironing a dress, Sarita's favorite fiesta costume of white cotton embroidered with bright red and blue flowers. She would be buried in it on the morrow.

Kate shook her head, wandering aimlessly around the kitchen as she tried to piece together the day's events. It didn't make sense. If Sarita had been the one involved with Rice, who would kill her? Rice might have wished to silence her. But why after all this time? And he was far away, hidden in his outlaw domain to the east.

Luz's sad, wistful voice brought Kate's attention back to the present. The subdued young woman spoke of her cousin and how they had grown up together. "She and I fought often, but Sarita was not really bad, just wild and lonely. She loved life, loved to dance, to wear beautiful things." She sadly touched the embroidery on the dress as she turned it on the wooden table and set the flatiron near the fire again to heat. "Why, she even wanted my job, to be near all the beautiful clothes and jewelry of the *patrona*."

Something niggled at the edges of Kate's mind. "Luz, did Sarita ever mention Doña Ellie's jewelry to you?"

"Oh, when the big fiesta was held in February at Twin Rivers for Don Adrian, Sarita was sent along with me. She helped me unpack the *patrona*'s things and admired them." A half-puzzled look came over Luz's pretty, round face. "She did ask me once if Doña Ellie trusted me enough to reveal where she kept her jewel cask."

Kate held her breath. "Did you tell her?"

Luz snorted in dismissal. "Of course! I know where it is kept. I am her maid," she stated with pride. "I told her it is always in the third drawer of the big armoire in Don Miguel's bedroom—" Flushing furiously, Luz interrupted herself. "But now, since the *patrona* sleeps next door, she keeps it in her small nightstand," she finished in an embarrassed whisper, not sure how much family gossip Don David's wife wanted her to repeat.

Kate's heart was in her throat. She had to have time to think, to sort this out and talk it over with David. Oh, pray God he came back soon. If Sarita had stolen the jewel cask, she was indeed involved in the abduction but she could not have written the note. Kate had learned that Sarita, like all the servants, was illiterate. Who had written it? Who killed her? Kate did not like the only answer she could think of.

CHAPTER
26

December 1853, Bent Fork

Will Bolton was drunk. It was scarcely six in the evening, but business was slow, his rheumatism ached in the damnblasted rain and what else was there to do but get a running start on the night? He leaned against the bar while Bernice sullenly poured another drink for him. When the squeaking front door announced customers, he turned to see Sheriff Verneer and a tall stranger. The stranger doffed his hat in the flickering lights of the room and Will paled; the heavy shot glass dropped from his fingers, spilling its amber contents across the scarred oak bartop.

"You! Sheriff, thet's Kane's kid, th' one what kilt the Clunes an' kidnapped my niece Katie. Arrest th' bastard!" His small bloodshot eyes shifted lightning quick between David and Ben. Something was wrong.

Placatingly, the sheriff grinned at Bolton, speaking in a soothing voice. "Now, Will, there's a mite more ta this here. It's not so easy done. Kane here claims Tom Clune, Lon Zeltman an' Rice Brighton all three snuck up ta his room an' tried ta shoot him in his sleep."

David's hard blue eyes penetrated Bolton's shivering hide. "Since Tom and Lon are dead and Rice is a wanted man, it appears to me, Will, it's your word against mine. And I've become a very respectable man, even have a friend or two in Sacramento and Washington." He looked across at the sheriff, who nodded in overeager acquiescence. Their little talk earlier had cleared any potential misunderstandings.

Bolton stood up, pushing his stocky body away from the barstool. "My word's good—mine and my Katie's. She'd tell ya, sheriff, if'n she wuz here. He kidnapped her right away from me, her only kin."

David closed the distance between them with one lightning stride and grabbed Bolton by the shirt collar. "You son of a bitch! Yes, sheriff, Kate'll tell you, if you like, how her dear uncle here sold her to Hank Clune! Kate shot Zeltman with Will's own ten-gauge and saved my life when I got Clune's brother."

"Yer lyin'. Kate's gone. What'd ya do with her, Kane?" Will was choking in David's fierce grasp. Suddenly, David released him and he fell with a lurch against the bar.

"I married her. She's at my father's ranch." David's voice was silky now. "Care to contest my word any more, Bolton?"

Sheriff Ben Verneer began to back out of the room. Kane had friends in high places and Bolton, a cantankerous old drunk of a saloon keeper, would have to fend for himself. "Leave it be, Will. He's friends with the governor, both U.S. senators—hell, no one'd give ya time o' day."

With that he vanished through the screeching doors, leaving a quaking, livid Will Bolton to face the menacing figure who now lounged with deceptive indolence against the bar. Bernice sensed the tension between the fat man and the stranger. She silently slipped up the stairs.

What was Kane's game? Bolton wondered. Nervously, he straightened his frayed, filthy shirt collar and appraised David with false heartiness. "Ya marryin' Katie an' all sort o' makes us kin. We might's well be friends, Kane." Bolton stood, thumbs in his belt, fast becoming more self-assured.

David continued to lean against the bar but let out a snort of derision. "My wife would never claim you as kin and I'd sooner be friends with a rattler, Bolton. At least they give warning before they strike."

"Now, lookee here, ya fancy dude—"

Will got no further before David's soft voice cut in, "I should stomp you to death, just like a rattler, Bolton. Kill you quick and clean to rid the world of a snake. Or, maybe I should let Kate do it. After what you did to her, she's the one with first claim on your polecat hide." He uncoiled from the bar and pushed the barrel of his Colt firmly into Bolton's protuberant gut. "And she has a terrible mean temper, my Irish wife. Just might save you some misery if I did you in myself."

"Please, Kane, I never meant no harm, please . . ." His voice broke into blubbering sobs.

Assessing Will's level of terror, David held him in that uncomfortable position for another few seconds, then said, "I might be persuaded to trade your greasy old carcass for one I want more." Will's small pig eyes darted up expectantly to the blue-black ones boring into him.

"Who did the Clune brothers deal with?"

Bolton's eyes almost popped from their veiny, fat-encased sockets. "They's real mean, Kane, an' too many fer ya ta handle. They'd kill ya," he whined.

"What's that to you, Bolton? Maybe they will, but if you don't tell me, I'll kill *you*, for sure. All I want is to find one of them. Rice Brighton." David's voice was deadly.

Will sputtered and shook in fear. "B-Brighton's a killer, Kane, he'll—"

"So am I," came the silky interruption. The sound of the Colt being cocked was deafening as it pressed in Bolton's gut.

"All right, all right!" Sweat poured off Will. "I cain't promise 'xactly when he'll be there, but ever two 'er three weeks he goes ta Santa Benita, meets a greaser named Mendoza." As soon as the words were out of his mouth, Will gasped in horror. He remembered too late that the Kanes were half "greaser."

"Go on." David seemed not to notice the slur on his ancestry.

"Wal, er, this Mendoza is a hand fer th' Q-Bar spread, hangs out at th' cantina, Las Escondidas. All th' rustlers who sell east 'n raid hereabouts git th' word on what's easy pickins from Mendoza.''

David nodded, uncocking the Colt and holstering it. "Bolton, you'd better be right about this, because if you lied to me or if you try to warn Brighton, I'll come back here and burn this sty to the ground, with you in it.''

As Bolton began to nod his frantic understanding and assurances, David quickly doubled him over with a punch to his ample midsection and another to his jaw, dropping the fat man onto the sawdust floor like a sack of turnips.

"Bolton, be glad I'm only half-greaser or I'd have hit you twice as hard!''

The world seemed to be spinning, whirling in a kaleidoscope of hazy colors, then fusing together into one pinpoint of light and pain. Oh, yes, pain. Somehow, sometime, it must end. Then, abruptly, it did, but the blurring spinning continued. Dr. Lawson's voice cut through it, fading in and out with Ellie's struggle to remain conscious.

"She can't have any more of that herbal concoction, Rita. I don't know what's in it, but I fear it may be slowing down the contractions.''

"But, señor, it dulls the pain and calms her.'' Rita's face, like the tight-lipped doctor's, was wavering at the side of the bed. Kate sat on the other side of the bed clasping Ellie's hand.

Slowly, Ellie focused her eyes, straining to see Kate, to orient herself. "Kate, how long—how long has it been?''

Kate smiled reassuringly. Her hand was bruised and sore from her tiny sister-in-law's desperate clawing grip on it when the contractions seized her. She rubbed Ellie's small pale fingers and spoke. "Not nearly as long as it seems. Babies take a long time to be born, especially the first one.'' Her eyes looked up at the doctor standing across the bed.

The doctor responded. "You must try to relax, breathe lightly when the contractions hit and let your body go limp. You're fighting Mother Nature, young lady, and that's always a losing proposition.'' His eyes were kind

and he, too, smiled at her. Kate, however, understood his
word differently than Ellie did.

Just then the cramping agony began again. Kate held
Ellie's hands, feeling her weakening. It was nearly dusk
and labor had begun just after daybreak. If only she were
not so tiny, so frail. Yet behind it all, there was a tough,
resilient core to Ellie Kane. Dr. Lawson, who had tended
her ills since she was born, told Kate that she was
deceptively strong. It was not as much her body as her
mind that had placed her in such grave jeopardy.

All summer and fall she had been depressed and restless; she had failed to eat properly and could be cheered
by no one. Dr. Lawson guessed the estrangement between his patient and her husband. Kate knew full
well why Ellie pushed food about on her plate at each
meal and cried herself to sleep in a lonely bed each
night.

Of all the goddamn times to go to his whore in town.
Kate swore vehemently to herself as she took a cool cloth
from Rita and bathed Ellie's forehead. Miguel had not
even come in from the range tonight. He knew nothing of
how his wife had spent the day. Finally, a scant half hour
ago, after dinnertime, a vaquero came to the house with
Don Miguel's apologies. He would not be present for
supper. Kate had never hated anyone in her life as much as
she hated Miguel Kane at that moment.

Of course, no one had eaten dinner. Alex paced like a
caged tiger in his study and Maria joined Father Sebastian
in prayer. *If only David were back.* The words repeated
themselves like a litany in Kate's mind, over and over. He
had been gone for three days now and she was worried for
him as well as in need of his assistance. If she had not
been so afraid to leave Ellie's bedside, Kate would have
ridden herself to Los Angeles and dragged that callous
bastard Miguel away from his harlots.

After another hour had passed, Kate was spelled for a
few moments by Luz, who gently sat at the young *patrona*'s
side. Kate rushed after the doctor, who had stepped outside
the bedroom door.

"How much longer? She's so weak she doesn't even cry out anymore." Kate's voice was anguished.

Dr. Lawson's seamed face reflected his own pain. He shrugged in bewilderment. "I simply don't know. She isn't moving the baby down the birth canal. I was afraid of this ever since last summer. Her spirit, her will, that's what's lacking. Ellie always had such spunk. I remember when she fell off her pony once when she was barely six years old. Cracked her head real good. I had to put a dozen stitches in—good thing it was all hidden by her hairline. She didn't even cry, only asked how soon she could see her pony to be sure it was all right! Now, it's as if she's not the same girl." He paused to look at Kate's pale face and huge green eyes. "Of course, Mrs. Kane, you've never had a child, so I expect it all seems worse to you than it is."

Kate's head snapped up. "Quite the contrary, doctor. Only a few months ago I suffered a miscarriage and nearly hemorrhaged to death. I know how it feels when things go wrong and I know something's definitely wrong with my sister-in-law and her baby."

He met her level gaze compassionately. "She may have to have the baby turned if it doesn't start down soon. That can be risky and very painful. I only do it when absolutely necessary. And to do it I have to have a woman's full cooperation and grit." He shrugged helplessly. "I'm afraid it would push her over the edge."

Ellie was lying in their big bed, warm beneath the sheets, asleep next to Miguel. She could feel his hand resting possessively over her waist, his beard scratching her shoulder. She turned to reach out for him, to embrace him and—he was gone. The pain, the pain came howling down, jarring her back into consciousness. She cried out his name in an anguish of loss. "Miguel, Miguel! Oh, please . . ."

Outside, Kate heard Ellie's feverish, faint voice and quickly turned to rush downstairs, leaving the stunned doctor standing by the door. *I'll drag that whoremaster home!* She practically collided with David as he entered the front door.

"Hey, Irish, I just heard I'm about to become an uncle! What's wrong?" Seeing her taut, furious face, his eyes flew upstairs toward the east wing of the house.

"Ellie? She's not—"

"No, she's *not* all right! Oh, David, thank God you're here! She's been in hard labor since morning and Dr. Lawson says she's no nearer to delivering the baby."

David's face whitened into set lines. "Where's Miguel?"

Kate spat a furious oath so vehement it probably caused the chapel candles to flicker. "In town, whorin' with his fancy madam! I was goin' to drag him back, or shoot him!"

David paled. Grabbing her shoulders, he asked hoarsely, "He's at Rosalie's, knowing what's going on here!"

Kate shook her head distractedly. "No, no, he rode out before daybreak, like always, and sent word back a little while ago that he'd miss dinner. He doesn't know, but he's damn well going to! She's crying for him, David! She needs him. That's his child and he owes it to her to be with her, the hell with their fights or whatever else he was tricked into believing."

David looked at Kate oddly as she said the last, then kissed her quickly on the forehead. "Don't worry. I'll bring him back. You tell Ellie her husband will be here!"

It took David well under two hours to reach Rosalie's. A small, pert blonde with yellow ringlet curls answered when he knocked, her big brown eyes alighting on him with anticipation.

"Well, hello sugar. Come in." Suzie had never met Miguel's brother. "Now, I *know* I can help you." She began to take his arm, but he pulled away, gently disengaging her greedy hands.

"Sorry, baby, not tonight. I'm looking for my brother, Miguel Kane. Where is he?"

His request for his brother took her by surprise. He didn't look like Mike. How could they be brothers? Then Suzie recalled just where Mike was and became very flustered. "Oh, well, you see Mike's—well, he can't be disturbed—he's indisposed—"

Before she could say more, a rumble of deep masculine

laughter, interlaced with a husky feminine chuckle, gave away Mike's location.

"I'll just bet he's indisposed!"

"You can't go in there," Suzie gasped, but before she could block his way, David had pulled the door to Rosalie's room open and stormed inside.

To say he was surprised would have been an understatement. David had believed the rumors about his younger brother and the beautiful madam, but somehow the scene before his eyes had a far more startling impact on him than anything he imagined. Miguel was sitting in a huge tin tub of water in the center of the room, leaning back with casual ease while Rosalie knelt in the water between his knees, languorously sudsing the thick black mat of his chest hair.

If David was startled, they were stunned. Miguel's face froze in incredulity and Rosalie gave a sharp, high-pitched curse and lunged for a velvet dressing robe tossed carelessly on the floor next to the tub.

David was the first to regain his composure and dryly said, "I know it's a long dusty ride to town, *Mike*, but I didn't know the customers here got such fancy service." He stressed the name Suzie had used. Mike, indeed!

"They don't, Davie, just special ones." Rosalie's voice was calm now but she still clutched the soggy gold velvet across the ample expanse of her breasts. Her eyes were challenging. "What in hellsfire are you doin', bustin' in like this? Close that door. If you don't mind, I only undress for one man at a time!"

David complied, giving the door behind him a quick shove. "Sorry you had such a long ride for only a bath, *hermano*, but I think you're needed more at home—"

At those words, Miguel straightened up and fixed his brother with a black scowl. "I never would have pictured you as a guardian of my morals, *mano*."

"Ellie's been laboring since daybreak to bring your child into the world. It's not going well, Miguel."

Miguel's face whitened and his hands gripped the sides

of the tub with crushing tightness. Abruptly, he motioned for Rosalie to let him get up.

With great haste they disentangled, she wrapping the soaked robe around herself, Miguel striding over to grab a towel and dry himself. He never spoke a word, just rapidly threw pants, shirt and boots on and flew past David, out the door, hatless and coatless.

David turned to follow Miguel, but Rosalie's voice called after him. "Let him go, David. I think he can use some time alone." She swore, furiously brushing at her eyes. "Why now, of all times, did this have to happen? He'll never quit blaming himself. How bad is she?"

David's jaw tensed and he said quietly, "Kate's afraid we might lose her."

"Oh, my God, no." Rosalie walked over to the side table next to the big bed and poured two generous shots of whiskey, then crossed the room to offer one to David. "It'll kill him, too. He loves her, you know."

"He's got damn peculiar ways of showing it." David gestured toward the tub with his glass, then downed the whiskey in one fiery gulp. "I'd better head back. My wife's put in one hell of a day and she needs me, even if I can't help Ellie."

Rosalie put her hand on his arm as he set the glass on the table. "Don't be too hard on him, David. He's always been harder on himself than anyone else has. Look, I know some things no one else does. It isn't all his fault."

"Well, it damn well isn't Ellie's fault," he shot back.

Rosalie shook her head impatiently. "I know. I tried to tell the young hothead that, but someone's done a great job of making her look bad. Given all the facts, I can't rightly blame Mike either."

"Rice Brighton," was David's laconic reply to her remarks.

Rosalie's hazel-green eyes widened, then narrowed in surprise. "What do you know about that polecat?"

"More and more and none of it good. He had someone in the big house steal Ellie's jewelry and plant a note luring her to where he kidnapped her. To find out who, I need to catch Brighton." He paused. "Now, if—if Ellie and the baby die—oh hell, I don't know if it's worth it, if my brother's worth it anymore."

"You don't mean that. He is and he and Ellie deserve the same happiness you and your wife have. If only she's all right!"

David observed her agitated pacing and pale face, her eyes glittering with unshed tears. It suddenly dawned on him. "You love him, too, don't you, Rose?"

She whirled in midstride and gave a quick, false laugh. "That's rich! Me old enough to be his mother!" Looking at his unbelieving face, she relented. "Oh, I guess in a funny kind of way I do. No fool like an old fool, huh? Look, I can't help him now, but he's gonna need somebody. Just be there, whether his wife . . ."

"All right, Rose." With that, he quietly stepped out of the room, leaving all the rest unspoken.

Rosalie had a lot of due bills outstanding in town. That fancy-talking friend of Mendoza's, the one who bragged about knowing all the big-time rustlers, should come for some fun any night now. He would tell her whatever she wanted to know, and suddenly Rosalie had an insatiable curiosity about one low-down sidewinder named Rice Brighton.

When Miguel stopped Dominican in front of the big hacienda, ablaze with lights, he wasn't even aware of Rafael catching the great beast's reins and leading him away, heaving in exhaustion from the punishing ride home. Neither was he aware of his own chilled body or the thin shirt that clung to his sweat-soaked skin. All he could think of during the breakneck ride was Ellie, his *pequeña*, his wife. He could see her silvery beauty, feel her softness, smell her lilac fragrance and hear her pleading voice: *Please hold me, oh, please, my love. You must still love me as I love you.* And he could see himself, pushing her away, lying to them both. He did love her still, always, no matter what she had done.

Practically tearing the front door off its hinges, he rushed in and collided with Alex in the foyer. Looking at his son's unshaven, distraught face, he moved quickly aside. "Upstairs, Miguel. She's in your room." As Miguel bolted up the steps two at a time, Alex's voice followed after him. "She said the first Kane heir would be born in his rightful place, in the master bedroom."

Before he even got halfway down the hall, he heard the door to his room open and Kate, who had heard Alex, called, "She's asking for you. Hurry!"

He strode past her quickly and entered the room where the small, pale body of his wife lay amid the sheets on their bed, the bed where they had probably made this child.

Dr. Lawson turned expectantly. This was the first time in all the months he had attended Ellie during her pregnancy that he even saw her husband. His first impression of the cold, arrogant Alvarez was quickly dispelled, however, when the young man knelt by his wife's side and took her hands. His low, hoarse voice was filled with love. It was obvious to the doctor that he cared for her deeply.

Just then the door again opened and Father Sebastian entered. "I think it is time, Doctor, for me to administer the last rites." Carrying the oil in a small, golden flask, he began to walk toward the still figure on the bed.

"No!" It was Miguel's voice, hissing in a fierce whisper, "Dammit, get him out of here! She's not going to need him. She'll be fine."

"Now, my son, you know we cannot chance such a thing. The teachings of the Holy Church are clear—"

"I'm warning you, Father, Ellie's my wife and I won't let you touch her. Get out!" Miguel stood up and walked with clearly menacing intent toward the resolute priest.

Sensing a dangerous confrontation that could only upset his patient, Dr. Lawson added his own persuasion, urging Father Sebastian to leave. "Don Miguel is right, Father.

His wife is not in that kind of danger. You'll only frighten her. Please. If necessary, I'll call you."

Father Sebastian was uncertain of what to do. Seeing Miguel's harsh, set face, he replied, "If she dies without the holy sacrament of Extreme Unction, it will be upon your immortal soul, my son."

"Let it be!" As the priest left, Miguel again knelt beside his wife and took her hands in his.

Ellie was fighting her way out of a fog-filled room, weighed down by a hundred clutching hands that tore at her with pain. But then she could hear Miguel's voice whispering love words to her. She could feel his hands; how well she knew the touch of those hands, so strong and gentle, entwined with her own. She opened her eyes to the dearest face on earth, gaunt and unshaven, but beautiful beyond belief. "Oh, Miguel, I knew you'd come. You had to come—" Breath was racked from her body as another contraction began.

"I'm here, *pequeña*. It's all right. I won't leave. I won't ever leave you again." He held her hands, trying to soothe her with his voice, his presence. My God, she was so haggard, soaked with perspiration, thin and hollow-eyed, her once lovely hair matted and tangled around her on the pillows. *Why didn't I notice how thin she's become?* She was tissue paper skin over frail bones save for her huge belly, now moving beneath the covers in an agonizing contraction.

"Just relax, Ellie, breathe in light, shallow breaths, don't fight it. You're finally beginning to move that baby and that's what we want." Dr. Lawson continued to issue crisp instructions, sensing a difference in her reactions now that her husband was here. Strange, sometimes husbands were helpful, sometimes not. In this case, he was obviously essential.

Afraid for her and in torture for her pain, Miguel looked across at the calm physician with a mute plea in his eyes.

"It's been a long, hard day, Don Miguel, but in the last few minutes, that stubborn young man or woman seems to finally be doing what's necessary. Your wife is small and first deliveries are always the most difficult. But she's been calling for you and now that you're here, well, just do what I tell you and we'll have your son or daughter born right enough.''

If there was condemnation for Miguel's treatment of his wife or for his tardiness in being at her side, it was not apparent in the businesslike tone of Lawson's voice. Miguel was here and that was that.

Miguel's own conscience, however, did not give him peace. As he held his small wife in his arms, talking to her, exhorting her to breathe in, bear down, do whatever the doctor asked, he admitted the depth of his feelings for the first time. What a sadistic fool he had been, punishing her all these lonely, wretched months, only to risk her life now because of his neglect, his cruelty! He forced himself to pay attention to the doctor's instructions, unaware of Rita and Kate, who were also following orders, bustling in and out of the room.

Finally, after what seemed an eternity to Miguel, the baby began to move. While Rita massaged Ellie's belly, Dr. Lawson guided the unwilling newcomer into the world. Miguel held Ellie in his arms as she bore down, expelling the child with great panting sobs of pain mixed with joy. Alexander Michael Kane was born.

''Don Miguel, take a look at your son.'' With that, Lawson deftly tied the cord, severed it and handed the screeching, sticky bundle to Rita, who quickly wrapped him in linens and presented him to Ellie and Miguel for a brief inspection. His little red face was screwed up for a lusty bawl. A thick thatch of black hair capped his head, marking him quite unmistakably Alvarez.

As Kate helped the doctor deliver the afterbirth and clean an exhausted Ellie, Miguel still held his wife. Her lips curved into a weak yet joyous smile and she murmured softly, ''I told her he'd be a boy, and an Alvarez.'' Then she was asleep.

Slowly, almost unwillingly, Miguel released her and laid her back on the pillows, kissing her closed eyelids softly.

He rose shakily, his face still ashen when he looked at Lawson. "Will she be all right, after all she's been through?"

The physician nodded. "Yes, I think so. There was no hemorrhage and the afterbirth came out clean and intact. She's just exhausted because of the time the birth took. Now she'll regain her strength quick enough. That boy's strong and healthy, too. You're a lucky man."

"I know," was the low response. With one parting look at Ellie, Miguel turned to where Rita was bathing his son in warm water. So tiny and perfect. His conscience smote him again with wrenching impact: *He's so obviously your son.* The bitter words he had flung at her last spring came back again as he looked at his child. What if she had told the truth? Did it matter now if she had lied?

CHAPTER
27

December 1853, Cien Robles

When Miguel came out of the bedroom, David was waiting in the hall, already having heard the clear, shrill cry of a baby. Before he could ask the question, Miguel answered it. "Well, *hermano*, you're an uncle." His eyes were haunted, but he was smiling.

"And Ellie?"

At this point, the smile broke and Miguel turned to brace his hands against the wall, resting his head on one arm. When he spoke, his voice was hoarse with unshed tears. "She's all right. The doctor says she'll live. Now I know, David, I know how it was."

Without a word more, David remembered their conversation of several weeks ago. "It's over now and she's well. You have a child—girl or boy?"

"A boy. He looks just like me, David. After all the things I said to her, the threats I made ..." His voice faded into silent misery.

David clamped a hand on Miguel's shoulder. "Quit tearing at yourself. We'll straighten out this tangle."

Miguel raised his head and looked over his shoulder at David. "You know, I found out something tonight. I don't really care what she did, if she was with Brighton. I love her anyway. I can't stop and I don't want to. I just want—"

Kate came out of the bedroom then, interrupting them. Immensely relieved at Ellie's safe delivery, she was still not inclined to be grateful to Ellie's husband, despite his timely arrival. "So, you'll forgive her now that she's presented you with a splendid heir, obviously a Kane! Well, I've news for you, *Don* Miguel. You have nothing to forgive her for! It's quite the other way 'round—if Ellie does choose to forgive you! Your little tart—I should say the tart here at the ranch—filched Ellie's jewel cask for Rice. Sarita did it! She was asking Luz about where Ellie kept it the day before your wife disappeared. If you'd bothered to question the servants, you might have found that out!"

Miguel stood still, fists rigidly clenched at his sides as Kate spoke, barely daring to breathe. If he had been gut-kicked by Dominican, he could not have felt more shock. It fit. Sarita's possessive jealousy and Rice's violent threats. All the pieces fell into place. Ellie was innocent.

Taking in his brother's anguish and shock, David spoke up. "Irish, this isn't the best time. We're all overwrought and bone tired. Let it rest until morning." David's voice was calm now, the cool gambler once more in control. He knew both Miguel and Kate were on the edge of breaking from emotional and physical exhaustion.

"But there's more and I want him to hear it. Sarita—"

"Kate! That's enough. We can't possibly solve this now. Miguel and I will tell the grandparents the good news. You go to bed yourself." David's voice brooked no opposition. Kate turned, with chin still belligerently set, marching down the hall to their room, skirt swishing in angry protest.

Clenching and unclenching his jaw for a minute, Miguel digested what Kate had said. *My God, what have I done?* Taking a deep breath, he said, "I'll tell Mama and Papa and Adrian. Go look after your wife, David. You're right, we're all too tired to think straight." He descended the stairs and went to Alex's study.

Unshaven and exhausted, Miguel entered the big oak door silently. Seeing him, both Alex and Adrian shot up from their chairs, frantic with worry. Adrian had arrived just an hour ago, but Alex had been waiting since early morning.

Miguel announced in subdued tones, "Papa, Adrian, you're grandfathers. My wife and son are fine. They're both asleep and I think we could all use some rest, too. If you'll excuse me?" With that, he turned and left them smiling at the splendid ending to such a terrifying day. Overjoyed, Alex went to the bar and poured two drinks for a toast.

"To our grandson!" They spoke simultaneously and laughed in schoolboy giddiness, as they drank, now weak with relief.

When Miguel entered the chapel, the scented candles made it hard for him to breathe. Father Sebastian and Maria knelt before the altar. Father Sebastian was absorbed in his prayers, but the minute Maria heard his footsteps on the narrow aisle, she stood and turned stiffly. *Pray God the child is all right!*

Smiling, Miguel took her clasped hands in his and said quietly, "It's all right, Mama. You have a splendid grandson and Ellie's fine."

Crossing herself in instant reflex, she felt a great weight lift from her chest. If the child had died, or even the girl—she could face no more guilt! Then she looked at her son's haggard face and asked, fearfully, "Is everything all right? The boy—"

Cutting her off abruptly, he said, "He's as dark as any Alvarez, if that's what's bothering you. He *is* my son. Ellie didn't go with Brighton, Mama. She was kidnapped. Sarita took her jewel cask and gave it to him. They arranged the whole filthy scheme and I—I believed it, God forgive me! I never even gave her a chance . . ." His voice faded.

Then he murmured, "I'd like to be alone, to try to pray, if you don't mind. It's something I haven't done in a while."

Father Sebastian nodded and took a speechless Maria, ushering her from the small chapel. "Come, Doña Maria, let us go see the new master of Cien Robles." He smiled warmly at Miguel as they left.

Very slowly, Miguel knelt and made the sign of the cross.

Miguel left the chapel just before dawn and slept until after noon. Father Sebastian approached him in the breakfast room as he ate perfunctorily, the first food he had consumed in over twenty-four hours. The priest wanted the child to be baptised in a few days. Miguel and Ellie had to decide on a name.

With leaden feet, Miguel approached their room, afraid to confront his frail wife once more. His own guilt gnawed at him and he needed time to think, but the issue of naming their son must be faced. He knocked.

Her call to enter the master bedroom seemed lost, echoing in the big chamber even as her tiny body seemed swallowed up by the large bed, the bed they had shared, the bed where their son had been born. However, Ellie looked surprisingly bright, flushed with the excitement of new motherhood. Luz had brushed her hair with arrowroot to clean its shiny length and given her a sponge bath. Then

Ellie had nursed her infant son for the first time. Despite the ravages of the previous day, she looked radiant to Miguel.

She took in his haggard, unshaven face and generally disheveled appearance. *So, now that he's assured of his son, he's contrite*. A part of her heart tore at the sight of his suffering, but she repressed it. Her own pain and sense of betrayal were uppermost in her mind. Mastering her conflicting emotions, she said, "I suppose Father Sebastian told you about the baptism. If he can't bury me, he can christen our child. One sacrament is as good as another, I guess."

Despite himself, Miguel smiled at her feisty irreverence. "Yes, he did say something about a name. Have you chosen one, *pequeña*? You were the one who suffered to bring him into the world. You should choose, not me."

Ellie swallowed hard, realizing his effort to reach out to her. He, too, had gone through hell, she knew. She answered, "That's hardly traditional. Your father named both you and David."

Darkening perceptibly, he replied, "Let's just say I'm trying to be a more reasonable husband than my father was."

His attack on Alex made her bristle with new hostility, giving her the courage to broach what she wanted to say. "I have thought for a long time about a name, that is, if you agree. I want to name him Alesandro Miguel." She took a breath and waited, then forged ahead. "It's your father's name and yours, too, but you do have the final say-so."

He nodded, smiling sadly at her. "I would never say no, Ellie. Thank you for the Spanish. It may soften the blow for Mama."

It did not. "Alexander Michael Kane!" Maria fairly shrieked. "You cannot be serious, to name the child after *him*!"

"You'll waken him, Mama," Miguel said softly, his eyes drawn to the slumbering infant in the cradle. "It's settled and it's her right. Alex was her only friend, the one who believed her when she spoke the truth. I didn't, neither did you. Anyway, it's Alesandro Miguel, a compromise of sorts.''

Maria left the nursery in a state of near hysterical anger, but Miguel sat for a while and simply gazed at his child, watching the tiny fingers flex and curl, the little mouth open in an *O* as he yawned. He was so delicate and perfect, this child, his son. The wonder of it washed over him again. Softly, he said, "What are we going to do, Sandro? What a mess your father has made of things. This is no way for you to start your life.''

David found him shortly afterward, sitting by the crib, gazing in hypnotic fascination, deep in thought. "Mama said you were still here, *hermano*. She also told me about the name. You doing a bit of extra penance?" David's tone was light, but he knew how delicate the situation was between Miguel and Ellie.

Bemusedly, Miguel looked up, then answered. "Hardly that. It was the name she wanted. She has the right. Papa treated her with love while I nearly killed her!''

David sighed. "You had a lot of help in your mistake. Rice Brighton's to blame, and that bitch Sarita. If she wasn't dead, I'd wring her neck myself.''

Miguel stood up, stiff after sitting in a cramped position for so long. "I'm even to blame for Sarita. If I'd kept my hands off the slut, she'd never have fallen in with Brighton." He fairly spat the name, his hate choking him. "Brighton's going to pay. If I can't make up for all the pain I caused Ellie, at least I can kill him for myself.''

Never in the most brutal battles of the war had David seen such naked hate as now suffused Miguel's face. His eyes were black, his jaw clenched like a twisting snake.

"I guess I can understand that. In fact, I'd like to beat the truth out of that bastard myself. He owes us both some answers. Like who killed Sarita and how he set up this whole rotten little scheme. The three days I was gone, I did a little detective work. Seems Brighton is tied up with a pack of local cutthroats near Bent Fork.''

Quickly, David outlined the information he had coerced out of Will Bolton. ''I figure in about a week, Mendoza and Brighton should be meeting in Santa Benita.''

''I'll be there, waiting.'' Miguel's voice was cold and level.

Early the next morning a most unexpected visitor arrived at Cien Robles. Her fancy landau jounced up the muddy, bumpy road and turned toward the corrals. Hair flying in a mane of loose brown curls, dressed in a simple blouse and skirt, Rosalie Parker hardly looked the premier madam of the area. She was disheveled and agitated. Leaping from the carriage, she questioned a startled Rafael. He could only point to the big stable where Miguel was saddling up. *What is* that *one doing here!* he wondered in amazement!

''Mike! He's in Bent Fork! Brighton!'' As she rushed to where he was tightening Dominican's cinch, Miguel whirled in confusion to face her.

''Rose! What the hell? How do you know that?'' He grabbed her arms in a steel grip, almost shaking her in his impatience.

''A lot of folks in town owe me. I started askin' around after you left the other night. A pal of Mendoza's sometimes comes to my place. Sally saw him down at the Bella yesterday. She had one of the girls there get him drunk and pump him. Seems Mendoza and Brighton are cuttin' some kind of big deal right now at a dive called Bolton's. Holed up there for a couple of days. I figured you and David might want to have a little talk with Rice.''

''Damn right. Thank you, Rose. I owe you, for more than this.''

Almost shyly, Rosalie said, ''I'm real glad about your son, Mike, and that Ellie's all right. Adrian St. Clair's talked the ear off half Los Angeles, telling them how handsome his grandson is.''

He acknowledged her words, his own face a mixture of

pride and wistfulness. "He's a fine, healthy boy. You were right about her, Rose. She didn't go with Brighton. I was a fool."

"Maybe so, but it's done and you have a family now. I don't expect to see you again, so you take care of yourself, darlin'." She turned to go before she said too much, then paused for a moment to add a final warning. "You and Davie watch out for Rice. He always was a polecat." She hurried toward her landau.

Before she could reach it, Miguel caught up with her. Grabbing her arm, he pulled her quickly to him and gave her a light, tender kiss. "Thank you, Rose. I'll never forget you."

Ellie felt much stronger that morning. She was still lightheaded and faintly dizzy, but Dr. Lawson assured her if she ate well and rested, it would quickly pass. He had not given permission for an unescorted excursion out of bed, but she was eager to see the outside. She put on a robe and walked carefully to the window. As she looked out, she regretted disobeying the doctor's orders.

There in front of the big corral sat Rosalie Parker's beautiful landau. After that humiliating day on Alavera Street, Ellie would have recognized the rig anywhere. When Rosalie walked quickly from the stables with Miguel in pursuit, Ellie stood rooted to the floor in sick horror. How could he? How could *she* dare to come here after all that had happened? A wave of blackness passed in front of Ellie's eyes. Steadying herself on a chair in the corner, she painfully slipped toward the haven of the bed.

Just as Rosalie had left, David had walked from around the corner of the stable. *What the hell is she doing here?* He was dumbstruck, watching Miguel kiss her and help her into the landau.

Miguel stalked toward the house after calling out rapid orders to Rafael, telling him to finish readying Dominican for a long ride. Then, as David caught up with him, he explained what Rosalie had found out. Without a word,

David turned back to the stable with further instructions for Rafael.

In the study Miguel was strapping on a gunbelt and checking the Colt in its holster when David returned. "Don't you think that's a little more my line than yours, *hermano*?" He gestured to the gun.

"It's my fight, David. He did this to my wife, to me. I'm going to kill him." Miguel's voice was flat. "I've had my share of target practice. I know how to use this."

David shook his head in disbelief. "Shit, kid, you could never shoot varmint coyotes or a marauding mountain lion. You think you could kill a man?"

Remembering the grim incident from their childhood, Miguel replied, "The puma was only defending her cub. She had a right to live. Brighton's different. I'll kill him like the rattler he is."

Watching Miguel calmly load one of the Patterson rifles from Alex's gun rack, David reassessed. "Yep, I guess maybe you will. Before you bust in and start shooting, though, there are a few things you might want to think about."

Miguel paused and looked expectantly at David. "Such as?"

"Who helped him besides Sarita? She couldn't write, but someone wrote that note to Ellie. And just maybe whoever it was decided Sarita would talk and killed her."

"Did they now?" Kate's voice was tinged with irony as she stepped silently into the room and shut the door which both men had left ajar. "And just how many people on Cien Robles can read and write? Who hated Ellie and wanted her gone just as much as Sarita?"

David blanched and shook his head. "No, I don't believe it. Her religious scruples . . ."

Miguel turned incredulously to Kate. "You can't think Mama would help that scum kidnap her own daughter-in-law—much less kill another human being!" It was less a question, more a statement of unbelievable outrage. "That's insane!"

"Then who, Miguel?" Her dark green eyes were wide, her gaze level as she looked from brother to brother.

Neither one would accept her accusation.

"We'll have to get Brighton. He's the key to the whole mystery." David took Kate in his arms. "Irish, Rosalie Parker just came with an urgent message."

She responded quickly, "I know, I overheard. Be careful, David."

Miguel broke in then. "This is my fight. You stay here and take care of the women. It's something I have to do by myself, *hermano*."

"Maybe you have the best claim on Brighton, but I have the first one. He tried to kill me two years ago in Bolton's cantina. If it hadn't been for Kate and an old ten-gauge, I'd be dead meat. I owe Brighton, too. Besides, he won't be alone. Mendoza and several other of his rustlers are sure to be there. Jackals like that always travel in packs. Like it or not, I'm coming along."

Miguel nodded in acquiescence, his eyes moving from David to an anguished, frightened Kate. They had their good-byes to say and so did he. "I'll meet you at the corral in a few minutes."

Soft morning light filtered across the room where Ellie lay. Silently, fearful of waking her, Miguel slipped in and closed the door. He knelt at the side of the bed, gazing at her lovely face, so childlike and delicately sculpted in repose, the thick silvery lashes covering her aqua eyes. Her hair was tossed across the pillow in a skein of curls, glistening palely in the dim light. Ellie's right hand lay by her head, its palm open and vulnerable while the left hand clutched the covers as her ruby and gold wedding ring winked in accusation at him.

For several moments he just drank in her beauty. Then, unable to withstand the desire to hold her in his arms if he continued looking, he lay his head down beside her on the covers for a moment. With the reverence of a priest holding the Host, he raised his face, took one loose, silky curl in his fingers and pressed it to his lips. Fighting for breath, he stood up and turned to leave as noiselessly as he had entered.

Ellie watched Miguel's retreating form, her eyes veiled by lashes which were thickened with unshed tears. She could still sense his presence so close to her, see him make the tender gesture with her hair and gaze so ardently and heartbrokenly on her face. She could smell the faint aromas of leather and tobacco, the musky male scent of him that she had always loved. As his long legs carried him quickly through the door, she studied his rangy body. Part of her longed to call him back, to recreate the magic spell of a moment ago. Yet another part of her could not forget that he had just left Rosalie Parker's embrace.

Crushed pride warred with desperate hunger as she held his image in her mind. Then she suddenly noticed a detail. The gun! Miguel had worn a gunbelt and a .44—something he never did. With a terrible sense of foreboding, Ellie leaped from bed, only to fight a wave of pain and dizziness at the sudden movement. She almost blacked out. More slowly, she made her way to the chair and scooped up a pale blue velvet robe. She struggled into it, then tied the sash with clumsy fingers and gingerly walked to the door.

By the time she descended the stairs and opened the big front door, she could hear horses' hooves. Kate was standing in the yard, watching Miguel and David ride Dominican and the palomino into the distance. Ellie's cries were drowned out. Only her sister-in-law heard her call Miguel's name. Kate ran toward the door frame where Ellie was falling to the floor.

As she focused her eyes and tried to orient herself, Ellie realized she was back in her bed in the master suite. "How did I get here?" She looked around in confusion, shaking her head to clear the persistent dizziness.

"Alex and I carried you," Kate supplied. "You almost cracked your skull before I caught you. Dr. Lawson warned you about getting up so soon."

"But Miguel left, wearing a gun! Oh, Kate, where were

they going?'' Her voice rose to a hysterical pitch, then dropped to a fearful whisper. ''He never wears guns, never.''

Kate looked at Ellie, unsure of what to say, of what Miguel had told her when he went to her room. ''Didn't he tell you?''

Ellie began to pull on the bedcovers nervously. ''He never spoke, just . . . I pretended to be asleep. Only when he left—I realized he was wearing a gun. I'm so damn weak, by the time I got downstairs, he was gone.'' The choked-back tears were evident in her hoarse voice.

Kate could see Ellie's guilt at the deception, but at the same time Kate could understand why she shrank from confronting her husband.

''They went after Rice Brighton, the young hotheads,'' Alex interrupted. Both women turned to face him as he stood in the door. He stalked angrily into the room, saying to Kate, ''She had to know the truth.''

''Why? Why now?'' Ellie was frightened and baffled. Too much was happening around her and she felt unable to cope with it all.

Kate told her what David had learned from Will Bolton and what Rosalie had just told Miguel that morning.

At the explanation of why Rosalie had come to Cien Robles, Ellie blanched. She had believed the worst about her husband, just as he had about her. Why couldn't they trust one another? And now he was going after Rice! ''Rice is dangerous, he's crazy, a killer,'' she blurted out.

Dryly, Alex put in, ''Half of California and parts east already are apprised of that fact, Ellie, including my sons. They can take care of themselves.''

''Ellie,'' Kate laid a gentle hand on her sister-in-law's arm, ''Miguel knows what Rice did. He knows Sarita took your jewelry. He couldn't just let it go. He has his own guilt and demons to exorcise. All we can do is wait.''

Alex snorted in disgust. ''Don't feel neglected because

Miguel didn't tell you, child. Both he and David chose not even to wake me. Kate's cry for help when you fainted brought me running from my bedroom in robe and slippers!" He was dressed now and obviously agitated. Grudgingly, he added, "I guess nothing was to be gained by fighting with me. It's something they have to do." He sighed and became pensive.

Kate thought to herself, *And something they have to find out, something neither one wants to face.*

CHAPTER
28

December 1853, Bent Fork

"Rice, yer crazy! Thet Kane's one mean greaser. You seen Morales. Kane busted him up, too. I know ya both hate him, but, shit . . ." Sam Mars lobbed a wad of brown tobacco in the general direction of a spitoon next to their table in Bolton's cantina.

Rice Brighton grimaced, unconsciously stroking his broken nose and scared right eye with his hand. It had become a nervous habit in past months. "I know how he can use his fists, but I don't plan on giving him another chance at me. Next time it'll be my turn to mark him up, real bad, so bad he'll beg me to kill him!"

Mars scoffed. "Easier said 'n done. He ain't gonna foller me 'n Mendoza."

Sam Mars was a thin, rangy man of middle age whose gaunt face and hollow eyes had seen more than he wanted to remember. He was worried about Brighton's wild talk. Even since the *patrón* of Cien Robles had nearly beaten Rice to death last spring, he had become a man obsessed. He raved about the woman, Kane's wife, and he brooded over his shattered looks. Considering Brighton had almost died from the beating, Mars figured he should think himself lucky to be alive, but Mars was a homely man whom women did not favor. He could never comprehend what Rice's smashed nose and puckered eyelid did to his vanity.

Brighton smiled, revealing several missing teeth. It would have been an ugly sneer, even if his mouth had not been disfigured. "I got it all figured out, Sam. That half-breed bastard's stinkin' rich, but his kind can never stand losing cattle. It's a matter of pride. If you, Mendoza 'n Morales keep raiding him steady for a couple of months, you'll pull in some prime steers. Then, just when he's fit to be hogtied, I'll lay an ambush for him. He always rides with his hands. I'll have a dozen armed men drag him to me. Juan'll be glad to help me finish him off."

Mars took a gulp of his whiskey and shook his grizzled head. "I don't like it none, Rice. None at all. Them Kanes is rich 'n dangerous. They got friends in high places. So's old man St. Clair. We're in fer a gallon jug o' trouble, mark me if we ain't."

Ellie brooded all day after Miguel and David rode off, reliving over and over that last tender gesture of her husband. Why hadn't she let him know she was awake? *Coward,* her conscience taunted her. Yet another part of her responded defensively. *He kissed that woman right in front of me!*

Early the next morning, after spending a restless night, Ellie sat with Sandro, gently rocking him as he nursed in blissful contentment. Kate came in and smiled wistfully at the picture Ellie and the baby made. How dearly she wished for a child.

"He is a love. Alex is so proud of him, not to mention your father."

Ellie smiled in spite of her pensive mood. "I guess Dad has told everyone in town about his grandson by now. Oh, Kate, every time I look at Sandro I see his father! I—oh, damn, I don't know!"

Young Alesandro fretted at his mother's sudden agitation. Ellie began to croon to him, kising him as she rose and carried him over to the dressing table where his clean linens were kept.

"You still can't decide how you feel about Miguel now that he knows the truth?" Kate took over the task of diapering the baby while Ellie refastened her dress and began to pace back and forth in the small nursery.

"Sure, he's repentant, after the fact, after he saw his son, after you told him about Sarita." Ellie stopped then and looked up at her sister-in-law. "But he was here when Sandro was born. Oh, Kate, I couldn't have survived without him."

Gently, Kate said, "Yes, he was here. They do seem to come to us when we need them, these Kane men."

"If only we trusted each other more. It's so complicated, Kate. It goes back to before we were married."

Kate's eyes filled with remembrance. "That's hardly unusual. It does for every man and woman, Ellie. It's what you make of your life now that counts. Forget the past. You have this young man to consider." As she spoke, Kate lifted Sandro up and cuddled him lovingly. He gurgled in delight, then closed his eyes and fell sound asleep.

Ellie took him from Kate and tucked him in the cradle. "I love you, my son, and I love your father. What will it take for me to forgive him?"

Will Bolton nervously hummed off-key as he sloshed the greasy dishwater over the glasses. Damn Bernice, asleep upstairs with Rice Brighton while he did her chores. As he thought of Brighton, his hands slipped on a glass and it plopped back into the water. Brighton and Mendoza never met here anymore—until yesterday. When Brighton's right-hand man Sam Mars and Juan Morales showed up, Will knew it was a big parlay and they would most likely not be in Santa Benita next week. He had sweated plenty over that last night. When David Kane found no one at Las Escondidas Cantina, what would he do? Keep his promise to burn this place with Will in it? Bolton shivered, cursing his everlasting rotten luck. Either Rice Brighton or David Kane would shoot him without a blink, Will was sure.

Julio Mendoza stared at Will. The elegant little pistolero was dressed in a fancy charro outfit trimmed in silver. He cocked one thin eyebrow at the fidgeting barkeep and dusted an imaginary fleck of dirt from his shirtcuff. *Dios,* how he hated to meet the gringos in this swill hole! "What are you so nervous about, amigo?"

"Nothin', Mendoza. Nothin'. Jest wonderin' when that slut Bernice'll be down ta do her chores. It's after noon 'n I got me better things ta do 'n wash beer glasses."

Looking with obvious distaste across the filthy barroom, Julio could imagine how well Will was washing the glasses.

Just then a tall stranger walked in, Mexican by the looks of his dust-covered poncho and dark, Hispanic features. He moved as if travel-weary, hunched over and stiff. Mendoza studied his face and decided he did not know the man who spoke casually in Spanish to Will, ordering a whiskey. The barkeeper quickly filled one greasy shot glass and waited for payment before shoving the drink across the scarred oak bartop.

The young man requested some food. Grudgingly, Will replied in his broken but serviceable Spanish. The Mex had money to pay. He waddled to the kitchen to get a bowl of last night's stew and some bread.

"I would check the food for cockroaches before I ate it, my friend. It has been sitting out in this place for some time," Julio said in Spanish to his countryman after Will disappeared into the kitchen.

The stranger nodded his appreciation and slowly walked

over toward Mendoza's table against the far wall. The place was empty except for the two of them.

"May I join you?" His smile was youthful and guileless.

Julio nodded and kicked out a chair. Just as the stranger took the proffered chair, something registered in Julio's mind. He had blue eyes! No sooner had the young man sat down than Mendoza heard the unmistakable click of a rifle being cocked beneath the table.

"Now, Señor Mendoza, you have a Patterson Revolving Rifle pointed at your guts. I can't miss, so if you don't want your chest severed from your legs, scoot back and toss the gunbelt on the floor. Pronto!" Miguel's voice was low, all the easy charm vanished when he switched from Spanish to English.

Will poked the fire in the soot-blackened fireplace and slung the iron kettle over it to warm. The grease on top of the stew was pale gray, at least an inch thick. Just as he was about to wedge a spoon in it, a voice interrupted him, familiar and deadly.

"I wouldn't waste my time, Bolton. I don't think my brother's hungry after all."

Will gasped and dropped the spoon.

"Which room is Brighton in?" Before Bolton could reply, David moved from behind the kitchen door and grabbed the fat man by his belt buckle. As he rammed the Dragoon Colt into Bolton's midsection, David spoke again. "Remember, cross me and I keep my promise. You go up in smoke with this dump!"

Bolton swallowed and gasped for air. "Ya gotta believe me, Kane. I didn't know they's gonna come here now! What's I s'posed ta do?" He whined as beads of sweat stood out on his forehead despite the December chill.

"Just tell me which room Brighton's in."

"The third one on th' right, Bernice's room."

Coolly, David replied, "All right, Bolton. I'm going to pay a little visit to Rice and Bernice. Who else is upstairs?"

"Jist Lil, down the hall. She won't bother none. Sick fer a week," he sneered in disgust.

"No other men here with Brighton?"

"Yeah, thet Mars feller and Morales, but they ain't here now. Rode out afore noon, I dunno fer where, I swear, Kane!"

After shoving Will Bolton, now unconscious, in a wood shed, David locked the door, then silently made his way upstairs, using the outside steps he and Kate had fled down two years ago. Carefully, he checked the other rooms, then went to the one Brighton occupied.

Rice lay on his back, arms behind his head, staring at the progress of a spider as it crawled slowly across the cracked adobe ceiling. Hearing the soft snore of the whore beside him, he kept his eyes straight ahead, unwilling to look at the cheap, rouged face, frizzy yellow hair and corpulent body of Bernice. God, what he'd give for Kane's blonde wife! The best he could get now was the likes of this foul-smelling slattern. Soon, though, he'd be rich and avenged on the Kanes and St. Clairs. Then he would live in high style up north and buy himself all the beautiful women he wanted.

When David kicked the door open, Bernice rolled over, flapping a pasty arm against Brighton as he tried to free himself from the covers. David's cocked gun stilled him very quickly. The woman began to scream hysterically. With a viscious backhand Brighton silenced her into hiccuping sobs, then faced his antagonist.

"Well, lookee what a Santanna wind blew back to Bent Fork. Still got that redhead with you, Kane?" His easy manner belied the inner turmoil he felt. Best to stall for time and hope his friends were about.

David stood against the wall after carefully scanning the room and seeing Brighton's gun on a chair in the corner, well out of reach. The smile did not extend to his sapphire eyes as he replied to Brighton's question. "I didn't bring Kate, but someone else downstairs is real anxious to see you. Get dressed. Ah, all but the gunbelt. I don't think you'll need it." David shook his head in mock concern,

eyeing Brighton's ravaged face. "On second thought,
maybe you *do* need a gun. No matter. You'll just have to
get by without it."

Brighton blanched, half in fury, half in fear, humiliated
to have the Kanes see his disfigurement. He realized
Miguel must be waiting for him downstairs. White-lipped,
he ground out, "I been planning to pay your brother a visit
anyways, Kane. You just saved me some time."

Both Julio and Miguel heard the commotion upstairs.
Miguel, sitting back in the corner behind the disarmed
pistolero, did not take his eyes off his captive. Mendoza,
however, stared in amazement as a hastily dressed, poker-
faced Rice Brighton stumbled down the steps into the
barroom. He was followed by a tall, yellow-haired gringo
whose gun was leveled menacingly at Rice's broad
back.

Seeing Miguel with a rifle on Mendoza, Brighton forced
himself to calculate. Sam and Juan were nowhere around,
but they would come back sooner or later. Stalling for
time, he spoke to Julio. "My friend, you haven't been
introduced?"

With a deceptively gentle smile, Julio nodded his head.
"No, Rice, I have not had the pleasure."

"Meet the brothers Kane, Don David," he motioned
behind him, "and Don Miguel." As his eyes met the
younger man's, Brighton felt an icy chill splash across
him. What had happened? How had they found him?

As if reading his thoughts, Miguel spoke first. "Señor
Mendoza, here, has some very talkative friends, Brighton,
especially when they're drunk in a whorehouse."

Brighton snorted, his anger turning on Mendoza. "Those
damn greasers of yours gave us away, Julio! I warned you
about Morales and Garcia and their big mouths."

Mendoza darkened, his hands clenching the splintered
oak table in anger at Brighton's slurs. "I would guard my
tongue, *amigo*. Right now, it would seem you need all the
friends you can find." His carefully chosen words reflected
not only his ire, but also made a veiled allusion to the
absent Mars and Morales.

Brighton calmed at this reminder, but still flinched at the hate he sensed radiating from Miguel Kane. "I didn't think it was part of your honorable code as Californio caballeros to shoot down unarmed men."

"We could let the Los Angeles sheriff hang you," David interjected cheerfully.

"And then again, I could finish what I started at your bandit hideout last spring," Miguel said very softly. "You still carry the reminders of our encounter, I see."

Brighton stiffened, then forced himself to act casual. "You got lucky, kid. That was once. I could take you now."

"You just might at that," David said. "Then again, you're older and fatter . . ."

He let his words trail off as he sauntered over to where Mendoza sat, leaving Brighton standing in the middle of the empty floor. Negligently, David pulled out a chair and stretched his long legs after sitting down. He kept his Colt trained on Mendoza while Miguel shed his poncho and deposited his rifle and gunbelt in the far corner. He crossed the room to Brighton.

"No surprises like knives, *hermano*. He was mother naked when I, ah, awakened him," David called out.

Brighton's bravado faded quickly as he recalled the cat-quick way Miguel had come at him before and the extent of punishment he had taken. *Jesus! He's going to beat me to death! Stall for time—stall! Get him riled so he can't fight so good!* A spinning vortex of ideas rushed through Rice's panicked mind and he blurted the first thought that came to him.

"Ellie have that baby yet? It got black hair or light?" As he spoke, he made a swift lunging punch, almost catching Miguel on the jaw, but the younger man sidestepped at the last second.

Miguel's legs were flexed and ready to spring like a panther. "It won't work, Brighton. You never touched my wife and we both know it. I owe you, though, for her pain. And I always . . . pay . . . my . . . debts." With each word, Miguel struck in hard left-right combinations at Rice, connecting with deadly accuracy. The scarred eye was bleeding once again.

Brighton swore, kicking a chair into Miguel's path to cover his retreat. When Miguel lost his balance for an instant, Rice used the opening to land a hard body blow.

As the exchange went on, David and Julio watched with seemingly detached interest. Julio's eyes strayed from the combatants to Miguel's discarded guns in the corner. Without shifting his gaze, David said crisply in Spanish, "Consider something else."

Nodding in comprehension, Mendoza returned his attention to the fight. "I forget you are only half-gringo, eh?" He laughed. Perhaps they would let him go. If not, he would wait his chance. Brighton certainly wasn't worth a bullet.

David watched Miguel's carefully timed feints and jabs score tellingly on his heavier opponent. Where the hell did the kid learn to fight like that? He was a natural. Then David chuckled to himself, recalling Blackie McGuire, the Boston Irishman who rode for Cien Robles. *Goddamn Irish always were scrappers!* "Not exactly Marquis of Queensbury, but he sure taught you well, *hermano*," David said aloud.

He felt relieved. When Miguel had insisted on facing Brighton unarmed this way, David was reluctant, but agreed, remembering Alex and Rafael's stories of Miguel beating Morales.

As he endured the punishment, Rice tried everything— throwing chairs, lunging headlong, hiding behind tables. Relentlessly, Miguel dodged, danced and pursued, raining blows on the outlaw in a steady, merciless torrent.

Finally, as he sensed Brighton's legs were about to buckle, Miguel toppled him to the floor and got a choke hold on his wet, torn shirt.

"Now, we do some talking. That is, Rice, if you'd rather talk than eat teeth. Who killed Sarita? I know she stole Ellie's jewelry for you. Who helped her set up the kidnapping?"

Brighton's head lolled to one side and Miguel shook him fiercely to keep him conscious. "Who, Brighton?"

Forcing his eyes to focus, Rice Brighton stared up with hate-glazed fascination into the face of his nemesis. He choked on phlegm, coughed it free, then spoke, relishing the message he would deliver. He hadn't known that slut Sarita was dead. Good riddance! But he did know how he'd get his last revenge on the Kanes. "Who'd you think helped us, you son of a bitch! The bitch herself. Your dear mama! She wrote that letter telling Ellie to meet me in the *arroyo*. She let Sarita take the cask. She fell right in with all our plans, you stinkin' greaser! Your fancy blue-blooded Mex mother sold her own son's wife to an outlaw. How do ya like it?" Brighton gave another convulsive cough and passed out just as Miguel dropped his head against the filthy, sawdust-covered floor.

Numbly, he looked over at David to see if he had heard, all the while remembering Kate's words to them before they left Cien Robles.

David, too, sat in shock. He could not believe it. It violated every tenet of her religion. Whatever her faults, she had always adhered to her faith.

Julio Mendoza took in the scene, realizing both Kanes were shaken by Brighton's revelation. Very softly he spoke to David. "I am very sorry for your pain, but I had no part in this. I do not kidnap other men's wives. Do you have a quarrel with me, *mano*?"

David looked back at the pistolero, as if seeing him for the first time. Absently, he replied, "No, Mendoza. You heard why my brother wanted Brighton. We have no fight with you." David paused, then added, "But *mano*, don't let us ever catch you with a Cien Robles steer, eh?"

Mendoza laughed and nodded. "*Bueno*." He stood up and slowly back out of the cantina. When they heard hoofbeats pound away from the livery down the street, David and Miguel knew he would not return.

Shakily, David walked over to his brother to help him up. Two pairs of dark blue eyes met in anguish.

Miguel finally broke the silence. "You know, *hermano*, it's strange, but on the ride here I had this gut feeling about what Kate said. I kept pushing it to the back of my mind, but it wouldn't let go." He paused, then finished helplessly, "I guess I already knew. I always took her side against Ellie. I could never see her jealousy, her fear, her hate." Shoulders slumped, he walked slowly across the barroom and strapped on the Colt.

Just as David began to haul Brighton from the floor, Sam Mars walked in the front door. "What th' hell—" Even as he spoke, he took in the sight of his semiconscious, battered boss. In a reflex action he drew his gun, getting off a shot before David's bullet slammed him into the side of the wall. Mars landed near a table and quickly knocked it on its side for cover. He was hit in the right arm, but used to a lifetime of such hardships, he gritted his teeth and prepared to shoot, ignoring the searing pain. If he could keep the stranger busy, maybe Rice could get behind the bar. Juan was down the street. Surely he would hear the fracas.

David dived behind a pile of broken furniture, losing track of Brighton, who now crawled laboriously toward the bar, a scant three or four feet away.

While Mars kept David pinned down beneath the rubble of furniture, Miguel quickly aimed the Patterson. Mars heard the click of the rifle being cocked and was aware of the second stranger for a split second before his death.

However, the exchange gave Brighton time to pull a wicked-looking butcher knife from a bar shelf. Miguel walked across the room, past the fallen Sam Mars, unaware of his enemy behind the bar.

David began to pick himself up from the debris when he realized Brighton was missing. "Miguel—"

Before he could complete the warning, Brighton lunged at Miguel from behind the bar in a berserk frenzy. He raised the shiny blade but never brought it home.

The force of the slug from David's Colt knocked him cleanly away from Miguel. David holstered his gun after he saw the widening crimson stain across the center of Brighton's chest.

"Saved a rope for the county," he muttered under his breath, turning his attention to Miguel. "You hurt, *mano*?"

"Damn bastard nearly got me. A close thing, David, too close. I owe you."

The longer Will Bolton sat in the wood shed, feeling the damp chill of December air cut him, the more his rage grew. He rubbed the bleeding lump on his head where David had struck him with his gun and cursed the Kanes with every oath he had ever heard. Rummaging around the dark, smelly little room, he searched for a way to free himself. After a few minutes he found a rotted board. Grabbing a piece of kindling wood, he began to pry the plank loose. With a sudden snap, it broke. He kicked it out and then applied the lever to the next plank.

By the time the shooting erupted in the barroom, Will was creeping cautiously toward the kitchen. Hearing it, he figured Mars and Morales must be back. That would beef up the odds against those damn Kanes! He rushed to the cabinet next to the inside door and grabbed his old Hawken rifle from its resting place. It was ready to fire and Will was in such a blind rage, he was itching to use it, despite his usual cowardice.

He burst into the bar in time to see David Kane standing next to Rice Brighton's body. It was all over. Brighton and Mars were dead. There was no sign of Morales. The Mex stranger that Kane said was his brother stood alongside him. All Bolton's consuming anger focused on David Kane, who took Kate, killed the Clunes, threatened and terrorized him.

"Goddamn you, Kane, you half-breed bastard!" Bolton shot at David, but his hastily aimed slug missed his target and hit Miguel, who pushed David from the line of fire. In one blurring whirl, David had his Colt free and fired point blank into Will Bolton's midriff. Two shots.

Before Bolton crumbled to the floor in death, David was across the distance separating him from his brother. Carefully, he stretched the long body on the floor, checking the seriousness of the injury.

Miguel looked up into David's face. "Now, we're even, *hermano*."

"Shit kid, I still owe you for running out two years ago. Just be still so I can get this bleeding stopped. Shame we had to bust up the place so bad. Katie probably owns it now."

His jaunty air did not fool Miguel. As David wadded neckerchiefs over the red stain spreading across his left side, Miguel took a breath and spoke again. "Get me home, *hermano*. I need to see Ellie."

David paused and considered. No doctor in Bent Fork. He could not be certain of the small, scattered towns between here and Cien Robles. If he could slow the bleeding, it might be best to try for home.

As if reading his mind, Miguel said, "Get something to tie this up and I'll ride." Then he passed out.

Juan Morales watched the tall stranger carry the blood-soaked body of Miguel Kane from Bolton's place and tie the slumping figure on his great black horse. *Shot up like that, you'll die long before you see your silver woman again, eh?* He chuckled malevolently as the pair rode away.

It had been a lucky break for Juan that he had taken the horses to the livery while Mars went to the cantina. When he heard the shooting, Juan cautiously approached the side window, arriving in time to see Will open up on Miguel and die for his trouble at the hand of the deadly blond gunman. Mars and Brighton were already dead on the floor. Julio Mendoza had vanished. A wise idea, Juan thought, deciding to follow suit now that his partners had been killed and the man he hated obsessively was guaranteed to die as well. Not wanting a shootout with the stranger, Juan rode hard for the rustler stronghold.

Ellie stood in the warm room, her palms damp with nervous perspiration as she straightened the covers on

Miguel's unconscious body for the hundredth time. He kept thrashing in his feverish dreams and kicking them off, becoming immediately chilled.

"No change in our patient, I see." Dr. Lawson's voice was brisk, neither worried nor falsely cheerful, simply stating a fact as he entered the master bedroom.

"No, but he tosses so much I'm afraid he'll reopen the wound. The fever and chills . . ." Her voice almost broke, but she stopped before she gave way to useless tears.

"It's to be expected, child. I dug a nasty .30-caliber slug out of him only forty-eight hours ago. That he survived the ride back here with all that blood loss . . ." He shook his head. "Young buck's tough as a mountain lion. We've just got to keep him as quiet and comfortable as we can. Keep lung fever from setting in and he'll make it all right. Miracle no vital organs were hit." He continued ruminating as he examined Miguel's side, changing the dressing while Ellie scrupulously attended to his requests for clean water and bandages.

When he finished, he looked at Ellie's pale face. "You look a bit peaked yourself. It's scarcely a week since your own ordeal, young woman. You need your strength to feed that baby, and both your men need for you to be well. Now, I prescribe some rest for you while the family spells you a bit."

"I second that, Doc." Alex came in and put his arm around her thin shoulders. "You go eat a bite of supper, then attend to my namesake. Rita has him all ready for his bedtime feeding. I'll sit the night with my son." He gave her a gentle push toward the door with the doctor's approval.

Looking at the worry etched in his dark blue eyes, Ellie realized Alex needed the time with Miguel, to try in some way to make amends for old sins.

She gave him a quick peck on the cheek and squeezed his hand. "All right, but if there's any change, call me at once!"

The whole family and Father Sebastian had been hovering around the sickroom since David brought his stricken brother home. Maria had at first dissolved into hysterical tears, then subsided into dry-eyed stillness. She kept her lonely vigil outside the bedroom, leaving only to look in on Sandro and go to the chapel. She was at her prayers now. David and Kate were resting. Ellie knew she needed to do the same. So did Alex, but his own demons drove him. Ellie understood; she had not left her husband's side since David rode in with him two days ago.

The light caused him to squint his eyes as he tried to focus them. God, but he ached, head pounding, tongue swollen, and pain in his guts—unbearable! Gradually, Miguel became aware of where he was, in his bed, *their* bed. So, David had made it home with him. He remembered little about the ride to Cien Robles through darkness and pain. He knew David had tied him on Dominican's back. He didn't recall anything of their arrival at the ranch.

Then Miguel saw his father standing by the open window. Had he kept a vigil all night? Alex's usually meticulous attire was wrinkled, his hair standing on end, as if he'd run his fingers through it over and over. Just then he did so again in nervous agitation. *He looks old and tired,* thought his shocked son. Alex was the *patrón,* always in command. He turned, as if sensing his son's eyes on him.

Upon seeing Miguel awake and lucid, Alex's unshaven face split into a joyous smile. He half laughed, half cried as his long legs ate up the distance between window and bed. "Damn, I knew that crepe-hanging doctor was wrong! Two or three more days before you'd wake up, he said!" His eyes were suspiciously shiny.

When Miguel struggled to push himself up against the pillows, Alex helped him. "Hurts like hell, doesn't it, son?"

Miguel grunted, then gasped. "Did Lawson take the slug out or that veterinarian who treats our steers?"

Alex chuckled. "You must be better. All I heard las

night was unconscious moaning. You figure you could eat something?''

"Yes, if I still have a stomach left." He looked down at the thick wad of bandages across his midsection.

"Doc said the bullet missed vital organs, but you lost a lot of blood. You need fluids. Ellie spent the last two nights cramming broth and water down your throat."

At the mention of her name, Miguel flashed Alex a frightened look. "She's all right? The baby—"

"They're both fine, but she is tired, weak from her delivery and now from taking care of you. I shooed her out of here last night. She should only have to handle one Kane man at a time." He grinned crookedly.

Miguel returned his father's smile, catching the warmth of the moment.

"I'll call Rita to bring some food. Whatever the doc left orders for you to have." Alex rose from the bed-side.

"Wait, Papa."

Something in the tone of Miguel's voice made Alex stop. Almost afraid, he turned back to face his son. "Yes, Miguel."

"I've made a lot of mistakes . . ."

"So have we all, son," Alex said gently.

"I promised to love and protect Ellie, yet I almost caused her death." Before Alex could say anything, Miguel raised his hand for silence, then went on, "I—I have a lot to tell her, and ask her, but that's for later. One thing she always wanted me to do was make my peace with you. I never could do that. I never believed you'd changed, even though I had. I was too full of hurt and pride. Maybe it took a bullet to knock some sense in me. Ellie was right about you and I was wrong."

"Oh, Miguel! You're far from the only one who's been wrong. I was, for so many years. Stupidly, blindly, I ignored you. Any man would be proud beyond words to have you for a son. I am proud." He paused and looked into his son's sapphire eyes. "We both love this land. Hell, I'm as much Californio as Yankee."

Miguel put his hand on Alex's arm. "And I'm as much Kane as Alvarez." For the first time in his life, Miguel admitted the fact with pride.

"I know that, son," Alex responded with equal pride.

When Rita answered the bell, she pretended not to notice that Don Alex's and Don Miguel's eyes were red. She cheerfully took an order for a hearty breakfast and bustled out to ask Don David to join them.

Miguel slept most of the day. The household was buzzing with news of his miraculous recovery. After Father Sebastian's premature attempt to administer the last rites to Ellie, he had not wanted to suggest such for her husband. Instead, he had spent the days and nights in ceaseless prayer for his beloved pupil. Immensely relieved to find his petitions answered, he remained in the chapel to celebrate a mass in honor of the young *patrón*'s return to health.

Doña Maria was in a quandary. What had that outlaw told her sons before the shooting? Did they know of her involvement in Ellie's abduction? She spent the afternoon in chapel, trying to pray for guidance, knowing it was time to confess everything.

The next evening she worked up her courage and approached Miguel's bedroom, only to hear male laughter. Miguel and Alex were recounting the incident of breaking Dominican to David.

"And there he was, leading that damn beast around the corral like he was a calf, gentle as a pet. Old Rafael just grinned while Joe Hooker about shit his breeches when Miguel swung up on that big black and trotted him around, smooth as silk." The pride in Alex's voice carried out to the hall.

"The ground never looked so far away in my life as it did that first minute," Miguel broke in laughingly. "I didn't know for sure if he'd dump me or run with me."

"Kid, you always could get horses to do whatever you wanted. Remember the time we stole those two geldings from Rafael's remuda . . .'' Maria retreated silently down the hall, her courage evaporated. All three Kane men united were more than she could handle.

Around midnight that night Maria awakened, assaulted by the guilt gnawing at her soul. Her only consolation was little Sandro. She spent hours just watching him, taking him into the courtyard for little outings. All the innocence and promise of his childhood cleansed her troubled spirit. Although she could not confess her sins to Father Sebastian, she had done so a thousand times to her beautiful grandson. When he cooed and smiled up at her, her soul found a measure of peace.

But the nights were difficult and something was particularly wrong tonight. Maria felt a portent of a dreadful event. Finally, she threw off her covers and rose. Donning a robe, she decided to check on Sandro. As she walked the long corridor to his room in the still, dark house, her sense of foreboding increased. Sandro was in danger! She quickened her footsteps.

Very quietly, she turned the handle of the nursery door and slipped inside, not wanting to awaken the sleeping infant. Ellie's room was adjacent to the nursery and the connecting door was always kept open. Now it was closed. Maria immediately went to open it. She stopped suddenly when a man holding a large knife moved out of a darkened corner to stand over Sandro's crib.

"Be very quiet, Doña Maria, or I slit his throat, eh?"

She turned her eyes to the crib. Thank God! Alesandro was peacefully asleep. "What do you want? Who are you?" she gasped in a frantic voice.

The big man chuckled and the cruelty of his deranged laughter chilled her to the bone. "You do not remember your servants, do you, Doña Maria? Your son, the *patrón,* he would have much more cause to remember me than you. He does not die easy, that one. I was sure he would be cold in his grave by now, but only yesterday my friend from Los Angeles brought me word he still lives." Seeing her stricken face in the moonlight, Juan chuckled again. "Ah, you understand my revenge."

"Mama"—David stopped short, seeing the ugly vaquero standing by the crib. He had been unable to sleep and had gone for a late-night ride. When he returned, he saw Maria go into the nursery and followed her. The last thing he expected to find was this brute menacing his nephew.

Morales said, "You—the *patrón*'s brother?" He kept his knife poised above Sandro's crib as he pulled his gun from its holster and leveled it at David. "So, I have Don Miguel's brother and mother at my mercy as well as his wife and son. Humm..." He appeared to consider.

Sizing up the situation, David stalled. "If your quarrel's with my brother, why not settle it with him?"

Morales's brutish features contorted in rage, then subsided into crafty cunning. "Why kill a wounded man—too quick and painless. Like that slut, Sarita. Bitch! I wanted to make her die slow for how she tricked me and used me. I waited for my chance for weeks. Just when I had her, someone interrupted me and I had to kill her quick.

"I have decided not to do that with the man who fired me and shamed me in front of all the men. No, much better to take his firstborn and his woman. The little silver one would not look at me before. Sarita told me how she favored me, but Sarita lied, and she died for it! Don Miguel will suffer more when his wife and son, mother and brother are all dead, especially the little one here." He looked at the sleeping infant almost reverently.

Realizing that Morales was mad and planned to kill Sandro, David took a desperate chance. He yelled a Spanish oath at Morales, drawing the killer's attention from the baby. At the same instant he reached in his jacket for his Manton pistol, simultaneously dropping to one knee and lunging to the side.

Morales would have hit him anyway but for Maria. As Juan trained his gun on the moving target, she flung herself in front of her son, taking the bullet in her back. David

fired around her. The .36-caliber caplock barked twice.
The first shot struck Morales's chest; then aiming more
carefully, David centered the last shot between the man's
feral eyes. Juan slumped to the floor in death.

Sandro was wakened by the resounding noise and began
to yell. He was unharmed, but Maria was gravely injured.

Ellie yanked open her door and saw David cradling his
mother lovingly in his arms. Quickly, she scooped up her
terrified infant and stilled his cries.

"Mama, it's going to be all right. Sandro's safe."
David stroked the silver and ebony strands of hair from her
eyes.

"And you, my son? He did not hit you?" Her voice was
faint.

"No, Mama. You saved us both."

Maria smiled. "You would have stopped him, David,
but at a fearful cost. I could not let you pay it. I have not
been a good mother to either of my sons, I think, but
perhaps this will help atone."

"Shh . . . Mama, I love you. Don't try to talk. We'll get
the doctor—"

She shook her head. "Too late, even for Father Sebastian." A look of peace came over her and she said, "Since
there is so much of his father in Miguel, I think perhaps
there is a little part of me in you. I love you, Dav . . ."
Her voice whispered away with her spirit.

David held her in his arms and wept.

CHAPTER
29

December 1853, Cien Robles

Maria Teresa Alvarez de Kane was laid to rest. Her family stood on the cold, windswept hill that December morn while Father Sebastian said the final prayers. Alex looked down at her small coffin, swallowed by the damp, rich earth of Cien Robles. Very slowly, he took the traditional handful of soil and crumbled it over the closed coffin lid. "Your inheritance, wife. It will be preserved. Our children will succeed where we failed. I thank you for them." He spoke in Spanish, so low that no one heard him but the sad old priest.

The funeral was small. Adrian and a few close friends from surrounding ranches came. Ellie, Miguel, David and Kate were the mourners.

David had been the most withdrawn, hurt deeply by the loss of a mother he never truly knew until the last moments of her life. Sensing the grief and guilt in his elder son, Alex walked down the hill with him. They went well ahead of the others. Miguel, still very weak, was walking haltingly and the pace of the women and other men was sedate.

After a few minutes of silence, Alex spoke. "I won't play the hypocrite and say I loved her, David. I tried once, but that was a long time ago. I am grateful to her, though."

"Grateful she died in my place?" David said the words as if they were torn from him.

Alex sighed raggedly. "We didn't do very well with our lives, your mother and I. The fault lay in both of us, but it hurt you and your brother more than either of us. I've known that for a long while now. I think she came to join me in that special hell for a time. It's not a good place to be, son. She made her peace, did what had to be done. Maybe it was her atonement for both of us. She neglected you while I tried to force you to be something you weren't."

They walked a few more paces and then David said, "Those were her words, 'perhaps this will help atone.'" He shook his head, trying to blot out the memory. "I would so much rather have had her live for me than die for me, Papa."

"Think of what you're saying, son," Alex said gently. "After what she did to Ellie and Miguel, do you think she could ever have forgiven herself? Would she ever have been able to accept Kate? No, it wasn't in your mother's character to change. She seized her moment to do something good, to make up to you for all the lost years, David. Don't deny her sacrifice with your guilt."

They stopped at the gate to the courtyard. The other mourners were far behind. David looked at his father and saw a side of him he had never seen before. "Thank you, Papa. I'm very grateful you're here."

With a choked voice Alex replied, "I might say the same, son."

David had a great deal to ponder as he made his way upstairs that night. The funeral dinner was over and the guests had all been attended to. Tiredly, he opened the door to their bedroom and saw Kate curled up in an overstuffed chair, reading. She had worked hard all day, yet looked fresh and childlike. He was overcome with a wave of tenderness. Coming up behind her silently, he softly said, "Irish," then bent down and kissed the side of her throat, burying his face in her thick hair.

Quickly, she turned into his embrace, letting the book

slide absently to the floor. He pulled her from the chair and she melted against him. He was exhausted and preoccupied, but she could sense an urgency in his kisses.

"Oh, Kate, love me, love me." She knew instinctively that he sought solace in her body and gladly gave it.

Gently she pressed her palms against his chest, shoving him down to sit on the bed, then helped him strip his clothing and boots. When she shed her velvet robe, he reached down and lifted the hem of her nightrail, reverently feasting on the beautiful swells and curves of her body, recently grown fuller. She fell back with him onto the bed. His hands cupped her breasts, then her hips. How perfectly they fit together, flesh on flesh.

With growing ardor, he rained kisses on her shoulders and neck, suckled her breasts and then pulled her down to kiss her mouth deeply. His tongue invaded eagerly as she accepted it and returned the caress. Realizing his urgency, she skittered her fingertips down his side and reached between them to grasp his hard shaft and stroke it.

"Oh, Irish, yes, yes." In mindless pleasure he rolled them on their sides and quickly thrust into her.

Overcome with love, feeling his need and his grief, Kate welcomed her husband into her body, sharing his pleasure, even as she shared his sorrow.

She arched against him and they slowly rode to the heights. Feeling the joyous communion of their joining, both lovers slowed the pace, languorously giving to one another. When Kate gasped and began a long, slow orgasm, David held her shoulders firmly and spilled his seed deep inside her. He felt renewed and at peace.

Slowly, their erratic heartbeats calmed and they gently held one another, unwilling to break the spell of closeness. David stroked her cheek and held her chin. Her green eyes were luminous and he drowned in their depths.

"Thank you, Katie. I love you." His dark blue eyes were clear and untroubled now. "You always heal me."

She caressed his lips, tracing their firm sculpted outline with her fingertips. "David, I've had something to tell you for several weeks, but so much has happened, the time hasn't been right . . . until now.''

Sensing what she was about to say, David slid his hand down and cupped a breast, heavier and fuller than ever before. With awe in his voice, he said simply, "Katie?" He knew.

She nodded in joyous affirmation. "If it's a girl, we'll name her Maria.''

Christmas was a subdued holiday that year and passed quickly. As the new year began, David and Kate hugged their joyous secret to themselves while Alex spent more time in Los Angeles attending to his shipping line. Miguel healed and grew stronger, but Ellie retreated from him.

When the brothers had ridden to Bent Fork, Ellie adamantly told Father Sebastian that young Sandro would not be baptized until his father returned. Then Miguel came home gravely wounded and a week later, Maria died. Now the child was over a month old and still not christened.

Finally, on a cool, sunny morning in January the priest confronted Ellie in the breakfast room. "*Patrona*, we must discuss plans for young Alesandro's baptism," he said earnestly.

Still uncomfortable in usurping her mother-in-law's role, Ellie was startled to be called "*patrona*." "Yes, Father, Sandro should be christened soon. Next Sunday will be fine, I think." She smiled at him and he surprised her by returning the gesture warmly.

Ellie did not feel at ease with the old priest who had been Maria's confessor for thirty years, but she was sympathetic to his plight, which in some ways was similar to Miguel's. Father Sebastian had been devoted to Maria Alvarez and her family since he was a youth straight from seminary. Now all the old Californio ways were gone, just as Maria was. He had been making overtures of friendship since Sandro was born. She resolved to be kinder to him.

But as Ellie considered Sandro's christening, she became upset. It meant she would have to discuss the arrangements with Miguel. It was customary to ask an uncle and aunt to be godparents, but she had to request Miguel's permission before she approached David and Kate. In addition, she had to write her father and inform him of the date. Her head ached with all the details.

Kate found her sitting in the *sala* that afternoon, rubbing her temples. "You really should get more rest, you know." Kate realized Ellie's tiredness owed less to her lack of sleep than it did to her unresolved conflict with Miguel.

"Oh, Kate, I was just going over plans for Sandro's christening. There's so much to do..." Her voice trailed off.

"You really mean, you have to face Miguel, don't you?" Kate asked, wondering if her sister-in-law wanted to talk. "Have you really spoken a word alone with him since Sandro was born, Ellie?"

Almost in tears, Ellie shook her head. "Oh, Kate, I'm so mixed up! I still can't sort it out and he's no help! He's been up and walking around for weeks, but he's never come to me."

"You've been sending pretty hostile signals to him, honey. Also, you might consider, as much as we had cause to dislike the woman, our husbands both lost a mother. There's been a lot of grieving in this house."

At Kate's thoughtful words, Ellie nodded again, considering the truth of the matter. "I guess I'm still afraid, too. Afraid to be hurt anymore."

On a brisk morning in January the two young women set out for a ride. It was Ellie's first real outing since Sandro's birth and she was flushed with excitement.

David was at the corral when they led their mounts out of the stable. They were a beautiful sight, Ellie silvery and tiny, Kate dark-haired and tall. David admired his wife's elegant, serene appearance. If she did not ride with Ellie's born ease, she had certainly made great progress.

As he watched the two laughing women, he called to them, "Now Ellie, don't get carried away and lead my city lady a merry race. She looks great, but she's still a beginner."

Ellie laughed. "I'm a little out of practice myself. Don't worry. We'll both be careful!" With that they were off.

As they trotted out of the yard and up the trail, David

watched them depart. Then seeing his brother emerge from
the stable leading Dominican, he turned in amazement.
"And just where the hell do you think you're going?
You've scarcely been walking for two weeks!"

Miguel grinned, but his eyes were sad, following Ellie's
retreat over the ridge. "You should know, *hermano,* a
Californio rides before he walks. I need to get my strength
back and I'll never do it sitting in the courtyard. Besides, I
know how you've hated riding out every day, doing my
work."

David grunted in admission, but he did not want Miguel
to reopen his wound.

Miguel stilled his protests, saying, "I'm not going to
start roping calves, if that's worrying you. Just a little ride
over to the main herd on the east section to see how the
new breeding stock's wintering."

"You're as much mulish Scot as Californio! That's an
hour's ride and you know it. It's too far!" Equal parts of
exasperation and admiration tinged David's voice.

Miguel answered by swinging up onto Dominican's
back. The effort cost him much more than he showed.
Damn his side! Gritting his teeth, he took a breath and
spoke casually. "Ride along with me in case I fall, then."
With a laugh he was off, although he kept a tighter rein on
Dominican than he usually did.

David swore and went for his palomino. Short of tack-
ling his brother to the ground, he knew he'd never change
Miguel's mind. Ellie and Kate had also ridden east. David
considered and shrugged as he spurred the golden horse to
catch up with Dominican.

"You wouldn't be a little anxious to accidentally run into
a certain little white filly and her rider, would you now?"
David grinned broadly. At Miguel's noncommittal grunt, he
changed the subject.

When they reached the herd, Miguel was sweating in the
cool January air. They dismounted and sat for a while in the
guise of watching the prize new beef cattle graze, giving
Miguel a chance to regain some strength. On the return to
Cien Robles the encountered the women on the east trail.

Ellie's eyes turned almost green in surprise to see Dominican's rider. What was he doing out here, after nearly dying a scant six weeks ago! A closer look confirmed her fears for he was haggard and perspiring. Feeling none too strong herself, Ellie was perversely angry with her husband for endangering himself.

"You have no business riding this far so soon," she snapped as they pulled close enough for conversation.

Miguel gave her a smile and touched his fingertips to the brim of his hat. "Good morning to you, too, *pequeña*." Then he looked over her flushed, shaking little body and added, "You don't exactly look in the bloom of health, either. We might take a break by that stand of aspen and rest a while." His eyes were searching, but she averted her face.

Quickly, Kate interjected, "David, just to show you that I'm not such a city girl anymore, I'll race you to the next ridge!"

Realizing her ploy, he replied, "All right, Irish, but I have to give you a handicap—say at least six lengths head start."

She snorted disdainfully and took off with him in tardy pursuit.

When Miguel and Ellie reached the copse of aspen, he dismounted, grimacing in pain. Before he could move around to help her, Ellie quickly slid from Moonlight, afraid to have his hands on her.

While they walked the horses over to the small creek meandering by the trees, he watched her. "You don't want me to touch you, do you, Ellie?"

She took a sharp breath, but said nothing to deny it, just walked ahead of him. While the horses drank, she patted Moonlight's neck and stood partially leaning against the little filly. She was tired and confused. Why did he have to come after her now?

Sighing, he knelt by the water and wet his neckerchief, then mopped his face. After a few minutes' painful silence, he said, "We have to talk, Ellie. It can't go on like this between us."

"I need more time, Miguel. I'm just not ready yet.

I—I'm still weak. This short ride convinced me of how far I am from being myself.''

He nodded in resignation. "All right. You can have your time, but we do have to have our son christened. Father Sebastian asked me if Sunday was all right. Will your father be here?''

"Yes, I just sent him a note yesterday. Will you ask David and Kate to be godparents?''

"I will, although I can imagine the protest Father Sebastian will make at having a Methodist for a godmother!'' He smiled and in spite of herself, Ellie could not help but catch his humor. She chuckled. It felt good to talk of everyday matters, as they had done in the past.

However, when he helped her remount, she stiffened involuntarily as his hands slid around her waist and arm. They rode back in silence.

David and Kate were greatly disappointed in the outcome of Miguel and Ellie's meeting. David decided the issue must be settled. He would have a talk with his sister-in-law the next morning.

Ellie listened to Alex and Miguel as they left the house. She was warmed by the jesting camaraderie of father and son, lovers of the land. Kissing Sandro's black curls, she laid him in his crib, then gazed fondly down at his sleeping face, thinking what a splendid *patrón* he would be.

David knocked on the open sash, then stepped inside. "Ellie, do you have a free minute?'' His smile was artlessly engaging as he glanced at his nephew, wondering to himself if his child would favor him as Sandro favored Miguel.

Ellie was uneasy over David's bemused state. After yesterday's unnerving experience with Miguel, she was wary. However, realizing that she owed her son's life to this man, and probably her husband's as well, she could not help but love David. She smiled to herself, ruefully recalling her initial hostility to her brother-in-law when he and Kate had arrived at Cien Robles.

"Why didn't you go with your father and Miguel?" she asked, trying to make conversation.

He made a face. "I've seen all the cows and calves I care to for the next decade, unless they're medium rare on bone china. At heart, Ellie, you are looking at a city boy. Papa and Miguel love the land, not this shiftless gambler."

She laughed. "Some shiftless gambler! You do need to get back to your business in San Francisco, though, don't you? I've watched all the traffic in messages and documents coming and going for weeks. I hope you aren't slighting your interests too seriously by staying on here."

He smiled and said, "Neither Papa nor Miguel has been in any shape to oversee the place. It's a family obligation, Ellie. Considering everything, it's not much for me to do."

"Considering everything," she said as they strolled downstairs, "you've saved my son's life and unraveled a terrible conspiracy that threatened us all. You've done a great deal, David, and I am grateful."

He made a gesture of dismissal with his hand. "That's not what I want to talk about."

"That's what I feared," she responded as they turned into the study.

David closed the door and motioned her to a chair. "Ellie, I'm not going to lecture you or ask you questions, but there are some things you should know. My brother loves you."

"Sure he does, David, now." Her voice was hauntingly sad.

"No, not just now!" He paced across the floor, then turned to face her, running his hand through his hair in a nervous gesture before going on. "Not—not just now, but even when he believed the worst, Ellie, even then he loved you."

She just stared in silence, uncertain and waiting.

"The night Sandro was born, I rode to Rosalie's to get Miguel."

She shot up from her chair as if the seat had just scorched her. "He was with *her*, that night of all times!" Her aqua eyes were flashing like blue fire.

Gently, David pushed her back into the chair, recalling Kate's similar reaction. "Easy, little sister, he didn't know what was going on here when he rode straight into town. The point is, he'd been on horseback since sunup and had just arrived at Rosalie's when I got there. I told him that you'd been laboring all day and were in trouble. Hell, he never said a word. Just turned chalk white and bolted out of the place. Rode that big black half to death to get to your side, too. Ellie, he wasn't even sure if the baby was his or Brighton's then! It didn't make any difference because he loved you. Fear of losing you finally woke him up to the truth of his feelings, feelings he couldn't deny anymore."

"Then it wasn't just seeing his son, knowing Sandro was his?" *It's too good to be true!* Then her joy diminished as she recalled the tender kiss between Miguel and Rosalie that she had witnessed.

"He loves you, Ellie. Believe it."

"Then why did he kiss her? Why did she come here after she knew Miguel had a son?" Her voice was an odd mixture of anger and hope.

For a minute David was puzzled about what Ellie meant. Then it hit him. Damn, she'd seen Rosalie that morning at the corral! "You mean the morning we left to go after Rice?" At her nod of dejected acquiescence, he said, "Rosalie came to tell us where Rice was."

"She could have sent a messenger! She didn't have to publicly humiliate me by coming herself. And, he kissed her, David. I was out of bed, walking for the first time. I went to the front window and I saw them."

David shook his head at the irony of it all. What rotten timing and ill luck plagued his brother and sister-in-law! "What you saw, little sister, was Miguel kissing Rosalie good-bye. She knew that he'd never be back to visit her. I guess that's why she came herself instead of sending someone. She's in love with him, but she knows Miguel loves you. They said their last farewell.''

He watched her reaction carefully. She sat bemused, unsure of how to respond.

''My brother is a very proud man, Ellie. Between the Alvarez and the Kane in him, he couldn't have turned out any differently. Do you have any idea what it means to a man like that to love a woman so much he can't stop, even when he thinks she's been unfaithful to him? It almost broke him, but he told me the night Sandro was born.''

''He said that?'' Her voice was filled with wonder. ''I—I have to think.'' She put her hands over her face for a minute, pressing her fingertips over her eyelids. Then she raised her head and looked at David. ''I never knew. I always thought he'd made the best of his forced bargain, I guess. That compared to a sophisticated woman like Rosalie Parker, I was just a pretty schoolgirl. You see, I—''

Ellie stopped abruptly, unable to reveal to David the sordid beginning of her marriage or her wanton abandon in coming to Miguel's bed that first time. She had come to him and because of that, she had never felt sure that he would have chosen to love her. Would she ever be sure?

With so much at stake, Ellie chose her words carefully. ''Tell my husband that I came to him the last time. This time he'll have to come to me.''

That afternoon, David strolled to the stable in search of Miguel. As he anticipated, his brother was rubbing down Dominican. After a few minutes of cursory small talk about the new stock and David's San Francisco business ventures, Miguel gave the big black an affectionate swat on the rump and walked over to the water bucket to wash off.

''You have something on your mind, *hermano*?'' He rolled up his shirt-sleeves and soaped up hands and arms carelessly while waiting for an answer.

David chuckled. ''We never could fool one another,

even when we were kids. Yeah, I have something to tell you. I had a little chat with Ellie this morning.''

At this, Miguel reached for a graying linen rag that served as a towel. His eyes never left David's face as he dried himself and rebuttoned his shirt. ''And . . .''

''I told her how you rode him,'' he gestured to Dominican, ''half to death to get to her that night Sandro was born.''

''What else did you tell her?''

''That you love her. What *you* ought to be telling her yourself!''

''She hasn't exactly been receptive to my overtures, or hadn't you noticed?'' Miguel walked over to the stall gate next to Dominican and put his hands on the bars, dropping his head down on one arm.

David said quietly, ''I know part of the reason why now.''

At this, Miguel's head shot up and he looked over his shoulder at his brother. ''She has legions of reasons, and I gave her most of them,'' he sighed.

''She saw Rosalie here that morning we left. Saw you kiss her right out there.'' David pointed through the big stable door to the front drive.

Miguel let out a unique mixture of Spanish and Anglo-Saxon profanity.

''I explained to her you were telling Rosalie good-bye. You *were* telling her good-bye, weren't you, Mike?'' He leveled his cool gambler's eyes on Miguel measuringly.

''Hell, yes, of course I was!'' he shot back defensively. ''You know, *hermano,* since you went straight and got married, you've become . . . very difficult at times.''

David laughed. ''Kate will take that as a compliment.''

Miguel, too, laughed for a moment, then sobered and looked at his brother. ''I want my wife back, David.''

David smiled. ''She gave me a message for you. Said to tell you,'' he paused here to remember Ellie's exact words, ''that she came to you the last time. This time you'll have to come to her.'' He looked innocently puzzled.

A slow smile suffused Miguel's face and his sapphire eyes blazed with deviltry. "If that's the lady's pleasure, so be it!"

Whistling, he left the stable with a great deal to plan.

CHAPTER
30

January 1854, Cien Robles

The day of the christening, Miguel dressed with special care in his most formal black wool suit, white silk shirt and red sash. He swore absently at the lingering traces of tenderness in his side when he tied the scarf securely around his slim waist. Running a brush through his dense black hair and then checking his jawline for any missed whiskers, he decided he would pass inspection. The chiseled hard planes of his face stared back at him from the glass, the dark eyes still holding a question. It was a question only *she* could answer.

He went to Ellie's room where she was nursing Sandro before dressing for the baptism. Her robe lay open and all she wore beneath it was a pair of lacy pantalets. "I see some things aren't such *pequeñas* anymore, Ellie." Miguel caressed her swollen breasts with an admiring gaze.

"Ooh! How long have you been watching?" She pulled frantically at her robe with one hand, attempting to cover her enticing breasts. Unsuccessful in closing the garment, she turned to the dressing table in the corner of the nursery and laid Sandro down. Furiously, she tied the robe and then began to unfasten his napkin. He was soaked as usual after his feeding.

Miguel came up behind her and watched over her shoulder. With a throaty chuckle, he gently pushed her aside, saying, "You're late, *pequeña*. Go get dressed. I'll change our guest of honor and Rita will be up to put his christening gown on in a moment. She just finished pressing it."

Mutely, she watched him. Of all the male arrogance, after scarcely speaking to her all week! Then she suppressed a wicked grin, surveying his finery.

"You, ah, think you can wrap him securely?" Her voice was dubious, and her trap was set.

He smiled down at the gurgling baby, knowing full well what she was expecting. It *had* happened the first time he changed his son. He proceeded.

Ellie stood, hands on hips, watching while he pulled the wet linen free. Boy babies had an alarming tendency to soak the object directly above them when they were exposed to cool air. Miguel's immaculate white ruffled shirt-front and red silk sash were in the line of fire. Gleefully, Ellie waited for the inevitable.

She was in for a surprise. As he removed the wet napkin, he neatly laid a dry one over Sandro's tummy. He then carefully wiped the child with a damp cloth and dried him. By the time he had the clean linens almost fastened, Ellie sputtered, "You! You've been practicing with him!"

Grinning over his shoulder, he spoke as he tied it. "Every day for a week."

Critically, Ellie surveyed herself in the big oval mirror as Luz dressed her. Her figure had certainly returned after Sandro's birth. Of course, she had needed to gain, not lose weight. The only part of her not wraithe thin had been her belly and that was nearly flattened now. The rest of her body had filled out as her appetite returned. For her tiny, fine-boned frame, however, her nursing breasts were really out of proportion, too big. But Miguel seemed to like them well enough. Remembering the devouring heat of his eyes on them, she felt a tingle begin deep inside her and suffuse her body with its warmth.

She was confused by Miguel's actions. After ignoring her so long he suddenly played the doting father. What did he intend to do? All week after her talk with David, she had waited anxiously for Miguel to approach her and he had not done so. This morning she decided that she must entice him.

When she finished the last inspection of her hair, face and dress, Ellie rushed from her room. Halfway down the hall, she forced herself to be calm and walked sedately to the stairs. Her heart, however, would not stop its trip-hammer beat.

Miguel stood at the bottom of the big curved staircase next to David, Kate, Adrian and Alex. He was holding Alesandro, dressed in his christening finery. When Miguel caught sight of his wife, he handed his son to Kate and walked halfway up the stairs to take Ellie's hand. His sapphire gaze raked her from head to toe; she was a vision.

The gown had just arrived from the dressmaker, a confection of the sheerest pink silk and gauzy lace, cut with a demurely high collar, but molded around her full breasts and tiny waist. The skirt was full but soft with a rustling overskirt of sheer lace. The long tapered sleeves hugged her arms and fitted snugly at her slim wrists where a froth of lace spilled over onto her hands. It was starkly simple yet so spring fresh and understated that it only emphasized her fragile beauty. She wore her hair down with a pale pink lace veil covering the curling silver-gilt hair. Beside her wedding rings, her only jewelry was the rose diamond pendant Alex had given her in honor of Sandro's birth.

Miguel kissed her hand, then tucked it under his arm to escort her downstairs. His smoldering inspection gladdened her heart despite her resolve to be angry at his high-handed ways.

She watched their son fuss in his long white linen

baptismal gown. It was softened and yellowed by age. Alex's own father had worn it, as had he, David and Miguel. With a sudden rush of hope, Ellie envisioned many more of their children dressed in it.

Kate carried her resplendent nephew to the chapel with David at her side. At one point when they were out of earshot of the others, he bent over and quickly whispered to her, "Do you think our child will want to wear this uncomfortable rig?" He chucked Sandro beneath the chin and elicited a gurgle.

Kate responded primly, "And why not? It's a family tradition, comfortable or not." Then she added impishly, "Of course, with my bein' such a heathen, do you think Father Sebastian will do the deed?" They shared a subdued chuckle.

The christening went perfectly with the rich, warm sunlight of morning pouring like liquid gold over the altar and benches of the chapel, bathing the celebrants with its benediction. Alesandro Miguel Kane cried once, a start of infant amazement at the cold water that touched him so briefly. Then he subsided at Kate's crooning voice. Adrian and Alex beamed in pride, Kate and David dreamed of their coming child and Ellie and Miguel gazed in fascination at the small wonder created from their love.

During the mass, Miguel and Ellie could not keep their eyes from each other. For Ellie it was like a strange yet wonderful reenactment of their wedding. He was dressed almost exactly the same, so splendidly handsome in black. But now he did not treat her with icy indifference as he had then. Her shy, admiring glances were returned with bold, considering ardor. By the time Father Sebastian pronounced the benediction, Ellie was sure her face was as pink as her gown.

The family celebrated at breakfast, admiring the baby and giving him lavish gifts. By then it was nearly noon. Ellie took her son upstairs to feed him. Shortly thereafter, Miguel joined her, but they could not talk in privacy. A succession of servant girls kept trickling in and out. Then

Kate came up to kiss her godson before his afternoon nap. Adrian, of course, had to give the boy a farewell chuck under the chin because he was leaving for town that afternoon.

After saying good-bye to his father-in-law and walking him to the corral, Miguel made his way back to the house. Never before had he been so aware of how crowded their enormous house really was! The only privacy he and Ellie might have was in one of their bedrooms. Yet he felt that was not the best place to talk, and talk they must. Purposefully, he climbed the back stairs, grateful for his returning strength.

When he entered the upstairs corridor, he could hear Ellie giving Luz instructions for dinner. Silently, he stepped into her bedroom from the door that adjoined his own. How long since that door had been opened the last time? He quickly slipped the rose velvet cape he'd bought her for Christmas off its hanger. When he heard Luz walk down the back stairs, he opened the door to the nursery and entered. Sandro slept soundly.

Ellie looked at the cape and back at him questioningly. "We'll have no uninterrupted time to talk in the house, *pequeña*." As he spoke, he slipped the warm, heavy folds around her shoulders. "Come, we'll take the back stairs and go where no one will know to follow."

She felt conspiratorial and excited as they stole from the big house and walked in the brisk January air toward the meandering fork of the creek. Just beyond a slight rise of land lay a dense stand of oaks and a pool. Early last spring, before their estrangement, he had taken her there to his childhood refuge. She felt it was a good place for them to go now.

They walked in silence for a few moments, glad of the cool, sunny afternoon, free of the noise and confinement of the house. Shyly, Ellie looked up at her tall husband, who slowed his long strides to keep pace with her shorter steps. He smiled down at her and she thought her heart would burst with the joy. Suddenly, she knew everything was going to be all right.

When they rounded the dense stand of oaks, Ellie gave a small gasp of delight at the scene that greeted them. Standing stock-still by the clear blue-green depths of the pool was a young deer. With one quick glance at the intruders, it ran off.

"How beautiful he was!" she exclaimed like a child.

Miguel smiled. "I used to feed the deer here when I was a boy. It bothered me that the men shot them, but when I got older and realized some of them needed the meat for their families, I became resigned."

"But you could never shoot one?" She understood.

He shrugged. "There was no reason. I was hardly in danger of going hungry."

He had brought along a small blanket. Now he spread it on a big sun-warmed rock next to the water and motioned for her to sit.

She looked up at the jagged outline of the trees towering against the brilliant azure of the sky. "It's beautiful here. I can see why you always loved it."

"It was my retreat from the world. David would come with me sometimes. We'd play hooky from catechism and fish."

She smiled. "I bet I can guess who was the instigator."

He nodded. "David was always the restless one, the rebel. Me?—I don't know." He watched the undisturbed depths of water and then knelt to pick up a stone and skip it across the pool, making ever-widening ripples. After a minute he looked up at her.

"Ellie, I've only begun to know myself in the past two years. I'm not who I thought I was."

"You're Alex Kane's son and you don't resent it anymore. I know that," she said softly.

He smiled. "You were right about him, *pequeña*. You were right about so many things and I was wrong."

She started to reach out to him, but he stood up and paced away. He had a great deal to tell her. Sensing his need, she subsided, sitting back to listen in silence.

When he was a good six feet away from her, he turned and looked at her. She appeared so tiny and lovely, all rose and silver in the early afternoon light. "I loved you the first minute I saw you, *pequeña*. Only, I didn't know it then. You see," he smiled, "I was expecting a meek, homely heiress. *Her* I could have handled! But you were so willful and so very beautiful. I was jealous then, and you're jealous now. Rice is dead, but Rosalie isn't. I want you to understand about her. David told me you saw us the day we left."

"What does she have to do with us?" Ellie was still uncomfortable with the subject of Miguel's mistress, not sure she wanted to hear what he had to say.

"It all began long ago, before I ever knew either of you. You see, *pequeña*, I never met many women when I was growing up. Papa and David were the charmers. Women flocked to them and ignored me. I retreated to my books, to this place." He gestured around the familiar landscape.

"That's why you thought you wanted to be a priest?"

He nodded. "That and a lot of encouragement from Mama and Father Sebastian. I could make a horse do anything for me, but ask a girl to dance?" He shrugged philosophically. "I guess I convinced myself I was better off as a loner. And I was sure Papa would give Cien Robles to David. Then when I was summoned home to marry you, my world was turned upside down."

She made a wry face. "I was a spoiled brat. I—I never explained to you about Rice. Dad told me he only wanted my money, but I thought he loved me. Just before we signed our betrothal agreement, I sneaked off to meet him." She cringed, remembering the ugly scene. "He tried to seduce me, but he wanted me to go ahead and marry you rather than risk being disinherited. I knew then Dad was right. Rice only wanted Twin Rivers, not me. I didn't think you wanted me either, that first day we met." She looked down miserably.

"Oh, *pequeña*, I was burning with jealousy over Brighton!" He shook his head in sadness, realizing what fools they both had been.

"If I hadn't told those stupid lies." Her voice was verging on tears. "I'm so sorry, my darling."

He knelt to take her in his arms, "Oh, Ellie, Ellie, little one, you have nothing to be sorry for! If I'd had the sense of a grown man instead of an inexperienced schoolboy, I would have known you weren't telling the truth. That's all over and done with. It's not the point now. What I want you to understand is how I feel about Rose."

He could feel her stiffen in his arms and he took her little chin in one hand and made her look at him. "We have to talk about her, *pequeña,* or she'll be between us for the rest of our lives."

Almost against her will she nodded.

"Rose was a friend to me, Ellie. She took a fumbling boy and tried to make a man out of him. She shared laughter and common sense with me, not just a bed. Rose always took your part, too, believe it or not. She told me you'd never go with Brighton, that you loved me, but I was too jealous and blind with selfish anger to see the truth. I was a fool. I hope you'll forgive a fool, *pequeña.* That day by the corral, I told Rose good-bye. I made my choice. Now I guess it's up to you to make yours. I'll always owe Rose, but I love only you."

He stood up, gently disengaging her arms from his. "I'll understand if you need time to think things over, after all I've done. I won't try to use sex as a weapon either. That's why I wanted us to come here, not try to talk in the bedroom. It takes more than being a lover to be a husband."

Ellie held her breath for a moment, taking in all he had said as he turned slowly to walk away.

"But it's not a bad place to start," she called after his retreating figure. He turned swiftly, and just as swiftly she flew from the rock and catapulted into his arms, giddy with joy.

Miguel held her tightly, running his hands up and down her back under the heavy cloak, burying his face in the thick silver-gilt hair that flowed over her shoulders. "Oh, *pequeña,* my little one, I love you, I love you."

Her hands clung feverishly around his neck, pulling his head down to hers, fusing their lips in a kiss that went on for minutes. Finally, gasping for breath, they broke the joining of the kiss and she whispered against his neck, "I love you, Miguel, and I want to make love to you, to learn to please you, every way." One silver brow arched delicately. "After all, if I'm going to replace Rosalie Parker, I have a lot to learn. Teach me, please?"

He groaned and took her lips again in a bruising kiss as he scooped her up. Lord! She was still as light as a feather, his tiny wife, his *pequeña*. Resolutely, he covered the distance from the pool to the house.

All thoughts of propriety obliterated, he carried her through the front door and up the wide, curving steps to the second floor and their bedroom. David and Kate were in the *sala* with Alex. All three stood silently as Miguel swept past with Ellie clinging to him. The lovers were joyously unaware of the onlookers.

After a moment Alex said dryly, "I think this calls for a drink. And, er, Kate, please tell the cook we'll be having a *late* dinner."

Once inside the master bedroom, Miguel slowly put Ellie down, still holding her small body closely to his. Deftly, he unfastened her cape and let it drop to the floor. After sliding her hair over one shoulder, he reached behind her to unloop the tiny buttons at the nape of her neck. There were dozens of them! Groaning in frustration, he persevered.

Ellie's fingers were busy, too, unfastening his shirt studs and sliding her cool, little palms inside the shirt to rub his furry chest. Then she moved her hands to his waist, untying his sash. She helped him off with his jacket, then his shirt. Ever so slowly he slipped a lacy camisole strap off one pale silvery shoulder, then the other. When he unhooked the two simple clasps in front, it fell, freeing her milk-laden breasts.

She stood still, proudly, as he feasted his eyes and filled his hands wonderingly, touching the globes tenderly.

"They'll only last until our son is old enough for other food."

"You're quite perfect, my love, either large or small," he breathed, bending down to kiss one pale nipple.

Ellie arched against him, loving the sensations that rioted through her body. She reached down boldly and began to unfasten his trousers.

Hoarsely, he murmured, "Boots first, *pequeña*." He picked her up and walked to the bed, stepping over the pile of clothing on the floor. He placed her gently on the bed, then peeled the lacy pantalets over her slim hips, down her silky legs, slipping them off. Slippers, garters and stockings quickly followed. "You're even more perfectly beautiful than before, if that's possible." His eyes drank in every delicate curve and hollow and his hands followed. She closed her eyes like a sunning kitten, letting him stroke her.

After a few moments, Ellie sat up. "Now, it's my turn," she said in a breathy voice. She pulled his unresisting body across her and had him stretch out full length on his back. Rising, she walked to the foot of the big bed and pulled off his boots and stockings. Miguel watched the delicious, shimmering bounce of breasts and buttocks as she went methodically about her tasks. He helped her ease the tight black pants over his narrow hips, grimacing when he rolled over on his injured side.

"Does it still hurt? Oh, you shouldn't have carried me!" Her small hand reached out gently to touch the light bandage wrapped about his midsection.

"You weigh practically nothing, *pequeña*. That didn't hurt. Oh, but waiting for you now does hurt!" With that, he pulled her down beside him on the bed and rolled over her, his rigid erection pressing between her legs.

Eagerly, she grasped the shaft and guided him inside her, opening herself and arching up to imprison him with her legs, which wrapped tightly around his hips. After all the months, he felt so welcome, so familiar inside her body. They began slowly, moving in ancient sync, but frenzied need so long denied quickly took over. He thrust into her with hard, fast strokes and she clawed at him, moaning in feverish, panting hunger until the stars and all the planets exploded behind her eyes. It had been so long since she felt the indescribable rush of orgasm. Ellie could not stop the tears that trailed from the corners of her aqua eyes. He watched her, thrilling at the sudden rosy blush that suffused her face, throat and breasts. Immediately, he followed her, spilling himself in wild abandon deeply within her.

They lay, locked together, breathing in frantic gasps, still caressing one another with hands and lips. Softly, he traced the trickle of tears on each temple with his fingertips, then kissed them dry.

Her eyes were still glittered like deep aqua pools when she whispered, "Don't ever leave me, my darling, I love you with my whole being."

"Never, *pequeña*, never." Protectively, he settled her into the curve of his arm.

She nestled against him but did not remain still. Very slowly and lightly she traced patterns with her fingertips across his shoulders and down his chest, marveling anew at the beautiful symmetry of his lean body. The black chest hair narrowed on his belly in an arrow descent to the dense growth of pubic hair. Her fingers followed it, then lightly skittered over the satiated phallus and went further down the insides of his long hard legs. She felt the tickle of hair as she ran her palms over the corded tendons and muscles of his thighs and calves.

Miguel lay back, letting her explore his body freely. She had never been this bold before. It pleased him and also began to arouse him once more. "Wanton little creature, aren't you?" His voice was a caressing drawl.

Ellie marveled at the wonders of male anatomy as his shaft, limp a moment ago, now rose stiffly under her playful ministrations. She stopped retracing her route back up his body, to circle it delicately, then stroke softly up and down with her hand. "You are so beautiful," she whispered as she felt her lips drawn to his pulsing core. On a few occasions he had made love to her this way. With hesitation, she bent over toward it. He very gently guided her as she took the hot, slick male flesh in her mouth. When she heard his sudden gasp she pulled away. "Did I hurt you?"

"No! No, just don't stop, *pequeña*! Please!" His voice sounded hoarse with pleasure. He guided her movements for a few moments, trembling with the urgency she evoked in him. Finally, he knew he could hold off no longer and lay back, convulsively releasing his fluid. It had never been this good with anyone but his *pequeña*. In amazement and tenderness he reached down and pulled her into his arms, kissing her softly.

"Was it all right?" She finally managed to say the words, pleased with herself yet mortified at her own boldness. *Let Rosalie Parker top that!*

He groaned. "All right! What do you think? I'm going to show you just how *all right* it was!"

With that, he pushed her up against the pillows, spread her legs, and slid himself down to nuzzle the silvery curls between them. She writhed and bucked in frantic pleasure until he held her little buttocks tightly in his hands, gently licking and sucking inside her velvety lips, bringing her to a searing orgasm. After listening to her sobbing and panting, he raised his head and arched one thick black eyebrow. He asked devilishly, "Was *that* all right?"

She gave a half moan, half giggle of sheer joy and pummeled at his shoulders and back. Like two playful young animals, they thrashed and rolled across the bed, then subsided to hold one another very tenderly.

For the rest of the afternoon, they alternately slept, then awakened to make love, first fiercely, then gently. It was as if they were trying to make up for all the months of lonely separation in a few hours' time. The early evening stillness was finally broken by a knock on the big oak door of their bedroom.

Miguel, engaged in kissing Ellie awake, raised his head and responded in Spanish, expecting Manolo.

Alex's voice on the other side of the door was laced

with dry amusement. "Personally, I'd be delighted if you two stayed there all night, but Rita informs me my grandson is getting rather fussy. Something about his feeding. And the rest of the family is waiting dinner as well. The cook is not a romantic, I'm afraid. But take your time." With that, he whistled jauntily and went down the hall.

Ellie shot up in bed. Her breasts were indeed full and tender once again. Of course, there was more than one reason for the tender nipples!

"Poor Sandro! How could I forget him?" she wailed.

Her husband's chuckle answered that question. He was around the bed, padding barefoot and naked into the adjacent room where he found a velvet robe for her. She fairly leaped into it and bolted across the two rooms into the nursery.

Rita was carrying Sandro, holding a small cloth bag wetted with sugar water to his mouth. Smiling conspiratorily, Rita said, "The little *patrón* would not be satisfied much longer with this." As if to prove her right he gave a lusty squall the minute she took the sack from his mouth and handed him to his mother.

Miguel and Ellie sponged off and dressed in great haste. They quickly slipped down the front stairs to make their tardy entry for dinner.

Miguel took her arm before they entered the *sala,* marveling at how unselfconsciously calm she seemed. He remembered her blushing, agonized shyness the first time they had to face the family and servants after making love. Now she was proud and confident. He leaned down and kissed her cheek just before they rounded the corner and appeared for inspection. She squeezed his arm in reply.

"Well," David raised his glass jovially, "at last we can eat! I hope the cook roasted a whole ox!" His eyes danced in delight as he surveyed Ellie's glowing face and the way his brother stared enraptured at her.

"I trust my grandson has been taken care of?" Alex interjected, neither deceived nor worried.

Just after the main course was served, David raised his glass of fine red wine. "I want to propose a toast to our children, the one here and the one on the way." He beamed with pride as he looked over at his brother and sister-in-law, then back to Kate, who smiled up at him joyously. Now that Miguel and Ellie were reconciled, Kate knew David had chosen the right time to tell everyone.

Delighted congratulations were exchanged and Kate informed the thrilled grandfather that his second grandchild would come in late summer.

"Of course, we'll be in San Francisco and Elizabeth Denton will deliver the baby. I trust her more than anyone." Kate squeezed David's hand under the table in remembrance.

"A midwife! No grandchild of mine will be born with a midwife! Why, they're more primitive in that damnblasted city than here in the wilds," Alex exploded.

"No, Papa, *Dr.* Elizabeth Denton is a fully certified physician and surgeon, from a fine eastern medical school. She's helped us before and we have implicit faith in her." David did not believe he could sway his father, but at least Alex subsided, muttering imprecations.

"This is a night for new beginnings." Miguel stood and looked lovingly down at Ellie. "And I, too, have a toast. To our ladies, gallant and beautiful. They give us our children and for that we can never repay them." He saluted Ellie and Kate, as did David and Alex. For a fleeting second the old man looked at the vacant chair at the end of the table.

Then he said, "I have something in the nature of an announcement to make. I know, David and Kate, that you plan to return to your home in that gold town. You've made your place there. Miguel and Ellie, you've certainly proven yourselves *patrón* and *patrona* of the ranches. However, I'm an old man with a shipping business in Los Angeles and I'm too tired to keep traipsing back and forth from here to there. So, I plan to move to Los Angeles and live in the city house. I'll be in semiretirement there, and most eager to entertain my grandchildren. The more, the better!''

Ellie interjected, ''But we'll miss you!''

Miguel, looking at his father, said quietly, ''You and Lorry are welcome to come home any time, Papa. You know that.''

David promised to fill their end of the bargain for lots of grandchildren. ''And you know, Papa, it's not too far from Los Angeles to that gold town we live in, either.''

Fearing his emotions might betray him, Alex cleared his throat and briskly assured them he'd be a frequent visitor to both places. ''Another thing,'' he said as he stood up.

David stopped him. ''I'll get it.'' He quickly strode to the sideboard where a long leather-covered object lay. He handed the bag to his father. ''You do the honors, Papa.''

Alex handed the bag to Miguel. ''Open it, son.''

Puzzled, Miguel looked from his father to his brother. Alex and David fairly burst with conspiratorial excitement.

When he slid the heavy iron rod from its cover, Miguel let out a long whistle and Ellie's eyes glowed with pride. It was a branding iron and its marker was the double *R* brand Miguel had envisioned for the combined ranches.

''Rio del Robles,'' he breathed reverently, looking up at Alex. ''How did you—?'' Then Alex's eyes went to Ellie, and Miguel knew the answer.

''I figure to have about fifty of them cast by spring rodeo. Adrian and I talked it over last month and agreed.''

David added, ''That seem all right with you, *patrón*?''

Miguel sat, feeling the cool smoothness of the iron in his hands. His heart was so overflowing he could not speak. Mutely he nodded, then managed, ''Yes, damn yes, it's all right!''

Alex watched the reactions around the table, then took a deep breath and said, ''A final toast, to my two splendid sons, the very best any man could hope for. I tried to bend you both to my will, but you chose your own roads, as men should. You've preserved our family's inheritance for your children. We are family, and we will never be strangers again.''

Solemnly they all stood, joining the tall old man with piercing blue eyes. David and Miguel raised their glasses, returning their father's tribute. Kathleen and Eleanor did the same. The winking candles on the long oak table gave a benediction in golden light.

Shirl loves to hear from her fans.
You can write her at
P.O. Box 72,
Adrian, Michigan, 49221.

By the year 2000, 2 out of 3 Americans could be illiterate.

It's true.

Today, 75 million adults... about one American in three, can't read adequately. And by the year 2000, U.S. News & World Report envisions an America with a literacy rate of only 30%.

Before that America comes to be, you can stop it... by joining the fight against illiteracy today.

Call the Coalition for Literacy at toll-free **1-800-228-8813** and volunteer.

Volunteer Against Illiteracy. The only degree you need is a degree of caring.

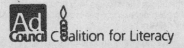

Ad Council Coalition for Literacy
